# STANLEY PARK

STANLEY

# P A R K

## Timothy Taylor

Alfred A. Knopf Canada

PUBLISHED BY ALFRED A. KNOPF CANADA

Copyright © 2001 by Timothy Taylor

All rights reserved under International and Pan-American Copyright
Conventions. Published in 2001 by Alfred A. Knopf Canada, a division
of Random House of Canada Limited, Toronto. Distributed by
Random House of Canada Limited, Toronto.

Knopf Canada and colophon are trademarks.

Canadian Cataloguing in Publication Data

Taylor, Timothy L.

Stanley Park

ISBN 0-676-97307-8

I. Title.

PS8589.A968S72   2001   C813'.6   C00-932428-3
PR9199.3.T39S72   2001

First Edition

Visit Random House of Canada Limited's website:
www.randomhouse.ca

Printed and bound in the United States of America

2 4 6 8 9 7 5 3 1

*For Jane and for my parents,*
*Richard and Ursula*

Timothy Taylor is a recipient of a National Magazine Award, winner of the Journey Prize and the only writer ever to have three stories published in a single edition of the *Journey Prize Anthology,* as he did in the fall of 2000. He is the author of *The Internet Handbook for Canadian Lawyers*; his short fiction has appeared in Canada's leading literary magazines and has been anthologized in such publications as *Best Canadian Stories* and *Coming Attractions.* His travel, humour, arts and business pieces have been published in various magazines and periodicals, including *Saturday Night.* He was born in Venezuela and now lives in Vancouver.

# AUTHOR'S NOTE

One strand of this novel is based on fact. In January of 1953 the skeletal remains of two children were found in Vancouver's Stanley Park. A hatchet was found with the bodies, which was determined to be the murder weapon. From the time the bodies were discovered until 1998, police believed the bodies to be those of a boy and a girl, aged between seven and ten years. DNA tests subsequently proved that the children were brothers. They have never been identified, no charges have ever been laid, and the case remains open.

# ONE

# THE
# CANVASBACK

They arranged to meet at Lost Lagoon. It was an in-between place, the city on one side, Stanley Park on the other. Ten years of rare contact, and they had sought each other out. Surprised each other, created expectations.

Now the Professor was late.

Jeremy Papier found a bench up the hill from the lagoon and opened a section of newspaper across the wet boards. The bench was between two cherry trees, the pink blossoms of which met high over his head forming an arch, a doorway. It wasn't precisely the spot they'd discussed—the Professor had suggested the boathouse—but it was within eyesight, within shouting distance. It was close enough. If he had to wait, Jeremy thought, settling onto the paper and blowing out a long breath, he was going to sit. He crossed one long, aching leg over the other. He fingered the tooling on a favourite pair of cowboy boots, ran long fingers through tangled black hair.

He sat because he was tired, certainly. Jeremy accepted that being a chef, even a young chef, meant being exhausted most of the time. But there had also been a family portrait taken here, on this bench, years before. Also early spring, he remembered; the three of them had sat here under the cherry blossoms. Jeremy on the one side, seven years old. His mother, Hélène, on the other. The Professor had his arms around them both, feet flat on the grass. He looked extremely pleased. Jeremy's mother was less obviously so, her expression typically guarded, although she made dozens of copies of the photo and sent these off to relatives spread across Europe from Ireland to Spain, from the Czech Republic to as far east as Bulgaria. Documenting settlement. He wondered if his father, who had no relations other than those in the photo, would remember this detail.

Now Jeremy lit a cigarette and watched an erratic stream of homeless people making their way into the forest for the night. When he arrived there had been seawall walkers and hotdog eaters, birdwatchers, rollerbladers, chess players returning from the picnic tables over by bowling greens. Then lagoon traffic changed direction like a freak tide. The flow of those heading back to their warm apartments in the West End tapered to nothing, and the paths were filled with the delusional, the alcoholic, the paranoid, the bipolar. The Professor's subjects, his obsession. The inbound. Four hundred hectares of Stanley Park offering its bleak, anonymous shelter to those without other options.

Of course, Jeremy didn't have to remind himself, the Professor had other options.

They had discussed meeting on the phone earlier in the week. When Jeremy picked up—expecting a late reservation, maybe his black-cod supplier, who was due into Vancouver the next morning—he heard wind and trees rustling at the other end of the line. Normally reticent, the Professor was animated about his most recent research.

"... following on from everything that I have done," he said, "culminating with this work." From his end, standing at a pay phone on the far side of the lagoon, the Professor could hear the dishwasher hammering away in the background behind his son's tired response.

"*Participatory* anthropology. Is that what you call it now?" Jeremy was saying. "I thought it was *immersive*."

"Like everything," the Professor answered, "my work has evolved."

He needed help with something, the Professor said. He wanted to meet.

"How unusual," Jeremy said.

"And what advice can I give on running a restaurant?" the Professor shot back.

"None," Jeremy answered. "I just said there was something I wanted to talk to you about. Something that had to do with the restaurant."

"Strange times," the Professor said, looking into the darkness around the pay phone. Checking instinctively.

Very strange. The stream of those inbound had slowed to a trickle. A trio of men passed, bent behind shopping carts that were draped and hung with plastic, heaped to the height of pack horses, bags full of other bags. Jeremy could only wonder at the purpose of them all, although the Professor could have told him that the bag itself captured the imagination. It held emblematic power. For its ability to hold, certainly. To secure contents, to carry belongings from place to place. But even the smell of the plastic, its oily permanence, suggested the resilience of things discarded.

Jeremy watched the three men make their way around the lagoon and disappear into the trails. He glanced at his watch, sighed. Lifted his chin and breathed in the saline breeze. It brought to mind the ocean beyond the park, sockeye salmon schooling in the deep, waiting for the DNA-encoded signal to turn in their millions and rush the mouth of the Fraser, the tributary offshoot, the rivulet of water and the gravel-bed spawning grounds beyond. Mate, complete the cycle, die. And then, punctuating this thought, the rhododendron bushes across the lawn boiled briefly and disgorged Caruzo, the Professor's manic vanguard.

"Hey, hey," Caruzo said, approaching the bench. "Chef

Papier." He exhaled the words in a blast.

He dressed for the mobile outdoor life, Caruzo. Three or four sweaters, a torn corduroy jacket, a heavy coat, then a raincoat over all of that. It made the big man even bigger, the size of a lineman, six foot five, although stooped a little with the years. Those being of an indeterminate number; Jeremy imagined only that it must be between fifty and ninety. Caruzo had a white garbage bag tied on over one shoe, although it was only threatening to rain, and pants wrapped at the knees in electrical tape. His ageless, wind-beaten face was protected by a blunt beard that fell to his chest. Exposed skin had darkened, blackened as a chameleon might against the same forest backdrop.

"The Professor," Caruzo announced, "is waiting."

Jeremy followed Caruzo between the cherry trees and around the lagoon. They passed down an alley of oak trees that stirred another memory of his mother. When they were alone—the Professor was often in the field on other projects, never explained—Jeremy and his mother would spend weekends here, feeding the animals. Bread for the swans, nuts for the squirrels. The racoons would take eggs from your hand and climb up into these same bent trees, crack their prize gingerly and suck clean the interior. Once a racoon bobbed its head in silent thanks before eating. His mother laughed for a long time at that. It was as happy as he remembered her being, ever. From his earliest memories right up to the day in October 1987 when Hélène Papier died, not long after his twentieth birthday. His father was again in the field. Jeremy had been seeking his own petulant distance, living on campus, playing in a bad rockabilly band called The Decoders and failing economics. When Jeremy thought of it now—ten years separating him from the events that had so tragically, so quickly, unfolded—it sometimes felt as if she had given up on both of them, all at once. In the middle of a dream turned left, not right. Taken her leave.

The suddenness of it sent Jeremy and his father flying across the world in different directions.

Caruzo marched ahead. He was chanting, as he would from time to time.

October 5, 1947,
The date of their demise,
When the things I saw in the trees and the sky
Made me finally realize,
It's the fir and the arbutus
Whose leaves will fall to meet ye,
And touching the soil mark the morning of toil
When the light it fails to greet ye.

"And now I singe, any food, any feeding,
Feeding, drink or clothing,
Come dame or maid,
Be not afraid, poor Tom will injure nothing."

When he reached the end of the chorus, Caruzo stopped on the path, held his hands out as if soliciting critical commentary.

"Food, drink or clothing?" Jeremy asked.

"How about a toonie?" Caruzo said.

Jeremy produced the two-dollar coin and they walked another fifty yards, over a small arched bridge and up to a trail mouth that entered the forest proper. A pay phone stood there. And since the Professor was still nowhere to be seen, Jeremy phoned Jules at the restaurant.

"How are you making out?" she asked him. She had the cordless phone tucked under her chin while she walked across the kitchen of The Monkey's Paw Bistro.

"It's all extremely strange," he said by way of an answer.

"Strange itself is not bad," Jules said. "All my father ever talks about are husbands and mutual funds. Turns out the evaluation criteria are similar."

She was trying to cheer him up, which he appreciated as always. "What are the numbers tonight?" he asked her.

"Twenty-six covers early. We have a six-top late. A few tentatives."

"Thursday," he said, exasperated.

"Walk-in Thursday," Jules said. Jeremy deduced from the steady scraping sound he heard that she was stirring the roasted carrot-ginger soup he had prepped earlier.

"I was going to use a bit of cinnamon in that soup," he said. "Is Zeena in?"

"Zeena, of course, is in," Jules said, and then, knowing he was trying to think about work as an alternative to what lay before him, she prodded, "Talk to me, sugar. How's he doing?"

Well, he's living in a park, for one. But Jeremy knew what she was really asking. "I can't be sure," he said to Jules. "He's not here yet."

"He'll show," Jules said. "Take the evening. I'll manage."

"Everything else prepped up?"

"Puh-lease."

"I made a demi from those duck bones. I was going to use that in the sauce for the duck breast with an apricot preserve...."

Sous-chef Jules Capelli met these instructions with long-suffering silence.

"Sorry."

"I got the notes," Jules said. "Now take the night and I'll see you tomorrow."

Caruzo had become the messenger. He could still cover great distances quickly on his long legs, and so he had been sent to set up this meeting, loping all the way across town to The Monkey's Paw to secure Jeremy's commitment in person. He returned with the good news, and a complimentary plate of lamb sausage and new-potato ragout inside him, retracing his steps through favourite back alleys, forest paths and finally to the Professor's camp.

"Yo hey," Caruzo called from the darkness, adhering to the protocol they had developed: Call from a short, respectful distance away. If there is no answer, come back later. "Hi, Professor," he called.

The Professor cracked the fly with two fingertips. He was sitting cross-legged in the middle of the little tent, sorting through piles of yellow foolscap pages. Each legal-sized sheet covered on both sides with handwritten notes, scrawled in pencil.

"Yo hey," Caruzo said. "Chef says yes. Jay-Jay is coming."

The Professor leaned out of the tent a little ways to catch the words. He was pleased.

"Five o'clock tomorrow," Caruzo said, nodding vigorously. "But hey," he continued, then stalled. The Professor waited while the big man squinted and relaxed his eyes repeatedly, milking out the thought.

"It's good," Caruzo said. "Jay-Jay coming."

"Jeremy coming is good," the Professor said, nodding reassurance.

"I'll meet him at the boathouse," Caruzo said. "Meet him, bring him in?"

"Fine," the Professor agreed. "I'll meet you both at the bulrushes."

"Right," Caruzo nodded. "Right." But he made no move to disappear into the dark, no move to find his way through the blackness to his own camp, so skilfully hidden for all these years. Instead he waited, a little nervously. "Do you want to talk?" the Professor asked, sensing Caruzo's mood. He quickly confirmed the presence of a pencil behind his ear, then felt around himself for one of his yellow legal pads.

He made a small fire. Then, as he had done so many nights since he discovered this place and the people in it, the Professor leaned back in the grass around the fire and only listened.

Caruzo spoke in the tongues of angels, although the fire of his words licked around the ideas he worked to express and often consumed them. Tonight again, he spoke of the children. "Their death pulled," Caruzo said, rocking. "The boy, the girl. Killed as they were. It pulled me and it sent me. Pulled others too. We were like the dry leaves, and their death was a puff of black air. For years I searched for them, and when I found them it all began." He gestured around himself at the park, the darkness. "From a leaf to a lifer," he went on. "That's me. A lifer to a leaf."

He burned himself out eventually and left as he typically did: without offering firm solutions to his riddles and without saying goodnight. He rose from his haunches, turned in the soft grass and vanished into the shadows.

The Professor read over his notes, then put the yellow legal pad back in the tent. He returned to the fire to watch it as the flames died. Since their last series of meetings, Caruzo had not untangled. So their deaths had drawn him here, the Professor thought, trying to work it through. The leaf blown by the evil event, the black wind. The leaf becoming a lifer, permanent. The lifer anticipating how he would one day, again, become a leaf. Was that it?

The Professor put his hands behind his head and stared up through the canopy of trees to find those pieces of the night sky that were visible. The fragments of constellations that, for those who could believe such things, would provide direction. He remembered how Hélène had disdained astrology, indeed most forms of the mystical. There was a certain cliché about the gypsy fortune teller with which she could not bear association. He learned this quickly after they first met. Nineteen fifty-six, Lyon. Hélène was living with her father and uncles, aunts and cousins, trying out city life after generations on the road. The Professor (not yet a professor) was over from Canada with his yellow pads and sharp pencils, observing. The first case study of a professional lifetime underway. His thesis named with some of the romance by which it had been electrified: *Romani Alighted: Remembering the Vardo*. Work from which all else had grown, the Professor thought now, branches sifting air above him. Their marriage, certainly. Hélène had been drawn to his interest in her. To his own unknowable history too, perhaps. Before his own father, now dead, there was only an expanse of unknown. A book of blank pages.

But the work with Hélène's family had also given birth to all his other work. Launched him across the anthropological landscape. Squatters in the Delta. Russian stowaways. The earliest Vancouver panhandlers who had peopled his successful book, *Will Work For Food*. Hélène might not always have appreciated her role at the root of things. And neither of them could have known how Stanley Park itself lay sleeping in their future.

The fire was out. The Professor climbed into his tent to sleep. He didn't dream of Caruzo. Didn't lie unconscious under images of Hélène's beauty, the unfolding of their years or even the October morning when he had awoken in the field with a very particular hollow feeling. The morning he had called Hélène, and the phone had rung and rung.

A welcome relief, this dreamless sleep.

In the morning he climbed down from the forest to the men's room by Second Beach. Familiar steps. He removed the pane of glass at the back of the locked building, as Caruzo had shown him long ago. He climbed in, washed, shaved. Then he spent the day on his favourite cliff, high above the sea in a salty breeze, thinking of how it might all be finally finished. Ten years later than expected, but one could not schedule tragedy or the irregular dawn of understanding.

When it was time to meet his son, the Professor pulled the fly-fishing net from his pack and walked down through the forest to the lagoon. At the trail mouth he stood in the shelter of a salal bush, eyes on the path. It was just before five. Caruzo appeared when he promised, leading Jeremy over the arched stone bridge and towards him. The Professor watched, but did not step from the bushes immediately, and the boy did as he would. He grew exasperated. His eyes found a pay phone nearby, a distraction. He stabbed the keypad with a finger, his back to Caruzo. Wishing, no doubt, to be anywhere but here. When he hung up, the Professor stepped from his hiding place, and Caruzo disappeared into the trees as agreed. The Professor enjoyed noting how the densely overlapping branches did not move as he entered the green face of the forest. Caruzo was merely absorbed.

"I can't stay long." These were the first words his son found.

"I thought maybe dinner."

"It's Thursday. I can't leave Jules alone."

His restaurant did not come up without mention of this name. "Oh, I'll bet you can," the Professor said.

They stood face to face in the falling light, the Professor's head just a degree to one side. The boy wasn't sleeping well, he thought. There were dark circles under his eyes. Black hair strawing this way and that. Was I wiry back then, like he is now? A little pale? They were still around the same six-foot height, the Professor observed, looking steadily into his son's eyes and thinking: I have not yet begun to shrink.

Jeremy thought only that his father looked better than he might under the circumstances. His eyes were bright, his brows pranced upward with good humour. True, his hair was dirty and his fingernails were black, and he was carrying an old wooden fly-fishing net pinched under one elbow for no evident reason.

"Perhaps you'll stay long enough to see me catch my dinner then," the Professor said. One needed darkness, he went on to explain. And so they sat on the bench and talked, circling but not meeting the matter at hand. Demand nothing, the

Professor thought. And so they talked about the Stanley Park game-bird population instead. A point of mutual interest, the Professor imagined.

"You eat duck?" Jeremy asked. A passer-by might have assumed he was about to provide cooking tips. Sear off the breast on a medium grill, skin side down. Render the fat. Finish skin side up, just a couple minutes. Sauce it and you're good to go.

But to which the Professor answered: "I've been here quite a few months and I didn't bring groceries. Have you eaten starlings?" He was aware that it sounded like a challenge. "Delicious, although you'll need two or three per person."

"I've eaten ortolan" Jeremy said, and then was irritable with himself for being drawn into the conversation on that level.

"Now, the mallard is a fantastically light sleeper," the Professor informed him.

Jeremy looked away.

"The canvasback even more so, fiendishly difficult to catch. The important thing is to learn a little each day here. Just a little. I spent a week trying to catch my first bird. A week. Do you know what I mean?"

"I have no idea what you mean," Jeremy answered. "I buy my ducks direct from a guy named Bertrand who lives on a farm up the valley."

"Although presumably someone catches them for Bertrand. Say though, I've been reading about you. Earlier this year. Anya Dickie's review of The Monkey's Foot. Brilliant job."

"The Monkey's Paw Bistro."

"Purple prose but a nice conclusion. How did the Dickie woman say it again?"

Jeremy sighed and looked out over the lagoon. The dynamic between them, he thought, didn't change much with the years, the location, or their relative mental health.

"'Crosstown Celebrates Local Beverages and Bounty,'"

Jeremy finally said, reciting the headline, which was also the lead line and the closing line of a typically enthusiastic Dickie restaurant review. She had been quite taken with the way Jules and he shared a passion for local meat, produce, cheese and wine.

"I could use that," the Professor said. "'Local bounty' is rather good. I think we share this passion, you and I."

Jeremy considered a retort along the lines of: "You and I share nothing but blood." But he imagined this approach would end the conversation. He would get no advice and have who knows what other effect on his father, and so he sat there and listened as the Professor elaborated on their supposed professional overlap, describing what he called "the stories of the residents." There was great deference in his voice. There had always been people here, the Professor said, solemn. There had been a First Nation, of course. Squatters later. Men who lived in trees. But this generation was the homeless, the new Stanley Park people. This was the story—collected lives and anecdotes, assorted obsessions and misfortunes—the Professor would now stitch together. The great Work-In-Progress.

"Is Sopwith Hill taking it?" Jeremy asked. A prestigious if aging textbook house, Sopwith had done the Professor's other books, some of these approaching mainstream popularity. Jeremy actually read one before the disastrous fall of 1987, before he fled to the culinary institute in Dijon. He couldn't remember the title, but he thought the Professor had spent three months in the downtown east side, interviewing panhandlers. Panhandling himself and living in a range of unsafe outdoor places, including under parked cars left overnight in a downtown parkade. Jeremy heard this story after the fact, his mother's bitter version. At one point (she had fumed) somebody had returned early to retrieve their car and had nearly run him over. He moved into an unused culvert behind the SeaBus Terminal at that point. "To be run over, that would maybe be the best to understand these people. These 'no-homes,'" she had said to Jeremy. "Only in dying like them, you can no longer write about them."

The Professor looked briefly away before answering the question. His son's tone registered doubt, incredulity. "They'll take it eventually." But his voice was a little tight.

So Jeremy sat back on the bench they had found, ran his fingers through his hair, which was in worse disarray than usual, a manic bristle. It was only appropriate that it started to rain lightly just then, fine drops hissing into the foliage around them.

"Fires," said the Professor, attempting to illustrate his point about learning a little each day. "Now there's something I knew nothing about. Thank God for Caruzo."

It was, for a moment, the single most unexpected revelation of the evening: The Professor could light fires.

They talked for over an hour this way, holding one another at a familiar arm's-length, both in their own way reflecting that Hélène was all the distance between them. Alive, she provided the bridge. Gone, she was the chasm itself. They might not yet have filled any of that emptiness, but a silver distance opened between them and the city. They sat, at the very least, in the same descending darkness, looking across the lagoon to the now gleaming towers of the West End, a parallel universe separated from them by the surface of the water on which slept hundreds of ducks.

"You stand watch," the Professor instructed quietly, when he deemed the time was right.

"For what?"

It was only his first visit. "Others."

Jeremy looked distinctly concerned.

"Not militant vegetarians precisely. More like the police."

"Oh, just that," the chef said. "Well, then: Charge."

Jeremy took shelter under a cedar. The Professor got

down on his knees and began to creep across the walkway. He held the old fly-fishing net in front of himself as he approached the clutch of rushes on the far side of the path. He rose to his knees and parted the papery stalks silently, the net aloft. Jeremy could make out several ducks within range. As he watched, all movement ceased.

And then the Professor merely fell forward, arm outstretched, pitching across the water. It was like a silent movie until a quarter second before his impact, when every duck within sixty yards burst from sleep and the lagoon simultaneously, and all previous tranquility, all silver thoughtfulness and reflection, drained out of the water in a spray of violent splashing. The air filled with black thudding shapes. Several birds left the water in a confused tangle and collided with one another, falling back into the lagoon. One fell onto the path in front of Jeremy, where it skidded, spun, seemed to glance at him in reproach before launching into flight again.

The one snared in the net, meanwhile, flew briefly in desperation, powerful wings holding it above water despite the Professor's full weight. Fighting. Flailing. Sinking suddenly. His father's head and upper body disappeared into the lagoon. He lay there, half-submerged, like he'd been shot. And then there was a gasping re-emergence, the duck now held by its neck, quivering, nearly drowned. The Professor breathing heavily. Water plastering down his hair, running down his face, his body blackened with it. He set the net aside, took the duck firmly in both his hands. He snapped his wrists sharply, cracking the neck. The bird was instantly still.

The Professor raised a finger to his lips. They waited. No celebration was permitted yet. The circling survivors reflocked above them, then homed in stupidly on another not distant part of the lagoon. As they swished to their new sleeping place the stillness slowly returned to the water.

Still no movement from the Professor, except a slight cocking of his head to the breeze. Listening to some small sound, measuring an intangible indicator that he knew from experience must either dissipate or return before he dared move. And when the Professor's variable fell (or rose) into the green zone, only then did they quietly scramble away from the lagoon, up through the grassy passageway to the Park Drive. Pausing just seconds at the edge of the new blacktop with its bright yellow markings for the angle parkers, then across this surface and into the cool forest. Even here they walked a distance without speaking.

When the city was almost inaudible, replaced with the sound of clacking cedars and moaning wind, the Professor stopped. "Ha ha," he said. Beaming again. He held his hands apart, in one the duck dangling by the neck, dripping water, beak and eyes serenely closed. "Look at that, would you? It never stops pleasing me to pluck from this forest the things that I need. Carefully and craftily I make my way."

He looked from his son to the bird and back again.

"And you are off to work now, I suppose," the Professor said, hoping he had stirred something. Guilt might do for now, although curiosity would be better.

"It's a nice bird," Jeremy heard himself say calmly, although his heart was pounding. Against his own better judgment he reached for the duck, thinking of cooking school and of France, of the ducks he himself had been taught to kill. Here, as the trees rattled against one another above them, Jeremy reached across his father to touch this duck, wanting to hold it while he knew it was still warm.

"Look at that. A nice redhead."

"Canvasback," the Professor corrected.

"Redhead," he said again, more emphatically.

"Oh no," the Professor said. "Definitely a canvasback."

"This duck," Jeremy said, irritated at their disagreement during this brief moment he had been enjoying, "is a redhead."

"This duck," answered the Professor, wincing now at the error, "is no redhead. With all due respect to your culinary education, Chef, I fear it has failed you here. There are pheasants, there are guinea hens and ortolans. Then there are park ducks. If you want to know about park ducks, I am, as they say, your man."

"Chestnut head—" Jeremy began.

"Cripes, Jeremy, shut the yawp just for a minute. Your red has a pronounced high forehead, a grey body and a much blacker tail. They are also a good deal less common around here, rare even. You see, my boy, I wouldn't have taken a redhead had there been a redhead to take. Which there wasn't, *ergo* this duck isn't."

At which point he took the bird back and slid it into a plastic shopping bag he produced from under his sweater. And without warning to Jeremy, he peeled off to the left and disappeared into the black forest between a towering stump and a half-fallen maple.

"This is ludicrous," Jeremy said, stopping and speaking emphatically to the empty pine-needle path. "I mean,…shit," he said. Here they were again, firing at each other in the blackness.

He looked up the path, down it, into the still darker forest, listening to the Professor moving away from him through the underbrush, the soft sound floating back. This moment would be the time to come to one's senses, Jeremy thought. To get the hell back into the city, to The Monkey's Paw, where twenty-six covers would be seated, conversation rising. Jules was probably now riding a wave of incoming appetizer orders, beginning to slam, the soundtrack urging everything and everybody onward into the night.

Or he could wait here. Thirty seconds from now the Professor would be gone. He might still be able to hear him, but he'd never find him. Not in that. In the darkness and the trees and the bramble. And the Professor wouldn't even notice, or he'd notice, maybe, but not be particularly surprised. He would forge ahead through this forest to his hidden spot.

(Perhaps he doesn't want me to see his spot, thought Jeremy.) Either way, he'd be fine. Just listen to him.

Somewhere up in the woods, the Professor was reciting a poem quietly. Jeremy had to hold himself very still to pick out the words.

"With an hoste of furious fancies,
Whereof I am commander,
With a burning speare, and a horse of air,
To the wildernesse I wander."

A challenge, of course, and it didn't get any quieter; the poem now came floating out of the swaying blackness from a single spot where the Professor stood, smiling and reciting, leaning his head back and looking towards the crack of black sky visible at the tops of the trees.

Jeremy crashed into the forest towards him. And when he found his father, they stood for a moment and looked at each other. Jeremy's favourite cowboy boots were past wet, the branches now reaching to soak his back and neck.

"Is this it?" he said. Through the trees Jeremy could make out campfires spread in the darkness around them.

"Not quite yet," the Professor said, motioning with his head that they should continue. He turned and hoisted a leg up to a foothold on a large root-covered rock, gripped the gnarled wood with his fingertips and disappeared over the top.

It was the root end of a gigantic tree, Jeremy realized. Torn from the soil by a gust of wind, torn up along with the huge boulder to which the roots had been clinging. Jeremy clambered inexpertly after his father and stood at the base of the broad trunk. It stretched out in front of them like a bridge, 150 feet long, silver in the moonlight. As they walked it bowed slightly beneath them. It surprised Jeremy, this slight bending of the massive trunk. He would have thought their weight was not enough to move such a great thing, a thing that vaulted them through the brush to a completely different part of the park. A denser part. A place that had no relation to anything that he had previously known.

"What we want is a fire," the Professor said from ahead of him, as they descended a slope.

And he lit good fires too, Jeremy discovered. After half an hour tramping through the damp and the dark, the Professor made a small hot fire in just a few minutes. Built with few words spoken, in a trench at the centre of his camp.

While the Professor changed into dry clothes, Jeremy squatted back-assed to the heat and considered that if he were abandoned here, he would be lost until morning. Perhaps even then. So busy a park, thousands of visitors a day. Never once had he felt lost in it, as he was now.

A map and a global positioning system would have revealed to him that he was not far from things that he knew. Just a couple of hundred yards off the Park Drive, near Prospect Point, in fact. Here a densely forested slope fell from the road, down to the top of a cliff that towered a hundred feet above the seawall and the ocean below. The Professor had found a clearing between the trees at the very edge of this cliff. There were tamped-down ferns and a tent built against the trunk of a cedar, a space big enough for one very still, very accomplished sleeper. And through the branches of this tree, and the others that umbrella-ed over the small clearing, one had a view of the harbour, freighters silent at their moorage, well lit. At the bottom of the cliffs and to the left stood Siwash Rock, which pillared fifty feet out of the water near the shore. A rock that was once a bather, legend had it, a bather honoured by the gods with this permanent place at the lip of forest that had been his home.

The Professor plucked the canvasback and drew it smoothly. He buried the entrails some distance away. He washed his hands and the bird with water from a plastic juice container. "Did you bring salt by any chance?" he asked, returning to the fire. "No matter, I have a packet left."

"How about string?" Jeremy asked. You might as well do it right, he thought. And when the Professor produced his string, Jeremy trussed the bird, tying it into the fork of a blackened Y-shaped stick. He buried the other end of the stick in the soft earth, supported it across a large stone and cantilevered the bird above the flames. By sliding the stone back and forth, the bird's height and roasting temperature could be very roughly adjusted. He sat back in the dry area of fern nearest the flames and folded his arms across his knees.

There was silence for some time. The bird began to glisten, then hiss gently. Finally the aroma was released: smoky, fatty, rich with oil. He twisted the stick a quarter turn.

"This is all quite illegal, of course," Jeremy said finally, aware that the comment was softened by his own complicity. But the Professor only looked at him as if he were a little slow for just getting this point. "All right," Jeremy went on, failing to resist a small smile. The duck smelled good. "How do you catch a starling?"

"Caruzo showed me," the Professor said, re-energized. "Peanut butter spread on top of a good strong epoxy from any hardware store. On a stick or a low branch in a relatively clear area, not too far into the forest. You can watch from quite close by; they are not a shy bird. Or scarce, for that matter. It works nicely, although you'll want to remove the feet before you cook them."

Jeremy rocked gently back and forth. Shook his head as if to clear it. "You clean them up like that?" he asked, nodding towards the juice container full of water.

"I take the starlings down to the men's room by the beach," the Professor said, "where I can spread out and do a good job." Now he was rummaging through his leather case, which he had slung up in the low branches of the nearby cedar. He re-emerged from the branches carrying a bottle of wine. "I bought this wine for you. A Rioja. You like Spain, don't you?"

"Never been."

"Right. France, was it?"

"France," Jeremy said.

The Professor uncorked the wine. Then he unsnapped a collapsible field cup from inside its pouch, telescoped it out, poured some of the red wine and handed it across the fire to Jeremy. He had a plastic cup for himself.

When they both had wine, Jeremy still did not sip. The Professor felt the pause and looked at his son.

"Participatory anthropology…," Jeremy began.

"Quite beyond immersion," the Professor said. "The next step, really."

Jeremy chose his words carefully. "I thought you had given this up."

"I had," the Professor said. "But I left something unfinished. Something I thought should be put to rest."

Jeremy wasn't sure he understood.

"My own celebration of 'local bounty,'" the Professor said, nodding towards the duck and smiling.

"Not funny," Jeremy answered.

"You don't like that we might be working on parallel projects."

Jeremy sighed and lifted the silver cup in the orange light that flickered around them. "*Santé*," he said. "To your health."

"*A la vôtre*," said the Professor, before drinking. "To yours too."

They charred the bird a bit on the back and the legs. It was tough to cook directly over such a low flame. Still, it wasn't badly done. The breast was crispy, the meat the texture of medium steak. The Professor cut them off pieces in turn, which they ate with their hands, sitting cross-legged next to one another in the dry ferns near the fire.

"It's not really cooking, I realize," said the Professor. "Perhaps with a salal-berry cream sauce we could tart it up to your customer's level of sophistication."

"Sure." Although: salal-berry cream sauce. Not bad.

"Salt?" The Professor dangled the packet at eye level.

Jeremy took the paper envelope of precious salt and sprinkled some across the piece of canvasback breast in his fingers. He chewed and swallowed. He took a breath.

"I'm just a cook."

The Professor glanced up. "Oh yes?"

"That's all," Jeremy said. "So I like local produce. So I like local rabbits. Whatever."

"Whatever? Meaning: no reason for this preference? No larger significance?"

"Of course it has significance. There just isn't any big—"

"Any big reason for it?" the Professor said.

Maybe not, Jeremy thought. He swallowed another mouthful of duck and held a greasy finger up in front of himself. "If somebody asked me, 'What are you trying to accomplish?'" he started, "I would answer that I was trying to remind people of something. Of what the soil under their feet has to offer. Of a time when they would have known only the food that their own soil could offer."

"Sort of a nostalgia thing," the Professor said.

"Make fun," Jeremy said, "but how would you answer the same question?"

"I would say," the Professor answered, "that I am here allowing the words of this wilderness to penetrate me, to understand what is being said by these people. Because I believe it is something that concerns us all, some more than most. You and I, for example. Or perhaps we are just ready to hear these words. You and I."

Jeremy looked away. Part of this answer was pleasing, the inclusion. The remainder was exasperating. "And what are those words exactly?"

"In aggregate, something along these lines:

With an hoste of furious fancies,
Whereof I am commander,
With a burning speare, and a horse of air,
To the wildernesse I wander."

Jeremy shook his head and sat back. "And to think Sopwith Hill won't commit to that."

"The stories don't come all at once, shrink-wrapped with a complimentary bookmark."

"Give me one. Just one to get a sense...."

"Well, there is this Siwash character," the Professor said. "He sits in the forest—a few hundred yards that way, near Siwash Rock—counting." Counting people, the Professor went on to explain. Nobody knew why, and the Professor had only spoken with him twice since arriving. Siwash made him tea both times, their dialogue polite, cagey. He had arrived, he explained, like so many others had arrived. "I am blown here," Siwash had said, running a hand over a waxy scalp, then pulling on an ear that appeared to have two lobes. "I was washed up on the beach like all the others. Crawled free from the wreckage of an imperfect landscape onto these perfect shores. I will never leave."

He liked maps. The Professor described how dozens had been Scotch-taped to the walls of the concrete bunker that the man called home. National Geographic maps of the earth's polar regions. A black starlight globe. Various cylindrical and conical projections. All these hung in the relative darkness of the concrete room, glowering obscurely from the shadows in a bunker that had once been a pillbox, an armed outpost on a rock outcropping above Siwash Rock. A vantage point from which the authorities once thought they could repel Japanese invaders during the dark and paranoid days of Vancouver's World War II.

But what about this counting? "Is there a number?" At their second meeting, the Professor tried to press down on this issue. He had decided the tea was China Black. "Is it a number you're waiting to reach? Like a thousand, or ten thousand?"

"No number," Siwash told him, and became elusive.

"Maybe a head count of some kind," Jeremy offered, intrigued by the idea. The map-lined pillbox in a public park was richly eccentric, certainly, but it sounded cosier than his father's set-up.

"Caruzo thinks it is a tally, yes. But even he doesn't know," the Professor said, nodding. In fact, Caruzo did not speak of Siwash often, and the Professor had never seen them together. He imagined it would be like having two evangelists in the same room. They could talk, but they already had views on everything, and their words were better directed at others.

"Caruzo," Jeremy said. "I suppose he is another story."

"I would think so, perhaps even the first chapter of a longer story. I understand you see him from time to time at the restaurant around breakfast."

"Yes, thank you. He's been a Friday regular for the past month. If you have any more people living around here who want free coffee and cigarettes and maybe a snack in the morning, you send them along."

"Those volumes you couldn't handle," the Professor pointed out.

"I suppose you sent him to see how I was doing?" Jeremy said.

"And you also sent him back with word that you wanted to see *me*," the Professor responded. "So we have both used him as a messenger, haven't we?"

They drifted into silence for a moment, the fire dropped to coals.

"I remember a photograph. The three of us at the lagoon," the Professor said eventually.

Jeremy looked up sharply at the mention of it. "Under the cherry trees."

"That's the one," the Professor said, smiling. He cut off some more duck. "You see how there is also a great deal of us held in this wilderness."

Jeremy didn't know what to think of that comment. They were silent for a few minutes.

"You wanted to see me. To ask me something, I suspect," the Professor said finally. "But I sense you are suddenly shy. Perhaps I can balance the scale by asking my favour of you first."

Jeremy nodded in agreement.

"I need someone in the city. Someone to do some research."

It surprised him. "Why not Caruzo?" he heard himself say.

"Well, Caruzo can't read, for one."

"Why not you?"

"Fine then."

"Sorry. Tell me."

The Professor took a moment before continuing. "Babes in the Wood," he said finally.

Jeremy waited for more, and when nothing came said: "Who are..."

"Who *were* murdered in Stanley Park, not far from here. Two children, conventionally understood to be brothers, although there have been different views on this over the years. In any case, two children, unsolved murder. Still, this story is not a murder mystery, understand. I am interested in the myths surrounding their death, about their bodies still being buried here in the park. About related matters."

"And when exactly?" Jeremy said, growing faintly nervous.

"Oh," the Professor said. "A long time ago. Fifty years. It was in all the papers at the time. Two little kids, murdered with a small hatchet in the park. Not half a mile from where we're sitting, in fact. The killer, never found. The reason, inexplicable. The repercussions..." And here the Professor leaned forward and looked at his son very closely. "The repercussions still spilling down through the years."

There was a second of silence.

"All right," Jeremy said. "What can I do?"

"I need details," the Professor said. "You could try the library."

Jeremy thought for a second.

"Yes?" the Professor pressed, canting a bit forward.

"Sure," Jeremy said. "I promise."

"There are stories, you understand?" The Professor was again looking directly at his son. "There is Siwash and there are others. There are individual stories written in code. Say mental illness, say what you like. But I have come to understand recently, very recently, that in these stories there are threads that weave together into a single chord. A single story lives at the centre of it all, and by this story the others might be interpreted."

"These kids," Jeremy said, voice flat.

"Their death. Perhaps."

Jeremy nodded, feeling helpless. A promise to do some research didn't sound like a lot coming out. Released into the dark air between them, it gained volume and weight, instantly.

"Well then?" the Professor said, thinking they should move on before the boy reconsidered. "Do tell." And with this comment, he laid back in the ferns, his head outside of the pool of firelight, supported in his two interlocked hands, elbows flaring out and framing his darkened face. A coal sparked and threw an instant of reflection into his black pupils.

"The Monkey's Paw is everything I want to do," said Jeremy, by way of introduction. "Jules and I work exceptionally well together. We understand each other precisely."

"Jules Capelli, yes. Plus, the alliterative Anya Dickie likes you," the Professor said.

Jeremy nodded. "That review helped us, I can tell you. We were in deep trouble there for a while," he said. Even thinking about it made him nervous.

The Professor waited.

"Money trouble," Jeremy explained.

"Ah, yes," his father said. He was not overly familiar with this kind of trouble.

"No matter how good people say we are, the downtown east side makes some people uncomfortable. That is, some of the foodies we would otherwise be attracting won't go there. Plus, what we do is not always cheap to begin with. A prawn raised in a vat in the basement of a factory in Singapore is about half the price of a fresh prawn from the Queen Charlotte Islands. Not as good, clearly, but cheaper."

"Fascinating," said the Professor, who was enjoying the ideological drama captured in the story. "It is inefficient, perhaps, to have your passion for local ingredients."

"Maybe that's it," Jeremy said. "In any case, I almost crashed the whole thing. It was close. Debts, credit cards, cheques. I'm bad with that stuff. And even now, it would be misleading to say we're hugely profitable."

"I see," the Professor said. "Now you feel pressure from the moneylenders, and it is distracting you from what you love to do, is that it?"

"Sure. Partly."

"And despite these pressures, you have little control over increasing your own business. So you simply cook well, remain devoted to your culinary principles, and hope that a lot of people will eventually come to appreciate your efforts and come to your restaurant and spend money, etc., etc."

Jeremy nodded wearily. "Basically. The strain of which brings me to the question."

The Professor sat up and poked the coals. "I'm listening."

"Dante Beale."

His father stopped poking the coals and looked at him. "What about Dante?"

"He's offered to invest. He likes the restaurant. He knows I'm struggling. He believes in what I'm doing."

"That barista boy," the Professor said.

"He *employs* baristas," Jeremy said. "Thousands of them too. Inferno International Coffee is huge—you have to give him credit for that."

"Credit," said the Professor, thinking back. "Isn't that what he gave you?"

"He guaranteed my bank loan. This arrangement would be quite different."

"I'm sure."

"This would be an opportunity to let someone else worry about the money for a change."

The Professor was skeptical.

"I know this is unusual," Jeremy said, "but I'm asking for advice here. You know him."

"I don't trust him."

"And you've been neighbours, friends, for what . . . twenty years?"

"I didn't say, 'I don't like him.' I said, 'I don't trust him.'"

"Explain."

"He's wrong for you," the Professor said, not quite explaining.

"It's a bad situation. Did I mention the bank is not happy?"

"You didn't, no."

"And Inferno is powerful. Big and getting bigger."

"I've heard. How many of those awful coffee shops are there now?"

"Hundreds. All over North America. He could really help."

"Dante will not help you do what you want to do," the Professor stated bluntly. "Dante is only one thing. He has always been the same thing in the many years I have known him. At one time I admired his focus, but now I see the man for what he is and what his worldview implies. Dante is a price. Dante is a sale. Dante abhors anything that is not a commodity. You, on the other hand...well, 'local bounty.' That's pretty good, actually. That's a pretty good idea."

"I agree but—"

"He is about only one thing, Jeremy. Mammon. The almighty dollar."

"Well," Jeremy said. "In those terms Dante is about $230,000 to me."

"Which means what exactly?" The Professor asked.

"The amount of my debt, more or less."

The Professor winced. "That's a lot, isn't it?"

Jeremy looked away into the darkness. It certainly was a lot.

"And the price for this timely assistance?" the Professor asked.

"Majority ownership. I work the rest off."

"I see. He then owns you."

"I may not be worth much without him."

"Bankrupt or not, I am under the impression you are exceptionally good at what you do," the Professor said, giving an atypical compliment, backhanded or otherwise.

"So, how should I respond to this offer?"

"*Turn him down*," the Professor said, articulating each word very clearly.

They were staring across the embers at each other. For reasons Jeremy could not yet explain, this answer was suddenly what he had expected all along. And he saw himself as a fool for having asked, for having thought that silence could be fruitfully ended between them. "That's it?" he said.

The Professor raised his eyebrows and shrugged.

"That's all I get after slogging through the forest to talk to you? Coming here in the middle of the evening?" Jeremy gestured angrily at the duck carcass, still hanging on the roasting stick, which toppled on cue into the fire pit.

The Professor responded calmly. "Did you want more advice or just different advice?"

The silence bristled.

"Why not talk to Jules about it?" the Professor asked.

"It's complicated," Jeremy said, but this reminder swamped his anger with different feelings. There would be problems here, he knew. And Jules was a little bit like the Professor in her commitment to the things she believed. "Me going broke wouldn't be doing her any favours either," he said finally, shaking his head.

"Even so," the Professor continued, "you would have held onto the one thing that provides you with stability and roots."

At which point Jeremy had to lie back in the ferns and laugh out loud. "Roots? Listen to you."

"All right, all right, keep it down," said the Professor. "I realize my present work puts at risk my credibility on the matter of stability, but if you just understood how important—"

Jeremy sat up straight. "Are you the voice crying in the wilderness?" he said. "I mean *the* voice." Then he lay back and let himself laugh some more. His father now allowed a small smile.

"You know, quiet is normally a good policy around here," the Professor said. "The attention one attracts is not always good attention."

Tell me about it, thought Jeremy.

# BECOMING BLOOD

What kind of attention was he attracting anyway? This question of Who They Were consumed Jeremy. As a preoccupation these days, it could be ranked only behind his father's mental state and the frantic contemplation of his own financial picture. It was an important question, Jeremy had long ago decided, because in the world of food you could be a Crip or a Blood, but you had to choose sides.

One of the American students came up with these names at the culinary institute in Dijon and they stuck. Crips versus Bloods. Crip cooks were critical. They fused, they strove for innovation, they were post-national. They called themselves artists. They tended to stack things like mahi mahi and grilled eggplant in wobbly towers glued together with wasabi mayonnaise, and were frequently suspicious of butter. Vegetarianism was an option for Crips but not for Bloods. Blood cooks were respectful of tradition, nostalgic even. Canonical, interested in the veracity of things culinary, linked to "local" by the inheritance or adoption of a culture, linked to a particular manner and place of being. Blood cooks liked sweetbreads and pot-au-feu. Bloods ate tacos, bratwurst, borscht. They used lard and as much foie gras as they could get their hands on. They made cassoulet to the recipe left by Louis Cazals and, depending on where the Bloods called home, they might like kimchi, salmon planked on cedar, fish stew with sausage, or twice-cooked duck.

Chef Jeremy Papier was Blood. He learned this truth about himself in his first working kitchen, although he didn't understand what he had learned until after he left France.

The kitchen was the Relais St. Seine l'Abbaye in rural Burgundy, where Jeremy worked for a year after graduating from the institute. The restaurant was named for a town, which was named for an abbey, which was named for the source of the Seine River flowing from a nearby ridge down to Paris. The designation *"relais"* meant you were either a filling station or a roadside restaurant, the latter in this case, a low building with multipaned windows, set back behind a gravel courtyard with ivied walls. Here the customers— very often German and Swiss families following the Seine to Paris—would park their Saabs and Audis and Benzes.

The *relais* was small, sixty-five seats around square tables with plain white cloths. To the rear of the restaurant the windows opened onto a grassy hillside climbing up to the edge of the Fôret de Gens, which ran down into the Ignon Valley. The forest was still full of boar and elk, many small etchings of which Chief Quartey had collected over the years and hung on the walls of his restaurant.

Chef Jacques Quartey himself was large—six foot six, close to 250 pounds—and appropriately fond of Great Danes. Two of his dogs would be wandering around the dining room at any given time, and Jeremy understood Quartey's total pack to include seven. They had been warned at school to expect initial disdain from any chef, particularly those who had been Michelin-starred and, even more so, those who had descended from four generations of similarly decorated culinary master sergeants. Still, it made an impression when Chef Quartey pinched Jeremy's letter of introduction into a long wick and used it to light the burners of the big range.

He said only: "Are you fast enough? Sometimes we are busy."

Jeremy knew he wouldn't be fast enough, no matter what accolades he had garnered at school. So he said: "I will be." Cagey, relying on the language barrier to obscure his meaning.

Chef Quartey handed Jeremy off to a somewhat more sympathetic sous-chef named Claude, who still wouldn't let him anywhere near the line. Claude, a five-foot-nothing pylon of culinary rigour, had Jeremy prep *mise en place*—all the ingredients and portioned materials required by the line cooks, which they would then arrange around themselves at their respective stations—for the first three weeks. The greatest portion of this daily prep routine seemed, to Jeremy, to involve leeks. Leek gratin, deep-fried shredded leeks, bistro leek salad—all these were *relais* standards. Of course, there were also shallots to mince, parsley to wash, sort, stem and chiffonade. Peppercorns to crush, chives to chop. Wine and brandy to decant into pour bottles. Bushels of tomatoes to roast and dice, celery roots to peel and shred or cube or cut paper-thin for crisps, depending on what Quartey bellowed out at his lecture each morning. Make mirepoix by the bucket. Fill the salt dishes. Wipe down the stations. Wipe down the stations again.

Week three climaxed with Jeremy participating in the making of a *relais*-style chicken stock that Claude described as *sincère*. Jeremy was never sure what this descriptor meant, except that his was a stock apparently based on no false pretences and that Claude had cruised repeatedly by, hovering at his elbow as Jeremy roasted the bones, sweated the mirepoix, then combined these with water, bay leaves and a halved head of garlic, and brought it all to a lazy bubble.

Week four, Thursday, Claude was absent for the dinner service because of a funeral. He made it clear the day before, having cleaned down his station, that the deceased was one of only three people for whose funeral he would miss work. (He did not name the surviving two.) Jeremy found himself promoted dizzily to the line. An appetizer and a main fell solely to him.

Quartey addressed the squab main course first: crapaudine. It was an old-fashioned presentation where the small bird was opened and flattened, legs tucked in to make a tight package. When it was roasted and garnished with bits of hardboiled egg for eyes, it did look faintly like a toad, the *crapaud* from which the name derived. Quartey described the plating in his typically efficient style. "Red pepper coulis to the plate. Our little toad here, please. Potato frite, like so." He showed Jeremy how to fan the frite starburst-style around the roasted bird, interspersed with roasted shallots and garlic cloves. Garnish with leaves of frissée. He gave similarly detailed instructions on the appetizer, sautéed langoustine served with curried cream. The positioning of the shredded leeks would be precisely the same, Chef Quartey emphasized, on each plate.

He would prep for the next two hours. Mirepoix first and foremost, always. Caramelized for the langoustine, which themselves had to be poached, shelled and diced. Green onions julienned, red peppers diced to a tiny diamond for garnish. Chicken stock reduced, flavoured with curry, mace and thyme, thickened with velouté, cream added. Prep for the squab meant roasting the shallots, the garlic and the peppers, which then had to be skinned and blended with water and more garlic into a coulis.

He looked up. Chef Quartey was watching him. "Messy," he said. And Jeremy saw that his station was littered with bits of julienned green onion.

Forty minutes before service, falling a little into the weeds, Jeremy opened up twelve squabs, flattened them with the heel of his hand on the board and tucked in the legs. He ran them onto a skewer, par-roasted them. At the pick-up, the breast would be crisped under the broiler and plated according to the chef's demands. At the call for shellfish, the langoustine and the caramelized mirepoix would be combined, sautéed and seasoned, piled in the centre of the plate, surrounded by a puddle of curried cream, garnished with the deep-fried leeks and red pepper diamonds, and slid into the window for pick up.

Maître d'hôtel Duclos reported later that a German family had applauded as he slid the plated squab onto the white linen tablecloth. The clapping made a sharp noise in the quiet dining room.

Chef Quartey said: "It is good Claude has only two friends left." But he smiled. Jeremy distinctly saw him smile.

Week five, Monday, Chef Quartey took Jeremy and three of the Great Danes into the covered market in Dijon early in the morning to pick out meat, cheese and produce. He asked Jeremy's opinion on something, a signal compliment.

"Name your favourite," Chef Quartey said, waving a hand over the seventy or eighty cheeses on display under the counter. They were standing behind the display case with the owner, who also addressed Quartey as 'Chef.'

"J'aime beaucoup le Reblochon, Chef," said Jeremy, naming a cheese from the Haute Savoie near the Swiss border.

"Excellent. I love Burgundy, but one cannot be fanatical about these things."

Sunday of week seven, on the one day the restaurant was supposed to be closed, Jeremy walked from the little hillside house he was renting down into St. Seine l'Abbaye to buy cigarettes at the gas station. "Gitanes, s'il vous plaît."

He walked through town, enjoying the almost entirely random way that streets began and ended. There were intersections of three streets, corners impossibly tight. He made his way over to the abbey. Inside, it was cold and gloomy, the altar feebly lit. He approached tentatively and stood, offering silence. Turning, his view was dominated by a twenty-foot-high crucifix, which hung on the wall above the abbey's main door. Staring into the nave from the back of the church, this Christ had an unusual companion: A skull and crossbones, like the pirate emblem, hung on the wall beneath his feet.

The dead. The dying. A family winnowed to two. But from what?

*Papier.* Jeremy let the name unscroll in his head—staring unblinking at the crucifix, at the skull—a name whose history lay in its own grave. His grandfather's first name had been Felix; Jeremy knew that much. Felix, who emigrated from Poland sometime in the 1920s, alone. Who had chosen a new surname on arrival. A truncated, Anglicized Hebrew surname, no less, although no Jewish lineage was ever subsequently acknowledged. For the few years the Professor remembered Felix on the scene, the Papiers had been Lutherans. After the disappearance, the divorce, the telegram relating news of his death, the story went with him.

"But we might be Jewish," a twelve-year-old Jeremy protested to his father. There had been a youthful period of genealogical interest, during which time Jeremy turned up evidence of Polish families with names like Papierbuch and Papierczyk. Papierovitch and Papierin. Jews all. Jeremy had been hopeful.

"Indeed. We might be. We might have this history. We are, for starters, both circumcised."

The Professor never spoke down to children.

"But that we cannot know our history for certain would be your grandfather's point, I imagine. He chose a surname. He chose this name with an intent, by a method, that is lost to us. You might think of it as the punchline to a joke Felix can no longer explain."

A hard concept to understand, then. The appeal of a given history—with the set of answers and instructions that Jeremy presumed came with such a legacy—had been so clear. Appealing still.

Outside the church in St. Seine l'Abbaye, Jeremy crossed the narrow highway that ran through the town, walking along the shoulder a short distance, smoking and inhaling deeply, squinting into the wistful, rose light of sunset. Contemplating personal history had made him lonely, only the second time since arriving in France. The first had been just before school began. He had gone to Lyon by train, again questing back through time. Seeking without any plan beyond wanting to find the building where his mother and father had met, where her extended family had lived. He didn't expect to find relatives; he understood they had long drifted away into the newly traversable landscapes of the European Union. But the idea of the building had appealed to him as an iconic place, a site he might identify with his own beginnings.

A site of important kitchens too, Jeremy understood. The kitchen of the large restaurant where his mother's father and uncles had worked as busboys and dishwashers. The kitchen at home in which they had eaten and in which his mother and father had had their first conversations. Jeremy carried a composite mental picture of it based on his parents' separate, scattered recollections. A cold tile floor. A wooden table big enough for the entire clan, where the Professor had done his interviewing—copious notes on sheaves of yellow paper, Jeremy imagined.

The young man was interested in the *vardo*, Hélène's father had explained to her. How some of them still lived, yes, although he also seemed interested in how they liked living in an apartment after having known the *vardo*.

Hélène told her father to tell the young man with his paper and pencils that she liked their apartment very much, and that she had been far too young to remember her short life in the wagons. But when she cooked dinner that night, it had been a stew of lamb marinated in yogurt and lemon juice. An old recipe, an open tribute. Tart and unexpected. The flavours contradicting themselves by being at once deep and light. Difficult to pin down. The Professor ate, watched her. Hélène looked away.

Handsome and beautiful, Jeremy imagined. His father described a small woman, with a precise figure, smooth dark skin, a large mouth and shining volumes of mahogany-coloured hair. His mother remembered a young man of strikingly intelligent eyes, angularity, likeable oddness. Jeremy wondered if perhaps she had also liked the young man's permanently erased history. They married in a civil ceremony. Her father's suggestion. The once-traveller now proud to wear his black city suit in front of the Justice, proud to wish them well, his daughter and her new husband. To bless their trip across the sea to Canada. To bless their remaining days with a touch of his thumb to each of their foreheads, a kiss on the lips. It was a serious but unsentimental goodbye at the Gare Part-Dieu.

As it happened, Jeremy never found either building. He had an address torn from the corner of an envelope found in his mother's desk drawer. Even so, no luck. The streets seemed to have changed. At a grocery store that looked to date from the same time, Jeremy stumbled over his words, asking about an apartment building that might have been across the street. A large restaurant that might have been nearby.

The man thought he remembered a restaurant. He didn't think it was a very good one.

"Pas Bocuse," he said, chortling.

He felt lonely then, riding the train back to Dijon. And now, school finished, work begun—in a very different part of the country, a place for his own new beginnings—Jeremy drew deeply on his cigarette and felt lonely a second time. He thought about climbing out of the valley and up onto the ridge above St. Seine l'Abbaye. From there he might have a view of the whole town. But setting out in that direction, he passed the *relais* and stopped instead.

To his surprise, there were lights in the window and cars parked in the gravel lot. To his further surprise, there were no gleaming salon cars. He counted instead a couple of dented Renault Cinq, a Citroën 2CV and several flat-bed trucks like those the local farmers used.

He went inside, and there Jeremy found that the dining room was noisily full. There was a scumble of country French conversation with no pause for his arrival. Nobody noticed him as he entered the room, except Patrice, their waitress from Pellerey, who was out front alone that evening. She came out of the kitchen with a chicken carved in the bourgeois style—cut up and reassembled for presentation on the table with a bunch of watercress sprouting from the cavity.

Patrice flashed him a crooked-toothed smile and gestured back towards the kitchen. When he went in, he found Claude sprinkling hard-boiled egg on a butter-lettuce salad and Chef Quartey plating a portion of langue de boeuf à la moutarde. Jeremy wordlessly pulled on his whites and his apron, washed his hands and, following Chef Quartey's nod, went over to help on grill. Much later, after everybody had gone and the broken tail lights of the farm trucks had disappeared up and over the hill, they all sat together out front for a snack and a nightcap. He returned Patrice's encouraging smile from earlier. He smiled at her Roman nose, brown eyes and black hair, and she smiled back. Chef Quartey poured them all more wine.

"Santé," he said, and tore off a piece of bread to dip into his own glass. "On the seventh day, Ger-ah-mee," Chef Quartey continued, pausing with something like respect and waving a paw around the empty room, "we serve the people with the rubber boots."

The words stayed with Jeremy as he walked home with Patrice, his arm around her shoulder, hers along his waist. The Rubber-Boot People, the people from here. Their simple words.

He woke up with the very earliest light, his hand on the strong curve of her hip. The light broke into the valley, through his window, across Patrice's brown shoulder, and there was, for a moment, utter simplicity and coherence.

He cooked seven nights a week from that point onward, eager for the seventh day when the stiff cardboard menu was put aside in favour of a chalkboard where Chef Quartey or Claude, or even Jeremy eventually, would write down their ideas. And during his few morning off-hours, Patrice began to show him the secrets of the surrounding countryside. In the Fôret de Gens above town, there were hollow trees in which the women of the village had once hidden pots of soup for resistance fighters. They never saw the men, Patrice told him, but they would return in the still-dark morning to retrieve their cold tureens.

Sometime later she took him to the source de la Seine. It was on the far side of the ridge above the town, the side of the ridge that faced away from the quiet of rural Burgundy and down towards the tumult of Paris. Here, in a little park of Parisian symmetry, a statue of the goddess Sequana guarded the famous source. She lay in a grotto built by Napoleon III, vacant eyes cast upwards as if imagining the City of Light, where this bubbling water would eventually flow under the Pont Neuf and around l'Île de la Cité and on to the sea.

In her direct manner Patrice only explained: "Here from the ridge flows the water that will wet the grass that the cows will eat to make the cream for your coffee when you leave me and go to Paris."

He climbed across the low iron railing that separated Sequana from her visitors.

"Ger-ah-mee," Patrice scolded.

He took a long step across the pool that surrounded the goddess, stood next to her, then climbed into her lap. She held him securely. He lay his head in the hard valley between her stone breasts and gazed out of the grotto at Patrice.

She was laughing. "Wait," she said. "Do not move now." And she produced a Polaroid camera from her handbag and took a crooked shot.

He remembered that after taking the photo, they heard the diesel snort of an arriving bus, trucking in the tourists from Paris to visit Sequana, to understand something of how Paris came to be.

"You must come out," Patrice said, holding the developing Polaroid.

"Tourists," Jeremy said, affecting a weary, spoilt tone. "I cannot bear them."

"I think the goddess likes the tourists better than you," Patrice said after he had climbed out. "They are maybe not so familiar." But they stood there for a few minutes longer and watched the picture become clear. It had turned out nicely.

Of course, he knew he had to return home eventually. Work visas aside, there came a month during which thoughts of leaving came up once a week, in each case riding sidecar on a sweeping memory of his mother's death. Of how she had launched him, sent him across the world to escape the vacuum of grief. To escape the palpable sense of guilt that emanated from his father at the funeral and in their few abortive conversations that followed. He had fled, Jeremy knew, and fled successfully, although now he heard the silence between them ringing. He sent a letter, a note really— part warning, part reassurance. *Coming home. Things are fine.* He enclosed the Polaroid from the source de la Seine, hoping it would help rebuild bridges.

"Well, you must go home then," Patrice said, looking out the window when he finally told her.

They went on one more long walk together, his last day in Burgundy. He suggested a parting visit to the source de la Seine, and Patrice looked at him curiously. It had just occurred to her that Jeremy thought that little park captured the region, with its gurgling brook artificially routed between the green benches, its gaudy statue and tour buses.

"Oh, no," Patrice said. But she laughed. She could let him take away this false impression. But he had a sweet way of looking at her, and he had lived here long enough that he deserved to know the truth.

She explained the geography of the area as they walked from the car down a small road, just a few kilometres north-west of St. Seine l'Abbaye. The ridge formed a break point in the countryside, like a continental divide on a small scale. To the west, the Seine ran its course to Paris, to the Atlantic, to places beyond. To the east, down the other side of the ridge, ran the Ignon River.

"The Ignon?" Jeremy said.

He hadn't even heard of it. He was, Patrice thought, such a boy. She took his hand and led him down an embankment next to the road.

It was quite different from the other side of the ridge. There was no signage, no park or statue. But at the bottom of the hillside, water emerged from the soil. From a hundred spurts and eddies coming out under roots and stones and a carpet of white flowers. The ground flowed with water that gathered and gathered again until it formed the top of the Ignon River flowing northeast and into the Burgundy countryside.

"The water of this region," she said, looking at him. "All around you."

The blood, thought Jeremy.

They stopped by the restaurant to say final goodbyes. Claude pumped his hand in the militaristic way he had, once up, once down. Chef Quartey clapped Jeremy's head in his hands and kissed him on each cheek.

"You will be," Chef Quartey said, looking for the English word, "exceptional."

Patrice drove him to the train station in Dijon, where they kissed a final time. She surrendered no tears, but said only: "Bonne chance, Ger-ah-mee."

The cheapest flight from Paris had a twenty-four-hour stopover in Amsterdam, where he wandered the streets without purpose. He drank glasses of beer at a string of cafés until he could feel nothing but a light humming throughout his system. He sat on a bench near the Prinsen Gracht, thinking of the *relais* but watching the trolleys. One after another they would arrive, brilliantly lit in the night air, the entire length of the train an advertisement for Nike or Panasonic or Kit Kat chocolate bars. People spilled from each car and joined the traffic tumbling down the canal roads into the bars and restaurants and smoky cafés. Amsterdam was teeming: slackers and clubbers and queens; the Euro-homeless now free to wander and be poor on the streets of any city in the union;businessmen in French blue shirts and gold ties; Amsterdam women who looked like whooping cranes, all hips and shoulders mounted high on gaunt black bicycles. And every three minutes, another train with another load of people, and another marketing message designed to address the tumult.

He felt sick. He imagined he had macroscale motion sickness that came from moving between St. Seine l'Abbaye and Amsterdam, such a great distance in so short a time. The next morning he hid in the Rijksmuseum for relief. He would have been happy only for some quiet, but he found instead three paintings that combined into a single lasting image of his entire experience in Europe.

*The Beheading of John the Baptist*. He stopped primarily to admire Fabritius's depiction of Salome, a frivolous aristocrat, which brought to mind the Audi or the Saab or the Benz that might as well have been waiting for her out front of the prison. But the image lingered as he moved on; Salome the patron had so airily inspected the proffered head as it dripped in front of her, held high in the hand of the workmanlike executioner, whose face reflected technical satisfaction in a distasteful assignment.

Bueckelaer's *Well-Stocked Kitchen*. It made him smile. A meta-image of thankfulness and plenty. Christ sat with Martha and Mary, surrounded by skewered game birds, Dutch hares, ducks, finches, pheasants, partridges, roosters, sandpipers, zucchini, cauliflower, tomatoes, grapes, artichokes, plums, cucumbers, lemons, apples, squash and blackberries. Jeremy imagined working with the large clay oven in the background.

Then: *The Threatened Swan*. Standing like a boxer, beak set to jab, wings cocked, feathers flying. Jeremy admired the bristling stance the bird took towards the attacker, knowing that in Asselijn's day, the threat might well have been a rookie cook like himself.

He walked the gallery many times, seeking out all the food pictures, all the glistening still lifes, but returned again and again to these three. The patron, the kitchen, the swan. As the clock marked off the few hours until departure, he stood in front of these images, one after another, and he found himself thinking again of his American friend who set to war the culinary Crips and Bloods. His mind swirled over his time in the *relais*, over his Sunday nights. Those loud late evenings when Patrice did not go home to Pellerey but consented to return to his bed with him. The hours and days he had spent with her in the forest above the town. The source d'Ignon. The true source of the region. It seemed that all his time in France had been captured in these images, triangulated. Fixing him like a crapaudine on the skewer of his own culinary training.

"These have been the years," Jeremy thought, reflecting now on his return to North America with new, unexpected enthusiasm, with something like zeal. "These years have made me Blood."

The Monkey's Paw Bistro was conceived of this conviction. It took him four years to raise the nerve and figure out how to raise the money, and a few weeks longer to convince his new friend Jules Capelli to join him as sous chef and pastry chef.

They had met only six months before, appropriately enough at the public market. He spotted her first. He was sifting through a basket of chanterelles, for his own dinner on a Monday night off. She was across the way, intently unstacking and restacking a pile of celery roots, setting aside ones that met some clearly exacting standard. His attention was arrested. She was about his age, thirtyish or a few years younger. Attractive, definitely, but she also emanated a quality he wasn't sure he could articulate. Something like strength and vulnerability at the same time. She had eyes too large for her face, almost sorrowful, but set under impossibly strong black eyebrows. A straight, austerely beautiful helmet of even blacker hair, blue-black, which she stroked gently behind her ears. And as he watched, she leaned over the stainless steel counter and auditioned the celery roots in her strong hands, the veins standing out in firm relief as her long fingers felt the rough surfaces. She held each one gently up to a nose that arched distinctly across the bridge. Smelling one in particular, she closed heavy lids over her eyes, finding the quality she sought. He held his breath, a chanterelle in one hand, halfway to the bag.

Jules felt this stare on her eventually, opened her eyes and turned to find it. Jeremy looked away sharply at her first movement. He found himself above the chanterelles again, found the one in his hand and began to move as normal, raising it towards the bag. And then—remembering what he had just seen but forgetting both himself and her actual presence five or six feet away—he raised the dusty orange, pine-needle-covered mushroom past the rim of the bag and to his nose.

Jules was looking surreptitiously around herself, having been unable to find the stare immediately. She was glancing back to her celery root when she spotted him. The guy in the suede leather coat, high cheekbones, dark eyes and thick, unkempt dark hair. He was staring back down at a basket of chanterelles, looking with faint recognition at the one in his hand. And standing, staring, his face had become dreamy. The mushroom drifted up to a spot under his nose, where he inhaled its fragrance deeply, taking a long, shuddering draw.

He opened his eyes again and dropped the chanterelle into the paper bag, apparently satisfied. At which point he noticed that she was looking back at him, laughing silently. He saw the

chosen celery root hoisted and sitting on the palm of her
hand, next to her shoulder, as if ready for shot put.

"Is that what I look like?" she asked him. "Like I'm trying
to get high?"

He reddened. He ran a hand nervously through his hair.

"You cook," Jules said. It wasn't really a question. He
looked tired. He was checking out chanterelles with a practised eye. He had a snip of Elastoplast around his left index
finger, right where you might take off a slice of knuckle if
you were behind on prep and not getting enough sleep. But
he didn't ask how she knew, just accepted that she had spotted him as a professional.

"My night off."

She nodded, eyebrows arched high. "From…?"

He told her about his work, sauté man at a popular tourist
restaurant with a steady-on salmon-and-prawns-type seafood
reputation. She was doing pastries and desserts at The Tea
Grill, a well-known and overtly experimental kitchen, the
kind loved by a certain glossy variety of critic and the finan-
cially enabled patrons that follow in their wake. A serious Crip
credential, but Jeremy was impressed.

They had coffee several weeks later. She called. They met
at Save On Meats, in a rough block of East Hastings Street.
Jeremy knew about the legendary Vancouver butcher—part
slaughterhouse, the band saws and heavy cleavers were in use
right behind the glass counters—but he hadn't known about
the little diner at the rear. It had a narrow yellow Arborite
counter that curved in and out to form conversational penin-
sulas. They sold drinkable diner coffee and enormous ham-
burgers for $3.50.

Jeremy loved it. He looked around the counter area with
a broad smile. Jules found herself pleased to have predicted
approval.

Save On Meats became a weekly thing, talking shop mostly.
He confided in her quickly, told her of the irritations and

rewards of his present work. He told of his ideas, his taste for the simplest, most direct and local cooking possible. "High-end urban rubber-boot food," he said at one point. He told her about the restaurant where he had worked in France, Chef Quartey, Claude, the cast of other characters and the surrounding countryside, which had all joined to inspire one single idea: The Monkey's Paw Bistro. He could almost draw the details of the room in words, so long had he lived with the vision. He told her about the slow-dawning possibility that he may have enough seed-investment money. He spoke of his so-far unsuccessful search for that one other chef he would need.

Jules nodded and listened over a number of similar conversations, watching his angular face work with enthusiasm around dark, shining eyes. She thought he was starting to like her, maybe he even had a little crush at this point. And she would have acknowledged a mutual attraction if someone had asked her. She would have admitted that once—the second or third time they got together—there had been a moment when she thought she was going to kiss him. A short lull in the conversation, very typical and comfortable. They were sitting on adjacent too-small stools. Jeremy shifted his weight, and their thighs rubbed. Jules turned with a smile, with a ready quip, just as he turned to her. They were staring at one another. Their expressions grew serious. And there it was, a hovering instant of possibility. Both of them floating in it. She looked at his lips, so full, so nicely formed. She could have. She would have.

But they didn't. From the start, Jules sensed a very different and possibly better way their relationship was directed. She liked this Monkey's Paw idea. She liked the implied day-to-day spontaneity, culinary theatre sports in a kitchen where two people could riff off one another. And she also knew that a professional relationship would scuttle romantic possibilities, no matter how their feelings were evolving. She made it a practice not to sleep with cooks in the first place, but turning up the heat with someone from your own kitchen was a truly ridiculous idea. Cooking was a twelve-hour day, more. You couldn't spend that kind of time together, dancing around the same prep counters, the same hot grills, literally rubbing against one another, and then go home to the same bed. Jules had tried it once—she knew. The experiment had been to good effect for exactly two nights, to bad effect for the additional two months it took to extricate herself from a life that had so physically, so intensely woven through her own.

Her evolving sense of their relationship was also rooted in her own irritations and rewards. She told him that there had been a time when she had wanted nothing more than the kind of job she had. The Tea Grill was new; it was highly visible on critical radar. At twenty-seven, coming out of cooking school after several years on the sales side of hotel catering, Jules felt she had to jump on board something moving, happening. Something on which a reputation could be quickly built.

"Hip at any cost," Jules said. Coming out of school it felt like there was no time to waste.

"And now?" Jeremy asked her.

"Turns out I don't want to be there." Jules wanted independence. Jules wanted to be known for her own work. "The restaurant gets raves, fine. I'd do something smaller just to establish my own personal connection with something good. Not huge, but good and my own."

Jeremy watched her eyes. Green. At once open, accessible and yet bottomlessly resolved. She was right about him. His interest had begun to migrate towards the romantic, although he had taken his time deciding. He hadn't had a girlfriend in the year since he started his most recent job. No dates even—too busy. Sex exactly twice, both with restaurant people, although not from his restaurant.

"There are a million things I can do," Jules was explaining. "An endless list of desserts that I can dream up and make.

They all taste good. Caramelized peaches with cumin infusion, brandy-yam ice cream."

"And there is liberty in it," Jeremy said, articulating what he believed to be her point.

"Sure. But I like key lime pie."

Jeremy considered this confession.

"The intent is spontaneity," Jules went on. "But the more I think about it, the more I imagine our creations to be the product of a 'spontaneity rule' of some kind. Like: Classic Ingredient A plus Exotic Technique B plus Totally Unexpected Strange Ingredient C equals Wacky Dish D. Sauce with something black or dark blue and you're good to go."

Jeremy was nodding.

"Everything *works,* clearly," she continued. "Crème de bourbon and lemon-grass tart is actually very good. But I sometimes think what I'm doing is totally... *incoherent.* That I'd rather make key lime pie."

"Key lime pie," repeated Jeremy (who didn't particularly like key lime pie, as it happened, but who could think of nothing more sumptuous just then, nothing more compelling, more richly personal than the *idea* of the key lime pie that Jules liked.)

"For example," Jules said.

It had not been since Quartey that Jeremy had had such a sweeping sense that somebody knew exactly what he was talking about.

She said yes a week later, to the question she had been anticipating. He started to address the harder choice this answer represented. "You know, one thing I've always thought about working together—you and I...." He stammered into a conversational cul-de-sac.

"You don't have to say it," she said quietly. "We both understand." There would be a measure of disappointment on both sides. It couldn't be helped.

And so, that spring, The Monkey's Paw did open. A narrow fifty-seater on Cambie Street in Vancouver's Crosstown neighbourhood, edgy but with cheap rents. They served bistro fare on a fixed price menu that changed daily with what could be found in Chinatown that morning. A restaurant other chefs would go to. Local but not dogmatic. It wasn't a question of being opposed to imported ingredients, but of preference, of allegiance, of knowing what goodness came from the earth around you, from the soil under your feet.

The typical dinner chalkboard read:

*Prix Fixe Menu:*
*$24.00*

*Down:*
*Pacific wild prawns*
*Saltspring Island chevre with toasties*

*Set:*
*Fraser Valley free-range duck breast, roasted*
*Lime-marinated sockeye salmon, grilled*
*All with inspirational sauces and seasonal veggies.*
*More details? Just ask.*

*Hutt:*
*Jules's increasingly famous dessert trolley. Get some.*

They riffed on sauces, using classical motifs: pear-mustard, chive-cream, shallot-ginger, roasted fennel. It was simple, coherent, Blood cooking in a *relais*-style room with six nights of Sunday nights.

They had two people out front—Zeena and Dominic—who worked the whole room without zones. Service was enthusiastic and knowledgeable. They went over each new menu item as a group before dinner service.

The room itself was simple: planked wood floors, a single vaulted front window next to a blue door with a centre brass knob. Tables and chairs from Ikea. North wall, brick; south wall painted dark brown to the five-foot mark to simulate wainscotting. The art work was haphazard, the product of piece-by-piece collection at local art-college auctions: etchings, woodcuts, off-kilter portrait photography and a large neo-classical still life with a menacing quality Jeremy couldn't identify. Jules donated three metal sculptures by a student artist named Fenton Sooner, who had gone on to enter high-profile collections, including (rumour had it) Steve Martin's. Stylized birds, thought Jeremy, who named the trio Heckle, Jeckle and Hide. They were worth more than all the other art in the restaurant combined, more than the furniture, but they held much greater value to Jeremy and Jules in the image of perseverance that they provided. Fenton Sooner stuck with it, completed the fraught transition from apprenticeship to recognition, and his crows were an emblem of gawky tenacity.

In the black-and-white-tiled kitchen, meanwhile, Jeremy and Jules had their fun at very close quarters. They had a single wood-topped prep area, an old Vulcan-Hart range with a chrome hood, where they worked side by side on the mains and the hot appetizers. There was an L-shaped pass-through in the middle of the room, where they rotated during dinner to deal with cold appetizers and salads. Jules rolled into yet a third position, desserts, as each evening wound to a close. With a dishwasher arriving late to clear the dish pit, there was barely room for anybody else.

The neighbourhood offered a shifting multicultural client base that nobody could consciously target. Film school kids in the mid-morning. (It was a financial necessity to open for the coffee trade.) Business lunches for the kind of businesses that embraced neighbourhoods in the earliest stages of gentrification: architects, designers, software developers. After work they had a bike-courier scene. And in the evening, a tantalizing trickle of those foodies and reviewers adventurous enough to dine out deep on the downtown east side, pushing up against the Hastings Street heroin trade. It was a colourful, kaleidoscopic place. Very Crosstown, very X-town.

And early in the new year, less than twelve months after opening, their efforts earned them the stunned, awe-struck, hyperbole-strewn praise of one Anya Dickie.

"Did you read the paper?" Jules asked him the morning the review hit the newsstands. "'Crosstown Celebrates Local Beverages and Bounty.' She likes us."

"She likes a lot of places," Jeremy said. Bloods could also be suspicious on occasion.

"Oh, very nice," Jules answered, pinning the review to the cork board outside the front door.

"She liked that tower of tuna and spinach and yam wafers topped with mango chutney at that cream-coloured Crip palace over in Yaletown. What's that place? The Tea Grill."

"Hey," Jules said, holding the door for him as they went back inside. "I happened to like that tower of tuna and spinach and...not yam wafer..."

"You can't even remember. Was it a fruit? A vegetable?"

"I didn't make it personally," she said, faux-haughty. "But I recall it was popular."

Jules Capelli was not a Crip, but she was different than Jeremy despite her sympathies to his cause. She believed, primarily, that restaurants were themselves organic. Crip, Blood, whatever it was you were consciously trying to do only had so much impact—you grew a reputation in the divinely haphazard way that trees grew roots and leaves. Being as small as they were, being as flexible, being as fresh sheet as they could be, every day, with a natural, loping and very personal spontaneity that suited her so well—these facts, Jules serenely held, told the story of how they had become Who They Were.

Of course, Jules didn't pay the bills.

People rarely set out to kite in a controlled way. More often financial kites soar out of sight with terrifying speed, the virtual string burning through your fingers. Jeremy could remember precisely how his own went aloft. It started with his line of credit at the Toronto Dominion Bank, $230,000 guaranteed by Dante Beale. He'd used the largest part of it to buy used kitchen equipment, Ikea furniture, glass and flatware, and decorate the front room. The remainder he had used monthly to buy fish, meat and vegetables. They were slow months, those first few, slower than he fully realized, and ninety days later—twelve weeks of black cod, salmon caviar, roebuck saddle, fresh rabbit and Saltspring Island chevre—the TD Bank rang to point out that his account was overdrawn by several thousand dollars.

He misunderstood at first, and asked cheerily: "Isn't that what a line of credit is for?"

His account manager, one Custer Quan, broke it to him more gently than he would have if Jeremy didn't have a heavy-hitting friend like Dante Beale and Inferno International Coffee. There was no more available credit, Quan explained. The Monkey's Paw was maxed out.

Jeremy remembered processing the news slowly, considering all the cheques he had written in the last twenty-four hours. Forty pounds of fresh sockeye salmon. Fraser Valley foie gras. A crate of arugula. Beck's from the Liquor Board. There were undoubtedly more that he didn't remember.

He promised Quan a deposit and hung up the phone, sweating, glad Jules wasn't in yet. And then it came to him, fully formed. He wouldn't have known he could be creative in this way. He took his TD Visa card—which, along with an Amex card, were the two other items Dante had facilitated—and drew a sufficiently large cash advance from an automated teller machine. Deposited this amount in his personal chequing account, which had been empty ever since he opened The Paw. And knowing there had to be something wrong with a manoeuvre so simple, he then deposited a personal cheque into his Monkey's Paw account to cover outstanding obligations.

He was still sweating, but the cheques would clear.

Nobody was the wiser until his maxed out TD Visa statement arrived at the end of the month. Then Quan phoned Dante, Dante phoned Jeremy, and Jeremy had to sort everything out again with another deposit that nobody could have anticipated. He had a bit of cash on hand by then, but he also had several new credit cards which he had applied for in the meantime.

"Do we need to talk about anything?" Dante said. But he was busy, Jeremy knew, and happy not to.

And with that, The Monkey's Paw kite was aloft and pulling hard, a ring of minimum payments chasing minimum payments. Jeremy paid the interest on the line of credit religiously, before any other obligation (and Dante was still his friend), so Quan continued to provide glowing credit references. Two credit cards became four, and those cards flushed out solicitations from still other credit cards until there was a cast of six, then nine unwitting lenders.

Things finally stabilized after the Dickie review. The Monkey's Paw began to break even about two days in three, a significant improvement and not too soon. By that time Jeremy had a petrified $200,000 line of credit, four Visas, three MasterCards and a Diners Club. He had other, unused cards in his wallet, which he had no clear idea he would ever need: Canadian Tire, Household Finance Corporation, cards that were sent to him pre-approved at unlikely levels. It occurred to him these might be needed in a crisis to make minimum payments on the ones that had come before. But as long as nobody cancelled a card on him or demanded immediate payment in full, Jeremy desperately calculated that he could keep this whole thing flying until The Monkey's Paw actually became profitable. Then he would slowly reel the kite back to earth.

What he needed was a break, some kind of special exposure to get the mainstream foodies into Crosstown.

His big chance in this regard might have been Brollywood, Vancouver's rainier version of the L.A. television and movie scene (and so christened by the flattered local press corps). The Monkey's Paw was no Le Cirque but, since the Dickie review, recognizable faces had been appearing occasionally from the cast and production staff of a television show shot largely in the Crosstown neighbourhood. *Last Chapter* was a show about all things paranormal, paranoid, concerning aliens, conspiracies or the sudden appearance of large amounts of ectoplasm. All this activity supposedly taking place in the new-millennial glow of an American city for which Vancouver was a cost-effective stand-in.

Jeremy had never watched the show, but that was hardly the point. *Last Chapter* was an international hit; it spawned rip-off shows, many of which were also filmed in Vancouver. It was all he could do to resist phoning the newspapers when one of the stars appeared at dinner and ordered something not on the chalkboard. One picture on page three, he thought. Michael Duke in The Monkey's Paw Bistro, Chef Jeremy serving. One Malcolm Perry thumbnail snap and they'd be made.

"Greetings friends." Jeremy had seen Michael Duke's car pull up and was ready for them. Duke was suited in brown chalk stripe, fedora pulled low, adhering to celebrity convention by being smaller than you'd expect. He wore unusually pale blue contact lenses.

"Hey there," Duke said, seeing Jeremy and extending a limp hand. As always, he adopted a sleepy expression and tone, which one assumed Duke felt was removed and sensual, but which veered dangerously near to making him sound like he'd sustained a head injury at some point.

Michael Duke was with Luke Lucas, no relation to George. Lucas was the producer of *Last Chapter*, a normal off-camera-sized man, but clearly Brollywood. You could tell from the black suiting with sterling silver bits. He was jowly but otherwise trim, thinning on top, a preserved fortyish with simultaneous softness and meanness in the features. With his manicured fingers that tapered almost to points, Lucas radiated an absurd, carnivorous health that Jeremy associated with the biz like which there is no biz.

When they were seated, Jeremy sprinted back to the kitchen to let Jules know. He wasn't sure why he bothered; she refused to be impressed by TV people.

"What do you recommend?" Lucas asked.

Jeremy suggested the roast duck breast with peach green-peppercorn sauce. "It's quite light, really. I'm sure you'll like it." Please like it, he thought.

"Luke is vegetarian," Duke murmured through a smile.

"I'll have the pasta," Lucas declared.

"That is made with squid, I'm afraid," Jeremy said.

On vegetarianism benchmarks, Lucas announced: "I don't eat stuff that can think. Squid can't think."

Jeremy checked back on them when they were finished, hands clasped earnestly in front of himself. They were talking about this 1996 Vancouver spring, which had yet to manifest itself in sunshine.

"It kind of...you know," Duke thought carefully about his choice of words, "...gets me down. This rain. Down."

"Rain or not, the thing I like about Vancouver," Lucas said, looking up at Jeremy, "you can make it look like any city on earth."

"I should go to Cozumel," Duke murmured to himself. "Sun will warm me."

"That was very good." Lucas was now looking down at his plate.

"Thank you," Jeremy said, pleased. "I really hope you'll both come back and try us again, and if I knew you were coming, I could prepare something vegetarian—"

"But when did you go Italian?" Lucas cut him off.

Internally, Jeremy winced. Fresh red and yellow tomatoes flavoured with minced capers, garlic, some lemon. Lightly sautéed squid. They were umido-inspired flavours, sure, but local everything except the capers. And here his target market had no idea that the dish was grown in this place, was *of* this place. Of the hard blue ocean full of this squid and that rain. Of the hands that gutted and cleaned and sliced and sautéed those squid, and the tongue that tasted it, and goddamnit, in the end it was better not to think about it too much because *You, sir, are a fucking Crip*.

"We try a lot of different flavours," he began, not sure where he was going with this equivocating response, but the question, thankfully, turned out to have been more rhetorical than anything. Already Duke was beginning to murmur about how maybe Tuscany would be better than Cozumel.

"Have fun in Tuscany or Cozumel," Jeremy said smiling, holding the door for them.

Jules, returning later to her theme of organic growth and spontaneous creativity said: "You're right in trying to make them happy, but you can't worry too much if they don't get it. The point is that in here—between you and me—that stuff just happens. Remember when Xiang started bringing in those Maris Piper potatoes? What did they become?"

Among other things, Jules was the queen of unexpected illustrations.

"Ten things we didn't expect," she continued. "Vodka-potato soup."

"Killer," Jeremy said, remembering.

"Roasted with the garlic cloves and lemon," she said. "Mashed with dill and mustard. Potato *galette*."

"You're right."

"So we riffed, baby. We get stuff and riff. That's what we do. That's how we stay honest. That's Who We Are."

"You're absolutely right," Jeremy said, inspired again.

"The thing about TV people…," she continued, assuming her self-evident-statement pose. She put a hand on a hip, still holding a spoon sticky with olive tapenade, her head tossed slightly back, eyes gazing at a spot above and to the left of Jeremy, where hovered (he was sometimes forced to presume) a cloud of obvious insights visible to the world but outside his own peripheral vision. "The thing about them is that they come and they go. Which is why they work on locations. So don't build your business plan around TV people unless you're planning to open a string of poison wagons, and Jay, my darling, I ain't slapping together falafels in the back of a poison wagon even for you."

Being contrapuntal was a good part of her significant appeal, thought Jeremy during these speeches.

"So, honey. What's tonight?" she said then.

"Chilliwack rock doves."

"And what's up with that?"

"Pear-brandy glaze," Jeremy said. "Roasted."

"You see?" Jules said, lifting her chin slightly, as if to capture the aroma of a typical Papier-Capelli idea.

She was so unimpeachably wonderful, he always had to pin reminder notes to these thoughts that they were friends, just friends. Although he allowed himself the pleasure, as she turned again to her tapenade, to observe how Jules wore her subtle oppositions physically. The black eyebrows and hair. The strong nose, firm square shoulders, athletic legs and powerful hands. These things opposed by a fragile, feminine mouth and vulnerable eyes, with their pale green irises forming the narrowest of rings around the pupils. Expressive in two distinct ways. Sometimes, watching her eyes, Jeremy thought he saw right back to the child that he imagined Jules had been. An odd, quiet and beautiful girl. Tough in the school yard. Stronger than the teasing boys from her grade-school classes. Streets smarter, then and now.

"The Snub notwithstanding, we have a good thing going," Jules was saying, gently folding the tapenade.

"The Snub," he said, shaking his head. It still annoyed him almost a full year later.

Just after opening, they had inquired about participating in a local foodie festival called Seasons of Local Splendour. The event was held on a farm—with the migraine-inducing name Garrulous Greens—where twenty or thirty local chefs and vintners would hand out samples from kiosks. Crowds of foodie and organic farming enthusiasts would descend on the farm, and mill about nibbling food, sipping wine and having their various epiphanies along the lines of: "The food I eat comes from the *soil!*"

It was a worthwhile event, one they felt especially suited to, but The Monkey's Paw was rebuffed. Jeremy got a letter saying thank you but that the slate was getting full of "the better known organic and Pacific Northwest restaurants." They received no encouragement to apply again next year.

Jules hadn't been fazed in the least. She pointed out that they were starting to get busy, that the people who tried them liked them and that they didn't need to prove anything to anyone. Their food was local, demonstrably local. Not braying about its localness, just doing it. And with that, the Seasons of Local Splendour Snub became a routine part of the kitchen banter.

"We have the food, sugar," Jules said. "The foodies will follow."

"Food is a language," Jeremy said. "We must keep our sentences simple and coherent."

"How about: Service in thirty," Jules said, as she moved over to the big aluminum fridge door, swung it open and disappeared inside.

It was just over a week since he had visited the Professor. Friday morning, and Jeremy stood on the steps of his apartment building, the Stanley Park Manor, contemplating the street with some dissatisfaction. It was drizzling, again. What was happening to their spring?

He was also feeling sleep deprived. The night before he had done a foolish thing. The four of them at The Paw would often have a drink or two after closing, frequently with lingering customers. But after these (thinking about making it to Chinatown by six o'clock the next morning), Jeremy would normally walk directly home. It took half an hour, but he enjoyed the cool after-midnight air and the sound of the city pulsing around him.

Last night, he reached the door of the Stanley Park Manor and looked past it, down Haro Street, to the black bulk of Stanley Park crouched at the foot of his street. And having failed to push aside thoughts of his father living among those trees—thoughts that were simmering, reducing and strengthening all week instead—that blackness at the end of the street seemed now to be waiting expressly for him. He yielded to the pull and walked the rest of the way down the sidewalk, to that point where the city abruptly ends and the park begins. That spot on the curb above the tennis courts, above the short stretch of grass. Above the portal of cherry trees. He walked down the slope tentatively, crossed the grass and stood under the trees, staring across the silver water of the lagoon at the forbidding forest. He turned back to the city after only a few such moments, frustrated, angered. And in this agitated frame of mind he had returned to Denman Street, piled into a cab, and gone all the way back across town to The Marine Club, the after-hours booze can of choice for a range of food and beverage industry night owls. There, Jeremy made diverting small talk and drank a number of large Irish whiskeys to smooth his nerves and ready him for sleep.

Down very late and up very early. Jeremy's emotional constitution felt like a chain of open links, waiting for some critical slackening of tension to disassociate themselves one from another and send them pinging off the pavement like a pocketful of loose change. He was up, at least. On the pavement in time to bus across town to Chinatown, kibitz with the suppliers, line up deliveries in time for dinner prep. And pay. Yes, there was that. He made a mental note to visit a bank machine and determine which cards had room.

First stop, coffee, but he walked by the Inferno Denman without looking up. Dante Beale was a decent man, whatever the Professor thought. A compliant financier. Still, Jeremy couldn't bear the bright-sheeted stare of the Inferno's front glass this early in the morning, its arched eyebrows of blond wood framing the window, the cheek-pinching bird-perch stools along the narrow window-counters not designed for newspaper reading but for gazing vapidly through one's own reflection into the flowing street. And above all of it, the ubiquitous Inferno Coffee logo visible from virtually any point in the city where a potential consumer might come briefly to light, a stylized godhead with a coffee, the steam from the cup sweeping and enveloping the face, providing the deity's obligatory beard and long hair. It could have been Adam's perspective on the Sistine Chapel ceiling, God offering not the touch of life but a hot cup of joe. Jeremy avoided looking at the Inferno Denman, just as he avoided drinking the over-roasted coffee Dante favoured for what Inferno ads trumpeted as its Italian richness and nerve-jangling strength. It was not Italian, rich or strongly caffeinated, Jeremy knew. Just burnt. And mostly Honduran, he understood.

From the cracked door of the Inferno bled the drying trickle of canned classical music (Vivaldi, always), barely audible. Dante's market research paying off, no doubt. The iced-gut violin strings of "Winter" having proved at focus groups to encourage the purchase of a peach Danish to go with the morning double-shot, skinny, extra hot latte. Following a similar rationale, the music changed in the afternoons to Blue Note compilations, nothing being an accident in the Inferno organization. Not the music they chose nor their conspicuous absence in Crosstown. Inferno didn't know the people in Crosstown yet; they hadn't been fleshed out in the catalogue of customer types to whom Dante felt confident he could sell, always sell, reliably sell every morning and lunch, to the extent that there was a business case for the investment in blond wood, canned music and barista training.

I don't grudge him his business plan, Jeremy thought, but two doors down, the Vivaldi finally diluted in the air behind him, he swung into Melchior's Coffee House instead. This coffee house was one of the many competitors that circled each Inferno like moons, although Melchior's was not a blatant rip-off. They had no blond wood, no bicycle-seat chairs either, instead a garage-sale assortment, beanbag to wingback. Second-hand dining-room tables were strewn with a frenzy of magazines toeing some line between hip and intellectual: *Paper, Interview, Flash Art, Z Magazine, Tikkun, Adbusters.* Jeremy noticed a copy of *Gud Tayste* lying prominently on the front counter, the millennial food magazine of choice for foodie-scenesters on both sides of the Atlantic. In a thick, large-format monthly with columns such as "The Chefosphere" (on new gadgets) and "Hack Your Food" (on twenty-first-century culinary developments), coquettishly named editor Kiwi Frederique championed something she referred to as "International Groove Food." Cripper than Crip, but Jeremy still couldn't help wondering how it felt to be hyped by people who could produce a magazine of such relentlessly cool, ravingly optimistic flavour. Invincibility came to mind.

In Chinatown he half-heartedly looked for a bargain but went with black cod anyway. He was imagining the roast shallot sauce already. He bought pork tenderloin as well, paid with a cheque, then walked back to the restaurant. Despite the drizzle, there were traveller kids sleeping in Victory Square park, one right at the base of the cenotaph whose inscription read: *Their names liveth evermore, / Is it anything to you, / All ye that pass by?* The words whispered out of the stone.

He started up the ancient Turkish coffee maker in the front room, and went to have a cigarette in the kitchen. "The Zone," as they called it, a cheesy name that stuck. It was a zone of perfect balance; he knew where everything was. His heart quickened with the first graceful touch of nicotine and, as he picked a stray piece of tobacco from the tip of his tongue, he let his eyes drift over the room. The Vulcan-Hart, the black aluminum sauce pots and skillets. Above the prep area were the knife racks, and there hung Jeremy's favourite indispensable tool. A ten-inch Sabatier chef's knife, engraved in tiny letters on the handle: *Chef Jeremy, We are reminded of our beginnings.*

Sabatier had been a name he'd encountered numerous times in France. Chef Quartey and Claude both used a range of these blades from the venerated maker in Thiers. But Sabatier had been out of his financial reach at the time, and so his father had surprised him with the presentation of this perfect gift on his return. A 1903 high-carbon knife, no less. Several hundred of these had been found by Sabatier in a warehouse attached to an old factory near Thiers. Here were oilskin-wrapped blades of matchless quality, never to be made again for the cost and craftsmanship required. Each thick blade entirely hand-forged—you could still see hammer marks on the blades—and each with a drawn tang that tapered down inside a blackened pear-wood handle. Jeremy's was also marked with an enigmatic stick-figure stamp, a devil running with a trident. Collectors had snapped them up.

And as the years had passed since his return, although it had not ushered in easier relations with his father, the Sabatier had evolved to become an essential in his cooking day. It became a toby without which the day might never start or be completed. And the sense of its shape and weight remained in his right hand after closing time. Now he passed his eyes across the antique blade and felt the reassurance offered by its dull gleam, a reassurance enabling him to turn his full attention to yesterday's mail.

Diners Club registered its reminder in wounded tones, about credit limits and payment due dates, the underlying implication that they wished they hadn't taken Quan's word for gospel. He was approaching a critical ledge here (and he was getting an instinctive feel for this ledge), the computer behind the words even now preparing the follow-up correspondence that would shift permanently to more formal language.

He stubbed out the cigarette and went into the front room to check the coffee. It occurred to him that Dante would not issue such a reminder and would never be wounded. If he suspected anything beyond a few struggles with the bank's line of credit, he didn't comment. The last time they spoke, he said instead: "Don't think of me as pressure; I want to relieve pressure. You need space to do what Jeremy does, to make the interesting food for the interesting people. I only want to give you that space."

Jules laughed out loud when she heard that. To say that she and Dante had not hit it off was to say that the angel Gabriel and Beelzebub had been uncomfortable seated at adjacent tables. The first time they met, Jeremy read it in her eyes. Bottomless distrust.

Dante had been on one of his typical, slightly possessive walkabouts, touring the kitchen, no matter how busy, sniffing things. Jeremy didn't mind particularly, or he had chosen not to mind, given that he owed Dante two hundred grand. Jules, not privy to this information, took a different approach. One more suited to her personality.

"Uh...," she said, skating down the range top, slammed, hair plastered to her forehead, fielding new orders and finding a man in a double-breasted suit hovering in the steam above a sauté pan of mushroom ragout. "Ex-cuuse me?" Shouldering into position.

He took the hint and left, not unmiffed. And when he came back later to say goodnight, chatting with Jeremy, he dropped another hint about the way they all might collaborate.

Jules disguised a smirk, poorly.

Dante nodded and took his leave a second time, feeling something he was not used to feeling: rejection. And, steamed just a little at this, he disappeared behind the shelving that obscured the door to the dining room but did not leave. He eavesdropped. Shameful, he knew, but she had tasked him to this point.

Jules did as Jules would. She talked up what they had. She reminded Jeremy of things they had planned together. Spontaneity. On-the-fly creativity. Urban rubber-boot food.

"Am I to understand you oppose the idea of Dante's involvement?" Jeremy said.

Jules spread her hands. *What can I say?*

Dante made to leave, quietly. Then she spoke again. So close, but no. Couldn't let it go.

"I oppose him," the woman chef said. "I don't like him personally. He's smarmy. He's after something. And I oppose what he stands for."

There was more. Inferno was polluting the city with sameness. Inferno was a cost model, an exercise in scale. Inferno was a celebration of everything they were not. Inferno was . . .

Dante made himself leave before Jeremy could respond. But he took pains, thereafter, to observe how Capelli held back Papier.

"Do you suppose she's a dyke?" Dante asked Jeremy. "Dykes are difficult. It's always politics with dykes."

"Jesus Christ, Dante," Jeremy said, angered.

"She has a very bad attitude." Then: "On the subject of which, do not swear at me, do you understand?"

These words put Jeremy on his heels. Dante had the voice

of a gangster when he needed it, suits and deep pockets to match. A pleasant, personable British exterior with a well of unexpressed violence hovering somewhere behind his eyes.

"You know, I happen to really love this woman," Jeremy said, not quite beaten down.

"Oh, listen to this, will you?" Dante said. "They love each other. If you're not getting scraped, it's not love."

"Jules and I are teammates. You have to see how that works, how the ideas and the creativity flow between us. I've felt this way since I first met her. She's integral."

"Jay, my friend, two things: First, I've seen the team in action, and I think she's a constraint. Second, she's mentally unstable."

"She's volatile and passionate. Sometimes creative people can be rude when they get interrupted at their work."

"Rude is fine; I'm rude. She hit me."

This was how the event had been logged. It was a shoulder, no more. True, Dante did step back from the physical contact with such surprise that he narrowly missed getting brained by the dishwasher, who was jogging by with a huge, aluminum, stock cauldron.

Jules said, not urgently: "Behind you."

Dante swivelled out of harm's way. Tripped on a crate of beets. Did not fall down.

It was close.

"Besides," Dante went on. "This Capelli, for all her personal complexities, won't be out of work for more than ten minutes. So you need feel no guilt."

Which served precisely to make Jeremy feel guilty, of course. Guilty about keeping Jules in sixty-five-seat Crosstown bistro when she could take her shining black hair, her beautiful strong nose and pointed opinions right back up the street to The Tea Grill or Jonah's, The Cedar Café or one of the others, up the street to any established kitchen you could name.

"And what would you do without me?" she once asked when he suggested she was a free agent.

"I could keep on going or go back to France," he said.

"France." Jules said. "France was school. We have what France prepared you for right here. What we wished for. And something with legs too. Those kids in the front window smoking roll-your-owns are bellwethers. They know when something is real and when it isn't."

Oliver Michaelson didn't know the kids in the front window from squeegee kids anywhere, but if somebody had ever asked him directly he would have said he hoped The Monkey's Paw was real. He hoped on Jeremy's behalf, godfather to his five-year-old son, Trout, university pal and once band mate. He hoped on behalf of Jeremy's financial solvency, which had been an ongoing issue over the years. There were certainly closer coffee shops to his loft office on Water Street, home of Michaelson Data Design, but nobody could say that he wasn't a faithful friend to those who warranted it. Plus, there was his wife, Margaret, who had been part of the university gang and since evolved into a devout foodie. She had been a steady customer of Jeremy's first, and suggested Olli do the same. Investment in a friend's business was one thing, an unwise thing in Olli's view (and he had thought about it carefully before saying no), but patronage wasn't too much to ask.

Olli pushed open the door of The Monkey's Paw at his usual hour, bang on seven, when the place opened for the coffee trade. He entered the long, dark space with the crazy art that his friend collected from local artists, and Olli smelled—with a nose that had grown canine-sharp since he quit drinking and smoking—both the coffee and a very slight dankness from the walls. He wondered how much the inevitable renovations would cost.

As usual, Jeremy was in the back, clattering around, when he arrived. Olli decided to wait at the counter quietly. He could have rung the bell that was left out in the mornings. But there was the odd occasion, coming to this place owned by an old friend this early in the morning, when he opened the serial port to a very short instream burst of nostalgia. It was, for example, provocative to entertain the thought of how they had stayed friends coming from the beginning they shared. Jay-Jay and The Decoders, from the school of toxic rockabilly. Jeremy played a hollow body electric, a position he fancied most amenable to being drunk during a performance. Moss Craven on traps (Olli hadn't heard of him in years). Olli himself played stand-up bass, poorly in fact but nobody at a Decoder gig knew the difference anyway. They each got a decoder-ring tattoo, felt so similar to one another in those months, in the weeks even, the days before they all launched off into their own utterly different futures. How did that work?

Jeremy came through the swinging door from the kitchen, glanced up sharply. Dragging his hungover ass around first thing in the morning as usual, thought Olli, not without a trace of jealousy.

Jeremy cracked a smile.

"Yo," Olli said, smirking a rockabilly smirk in return. "Gas me up."

"Decoders, go," Jeremy answered. And after they had shaken hands, he tapped out coffee for the double espresso Olli favoured, burped out two black bullets into a to-go cup, the whole time watching his friend with one eye. Olli drifted in his presence sometimes, Jeremy had observed, sweeping his eyes around the room as if trying to remember something. This morning Jeremy was checking surreptitiously for indications of how his godson was doing, before committing to the question. Trout had health problems from the start, and a heart condition that persisted. They were the model sick-kid parents, Olli and Margaret, hyperattentive without betraying the least sign of it. At dinner parties over the years, Jeremy had noted how things might get raucous but the radar was always on, scanning for a signal from the loft bedroom above.

This morning, as Olli waited for his coffee, Jeremy found himself thinking that his friend was showing signs of strain.

Even before he got rich, Olli always looked rich. He had good posture, for one, a lean athletic frame for a guy who didn't go to a gym until his late twenties when he was a recovering alcoholic. He wore wide-shouldered, fitted Italian suits and big, off-white, made-to-measure shirts with two sharply pressed front pockets. Wide colourful ties. Then CommotionWorks bought TroutWorld, his original software development company (before CommotionWorks went spectacularly bust). Olli pocketed the cash, looked like a genius for timing, and didn't really change that much. Margaret picked them out a penthouse loft in Yaletown, and they both kept on working as hard as before. She was a seismic engineer, and her firm was involved in half the upgrade projects happening across the city (ongoing, frenetic preparation for The Big One. Jeremy thought there was something increasingly millennial about it.) But money didn't stabilize the tectonic plates or Trout's heart, and they both carried on carrying on. Emblematic of this fact, Olli stayed with the sharply creased, made-to-measure, two-pocket shirts, just like he was still looking for that first $2.35 million.

His money only came up once that Jeremy could recall, and the memory always embarrassed him. It was in the early years of his planning for The Monkey's Paw, before Dante. Jeremy's cheapest conceivable vision of the place could have been realized for one hundred grand, but the answer was still no. Polite, but firm. There was money, Olli had explained, and there was liquidity. Lots of the one didn't necessarily mean lots of the other.

"You see," Olli said, sitting stiffly in his office chair, running fingers through his short sandy hair, turning to glance at a huge monitor on his desk that had given a cock-a-doodle-doo to signal incoming e-mail. "From the standpoint of cash, we're both broke."

Had Olli stopped there, Jeremy would have left resentful. He would have walked out the door thinking, Well, if you're going to be broke, I suppose it pays to be rich first. But he remembered taking a minute to digest the words, looking out over Olli's shoulder to the sunlit inner harbour. The stacks of shipping containers made a colourful quilt against the high blue mountains on the North Shore. And Olli, sensing a distance grow briefly between them, leaned forward on his elbows. "Jay-Jay," he said sincerely. "You think I'm being cold about this."

"Nah," Jeremy said.

"You do, but you're wrong. A) I can't afford it. I simply don't have one hundred thousand dollars, and I've borrowed all the money my bank is comfortable lending, trying to do this thing that I'm doing. And B)..."

It wasn't exactly a stand-up-come-around-the-desk embrace, but Jeremy felt the warmth.

"B) I can't afford us getting into a big fight, having a falling out. Trout ending up without a godfather."

"Why would...," Jeremy started, but he knew the risk better than most people. What were the chances of going down in the restaurant trade and losing your investor's money entirely? Fifty, sixty percent?

Olli had leaned back in his chair and done something Jeremy hadn't seen him do since university. He reached for his smokes. Of course he'd quit and didn't have any cigarettes on him—they both knew that. But in that moment, flustered despite appearing otherwise, Olli's fingers went to the lip of one of those sharply creased front pockets on his made-to-measure shirt. They found the seam of cloth, realized their own mistake and quietly withdrew to the desk top.

Jeremy now finished the espresso, added the two teaspoons of brown sugar he knew Olli liked. Stirred it and handed it over. Olli went into his pants pocket for change while Jeremy looked again at the familiar shirt.

Ironed badly, he thought all at once. That was it. There was a crease stamped across one of the pockets and a brown mark on the collar, which was splaying out the jacket at the back. In a cascade of details, Jeremy redrew his mental picture of Olli. He was looking *frayed*, that was it. A little mad, although in a nice, middle-class way. He knew Olli had given up drinking years before, less than a year after Trout was born, in fact, but he was giving off a combination of jerky signals that Jeremy associated with drinking. (Madness accompanied his own hangovers. In Jeremy's case this sense was sidecarred to a careening paranoia and a kind of gyroscopic rigidity in the brain, centred somewhere in the cerebrum. He'd try to look sideways out the bus window and something would strain against realignment. Push his eyes back to the front.)

He checked out Olli's eyes. They were clear but watery. He could be using Visine.

"So, tell me about Trout," Jeremy asked.

"Oh...," Olli said, scratching his head. "He's painting dollar bills. Perfect replicas of U.S. dollar bills. We have 133 now."

Jeremy smiled. He had some godfatherly pride in the strange creativity this project suggested, and he might have liked to hear more about the boy but Olli, as usual, had to fly.

"Dinner Monday?" he said, extending his hand. "Margaret wants to show off her new Aga."

"Sure, and wow," Jeremy said. He preferred a flame himself, but he was aware how much an Aga cost. They shook again, a short firm shake like Claude's. Like the ones you earned from countermen in French cafés but only after months of patronage. These patterns were important, Jeremy thought after Olli had left, although this comfortable thought was unsettled somewhat by the pattern suggested by his next customer.

Jeremy kicked a cowboy boot up on a chair behind the counter, ran an elbow across his knee. "Caruzo," he said.

There were many horsepower of something coursing through Caruzo. He panted out his words in anxious, breathy gasps, and was frequently helpless to movements that flashed through his limbs. He bobbed on his feet. Head-faked. Dodged invisible punches.

"How about a cigarette?" Jeremy suggested after watching Caruzo for a while. And he pulled one out, lit it and handed it across the counter to Caruzo, already looking past him to his first film students of the day.

"Hey, Jay," one of them said, angling around Caruzo, who stood adrift in front of the cash register, sucking on the smoke. Bobbing. "Coffee. What do you want?" he said to his friend, who answered in the slow, cadential speech of the recently stoned.

"You got eggnog lattés?"

Jeremy sighed. Wherever did people learn to like this stuff? The Inferno. "Not now. Not ever," he said.

"Just give him a coffee," the first one said. "Do you, like, have the fritters going yet?"

"Not until ten," Jeremy said.

The kids took their coffee to the front window, laughing. At Caruzo, no doubt.

"Yo Jay, yo Jay," Caruzo said. "How about a coffee? You got just plain coffee? Coffee?"

"I think so," Jeremy said. "Black, right? That will be twenty dollars please."

"Damn. Left my wallet in the park." Caruzo took the coffee and started to laugh at the regular joke they shared. A hiccuping, belching, farting sound. It sent his shoulders jogging, produced white flecks at the mouth corners and, more often than not, jarred a little pendulum booger out to the edge of his upper lip. Sure enough, there was the booger.

"Oh right, I forgot. You don't *have* any money," Jeremy said, slapping his forehead.

"Hey, I got money. I got money, you know," Caruzo said, who had now spilled coffee on himself, the counter and the floor. "Just not on me. It's not on me. Hey Jay, though? Jay, I am a messenger."

"Here's a napkin, blow your nose. How about a seat?"

He led Caruzo across the room to a table against the brick wall. They sat down together, and Jeremy waited while Caruzo blew his nose, elaborately examining the contents of the napkin. Blew again. It was a big nose, like a sap extrusion on a cedar trunk. His eyes were a faraway storm colour, against which it was hard to pick up the pupil movements.

Finished finally with the napkin, Caruzo delivered his message. "The Professor is asking after you. Asking after you, Jay-Jay."

"I see," Jeremy said, glancing around the room.

"Babes in the Wood. It's all about that, Jay, nothing else. Babes in the Woods, most of all. Needs to know soon, right?" Caruzo was staring at him intently. Staring through him. "Needs to know what you found out soon, Jay."

"Fine, Caruzo," Jeremy said. "Tell him I'll be down to the library next week."

Caruzo was a permanent jangle of ticks and repeated words, but he went absolutely still with this answer and spoke the first complex, non-fragmented sentence Jeremy had ever heard him speak. "The Professor was expecting that you would have done the research by now."

It made an impression. Jeremy said, "I promise I'll do it this weekend."

Caruzo nodded slowly and seriously.

"Caruzo?" Jeremy said, trying out something he'd been wondering. How did you go about asking questions of a person like Caruzo? What did his father hear?

"Jay?" Caruzo said back, all ears.

He couldn't think of any better way of phrasing the question. "What do you and the Professor talk about, Caruzo?"

"Oh. Phhhhht," he shrugged, snorted, boogered on himself again. He was talking through the napkin, eyes bulging from the incomprehensible activity that surged within. "Well, he's writing. You know. Writing. Always writing. And listening too. Always listening. Listening and writing. Writing and listening."

"About what, though?" Jeremy was beginning to see how these conversations could be trying.

"It's like Siwash, Jay-Jay."

"It is?" Jeremy said. There was always the danger Caruzo would unspool on you. Only once had Jeremy been forced to ask him to leave.

"He's, like…," said Caruzo. He was holding his hands apart now, palms inwards, as if trying to contain something. An idea. Hold it in its invisible box so he could see it. So Jeremy could see it. "He's, like, counting. Waiting. Counting. Waiting. Like the Professor, only the Professor is writing. Listening. See? The same."

Caruzo grabbed his hand. Uh-oh. The brown fingers wound around his own palm, fingertips clamping almost at his wrist. They had no fingernails, Jeremy could now see. Only pads.

"Signs, Jay-Jay."

"Signs?" Jeremy said.

"Signs and signals. Signals and signs. From somewhere. Signs of life. Signs for life. I believe in the signs, Jay-Jay. I really believe in these signs."

Caruzo let him go and they both got up.

He had customers, more film students. More coffees. Later smelt fritters and house tartar mayo. What was for dinner tonight? Black cod, of course. He was going to have to prep himself a little roasted shallot sauce then, wasn't he?

"I'll tell the Professor. Your promise," Caruzo shouted

from the front door, startling everybody in the place before disappearing out into the drizzle.

"Sorry," Jeremy said. "He's a family friend." He took their orders, glad suddenly, overwhelmingly, that there was a morning service. What other signs did he need? And what would he be doing without them? Sleepless in his apartment, looking out over the park and wondering.

"Iced tea, please."

"Made here," he said automatically, distracted, smelling her before he looked up, a blend of patchouli and CK.

"Smelt fritters yet?" she asked.

He looked finally. Fantastic blue eyes, angelic face. Had he seen her before? He thought so, once or twice. She hung out with the design students. He had looked before but looked away. A bit young, twenty-two, twenty-three. "Fritters," he said. "Everyone wants fritters. I throw them on ten-ish. What is it now?"

She consulted a gold nurse's watch pinned to her black velvet pants. Narrow shoulders, small round head with short white hair, tiny lobeless ears. Scrubbed-clean symmetrical features and frosted coral lips. She wore a tight orange sweater with blue athletic stripes around the right sleeve. North Star runners. Faux school gear strapped tightly around a Barbie from the toy section of the 1978 Sears catalogue.

"Nine-ish," she said, a tongue stud glinting as she spoke.

She was waiting for his answer. He could feel the appraisal. Of his decoder-ring tattoo. (His was on his right forearm, Popeye-style. Olli had demurely gone for the shoulder, invisible most of the time.) Of the cowboy boots and Wrangler jeans he typically wore before dinner service. He saw her take it all in. And when she looked back up to his face, she laughed a little through her nose. Laughed as if she had just had an idea that pleased her.

"Close enough," he said. "It'll take me about twenty minutes."

"I'll be in the window," she said, still smiling.

"And the name?" he asked, his pen hovering over the pad. He might need it to call out from the counter. It was a good idea to get it.

"Benny," she said. Then she walked away slowly. Moved across his oak planks towards the high arch of his front window. Split up into its many panes, each one now crying streams of spring rain onto the pane below. Streams that pooled at the base of the brick front wall and ran off down the sidewalk vaguely seeking the sea. The sky was coming down now. There it was on his window, outside his door. Tapping audibly on his glass above his oblivious slacker customers (who rocked back in their chairs and blew smoke upwards, laughed loudly all at once, and did any confident thing that came to mind).

Oblivious but for one, who folded her arms across her rib cage under her sweatered breasts. She lowered her chin as if to listen to the current monologue, lids set in an expression of rigorous boredom. But with her head turned slightly to observe Jeremy at the back of the restaurant, to assess whether the ray she had beamed out had been received.

He had finished entering her order, taken his boot off the chair behind the counter and walked over to the kitchen door. He had his hand on the wood, leaning forward to push it open. But he was thinking about something. Benny waited.

He turned and glanced back.

Benny caught the glance and turned her head slowly back to the conversation, betraying no satisfaction, although she knew. Of course she knew.

Jeremy turned his head more quickly and went into the kitchen. He put the smelts in salty beer batter almost as light as tempura. And when he lowered the basket into the fryer, the oil frothed around the slender fish. They would crisp down in a few minutes into a crunchy mouthful, which, dipped in tartar mayonnaise, rivalled any french fry.

"Benny," he called when they were ready. She got up slowly, came over.

"Thanks, Jay," she said. "So, like…" She ate one standing there. Dipped it in the tartar mayo and took it gently between her teeth.

"They're hot," he warned.

She chewed it gingerly. "They're delicious."

"Thank you," he said. He described the process of making a smelt fritter, knowing the magic implied. The magic of how the fritter was conceived (art). The magic of how it was tossed together back there, out of sight, in just a few minutes (craft). The magic of its taste now (alchemy). What was that spice? A bit of powdered ginger, in fact, one of his few trade secrets.

Benny ate another one, standing there, looking at him and listening to all that he said. And later, as she and all of her friends clumped to the door, she appraised first that he was watching before she turned and smiled again. She waved a wiggling-finger wave and mouthed very distinctly: *I'll be seeing you.*

He waved back—she was gone. The Monkey's Paw was now empty, and there was sixty-eight dollars in the till. He had held it off all morning, but now he stood behind the counter and felt a wave of fatigue break over him. He struggled to banish an image of a night-lit lagoon from his mind, and forced himself to remember Benny's glance and wave instead. Better that, he thought. Better to be incrementally cheered. Cheered despite hemming debt, despite a hovering blackness, a sense of things going steadily out of balance. Cheered by the simple fact that a raver angel named Benny liked him, liked his smelt fritters. He made it, she got it. Was there a better chemistry?

Jules came thundering in just then. Her timing perfect. He could dig down and find his strength, but hers spilled to the surface, always.

"Hey, babe," she shouted, and slapped him hard on the butt as she passed. And with hardly a word, they were swept up in the momentum that would build towards lunch, through the afternoon and on to dinner. The kitchen came alive with the slam of the oven, the scrape of the fridge door and the clatter of pots and knives. Astor Piazzolla materialized in the air as Jules popped in a stack of her eclectic CDs, and a spike of energy entered the collective bloodstream.

When they were prepped and Zeena was in, before the first lunch tables were seated, Jules poured a glass of soda water and leaned against the cutting block. She sipped and watched him adjust seasonings for a moment.

"You look a little tired," she said.

He nodded.

"How's Dad?" she said, reading him perfectly. No surprise.

He didn't say anything.

"Ah, come here, honey," she said. And she put down her glass and hugged him. Hard (she was strong). Squeezed his bones together, made him feel weak but safe. Safe in a place that smelled like caramel, like lightly scented soap. Like the solid breakfast he never had.

Benny took an active interest. Jeremy had the quality, she decided. After all these years of going to design school, working survival jobs, she felt she was in a position to recognize that this guy—not bad-looking with his impossibly messy hair and despite the cowboy boots—this guy had the quality of actualized self. Needs, freedoms, known desires, a creative centre. Benny was often impatient with her peers for lacking all these things, for being not yet formed. Everybody grew up late these days, lived at home for years too long, became adults at thirty. Benny had been supporting herself since sixteen and prided herself on only dating adults. Her friends may have noticed that she suggested The Monkey's Paw more often now. (Or they may not have, it didn't concern her.) But she never mentioned his name, just said something like: "I'm at The Paw around three. You coming?" Everybody always came. They were sheep. They filled up that front window and ate smelt fritters, and she only cared that she managed to talk with him each time for a few minutes. He had noticed, she knew that. The chef had definitely noticed.

One time she got him at the front counter and manoeuvred the conversation into dates. Good ones, bad ones. She invented a bad one from the night before to get things rolling, although she kept the details sparse so as not to create something, somebody, he might view as competition.

He offered a bad one in return, from years before. But he also described a good one. A time when he took a girlfriend on a surprise trip to Ucluelet. He phoned her up on a Thursday; they left on Friday morning. They stayed for the weekend in a cabin on Long Beach with a fireplace and a tiny, rudimentary kitchen. Benny could not keep this story inside herself. A week later she was talking to a girlfriend and she said, with little preamble: "Imagine you had a boyfriend who phoned you up and said, 'Let's go to Ucluelet for the weekend.'"

Her friend looked at her very blankly indeed.

"Like as if…," Benny started, "as if any twenty-three-year-old guy would *ever* do that."

She went from being a new face to an almost daily face in a handful of weeks. He didn't mind that she acted like they'd known each other for months and months. He didn't ask why. She was an appealing cluster of contrasts. Hip. Overtly ambitious. Deferring. Argumentative. She was a schoolgirl, sure, but she appeared to be getting on with things.

"What do you study?" he asked her. She was picking up her smelt fritters, lingering as she did now at the counter while her friends shot the breeze and blew smoke rings in the front window.

"I've told you," she scolded. "Design. I want to be a designer. I *will* be a designer."

But one needed to pay the bills, and so there was Canadian Tire, where, in six years of part-time employment, she had reached the rank of floor supervisor. He succeeded in not laughing the first time she told him. With her white spiky hair, Benny in a Canadian Tire uniform was a dissonant mental picture. Still, he was impressed by the evidence of practicality. Her diligence in paying her own way. What had he been doing in his early twenties? Getting drunk at Decoder gigs. Fighting with Olli and Wes about the album that never got made. Completely at odds with the idea of a game plan. Even now, Canadian Tire was what? An unused credit card. An untapped source of cash. An emblem of his irresponsibility or his bad business sense. Of deepening trouble.

The mail was not improving but it was that time of the month. He was shuffling through a stack of envelopes. Mid-morning, a Tuesday. Benny hadn't been in because she was working, but her crew had gone, and Jules had arrived in front of her own personal ridge of high pressure. Clouds were scattering. There were a number of thick statements in the pile, the envelopes reassuringly hefty. When they closed your account, Jeremy imagined, you received only a slim letter.

He set aside the statements to consider later. At the bottom of the stack there was a Postal Announcement Card. He checked the optional boxes across the top of the card for clues as to what was waiting for him. It was not a parcel but registered mail. Not good.

They had a medium lunch service, enough to be encouraging. When it was finished, Jeremy borrowed Jules's old Impala station wagon to run some errands. In truth, a single errand, but he kept it to himself.

In the main branch of the post office, the ceilings of the

central hall were so high that a single trapped bird could not be captured. They had tried food, drugged bait, nets and finally BB guns, at which point *The Vancouver Sun* did a soft feature. There was a minor public outcry, the result being that you could now, if you were very lucky, get shat on by a starling while standing in the interminable line.

Jeremy retrieved his letter and walked to the marble side counter. He was already muttering the words: "Damn, damn, damn, damn." It was a very slim envelope.

One sheet only. He spread it flat on the countertop, and read: "We regret to inform you that your account with Royal Bank Visa has been closed and that all borrowing privileges..."

Jeremy took a deep breath and let his eye skip down the page.

"...$5,243.50, including interest. Payable immediately."

He let the breath out, his eyes unfocused, staring through the page, through the countertop, as he processed this news. Very bad news for a kite, he knew. You could not simply remove fifty-three hundred dollars from the soaring, madly circling stream of payments without threatening to crash the whole unstable contraption. Nothing from Peter meant nothing for Paul. The money, or at least some portion of it, would have to be replaced.

Jeremy let his head roll back until he was staring directly at the ceiling. Above him he saw the starling, sitting on the corner of a bank of neon lights. The bird was looking at him, head cocked over as the Professor liked to do.

He checked the time. They were rocking towards dinner now, in the ascending part of the long crest. Jules had the dinner prep list. It wasn't entirely fair to leave it all to her, but by the time he got back, in a couple hours with any luck, there would be a crowd of bike couriers drinking after-work beers (hopefully a lot of beers). The CD player would be going up a notch in volume every half-hour, shuffling between Piazzolla and Hüsker Dü, Gavin Bryars,

Carlisle Floyd. Sawing from world to metal to experimental to American opera, giving the place an off-kilter cultural shuffle they were cultivating to go with the rooted, local menu.

He pulled out his wallet and inspected his cards. Fifty-three hundred dollars. From where? Amex might work for a thousand or two in an automated teller machine; he had never tried it before. But he pulled himself up short before considering the idea any further. Credit cards were common, vulgar he sometimes thought, but Amex still held a certain undeniable caché. Dante had arranged it, for one. And out of respect, Jeremy did not use the card, ever, except to facilitate the awkward moments brought on as he strained the limits of other cards.

"The Visa card has been declined, sir." He had heard these words on more than one occasion.

Jeremy might protest politely here, then offer the gold card.

"I'm afraid we don't take American Express." Pause. And then more often than not the clerk would mutter, "Oh, forget it. We've been having trouble with the lines. Just sign here."

But even if Dante were not considered, Amex had to be revered because Amex had no limits and no credit terms. Jeremy thought of it as the Great Satan of credit cards. You could buy a yacht on the third, but if you hadn't paid by the thirtieth Amex would most certainly, most utterly seriously, come hunting through the world for only you. Sifting through the stones of every city in every nation.

Amex was out of the question, which left only a couple of options. Household Finance Corporation. Canadian Tire.

He withdrew the card and thumbed the edge. He thought of Benny, but also of the sprinklers and the lawn furniture he did not need. The cash that he did. He disliked what the situation demanded of him. Creativity, sure, but also guile. And he disliked even more the revelation of this creativity and guile within him. But what other option was there? The Monkey's Paw had to be worth the effort. The card had a pre-authorized $2,500 limit, enough to buy time, certainly. It was offering its assistance.

He put the red and white card in his front shirt pocket.

At the store on Burrard Street he leafed through the catalogue, looking for a single expensive item that could be transported without too much difficulty.

"Marine batteries?" He asked a clerk finally. "I need a dozen."

Black, plastic-cased behemoths with steel cable handles, marine batteries weighed eighty pounds a piece but were also, crucially, $175 each. A dozen with appropriate taxes came in under $2,500, he calculated by hand on the white margin of the catalogue.

"You must have a fleet," the guy laughed, as they humped the batteries from the shelf onto a flat-bed dolly.

At the counter, the look on the young woman's face suggested that she didn't care if he was buying twelve barrels of ten-penny nails for the purposes of shrapnel-bombing the provincial legislature. "That's $2,394.63 with tax," she said. Bored.

He made it under the limit and, heart pounding, flourished the card from his breast pocket like he'd been popping in and out all afternoon buying pulleys and 10W40. Pliers. Sets of goggles. Whatever it was ordinary Canadian Tire customers bought on a Friday afternoon.

She swiped the card. Ran its hard edge through the magnetic slot, and Jeremy thought: That's it. My relationship with Canadian Tire has changed. We're *sleeping* together. Now everything will be subtly different: the way we speak on the phone, our letters and our conversations. He signed the slip, took his receipt and left.

Second stop, Canadian Tire again. Not the same store, naturally, but a different location, where he would return the batteries and try for a cash refund. This ruse involved convincing the clerk that the purchase had also been cash, which made the whole operation highly time-sensitive. By the next business day, even a couple hours later, the purchase would show on the card. And so Jeremy was speeding, driving far across town to the Canadian Tire where Benny worked. Her location seemed the logical choice. He wasn't expecting any help from her—in fact, he was hoping very much he wouldn't see her at all—but if it absolutely did not work, if the clerk refused to bite and called in the floor supervisor, well then, at least Benny might understand that it wasn't stealing.

"What was wrong with them?" It was the first question the kid asked him. They had already unloaded the batteries and trucked them back into the store.

"Voltage." Jeremy winced internally. The full extent of his knowledge about batteries was that they were rated by voltage. The young cashier glanced at him and down to the receipt again.

"I'll ring it through in that case," he said cheerfully. "The system will credit your card."

"I'm sorry, but I paid cash," Jeremy lied, and looking up just as he said these words, he caught his own reflection in the shoplifting prevention mirrors and grew red with embarrassment.

"Well, the receipt shows a charge to your account. Here's the card number." The cashier pointed to the top of Jeremy's receipt.

Jeremy pretended to think. "I presented the card for the discount," he said finally. "I suppose the other cashier must have keyed in the number."

"Darn," the cashier said. "I'm new."

Jeremy stared down intently at his own hands. "I'll tell you what," he said after a second or two. "Why don't you phone and get the card balance? It should be zero. Since I didn't use the card to buy them, the batteries won't show."

Please don't show, he thought.

The cashier waffled, but finally picked up the phone. He looked greatly relieved when he hung up. "The card balance is zero," he said.

"All right," Jeremy said, smiling broadly. "I told you."

"Now I just need a signature from a supervisor for the cash."

No go. Well, it had been worth a try. "Sure," Jeremy said, wiping his forehead with his handkerchief. "Call Benny. She's working today, isn't she?"

The batteries were in the store. No crime had been committed, not that he knew of anyway. He waited, frozen at the till. She came right up next to them and put both her hands firmly on the counter. Patchouli and CK gently filled his nose. Benny looked at the cashier, then up to Jeremy with evident surprise.

"Jay," she said, smiling but confused, even reddening at seeing him in this setting. "What's up?"

The cashier tried to explain it all while Benny read over the receipt and while Jeremy stared at her profile and could not help but wish to be anywhere else on the planet but here. How sorry to be busted in this undertaking, by this slightly ramping nose. This perfect ear.

They went to the manager's office together. It was her calm suggestion, the redness of embarrassment or pleasure gone from her cheeks. "Marine batteries?" she asked when the door was closed behind them. Her voice was flat but her eyes fully animated and locked on his own. "Twenty-four hundred bucks? Come on."

It was Jeremy whose face was now burning, but he kept quiet. He didn't have anything to add that would change her mind if it were made up already.

"Do you scam the card company too?" she asked, growing curious. Trying to work it out.

"Oh God, Benny. No, it's not about that."

She looked at him very carefully while he explained to

her what it was about. About a need for cash or, more accurately, a need for time. And he told her much more. He told her about The Monkey's Paw, not just about its financial struggles but about what it stood for. The creativity. About the amount of himself that had been poured into it even before it was opened.

She looked at him slowly throughout his explanation, her arms crossed under her breasts again, nodding slowly as it dawned on her what, under the circumstances, might be born of conspiracy. She felt a flutter of excitement she did not reveal. A sense of the connection that could be made, the links forged. She had set out to do it herself, she knew, although she could never have predicted how it would be realized. He had come to her.

Jeremy finished his piece. She chose to scold first: "Whatever you're doing, you're doing badly. How much cash do you think is in those tills? Not three grand, I can tell you that. You really disappoint me."

He looked down at his boots.

"I've worked here since I was seventeen," she began again, her expression now very serious, although her heart was pounding. "Since I moved out. Six years. They trust me."

"I am sorry this thing happened," he said. "I'm leaving now. Your batteries are back in the store. Nothing has been—"

"This place has paid for everything I've done," she went on, interrupting. "Travel, school."

He watched her numbly as she rifled through the desk, extracted a key and turned to unlock a heavy filing cabinet against the far wall. There was obviously a risk, she assessed, but manageable. Petty cash for a large refund was not inconceivable. She pulled an envelope out of the middle drawer, turned and put it on the desk between them.

"Benny—" he said, meaning to go on and refuse this assistance. But she cut him off.

"Unfortunately," she said, putting one hand on her hip and holding the other out palm up, "unfortunately, as it happens— bad call on my part—Todd called in and found that the card balance was zero, and since I'd just come on shift and was busy with ten other things, I checked your driver's licence to make sure the card was yours and gave you your cash back."

She blinked her eyes at him. Then she unwound the string binding on the flap of the envelope and counted out the cash. "Two thousand, three hundred, ninety-four," she said when she was finished. "I owe you sixty-three cents."

"I don't know," Jeremy said, breathing a little raggedly. "I mean, fine, but—"

"Take it," Benny ordered, and he did.

She walked him out.

"Thank you," Jeremy began, but he wasn't entirely sure what she had done for him. The quality of the favour.

"You know where I want to go," she said, ignoring the fumbled thanks. They had reached the Impala, and Benny leaned comfortably against the front fender. "What I want to be."

"A designer," Jeremy said. "And I know you're going to be a good one."

"What I'm trying to say is," Benny said, "I know what it's like to have ambitions. To want something. To work hard for something."

Jeremy had to smile a little. "You have a twin who hangs out with a bunch of slackers in a little restaurant in Crosstown all afternoon."

Benny was making no apologies. "That alter ego might turn out to be a good investment."

Jeremy fingered the cash in his pocket. "What am I going to do with both of you?" he asked finally.

To which Benny replied: "What are we going to do with you? is the question."

He put his hands up to his chest then spread them wide. "I'm open to suggestions."

"You should be careful, I have a few." And with these words, Benny got up off the fender and kissed him. A cheek kiss, a friend kiss really, but it had a certain forcefulness he wasn't sure he recognized as friendly. It left a little damp mark, a smudge that he could still feel in the car. Driving uptown, across the Granville Bridge, Jeremy found himself smiling. Grinning uncontrollably.

He stopped at a Royal Bank machine and counted out twenty-two hundred dollars cash onto the sill of the kiosk. He punched the keys slowly, doing what he had to do. The machine took the money without gratitude. He kept $194 for Xiang, who by now took only cash. He wasn't ahead— Jeremy understood well—down half a Royal Bank Visa and up one whole Canadian Tire. But he was aloft. With these few small manipulations, the kite was again pulling tautly at the end of its lengthening tether.

Onward to Crosstown. Dinner service was accelerating towards him as he plunged through downtown. Past the Inferno Granville with its smell of burnt coffee and its canned jazz.

He found a parking spot right across the street and looked admiringly at his restaurant. There they were, his bike couriers. Sitting in the front window taking in the sun, which had just broken through and was streaming down, a golden wash of promise and fortune over The Monkey's Paw Bistro.

He walked in at full speed, into a room of good smells he could read like written words. There was a white fish stock. There were roast shallots. It was all coming together.

"Hey, Jay," one of the couriers said.

"Dino," he said, turning around walking backwards through the restaurant towards the kitchen door. "I have some cooking to do, sir, but *you* are having a round of beers on me. Zeena! For Dino, givin' it away here."

The couriers were grateful. They cheered, something along the lines of: "Yay, beer! Beer is good. Uh-huuuuh."

And Jeremy was laughing at the moment his back hit the swinging door into the kitchen, the moment he collided with Zeena coming the other way with a tray of coffee mugs. The mugs hit the floor and shattered into about two hundred and thirty thousand pieces. Nobody was hurt, and it was lucky it happened on the other side of the pass-through, well away from the range top, or it would have been fish stock and roast shallot sauce from scratch.

# TWO

# DANTE BEALE

Summer came. Cherry blossoms gave way to rich purple leaves. The sleeping bags multiplied in Victory Square. Crosstown smelled like pot and moved like a trance. Crowds spilled out of the Cannabis Café and Fabrek's Falafels, and the streets were full of young travellers and rivulet-haired, round-faced women in hiphuggers. The neo-hippie. The zippie. The raver. The punk. Jeremy found there was boundless optimism to be absorbed from every passing nose-ringed face, every busy Hacky Sack-obstructed street corner.

Plus, they were getting the foodies out. In the last week of June, they were slammed.

Thursday, in particular, they got hammered. You couldn't predict these things. There was a tremor out there, somewhere, in the substrata of the foodie psyche. Late in the afternoon, just as the summer light took its first dip towards the horizon and the end of the day came into sight. The shock waves rippled out, shaking through the molecules. A fine effervescence, a singe of electricity, spreading in great concentric circles, piling up energy in front of itself.

The first small wave broke with a phone call, which rang at The Monkey's Paw as Jeremy arrived after his afternoon break. Zeena answered it and winked hello at him. Four-top. Moments later, from the kitchen, he heard it ring again.

"Got a system moving in," Zeena said, her pen hovering above the blue leather-bound reservation book on the old walnut sideboard.

You could almost feel a breeze. Tonight was going to slam.

Six o'clock, Dino and the couriers were still there, several of them loudly drunk. Jeremy was smiling in the kitchen listening to Zeena kibitz out front and collect $12.95 a pitcher. Jules and he were wordlessly prepping, feeling the swell.

He smiled across The Zone at the back of her head; she was hunched over a floured board making puff-pastry sarcophagi, which, when baked, would be stuffed with goat cheese, tomatoes that she had dried earlier, and topped with green-onion marmalade. Appetizer number one, which came out of the ether earlier that afternoon.

"Fantastic onions," Jules had said when she saw them, the idea already forming.

They were cheap, Jeremy thought, but did not say. He was pulling in the reins a bit, not sure he would survive another card cancellation. Sensing this lately, Xiang would eyeball him as he navigated up and down between the bins at the Happy Valley Market on Cordova Street and say something like: "California artichokes. High quality. Good price." Or: "Florida strawberries. Whole bag. Ten dollars." Referring to some huge surplus item he was trying to unload before it went off. Jeremy might still find the local material he was looking for, but more often than not now, if the offer was good, Jeremy would have a look at the item and dicker his way to a price.

"Cash," Xiang would say.

"Visa?" Jeremy would try, with a narrow smile.

"How about...for The Monkey Paw...cash," Xiang would say, as if it were an idea that had just occurred to him.

Jeremy was working on the other appetizer, salmon in phyllo with roasted garlic and red-pepper coulis. The stock for the coulis was made with the salmon carcasses and was steaming luxuriously on the back of the range, giving off a rich velvety aroma and, to Jeremy (he kept it to himself), a slightly rancid back-flavour of burning plastic. CIBC MasterCard was now carrying another few hundred dollars' worth of wild sockeye picked up at another supplier. But not even in his present, frugal frame of mind was Jeremy going to buy farmed salmon.

"What's with the canned peaches?" Jules called from over by the cooler. She was holding a can in her hand. Product of Mexico. Several flats of them, almost free.

"Today they're for the guinea hen," he answered, without looking up. For the most part, the minor adjustments had escaped her notice, but now Jules looked over at him in a way she intended to communicate dissatisfaction, confirm she didn't find canned peaches minor.

"I have them soaking in peach juice and some grappa," he said, sounding guilty already (although he continued to lay out his phyllo). "I'm going to grill them with fennel seeds. I stole it from Umberto."

"Canned peaches," Jules said again, shaking her head. "They must have been a bargain." And she smacked the can back into its place.

It chafed. She was the less dogmatic about these things of the two of them, normally. But her reaction made him feel like he was betraying them, or her. It made him think about the impossibility of doing this work alone, of coming up with ideas day after day without her. About simply being without her.

She came over finally, before service. He grilled her one of the hen breasts and she ate it off a saucer, standing right next to him. If it hadn't worked she would have told him, but it was tender and the peach juices glazed to a beautiful bronze.

"You really stole this from Umberto?" she said, chewing.

He shrugged. "I was browsing the cookbook section. Let him sue."

She raised her eyebrows and wagged her head back and forth. She withheld overt approval even after they sold out, but up front the hen with Mexican canned peaches went down huge. He glanced at his watch near to eight o'clock as he put the last one on the grill. He had a dozen going and another half dozen appetizers waiting on the stainless steel counter for Zeena and Dominic. And down the line a way he watched the strong back of his strong friend as Jules cut portions of roasted lamb leg, mounding each thick slice with the soft mixture of bacon, spinach and shiitakes cooked in brandy and butter. Garnished with paprika and grated Parmesan cheese.

Zeena burst in and took two soups and three goat-cheese fills, balancing the plates up her arms. Then she stopped just before leaving the kitchen, turned to look at them both, speaking over the soundtrack that suddenly surged from the background. Mingus. They were rocking.

"Cute guy at eight says great chicken," she said.

"Guinea hen," Jules and Jeremy said in unison.

"Zeena, please tell the man to leave," Jules said.

"We want him out of here," Jeremy repeated, pointing with his tongs as Zeena smirked.

"And can either of you make a couple simple green salads?" she asked.

"Simple green salads," Jeremy said, raising an eyebrow.

"Brollywood," Jules said. "What do they want for dinner? No, let me guess. Guinea hen, no skin, poached. Plain rice."

"Close. He asked if you could make a seafood omelette, egg white only. Said his name is Dante Beale. He knows Chef Jeremy. Table ten with a friend."

Jules registered the name. "Is that guy still sniffing around?"

"Apparently," Jeremy said. The words were a bit more cavalier than he felt, but in the weeks since Dante and he had last discussed partnership—Royal Bank Visa and the Canadian Tire near-death experience notwithstanding—Jeremy had felt a surge in confidence. He attributed the improved outlook in part to the Professor's advice, although he was banishing thoughts of his father. They only made him feel guilty about not having done the one thing requested. Babes in the Wood. He simply didn't have the time. He was up early, worked all day, and the library wasn't open at one in the morning when he finally crossed town on his way towards bed.

"Tell Mr. Beale and his companion that I will prepare their salads and be out in a moment," Jeremy said.

Zeena left the kitchen with her armload of appetizers.

"What does he want?" Jules tried again.

Jeremy pretended not to hear the question, and after he'd plated the pieces of hen—a portion of dark meat and breast meat on top of a disc of roasted polenta, warm peach garnish, a splash more grappa and a twist of fresh watercress— he slid the plates onto the pass for Zeena. Then he went over to the cold appetizer prep table and made two very simple salads, fresh spinach and butter lettuce tossed with a tablespoon of red wine vinegar and walnut oil, topped with a sprinkling of diced hard-boiled egg, sesame seeds and cracked pepper. He wiped his hands, straightened his chef's hat and carried the plates out himself.

In the dining room he liked what he heard: the low-flame roar of the conversational furnace. You could almost feel heat off the jostling movement of so many minds and tongues and egos in such a small place. A round sensation, Jeremy thought, like a whiff of cognac. A couple of heads turned as he came out past the back service station, where the old coffee machine sat, and entered the main room at a measured pace. A couple of approving nods, which he returned, smiling. Someone tinked a glass and a woman laughed lightly. Jeremy smiled again and locked his eyes on table ten.

Dante's head was, as always, leaning aggressively into a conversation. In another life, were he less interested in commercial domination, Jeremy thought, Dante would have made a decent drill sergeant. His once dense black hair receding radically in front, Dante had gone for the Bruce Willis shave down. This complemented his grenade-shaped head, nose by Uzi, jaw and eyebrows straight and blunt. The overall effect was a simmering, dangerous aroma, a sense that from his fatless frame—Dante was near fifty and only five foot six, but triathloned and Tai Chi-ed into lean perfection—might burst an unexpected and brutally effective assault. A head butt. The heel of a palm slammed without warning up into the spot below your nostrils.

He dressed in suits, always, which Jeremy understood were cut into the double-breasted V-shape he liked on Saville Row. Shirts made in Jermyn Street, dazzling white with French cuffs and widely spaced, razor-thin stripes in bright orange and blue. Spread Windsor collar, often without a tie. Crockett & Jones lace-ups. He was an elegant thug. A man who started carrying Irish linen handkerchiefs at age thirty, after his first million. Pounds sterling, that is. The nest egg that he brought from London with him—brought with his no doubt conscientiously acquired posh accent—and with which (the date was 1975) he launched his ideas for the commodified coffee experience on the unsuspecting Pacific Northwest. The Inferno sputtered for two or three years, and then it simply caught fire. Nobody saw Dante coming. Business in Vancouver had only recently profiled him (his arm around two of his handsome baristas—he was a team guy). And here he was now, quite indisputably The King of Coffee.

He saw Jeremy approaching. It was not apparent that the mouth moved into the shape of a smile, certainly not broadly enough to show teeth or crinkle cheeks, but it did move subtly to a less intense disposition.

"Will you look at this," Dante said as Jeremy put the plates down on the table. His dinner companion was close to Jeremy in age, wearing a steel grey, zipper-fronted suit with a white T-shirt underneath. He was tanned, with strong features, and he'd shaved his full head of hair down to about Dante's length, perhaps out of sympathy.

"Jeremy," Dante said, reaching up his hand to shake Jeremy's. He certainly didn't bray his dominance around like a drill instructor, but used instead a comradely, insinuating tone. A team leader's tone. "How are things?" he asked. His eyes matched the gun-metal sheen of his suit and he stared fixedly, with almost startling interest, directly into Jeremy's own eyes.

"I am very well, Dante. Welcome to you both," Jeremy said, involuntarily adopting the same posh, conspiratorial tone. And released by Dante, he reached over and shook the other man's hand, who at least pulled his ass an inch off the chair as he shook.

"Glad to know you," the man said.

"Meet Philip Riker," Dante said. "I stole him from Nike a number of years ago. A one-man Inferno SAS, Philly is: special projects, Internet presence, competitive intelligence, strategic visioning.... I am essentially forbidden to do a thing without the Philly say so, isn't that right?"

Philip grinned and showed teeth. "I am the idea hamster," he said.

"Well...," Jeremy said, clasping his hands in front of himself, welcoming them both with his warm, benign presence. "Plain green salads. Tossed lightly in walnut oil. I hope you like them."

"They'll be just fine," Dante said, still staring him down.

"Sorry about off-menuing," said Philip. "I never eat anything on the sheet."

"My pleasure to do something for friends," Jeremy said, and suggested a crab omelette for a light main course.

"Philly?" Dante said.

"Yolks?" Philip asked.

"Normally," Jeremy said.

"Dante shouldn't eat yolks," Philly said.

"Egg whites it is, then," Jeremy said, nodding very seriously.

"And a bottle of Pellegrino," Dante said, waving his hand to dismiss the topic. "I see you're full. How has your week been?"

"Good. Tuesday and Wednesday, both good nights."

"I am very pleased," Dante said, and he settled back in his chair to get a better look at Jeremy, who despite the height advantage and the fact that he was now standing towering over the table could not help but notice the comfortable way Dante maintained possession of the space around himself. Philip was looking intently across the table at his master. Jeremy, chef's hat adding useless, duncelike feet above his head, was inclined politely forward to catch the stream of quiet, approving praise that now flowed from Dante. And around them, Jeremy could sense, the room had begun to shift its gaze downward from him to the seated speaker. Who's the chef talking to? What are they saying?

Dante had finished what he was saying with a shake of his head and the words: "I am truly jealous of you, Jay." Then to Philip: "I am jealous of this man, just as I am jealous in general."

"In general you're covetous," Philip said. "It's different."

Dante acquiesced with a smile. "But there is such a spirit of creativity here. It would be something to covet, wouldn't it?"

Jeremy started to answer—he was thinking of saying something about how Jules took one look at the green onions and saw her evening's creation blossom in front of her mind's eye, a creation they might like to try, in fact—but Dante only gave him half a beat and he missed it.

"Of course there is," Dante said. "And that is rather special, these driving, youthful ideas full of passion and power. I see you having real chances to be huge."

"Thank you," Jeremy said, although confused by the quality of Dante's praise. (*Huge?*) "We are very pleased."

"You very well should be," Dante said. "And we are doing our bit."

Jeremy waited for it, finding he was thinking all at once about getting back into his kitchen. A glass of wine might be nice, and the continued cooking of dinner for ordinary hungry customers.

"I got you into *Gud Tayste*," Dante said, taking a sip of his water.

"Sorry?" Jeremy said. His attention swivelled sharply back to the table. "The magazine?"

"The same. You know the 'Global Village' section they run?"

Of course he knew, and he nodded mutely.

"They're doing a Pacific Rim feature. Do you have any idea what their circulation is?" Here he glanced across at his younger colleague.

Philip responded without looking up: "250,000 world-wide. They're huge in England. Sweet demos. Average income coming in at something like a hundred grand U.S."

"Hip with money," Dante said, smiling meanly. "Travel budget, Philly?"

"A lot," Philip said, starting on his salad.

"Average number of languages spoken?"

Philip looked up from his plate. "Two and a half. The one with the most research rodents wins."

Dante looked up at Jeremy, suggesting a response would be appropriate.

"So, what...," Jeremy stammered. "Have they been through here already?"

Dante laughed out loud, some heads turned. "Of course not, Jeremy. But they only review who they like anyway."

"And..." He wasn't sure how to ask this question without seeming ungrateful, but he came up with: "And why would they like me, exactly?"

Dante sighed, disappointed that Jeremy didn't just thank them and leave. "Jeremy," he said finally, "journalists only know what's hip because people tell them what's hip."

Philip took the tag. "They're hot on this dawning of the Pacific Century idea. We just shot 'em some of that stuff. Shot 'em some of that stuff on a slant. Don't worry, it's all messaging. Keywords to take out the demographic target."

"Well, thank you," Jeremy said. "Thanks both of you, very much."

"How's your father?" Dante asked politely, moving the conversation along and inclining a little forward as he spoke.

Jeremy stumbled on the question, guilt leaching into his consciousness. "He's fine."

"We used to play chess on the odd Wednesday, he and I," Dante said. "But it's been several months now. Seems I keep missing him."

"Oh, he's around," Jeremy said, growing nervous with the questions. He had the absurd passing sense that Dante knew of his father's whereabouts and disapproved. Where was his father right now? Sitting cross-legged at the fire, duck grease on his chin, eyes animated as he talked with Caruzo about the Babes in the Wood, Siwash or one of the other tangled stories that consumed him.

But Dante only reached out his left hand to shake Jeremy's. He stayed seated, and Jeremy gripped the proffered hand, which fit awkwardly in his own and made him feel like they were holding hands, not shaking at all. Dante squeezed tightly.

"I am really happy about how things are going here," he said smiling. "And I am not surprised either. You are really very good."

He was shaking Jeremy's hand slowly back and forth, his fork squeezed in the fist of his other hand.

"Will you call me this week?" Dante asked, releasing him. "We could talk..."

"I killed 'em," Jeremy called to Jules as he burst into the kitchen.

"Yolkless omelettes and canned peaches," she said without looking up from the grill. "Who would have thought?"

They ran late. The last table was finally gone after midnight, and Zeena locked the front door. Dominic turned up the music, and they all danced in and out of the kitchen carrying

dishes and trays. Jeremy offered to make a late family meal
and set a table for them.

"Frittata," he announced, sliding a large plate into the
centre of the table and beginning to cut slices. "Made with
both the yolk and the white."

"Wine, please," Zeena said, holding out a water tumbler.

Jeremy got a bottle of Spanish red for them and poured.
Standing there with the bottle in his hand, their glasses full
and rising to their lips, he said: "I love you all."

"That's sweet, sugar," Jules said, and then to Zeena:
"How'd it go?"

"Awesome," Zeena said.

They ate. They helped the dishwasher clean up. Afterwards Zeena and Jules danced because Dominic had to
leave and Jeremy didn't feel like it. He was on his fourth
glass of wine, his fifth even, and found himself struggling
to relax into the pleasant feelings he normally felt at this
hour. He enjoyed watching the two of them tango around
the kitchen to Astor Piazzolla, their faces glowing red.
Stopping to smoke a joint Zeena produced from a pill bottle in her purse, then tangoing off again across the tiles,
laughing. The truth was, he loved this time, when they ate
what he fed them, as much as any other time he could
imagine.

But he was thinking about unkept promises too, each sip
of wine deepening a pull like gravity that was overwhelming
his enjoyment of the moment, and the more practical impulse
to get to bed and rest up for what would hopefully be an even
busier Friday night.

"Let's go to a club," Zeena said.

"Yes," Jules was saying. "Let's all go to a club."

A good Thursday behind them. Dollars in the deposit
pouch. Dante's partnership less a foreseeable requirement now
than at any time since that first phone call from Quan three
months after opening. There was every reason to celebrate.

And here I am, Jeremy mused, thinking only that the Professor would like to hear about these developments.

"I can't," he said to Jules and Zeena. He called them a cab, gave the driver ten dollars to get them up into Yaletown.

"You're a terrible bore," said Zeena.

"Bye, doll," Jules said, and she leaned out the door to peck his cheek, but Jeremy caught the back of her neck with one hand and gave her a good hard kiss. She pulled the cab door shut, looking back at him curiously. Just before they bounced out of sight at the end of the alley, they both waved out the back window. Two little white hands.

He locked up quickly and walked up through Cross-town towards the density of downtown. The streets were shining, and the prostitutes were floating at the mouths of alleys like salmon waiting for their turn to run the rapids, tired but determined. He strode across downtown, picking up steam and speed as he sipped from a wineskin he had topped up with Sangre de Toro before leaving. He couldn't explain his mood as he loped down through the West End, among the apartment buildings, and passed his own without a glance.

The lagoon was black. He wasn't sure he could even see ducks out there at all. He stood at the cherry trees, sipping from his wineskin, wondering what to do next. And then he pushed himself off between the trees, down to the path, where he started off at a trot for the far forest.

He began by looking for the spot where they had caught their canvasback for dinner, the only way he could think of beginning to retrace his steps and find the Professor's camp. But no single cluster of bulrushes was particularly distinguishable from any other. He tried searching for anything familiar, going first one direction and then another along paths that petered out in a few yards or wound away in the wrong direction. Above him a milky moon was trying and failing to squeeze its light down through the branches, and Jeremy stumbled pointlessly in circles and drank still more from the wineskin.

He found one trail that looked like the right one. He followed it into the forest, counting steps, trying to imagine where the sudden turnoff had come. Imagining the point from which he had stood and heard the song sung low: *With an hoste of furious fancies, / With a burning speare, and a horse of air...* And when he was sure he'd found the spot, he slogged deeper into the dense brush and realized he had found... well, nothing. No tree root, no upturned boulder. No place to climb onto the back of a great fallen cedar to observe the forest lying about him, to highway through the darkness to secret places. Instead, hanging bushes pressed down onto his head and shoulders, forcing needles under the collar of his jacket and down between his sweating shoulder blades. Forced him to see his own hand in front of him now, slashing uselessly at the darkness and the salal leaves with the Sabatier.

He froze, seeing it. He sobered. He woke up from a kind of sleep, feeling the familiar weight of it in his hand and the strong immediate sense of what a bad idea it had been to return to the kitchen, to find the magnetic knife rack without turning the lights back on, to feel it out with his hands, gently, wrap it in a tea towel and stick it in the waistband of his pants.

"Jesus," Jeremy said aloud. "What am I doing?"

He stood still for many minutes. Listening to the forest. Sounds became apparent among the trees, sounds beyond the steady hiss of leaves and needles brushing one another, sounds coming through the million frictions in the canopy above. Voices. The sound of movement, of life and activity. It couldn't be the Professor. Jeremy knew he had not accidentally stumbled so far up into the forest. Accidentally found a spot which had taken them thirty minutes of walking from the lagoon, after which he had been so disoriented he couldn't have pointed a finger in the direction of downtown. Only the ocean had given him any bearing. That sliver of water from high on a cliff.

There was no cliff here. He was at a low point, somewhere near the park's epicentre. And around him rose the forest, full of life. He was at the bottom of a well of hidden activity. He pushed the knife back into his waistband, took another long drink of wine, and considered he was lost and did not care.

There was a nurse log covered in moss and ferns lying on a low ridge that ran away to his right. He climbed along it on his hands and knees, peering ahead. And as he crawled, he saw the flicker of campfire come winking through the trees, first from his right, then his left. Voices became clearer. He could make out the peculiar feline mewl of a baby crying.

A guitar plucked in the near distance. A metal pot scraped against a rock.

He crawled further. At a fire through the forest ahead he identified the source of the baby's cry, quieted now in the muffle of a heavy blanket, held in the arms of a bent figure, a woman, crouched near familiar low flames in a narrow trench. The woman rocked the child, sitting on the ground near the heat. As he watched, there was a disturbance in the brush on the far side of the fire, and two men emerged from the darkness and entered the low ring of light. One looked carefully into the darkness, his eyes passing slowly over Jeremy hidden in the blackness, while the other crouched and opened a black plastic bag. He removed items for inspection. Food, Jeremy realized. A pastry box, some apples. And then small grey shapes laid next to one another in a furry row. They were squirrels.

The two men warmed their hands in front of the flames while the woman spoke to them in a quiet, steady tone and rocked the baby. Jeremy sat in the darkness straining to hear, far enough outside himself and any experience he had ever had to pause and consider that he was eavesdropping, peeping like a Tom, hovering like a ghost, or a god, or a conqueror in ambush.

It wasn't English, but an entirely unfamiliar string of sounds. Like insect sounds. Clicks and whirrs pushed from behind the tongue, hissing fricatives spilling into the still air. Popping epiglottis, singing in the blue night. An ancient-sounding tongue that mirrored the sound of cedar branches hitting one another in the wind overhead, or the sound of wave slaps on algae-ed stone, the sound of sappy softwood popping in a dying fire.

After they were finished talking the figure holding the baby passed it, wrapped and invisible, to the younger of the two men. Then moved with the woman into the spill of darkness beyond the ring of fire, gently entwined and rolled to the ground. Jeremy could hear the crack of twigs on the forest floor, and see the two shapes briefly writhe, find their positions against one another, then steady into a shared rhythm. It took him a moment to realize what he was now watching. Not specifically intending to see anything, and now having seen and heard more than the three figures might have wished him to see. And, as if to confirm this impression, the solitary figure by the fire placed the baby in the fold of some ferns and slowly rose from his haunches. He turned from the fire so slowly that Jeremy had to watch carefully to see whether he moved at all, and when he was facing Jeremy, facing the darkness, he began to inspect the forest with studied interest.

Jeremy backed slowly down the nurse log, careful to thread his legs through the bristling huckleberry. The baby re-commenced its crying, its slow wail spilling after him. The fresh red eyes pinched shut, feeling the night and the fern and forest around itself. Feeling the heat of the man's chest as he turned and scooped it into his arms. Sensing me here, Jeremy thought, and joining its voice were the sounds of the forest that followed him in his retreat.

Then the cry split into two, and he felt drunkenly certain that what he had taken for a baby had, in fact, been two babies. He climbed down off the log, and as he generously spilled wine onto the front of himself and down his neck, his thoughts spilled one onto another. He began to walk slowly, examining the forest around him with minute interest. The base of a tree here. The bend of a salal bush there. He felt the natural looping of his own path through the landscape. He made large useless circles through the trees, stopping now and again to replenish the inspirational buzz in his head with a draw on the wineskin. Circling. Circling.

"Where are you?" he said at one point, talking to the darkness, the living and the dead that it held.

The forest finally rejected him, burped him up on the edge of the lagoon, tired and sobering up badly. His path had traversed the park from firelight to firelight, through the un-marked graveyard of the forest floor to a bench on the famil-iar pathway around the lagoon.

There were half a dozen Canada geese sleeping nearby, silent in the nighttime cool. And in the dark, as the last of the wine burned itself out inside him, Jeremy pulled the Sabatier out of his waistband and balanced it in his right hand, enjoying the dull light that the blackened carbon-steel blade still seemed to shed. The secret of the knife was its hand-forged, feathered tang, which gave it legendary balance. But Jeremy wondered now if its secret was also that a father had presented it to a son on his return from afar, and that it now filled the son's hand weightlessly like a talisman. The Professor, meanwhile, slept soundly in the blackness behind him, dry under the plastic sheeting, in need of little. His fire would be smudged out, the embers buried in wet fern. Somewhere in the forest nearby would be duck bones, slowly disappearing into the mouths of ants and beetles, into the gullets of crows and the stomach of the earth itself.

The forest inhaled. It grew darker. The sound of voices had stopped or gone away. He sensed the subsuming pres-ence of the park instead, the silent and perpetual riot of growth and decay going on all around him: in ponds, in the trunks of cedars, in between the nurse logs where the ivy and the foam flower spread, in the secret paths of snails and squirrels. In the other secrets held in the forest floor.

He woke with the sun, which slanted in between the towers of the West End, prismed itself off the tall aquarium-green glass of the monolithic condominium that stood at the foot of Haro Street. He woke stretched out on a park bench.

He started sharply, sat halfway up. "Gawd."

A glance at his watch revealed that it was five in the morning, but also that something was wrong with his eyes. His vision was obscured, his eyelids unreasonably sticky. He put both hands up to his face, rubbing free what seemed like a resin of some kind, a spray, a coating on his face.

His hands came away flecked black.

"Jesus." He was sitting straight up now, brain tumbling, starting assessments and rejecting them. And then, continuing to rub his eyes, his face, he felt a faint throb begin across the bridge of his nose. Pain that punched through the dull ache in his head. Pain that produced a new set of red smears across his palms. His own blood. Dried and fresh.

The flow had been opened again.

"Oh, gawd," Jeremy said again. And now he planted his feet on the ground and fished in his pockets for a tissue. A branch, maybe? He thought he remembered the slash of a salmonberry cane across the bridge of his nose. The irritation momentary at the time. Fleeting. And now.

Now there was blood on his hand, on his cheek and chin. In his hair. There was new blood dripping from his nose to his chin, and from there to his shirt.

He jogged around the lagoon, head aching, two fingers pressed to the cut. He jogged under the purple cherry trees, up the hill towards home. Past the green monolithic condominium with its million-dollar suites. Without looking at it, eyes to the pavement ahead, he remembered a story about an old woman who had lived in the walk-up co-op that had previously occupied the lot. About how the developers had been forced to buy out every aging co-op resident at exorbitant prices and how she had held out. She didn't want the money, only to stay living on the same spot. And how in the end she had settled for a suite in the new building. She would take no cash, only a suite, which would allow her to keep a nail-hold on the land that held so much of her. A tendril of remaining connection snaking down twenty stories to the ground from her half-floor, 2,400-square-foot condo with its marble and hardwood and stainless steel kitchen. She held out. She faced down the monolith, and she remained.

It was the bridge of the nose. A horizontal boxer's cut. Not deep but well supplied with veins. He stood with toilet paper mashed between his eyes for a full five minutes before the blood hardened enough to hold his pulse without breaking. He found gauze and tape. He fashioned a bandage, thought about his next move for a full ten minutes. Then went to bed.

He missed the morning service. It was a hundred dollars' worth of coffee and Nanaimo bars, fine. It was also the first time in his life he'd not been in a kitchen at the time he was supposed to be.

"Your father OK?" Jules asked, first question, when he phoned. A death in the family might explain why she had to let herself in, might explain no breakfast service or how it could be that Jeremy was ten minutes away from being late for lunch prep.

"Yeah," he said. "Um..."

She waited.

"I'm running behind. Something unusual. Something I promised to someone. It's a one-time thing."

Of course it was fine, Jules assured him. Speaking quickly.

He phoned in the orders. Also a first-time thing. Xiang cooperated only with much cajoling and many reminders about the long period of cash payment The Monkey's Paw had endured. He agreed to take a credit card number, to be followed by a cheque. And so Jeremy compensated by ordering more from everybody than he needed. Salmon, thick-cut pork chops, lamb shanks.

"How about mushrooms?" Xiang asked him. "Chanterelle, very good."

"Sure. Four pounds of those and some eggplant."

Then he went to the library. He stood outside the building for a moment, considering both the task before him and the new building itself. Vancouver had replaced its old library, and Jeremy still missed it. Certainly it had been cramped and a bit dusty, but it had also been an architectural rarity from Vancouver's early boom days. Crisp sheets of glass opened the inside to the outside. He remembered how, from the opposite street corner, you could make out people reading, taking books off the shelves. People from around here using their library as it was meant to be used. This late-modernist gem had now been converted into a Virgin record store and a Planet Hollywood.

The new library, meanwhile (in front of which Jeremy now stood), was built to resemble the Roman Coliseum, complete with arches and pillars in a ring around the central building. Overt unoriginality aside, Jeremy was offended more by the greasy pizza fumes. In their infinite commercial wisdom, the developers had opened the atrium outside the library to retail activity, the first, very prescient, client in which had been a pizzeria. Nothing wrong with street pizza, Chef Jeremy thought, just this particular street pizza, which went beyond fast and cheap and standardized, and was striving also for the exotic, the novelty niche. Wolfgang Puck meets the Inferno Franchising Group: pineapple, pine nuts and Chinese sausage, or spinach, blue cheese and maple syrup. A commodified splatter of culinary incoherence on a shingle. Jeremy tried meatball and green olives once and couldn't swallow his first bite. He had to walk gingerly outside, holding this mess in his mouth, the rest of it at arm's length in one hand. He felt like a kid who'd wet his pants, hobbling stiff-legged for the wash-room. Outside he leaned over a garbage can and deposited this tapenade of ground beef and dough and pimento-stuffed manzanilla olives onto the cans and newspapers therein.

He took a breath and went upstairs.

"Babes in the Wood," the librarian at the history desk said to him. "Nobody wants to know about Babes in the Wood any more."

The librarian was staring right at the bandage between his eyes.

"Some people do," Jeremy answered.

"Well, not many people. There was a little spate of inter-est in the sixties."

He was bearded, wore thick glasses with heavy black frames and what looked like hospital greens. He used a wheelchair.

"The sixties?"

"Flower power and all that crap. Some of these hippie academic guys kind of dug the image of the little kids in the forest. Forever free."

"Are the bodies still in the park?" Jeremy asked, raising his eyebrows.

"No," the librarian said, with something like distaste. Ejecting the negative syllable and smirking at the question, shaking his head. "They were found by a city parks worker. Bodies went to autopsy."

"I see."

"You don't know the story?"

"Not really," Jeremy admitted.

"It's a quick study. Nineteen fifty-three. A city works crew is clearing bush up on Reservoir Trail in Stanley Park. They uncover two little skeletons buried in the leaves."

Here the librarian paused for a second and scratched his beard. Then he reached under the desk and pulled out a red cardboard Closed sign, placed it on the countertop and wheeled himself out from behind the desk. He beckoned to Jeremy and pushed himself towards the elevator.

"Social Sciences," he said when they were inside. "They have a file of related stuff. Research?"

Jeremy nodded. "For a friend."

"Albert Tong," the librarian said.

"Jeremy Papier," Jeremy said, reaching out his hand.

"Not me. The guy who found the bodies. I'm Gil."

They shook.

"So Tong finds a human skull. Bits of clothing. A little lunch box. He calls the cops, of course."

Here the elevator dinged their arrival at the right floor. Gil wheeled out in front of Jeremy, talking over his shoulder. "They dig around some more. They uncover the skeletons, still fully clothed. And then, buried with the skeletons, they find a shoe. A single adult shoe. Also a fur coat."

"The killer's?" Jeremy said.

Gil shrugged. "You might think so."

At the Social Sciences desk, Gil greeted the woman behind the counter.

"Nobody was ever arrested?" Jeremy asked.

"Nope. Some people came forward who had been in the park around that time and thought they saw a woman with two little kids, a boy and a girl. The cops did a country-wide search for anybody who knew about a brother-sister set gone missing. Sifted through hundreds of tips. Didn't amount to much. Which might be explained by the fact that a couple years ago DNA testing proved the kids were brothers."

Jeremy nodded. "But the bodies. Not there any more."

"I once heard rumours but it's urban legend stuff. They dug up the skeletons and took them to the morgue. That's generally what cops do, as opposed to leaving them lying around."

The woman returned with a thick brown envelope. Gil wished him luck and wheeled off to the elevators.

In a nearby carrel he hefted the large manila folder, which was tied shut with waxed string wound around two paper discs. Inside, there were dusty newspaper clippings stacked in sequence. At the bottom of the pile there was also a sheaf of pages with handwritten notes. A dozen messy pages. Almost indecipherable. Still, he leafed dutifully through the pages, moistening his thumb as he went, words slipping past unread. When he reached the last page, he realized he hadn't processed a single sentence and felt honour-bound to read the last words in full. They read:

*I will remember the following strange words: "... meant to be together. Just as the two were drawn from the same soil, so too must the same soil hold them, and through it must they be reconciled."*
*The others are drawn to his vigilance.*

Jeremy shook his head, baffled. It could mean anything. He yawned and ran a finger down the envelope's contents list. The newspaper articles were neatly listed. No mention of the handwritten notes. So that was it, he decided, nodding. The latter-day addition of some random nutcase.

He started at the top of the pile of newspaper articles, grateful for the frank broadsheet English. There were still gaps in the story, large unknowns, but over the years an accepted frame had fallen around the newspaper account of the Babes in the Wood. Two children, maybe five or six years old, brutally murdered. The decayed bodies were discovered by city parks workers in 1953. Over an unfocused picture of a clearing in a forest, *The Province* had superimposed a cutout photo of the murder weapon, found at the scene. It was a rough, two-headed axe, one head the conventional vertical blade, the other a square mallet. Other articles confirmed that the weapon was a lather's adze and that it matched the broken opening in each of the skulls perfectly. Also found at the scene: a woman's fur coat and a single red loafer.

The murderer's trail, however, was long cold. Police searched fruitlessly for further clues, learning little that wasn't evident at the crime scene until the appearance of one Miss Harker.

Jeremy's finger, tracing down the newspaper column, had just reached a large pencil star in the margin next to the words: *The Witness*.

A young woman—a girl, really—she was only sixteen at the time. But she had been in Stanley Park on October 5, 1947, and had seen a woman with two kids (a boy and girl, she thought) and then, sometime later, without. She hadn't thought of it further until those six years had passed, the parks workers made their grisly discovery and the story first hit the press. Her family had since moved to Toronto, but she read the news accounts and contacted the Vancouver City Police. She told them what she had seen that day. It dated the murder, but in the end, provided no substantial lead.

Perhaps as a result of this frustration, an accepted theme had developed in the small body of Babes in the Wood literature. The articles were inevitably printed in October, the anniversary month, and most of these cast the murder as an at-once tragic and inaugural event in the city's history. For Vancouver, the first of the self-inflicted wounds North Americans would come to associate with late-twentieth-century urban life. Murder, burglary, arson, carjacking, child abduction, rape, stalking, the drive-by and the home invasion…all these would follow. But the murder of those two children ushered this unsettling aspect of modernity onto the stage of Canada's third city, quiet at that time in its West Coast rain forest. Gently dozing in the mists that rolled in off the as-yet toxin-free and salmon-filled ocean. And thinking of it each year, or more accurately every ten years or so, the press in Vancouver would disinter the tale. The journalists would open their articles sounding as perplexed as they had been the first time. They would run over the tragic facts, grafting on the pale analysis of sociologists or psychologists or members of the still-stymied Vancouver City Police Unsolved Crime Unit. And they would finish as perplexed as they began, as perplexed as they would be for Octobers stretching into the future. Flipping from article to article, Jeremy was forced to consider a calendar of civic passage, guilt and confusion, tracing itself up through the decades.

"Interesting," said Jeremy aloud. Then, conscious of the time, he slapped shut the file folder and returned it to the librarian.

He walked briskly down into Crosstown. The sky was high, and there were ragged clouds moving rapidly seaward despite the breeze being light on his face.

Jeremy was filled with two contradictory feelings. One was tangled excitement about having something to report back to his father. The other was anxiety, which pulled him to a jog as he descended the steep part of Homer Street. A feeling that only resolved to relief when he rounded the corner onto Cambie and saw The Monkey's Paw façade. He stopped in the street, opposite, and admired it as if it had been resurrected from the ashes.

"Some tea?" Miss Harker had suggested.

The Professor was thinking about tea, having just tried to make the salal-berry variety. He was thinking that this was one of Caruzo's innovations that didn't work terribly well—it stained his lips dark purple and tasted like hot water for the effort—when the memory of Miss Harker coursed through him.

"Cookies?" she had pressed.

He had declined her tea and cookies at first, but she firmly re-offered. A twig of a woman with a stubborn streak and an unblemished memory of the day. If they were going to talk about this matter, she was saying in effect, they were going to have a nice cup of tea and a biscuit while doing so. He settled into one of the plastic-covered couches in her front room.

"We read about it in *The Toronto Star*," she told the Professor when she returned with the tray. "'Babes in the Wood.' From our little Vancouver. It was horrifying."

There had been the press to remind her thereafter. Newspapers tracked her down and phoned from across the country. There had been interest from a television show at one point, years later. She turned them down.

He was her first professor, she had told him. Psychology, was it?

"Anthropology," he said. And to explain his interest in her version of the story: "A farmer touches the earth in his fields. He thinks, This land is mine. A person in the city too, they walk their favourite streets, they visit their favourite parks."

Miss Harker nodded with recognition.

"Others are homeless, unrooted by choice or force," the Professor continued. "I know a man without a home who lives in a place where other people park their cars. He knows his city like no other person, from the inside out and at all hours. But he cannot let himself attach to any one square foot of it more than any other. He cannot afford it."

Miss Harker nodded with a little less certainty.

The Professor sipped his salal-berry tea, remembering her hesitation. He dabbed his mouth with the edge of his sleeve, let the hot liquid slide into him and warm him.

"I am interested in these different connections," he had told her. "The connections between people and the places they call their own. I am interested in how these connections are forged and broken. And how, for some, the connection refuses to break."

Miss Harker considered this comment for a moment. "When I learned we were leaving Vancouver," she said finally, "I grieved like a sister had passed on. Of course, I was very young."

"October 5, 1947," she began. Her family's last day in the city. Her father was an Anglican minister, and had received notice of a move. There was no question whether or not he would go. Never mind her friends, her school. Never mind that she had a sweetheart.

"Never mind my connections to that place," she said.

On her last day in the city, Miss Harker walked down from the rectory on Jervis Street to Stanley Park, her favourite place in all of the city, a place that was pure and unimpeachably good. "More like a church than a real church," she said to the Professor.

She walked and walked, crying often. She crossed the entire park, through the forest to the Burrard Inlet, where she spent some time pulling flowers from the grassy bank and throwing them into the sea. Eventually, she began to hike back through the forest to the city. It was late morning as she climbed up and away from the grey inner harbour, climbing up into the rich greenness of the forest, breathing deeply, feeling a little restored. She stopped to catch her breath at a corner in the trail. The moss-covered trees arched overhead, enfolding her. The forest was hushed. The soft red earth of the trail made no sound under her feet as she looked all around her, resolving that she would remember everything about this instant of stillness.

That was when the children burst into view, startling her as they rounded the corner and tumbled past. A little boy and a little girl, she said. They were wearing red plaid hunter jackets and leather aviator caps, goggles riding high on their foreheads. They were excited, happily screaming back and forth between them in a language she didn't understand. A language of their own? she wondered at the time.

Miss Harker stared after them, then turned to see the woman who followed. Her eyes tired, face unsmiling. She scuffed along the path in bright red loafers, holding a short fur coat tightly around herself. And as the woman brushed past, Miss Harker could see that she carried a small hatchet. She could have touched it. It had a small chip in the blade.

Miss Harker set down her teacup. "After they were gone, I became frightened," she said.

"Why was that?" he had asked her.

She didn't know. Her hand rested on a doily that covered the arm of her chair. Her fingers touched the embroidered cloth and leapt back into her palm, again and again, as if the material were burning hot. Her hand began to tremble, just slightly.

There had been something, someone. She couldn't be sure. She felt embarrassed at it now, mortified then. Of course, she hadn't told anyone.

"Someone else?" the Professor tried. "Someone else there?"

No. Yes. Maybe. She had been suddenly spinning in a cool mist of new feelings. An apprehension of her impending departure that was so real, so close, it was as if she had been separated from herself. As if the passing children had carried off the part of her that had known this place, known Stanley Park. Carried her up the trail with them, around the bend, out of sight. Their voices absorbed by the forest, to be, all of them, absorbed.

She fainted. Or she must have. She woke up lying on her back in the soft red earth, the forest rising above her. It seemed to her that the air had grown dark. And all at once there had been faces. Or the sense of faces in the woods. Faces and forms. The sudden, immense sound of a thousand people hovering in the air nearby. Thousands of human sounds singing to her out of the blue light, sounds that came in off the paths and through the leaves and blended into the air around her.

There had been a young man, after that. Skinny and rather ragged. He could only have been about her age.

The Professor set down his own teacup and sat forward in his chair, leaning in, eyes sharp.

"He looked down at me as I lay on the trail. He touched my forehead. I know so because there was a dirty smudge there later. I struggled to sit and he vanished into the woods."

She walked quickly to the zoo after that, she told him. She stood at the monkey cages and smoked a cigarette. "I was occasionally naughty."

Late in the afternoon, having smoked through her fear and forgotten her anger, cried herself dry of tears, she returned to the city through the rose gardens. The grass was green but the bushes had been clipped back, sharp stalks coming up from black soil. Overhead, the sky was wool. She wound her way through the empty beds and borders, down towards the road. She turned to look a final time.

The woman stood at the top of the rise, fifty yards away. She looked dishevelled now, even at a distance. Her fur coat was gone. Miss Harker remembered watching her cut across the flower beds at a slow, limping run, eyes on the horizon, seeing nothing. One bare foot sunk into the soil, again and again. It was pasted with black earth. The woman was alone.

The Professor didn't move for several seconds after the story came to an end.

"I was just a girl," Miss Harker said. "Resentful, melo-dramatic about my own affairs." She felt uprooted and alone. And that night she thought about what she had seen and put it all down to the sad wreckage her sixteen-year-old world had become.

The Professor was frozen at the memory of it, his salal-berry tea long cold. He remembered holding his breath as she described these moments, and he was holding his breath again now.

He exhaled, then took a deep breath of fresh sea air.

"We got a ton of stuff," Jules said when she heard Jeremy arrive. "Gorgeous chanterelles." She did not look at her watch.

Then she turned around.

"What the hell happened to you?"

He pointed at his nose. He made a gesture.

"Cut," he said. "Branch." And then he began looking around himself as if trying to remember where things were.

Jules turned back to her prep. "How'd the favour go?"

"The Professor," Jeremy answered. He didn't want to get into it.

Jules stopped cleaning mushrooms and stroked her hair back behind her ear. "Who just phoned, by the way," she said. "He wondered if you could see him Sunday."

Jeremy was walking away from her as she spoke, towards the walk-in. But he stopped abruptly, turned to the prep counter, put his fingertips on it for balance.

He heard what she had said, but wasn't looking at her. He made a move towards the dish pit and stopped again, staring into the empty drying racks, stranded in the middle of the tiles with a hand on his chin.

Jules glanced over. Curious. Not saying anything.

"So, what's on tonight?" he asked finally.

Jules put her knife down. "Take a sniff, Chef," she said. The kitchen was fragrant with simmering wine, bay, thyme and allspice.

He breathed in as instructed. "Lamb shanks."

Also: salmon with dill beurre blanc, pork chops in Calvados and cream. Both with a choice of new potatoes or roasted garlic polenta. One pasta, farfalle con funghi.

"Four mains?" he said.

"I had to do something with it all," Jules answered. And as she ran over the appetizers, she watched him look around himself, failing to find his place. There was copious eggplant, which she was working into eggplant caviar for stuffing into tiny tomatoes, she explained.

His eyes were drifting oddly. She tried to follow his gaze, but if he was looking for something, there was no pattern to the search. His eyes went to the walk-in, across the tiles beneath his feet. To the door into the dining room, to the range top. But when he found the knife rack his gaze settled briefly, and then his eyes went round, his mouth opened slightly. His breathing quickened.

"Oh God," he said as a memory bloomed within him. "Oh God, oh God, oh God." It had been insane to bring the knife. Something he could not afford to lose, staggering around drunk in the wet salal, slashing and cursing.

Something that could be taken from him while he slept.

"Jeremy?" Jules said, coming towards him. He was staring over her shoulder still, one hand gripping the prep counter. She looked again to the knife rack. There were the Wurstof Trident filleting knives, carving and paring knives, and other blades they had each picked up over the years. All in the places where they were used to seeing them, and being so, highlighting the empty space at the centre of the rack.

"Where...," Jules started, knowing immediately. She turned back to him, put a hand on his forearm. "Jeremy? Where is your knife?"

"I can't...," he started. "I have done... so stupid. Last night. Oh Jesus."

"Jeremy," she said sharply, trying to get him to make eye contact. "You went to the park?"

His hands were at his face now, balled fists in his eyes.

"What the hell did you do?"

"Oh Jesus."

"Talk to me."

"I didn't mean to, even. I literally didn't see it in my hand until I was there. In the forest stumbling around."

"Stop it!" she shouted. "What happened?" She reached up and removed his hands from in front of his eyes. Put her own hands on either side of his face.

"I slept there," he said. "Someone stole my fucking knife!"

Jules let her shoulders round slightly in relief. "Stolen? All right, we'll go look for it," she said, knowing that it would be long gone. He got teary. He was embarrassed, but he could not stop it. She hugged him.

"My father—I was there looking for him."

"I know, I know," Jules said.

"I'm such an idiot," he said, and he buried his face in her shoulder.

"You are sometimes," Jules said. She put his apron around him, tied it up and steered him by the shoulders over to the prep counter with the half-made melizzano. She showed him where the tomatoes were. She put a Henckels nine-inch chef's knife in his hand and a steel in the other. She fetched a paring knife and laid it on the cutting board next to him.

"Note the time, Chef," she said, still kindly, but also feeling a tickle of impatience. Knowing he would be useless, she undertook the placement of the lost ads herself. While Jeremy stood at the counter, cursing his own stupidity, she stared down at a job that had to be done.

"Lost near Lost Lagoon early Friday morning," she said to *The Province* classified ads desk. "Unique chef's knife. Sabatier. Devil's stamp. Engraved on the back of the blade. High sentimental value. One thousand dollar reward. Phone ..."

"What?" he said from across the kitchen, turning towards her.

"Where would you find another one?" she said, not even looking back. Dialing another number already. "Lost ads, please." *The Sun, The Province, The Straight, The Courier, The Kitsilano News.* It took her fifteen minutes and she was back on prep. Dinner service marching towards them both.

They were full through to ten, ten-thirty even. Compliments flowed back through Dominic and Zeena. The music pulsed along, jigging and jagging. Gypsy Kings. Jimmy Smith. On towards eleven o'clock Jeremy thought he heard a snip of Alice Cooper in there somewhere. He tried not to look at the knife rack. He tried not to feel the absence of its heft in his hand.

"There's someone here to see you," Zeena said. "A girl."

She was at table seven, sitting a little sideways, a shoulder leaning into the exposed brick. Dressed in tight black velvet. Or was it purple? It was, in any case, one of those in between colours that drew the eye tightly to her, and down her length. From the short-sleeved, vampy, cleavage-enhancing top, across the narrow waist to where she settled into the chair, the fabric of the pants still holding her tightly (holding his eye) down the crossed legs to just below the knee, where they flared. She had high black boots on that covered the calf, laced up along a lattice of chrome eyelets.

Benny was smoking and drinking a martini. Rocks. Twist.

"Hello," he said

"Hello," she returned slowly. Showing him the stud.

He leaned down and kissed her on both cheeks, then he sat opposite. "You look great."

"Thank you. I feel a little out of myself. I feel a bit make-believe. Of course, my day began strangely—you weren't open this morning."

"I slept in," he said. "I wish now that I hadn't. But I did."

"I forgive you for sleeping in." Benny was looking around the restaurant. "There is a different crowd at this hour."

"My foodies, or what's left of them. We were full earlier." He was leaning into the table. He straightened up a little and said: "I'm glad you came down."

"I was thinking about you this afternoon," Benny said.

He didn't answer, waiting for her. She smoked deliberately.

"They fired me," she said eventually, exhaling.

Jeremy felt the news pass through him and felt immensely tired. So tired that he removed his toque, leaned forward and put his forehead on the tabletop.

"Damn," he said. He could feel the tablecloth biting a fine pattern into his skin.

"Lift your head up," she commanded in a low voice.

He did as he was told.

"There is no point in worrying now," she said after he had replaced his chef's hat. Ice cubes clinked in her glass as she finished the martini. "What's lost is lost, right?"

He laughed a half laugh. How right she was. "Look at you," he said.

"You don't like it?" Benny said, glancing down at her velvet, shrink-wrapped self.

Jeremy stared at her body, as he had been authorized. "I like it very much," he said.

"All right then," Benny said. He ordered her another martini from Zeena, who was watching them carefully.

"Get back to work," Zeena said to him playfully.

"Not just yet," Benny said.

Zeena left them.

"Tell me what happened," Jeremy asked her.

"They called me into the manager's office. They said, 'We're very disappointed in you....'"

"Shit. I am—"

"Forget it," Benny cut him off. Her emanations were shifting minutely between sexual invitation and anger. Back and forth. "So I lost something—maybe I found something else already. It took me a whole day to find other work."

"Tell me what they actually said."

"That Jeremy Papier is a thief."

"But I'm not."

"That it might be fraud...that if you didn't pay them immediately when they wrote to you that they might well get the police involved, in which case it was going to be hard for them to say exactly whether or not, under the circumstances—because I'd been a really good employee up until then—whether there would be reasonable grounds to charge me too."

She stopped just as she ran out of breath.

He glanced around and saw that they still had a few tables left, one of which, having noted that the chef was in the dining room, was smiling and nodding in his direction. He returned the smile.

She lit another cigarette and eyed him. "You have to go," she said.

He didn't get up right away.

"You have work to do," she said. "Not to worry, I'll stay."

He looked at her once again down her velvet length. She grew sharper with each thing she said, more desirable. "I'm glad," he said. "We could go for a drink in an hour or so. Are you hungry?"

Benny craned her neck to look at the chalkboard. Zeena had scratched up the prix fixe menu—two appetizers, four entrées—in her signature Gothic block caps, with needless umlauts and tiny spear-tips capping the upstrokes on the odd lower case *h* or capital *N*.

The salmon was gone. So were the lamb shanks.

"I think I want a pork chop," she said like the word amused her.

"Grenadin de porc Normande for the lady," he said, standing and bending slightly at the waist.

"No," she said.

He stopped momentarily in surprise. She knew what it was apparently.

She skewered him with a return glance. "I am familiar with Calvados. And not incidentally, allergic to apples."

"I see." He was thinking how the dish could be prepared quickly a different way. "Do you eat mushrooms?"

She did.

"And what do you feel like drinking?" There was a reliable way in which people revealed to you what they really felt like having for dinner. It was half the fun of cooking, this investigation. "Something new," he said, taking a step for her. "Something to discover on the day you lost something else."

"All right," she said, smiling and compliant now. She would let herself go with whatever he had in mind for her just then.

He went back into the kitchen. The dish-pit guy was in, starting on the cycle that would return all of their plates and pots and skillets and cutlery and glassware to its proper metal rack for reuse in the morning. Most nights up until now, they hadn't stretched the limits of their inventory. Tonight, and several nights this week, he mused, by the end of the evening they were running out of one tableware item or other. He felt a satisfying sense of pushing snugly against their capacities.

Jules smiled at him, wiping her forehead with the back of her hand. She was assembling a small selection of cheeses on a bed of arugula and purple kale. He watched momentarily, as he often did in the wind-down section of the evening, enjoying the movement of her strongly veined hands. Their sureness. It occurred to him that there was no cook in the world that he really admired more than Jules Capelli. Her simple understanding of the food universe was as stable and sure as Pépin. She laid out a wedge of Brie de Meaux, a small block of Pont l'Evêque and a piece of Saltspring Island chevre.

Tom Waits trickled through the overhead speakers into the kitchen and the dining room. "Semi Suite." He turned to Benny's dinner. He would make something *à la minute*. One dish uniquely for her.

He scooped up a skillet in one hand and let it bang onto the black gridded top of the range. He went to the walk-in and found the few remaining pork chops, which had been put away. He removed one, then picked a large bottle of Chambly La Fin du Monde. A Trappist-style Quebec beer, one of the best in the world as far as Jeremy was concerned. Benny would never have tried it, and he guessed that she would not believe that such delicate effervescence could come from a beer at all.

There were still sliced chanterelles and shiitakes, diced onion, cream, garlic, crushed pepper, all prepped and in containers next to the stove top. *Mise en place.* He poured Benny a glass of beer, watching the uneven bubbles forming in the firm head, letting the foam rise a good half-inch above the rim of the glass. Then he poured off a cup of beer into a small bowl and put it next to the other prepped ingredients, put the tall bottle next to the glass on a serving tray, slid them onto the stainless steel pass-through for Zeena.

"Table seven, sweetie," he said.

"Your new gal, Jay?" Zeena said. He could tell she was looking forward to her post-action joint.

"How'd it go out there?" Jeremy asked back, pretending not to hear the question for which he didn't know the answer.

"We rocked," she called back over her shoulder, pushing through the swinging portholed doors and into the dining room. "OK tips. Got hit on twice."

When the pan was hot he added a knob of butter and some oil from a plastic, red-nozzled bottle, let it heat through and foam while he vigorously salted and peppered the chop. He dusted it with flour, then gripped the protruding bone with tongs and pressed it down into the foaming fat. When it was browned on both sides, he tested its firmness with his thumb, pushing gently on the flank of the hot chop, pulled it out and onto a small plate that he slid into a low oven. A few onions went into the pan, a grind more pepper, chanterelles and shiitakes sliced thin, some minced parsley. He tossed the mixture, letting it slide to the far edge of the pan, pulling it back and up towards him, which made it break loose from the slick surface and turn over before landing. He let it cook through, whistling with the music—they had segued from Tom Waits to Tom Jones. When the mushrooms were starting to brown, he added a bit of garlic and the beer, swirling the contents of the pan to mix them while they boiled. A knob of butter to thicken the sauce. A new dry side-towel before grabbing the chops out of the oven. Back they went into the sauce, half-covered and slid just slightly off the flame.

He chose new potatoes for her, much better with the beer. He laid down a bed of the browned mushrooms in their sauce, nestled the chop on top, triangulated with three of the waxy yellow potatoes, sprayed the plate with more parsley and carried it out himself.

"Grenadin de porc au beurre La Fin du Monde," he said, sliding it onto the table in front of her.

She inhaled the steam, her eyes closed now, enjoying the aromas.

He watched her for a second, then leaned over her and kissed the top of her head, his lips gently brushing the white blond hair. The first time he'd kissed her. And seeing down the front of her, past the bulge of cleavage, he admired his creation sitting warmly on the plate, made with his own hands.

She looked up at him, her neck craning back.

"Where'd you get a job so soon?" Jeremy asked.

"At an Inferno," she said smiling. "I'm a barista now. Kiss me properly."

Which he did, although quickly, sensing at least one of the remaining tables watching, and feeling a mixture of feelings. One, familiar and not unpleasant: a gonadal, possessive stirring against the inside of his pants. Something actually moved down there. Another feeling hovered outside of him. A feeling of circumstances aligning, in a portentous way that refuted free will. The trees in Stanley Park had swayed above him in the same black way that he and Benny now just briefly swayed together.

The third feeling was hard and metallic, startling against his lip and, for the merest of instants, under his own tongue.

Sunday he ran errands. Dry cleaning, some shuffling around of withdrawals and deposits; they had a good week, and he had a few thousand dollars to wind the kite in tightly a turn or two. He bought milk for home. Bought some stamps. All of these activities an elaborate stalling tactic to avoid a trip he knew he was going to make.

It didn't matter that Jules had placed the ads. It didn't matter that the markers had been set out that might lead his lost treasure back home. It was gone in the way that the recently departed are gone, their presence still burned on memory's retina. He would look each time he passed the familiar spots, the knife rack, the wooden chopping surface. He would look involuntarily, expecting to see it miraculously restored.

He brought the Sabatier papers of certification to Bloom's, a high-end knife shop in the basement of the Hotel Vancouver. Sigmund Bloom looked these over with some curiosity.

"This is a very rare piece you have."

"Had," Jeremy said with a pained expression.

Bloom looked up expectantly. With such timeless artefacts, items fully expected to outlive your grandchildren, there are only strange and noteworthy ways for them to require replacement.

"I lost it," Jeremy explained.

Bloom winced. He picked up the papers again, hoping to see something that would improve the situation. But he shook his head finally and said: "L'Enfer was an unusual factory. They were situated at the base of a waterfall on the river Durolle, in the Thiers region of France. It was the least desirable location on the river, hence the name. Rumour had it that the owners of the factory collaborated with the Nazis during the Second World War. Bayonets, you understand. Their output was duly shunned afterwards, leaving a warehouse of unsold items to be discovered in later years."

"Hence the name?" Jeremy said.

"It was nearly under the waterfall. I understand the noise in the factory to have been constant and oppressing. The factory took the name Le Creux de l'Enfer, which roughly translates as 'The Pit of the Inferno.'"

Jeremy processed this description. "'The Pit of the Inferno,'" he repeated, staring at the jeweller.

"Yes," Bloom went on. "Or 'The Depths of Hell,' if you like. That is the better translation, in the sense that *fer* means iron, and *enfer* may be construed as 'in irons' or 'in captivity,' hence 'Hell.' Still, I like 'The Pit of the Inferno' better, since the sound made by the constant pounding of the Durolle over the waterfall, combined with the wail of the grindstones, must have sounded very much like the roar of a bonfire. Imagine working in such a place. You'd go mad."

"It's remarkable really," Jeremy said. "'Pit of the Inferno.' How can we be sure that my knife came from that factory? Sabatier had a lot of factories in the region."

"The blade mark," Bloom said. "A little devil stick figure running with a trident."

Jeremy nodded slowly. "That's the one."

Bloom shook his head sympathetically. "The trouble is, there's little chance you'll replace such a blade, short of buying from another collector."

"It has to be replaced," Jeremy said. "Not necessarily with Sabatier, but a blade of real quality."

Bloom ran through some high-end options. Wurstof Trident, Sabatier's present Maître de Cuisine line. "At the very high end," he said. "There are also handmade knives coming out of Japan. The zirconium-oxide ceramic blades won't get dull for decades, literally. They also don't oxidize like your old carbon-steel blade, and they're stronger and lighter."

"How much?"

Kyocera's KC-200 black ceramic, hot-pressed, six-inch chef's knife with a wooden handle retailed for $522.40, including taxes.

"And they go up from there."

Jeremy raised his eyebrows. Something about his curiosity in the best, in the most expensive, captured Bloom's imagination, and he went behind a glass partition into the rear of the shop, where he dialed the combination on an old green safe.

Bloom returned with a black wooden box and set it gently on the counter. Opened, the box revealed a blue satin lining, and on this satin lay a most unusual blade. A nine-inch chef's knife. Absolutely black from the point to the butt of the handle. It seemed to absorb the light.

"Fugami," Bloom said. "Made with extraordinary care, in batches of sixty only three times a year. The ceramic compound is thirty times harder than similar knives. Maybe the Kyocera will need sharpening in a couple of decades, but technically speaking, this Fugami will not need sharpening until sometime early in the fourth millennium."

Jeremy exhaled. He didn't want to hear the price.

"Are you a collector?" Bloom asked, gently anticipating the unasked question.

"No," Jeremy said. "I'm a chef."

"You do not need this knife." His voice was paternal, dissuading, and he made a small motion to close the box. But Jeremy reached out quickly and touched the black wood, and Bloom's hands dropped away. Jeremy pulled the box across the glass counter towards himself, removed the blade. The Fugami nestled firmly into the meat of his palm, nearly weightless.

"Thirty-two hundred dollars," Sigmund Bloom said.

Jeremy actually gasped. In part it was an expression of impossibility. There was no way he could consider such a purchase. The Monkey's Paw just now making its first small steps towards profitability. At the same time, it was perfect that the blade should cost an amount approaching the threshold of physical pain. Perfect that he should suffer for it— Jeremy's mind was spinning forward as he held the knife in his hand—perfect that for the loss of his Sabatier he should put himself again at the lip of the volcano, yes, staring down into the inferno itself, and with penance and risk-taking restore his talisman.

"You must think about it carefully," Bloom said after a few seconds. "Take some time." He left Jeremy standing there and went into the back room.

Jeremy pulled out his wallet, instinctively running his thumb down the edges of the cards. Even with a good week under his belt, even with the kite pulled in a few turns, none of them had that much room.

Bloom returned in a few moments.

Jeremy took a deep breath. "Do you take Amex?" he asked.

He dropped the knife at his apartment and went to meet the Professor. They walked to a different place, a clearing where the earth was reddened with decaying cedar. It wasn't a secret spot, but a place where they could sit together on a log and look like any other two people stopping for a breather in the middle of a long walk.

"Well, what has happened?" the Professor said. He was dirtier, Jeremy noted, and today he seemed slightly agitated.

"The rumours of them still being buried in the park," Jeremy began, "these are urban legends."

"I see," the Professor said, nodding. Not surprised.

"They were killed here, though. October 1947 is the agreed month."

"I see. I see."

"And a witness came forward," Jeremy said, watching to see what effect this information would have. "A Miss Harker. She apparently saw the murderer."

"Yes?" The Professor said, very focused. "And what else?"

Jeremy scratched his head.

"What else did she see?" the Professor prompted.

"The kids?" Jeremy said. He had the feeling that he was being tested.

"But what else, anything?"

"I'm sorry," Jeremy said, not understanding.

"In the park," the Professor said, exasperated. "She saw someone...."

And then he stopped and looked away, realizing that Jeremy had nothing more.

"There are a few newspaper articles," Jeremy said. "I read them. There are also some notes, which I didn't have time to read."

"I see," said the Professor.

It occurred to Jeremy that he had wanted to appease, to make done with what he had promised. "I closed the restaurant for the morning to do this for you," he said.

"Your sacrifice is appreciated. So, nothing else to tell me?"

"Business is better," he said. "If I hold Dante and the bank off for another couple months, maybe the decision won't be needed."

The Professor glanced at him. "That would be nice, wouldn't it?"

They drifted in silence for a moment.

"Will you at least read the rest of the file at the library?" the Professor asked quietly.

Jeremy bowed his head. "I'll try," he said. "But you understand that it's really important I focus on The Paw right now."

The Professor nodded slowly.

"I came looking for you a couple nights ago," Jeremy said.

The Professor registered surprise.

"I saw some people around a fire."

"Did you really?" Now the Professor was smiling.

"Two men, a woman and a baby. They spoke a strange language."

The Professor actually clapped his hands. "Brilliant. Strange how?"

"Popping. Hissing."

"You have seen and heard a great thing," said the Professor.

"An ancient tongue. An aboriginal language, nearly extinct. I had heard there was a group sleeping in the low area just west of the lagoon."

"That's them," Jeremy said.

"Cultural holdouts," said the Professor. "These people are taking a last stand. Homing in on a place that cannot be taken from them. You see, their language belongs to this land. The words themselves are linked to specific things: a bend in a creek, a bank of stones, the old Beaver Lake salmon run. They've moved back, this small family or group of families, however many there are, to the place from which they cannot be driven."

"Well, they could be. You're not allowed to live here."

"Yes, of course," the Professor said. "But the land itself cannot be taken. This great locus of civic pride, this Stanley Park. It can't be expropriated, built up, paved over, strata-titled. These speakers of an ancient tongue, their actions are the sociolinguistic equivalent of taking sanctuary in a church. These woods, this is the church."

The Professor was animated. His hair tufted out at the sides as he spoke. "And you don't see the connection at all, do you?" he said, after a few seconds of silence.

Jeremy didn't, although he found himself reluctantly interested.

"Each of these new arrivals will forge their own connection to this sanctified soil," the Professor said. "The Babes in the Wood were only the latter-day genesis of matters."

"What about Siwash?"

"Siwash counts everything that passes," said the Professor, his face wide open with wonder. Dogs, joggers, bladers, pedestrians, bikes. Everything, the Professor theorized, was being catalogued.

"Why?"

"Oh dear, I am disappointed," the Professor said.

"How should I know?" Jeremy answered, defensive.

"If somebody were to ask me, What am I trying to accomplish?" the Professor said, in a strangely flat, dogmatic cadence (it took Jeremy a moment to appreciate that he was being mimicked), "I would answer that I was trying to remind people of the soil under their feet. Of a time when they would only have known what that soil could offer."

"Or words to that effect," Jeremy said, but he gave a half-smile in acknowledgment of the impersonation. It was pleasing that his father remembered something he said well enough to repeat it under these circumstances, even half-right and miles out of context. "You only forgot the part about food."

"Ah yes," the Professor said. "It's all about food."

"I'm a chef. It *is* all about food."

"No, it isn't. It's about roots and place. It's about how people relate to the land on which they stand. In our rootless day and age, our time of strange cultural homelessness—and worse, our societal amnesia about what used to constitute both the rewards and limitations of those roots—I wonder if we might look to these homeless," and here the Professor extended his thin arm, pointing into the park to signify all of its occupants, "to find an emblem of the deepest roots of all."

Jeremy considered this for a moment. For an instant, he had thought the Professor said *culinarily homeless,* a provocative phrase. He asked about Siwash again.

"Perhaps he's marking the passage of these various visitors over this ground," the Professor said. "Their movement across the soil of which you so eloquently spoke."

"Why would he?"

"There may be a number he is waiting to reach," said the Professor, looking disappointed with Jeremy for not trying harder.

"What number?"

The Professor rolled his eyes. "Well, we won't know that, will we? Perhaps it's a running total with some significance trigger, a value above which something will happen."

"Something might happen? That's comforting."

"Perhaps not," the Professor said, then changed the subject. "So, do you know how to find your way out of Stanley Park?"

Jeremy thought he knew. They hadn't come very deep into the forest. He looked around himself, about to answer the question seriously before reading the playfulness in his father's question.

"No, Professor," he said. "How do I find my way out of Stanley Park?"

"Why," the Professor responded, "you just follow the psychopath."

# THE TREE OF KNOWLEDGE

"Where is she?" Margaret was fussing, something she didn't like to catch herself doing particularly. But as soon as Jeremy came in she was taking his coat and offering him a drink. She was shooing Trout off the kitchen table. Apologizing for the mess (although there wasn't much of one by post-weekend standards) and in advance for the dinner.

To Jeremy's nose, everything smelled competently Silver Palate tasty.

"I told you to clean up your paints honey," Margaret said to Trout. Then to Jeremy: "Drink?"

Trout looked up and smiled faintly when he saw Jeremy. He lifted one arm draped in a painting smock. A silent, open-palmed gesture Margaret had seen him use so many times. Maybe it was inspired by *Star Trek*, she thought, although it seemed less like Unitarian go-forth optimism and more conventionally priestly. A televangelist, maybe.

Jeremy returned the blank hand of friendship. Trout lowered his head again to the work open on the table in front of him. First he gazed at it, then he moved his head slowly to consider the colours on his palette and those in the painting. Margaret frowned as she poured Jeremy's drink. She asked him again about Benny.

"Coming in an hour," Jeremy said. "She works until eight."

"Canadian Tire, you said?" Margaret answered. She couldn't keep the little smile off. She wasn't disdainful; she just found the detail cute. He had produced such a series of odd dates over the years since they broke up. Jeremy's epic love poem of alternately fragment or run-on sentences.

"She left Canadian Tire," Jeremy informed her. "It's a bit complicated, but she had another job in less than a day. Barista at the Inferno Pender. She's one of those people who can't be unemployed."

Margaret allowed her eyebrows to rise with approval. That last part was new, the industrious-sounding part. And Margaret, treasurer of the Western Canadian Women's Business Association, believed in the power of feminist industry.

"One Bushmills," she said, and slid a tumbler across the kitchen island. Then she stopped, her slender hands briefly motionless on the thick wooden counter, looking with more genuine exasperation at Trout, still at the table. He had just dipped a brush methodically, having settled an internal debate about colours, and was applying the result to a very precise place on the paper. Silently industrious himself, she thought. "You know," Margaret said, more to herself than to Jeremy, "maybe I'll have a drink."

Fussing definitely wasn't her. Fussing was household angst jazzed on oolong tea. It was reasonable to Jeremy that seismic engineers didn't do fuss, especially those doing their work along the Pacific Rim's Cascadia Subduction Zone, where popular science would have it that everything from Portland to Vancouver was spectacularly overdue for obliteration. In the Cascadia Subduction Zone, the oceanic plate was slipping irrevocably under the North American continental plate. Maybe only ten slips in the past three thousand years, but each one rumbling for minutes at a stretch, releasing energy at some point past what the Richter scale had been designed to measure.

So Margaret didn't fuss about the future like everybody else but planned dispassionately instead. Margaret made a significant mark on the landscape (her firm was tearing up and reassembling buildings and bridges all over Vancouver), but she did so merely by spontaneously acting out who she was. She premitigated damages by designing such things as seismic gas-flow cut-off triggers, shock absorber systems. Restraining cables for heavy objects and the crafty reinforcement of fifty-year-old bridges. Jeremy's favourite example was the strong-motion network.

"What does it do?" he asked her once. They had been shutting down The Paw together. One in the morning, something they did when Olli went to Palo Alto or Redmond overnight and Trout was with a neighbour. Her foodie friends would leave, and Margaret would stay behind to drink grappa and talk.

"It measures strong ground motion so we can analyze the quake afterwards. Statistically speaking, there is a significant probability that we'll have a subduction quake in the next 150 to 200 years. It'll be massively destructive, we know that, maybe a thousand Loma Prietas combined. And no one's ever measured something like that. How the ground moves, directions, speeds, distance, which plates."

"Who's going to be around to read the meter after all that?"

"Well, someone will survive. We're not *all* going to die."

She actually got upset with pop science's apocalyptic interest in The Big One. "What a name," Margaret would say, with visible disdain. Subduction quakes in the Pacific Northwest are all pretty big, baby—they just don't happen that often. "Throwing darts at the millennial calendar is less useful than, say, four gallons of water a person and heavy-soled shoes under the bed."

"For what?" Jeremy asked.

"To drink, duh."

"I meant the shoes."

"Oh," Margaret said, looking at Jeremy seriously. "Earthquake. Glass. Think about it. Heavy soles."

She went and got herself the drink. Trout had finally risen quietly to his feet. Jeremy turned to watch the little boy as he stared down unsmiling at his painting. He looked at the tip of his paintbrush, wiped it on a stained towel and packed up his kit. When he was finished he took the painting gently by its two upper corners and, holding it out from himself, swung it slowly back and forth to dry it. There was no point fussing with this kid, it occurred to Jeremy, his movements were so simple, so unswervingly predetermined. So like his mother's.

Jeremy looked around himself now and registered how even the layout of these two-thousand-square-foot Yaletown lofts resonated with a particular kind of architectural certainty. Steel cable railings along the edge of the overhanging second floor. A concrete and aluminum spiral staircase. Exposed steel beams, the centre ones still with the tracking for some kind of monster crane. The kitchen itself more slick by far than The Paw's, everything top end. Aga. Calphalon. Cuisinart. Good Grips.

Margaret turned away from him now and held a crystal tumbler under the ice dispenser on the front of the aluminum fridge, came back to the island and poured herself some Stoli. Took a big sip.

"Cheers," she said. "And hello, by the way."

"Hi." He laughed at her. Standing there in her long black skirt, cream sweater. Pearls. Apron with the Microsoft Windows95 logo (an ironic gift for Olli, no doubt). With one hand aiming the tiny matt-black remote at the stereo and sparking up a Tony Bennett CD. In her other hand the glass dipping over dangerously, bracelets falling down her slim arm towards her elbow. She had beauty, thought Jeremy compulsively as he watched her. She owned it. Somebody or something had bequeathed it to her. He imagined there might have been a ceremony involved, at which some quiveringly perfect, angelic being spoke silver words: "You shall have beauty, daughter. You have been chosen."

"So, what's she like? She cute?" Margaret said.

"Can we talk about something else?"

"Don't be shy, it's me."

"She's very attractive, in an odd way."

"Odd how?" Margaret asked, smiling internally at the description. Weren't they all? Except Jules, of course, but Margaret sensed that Jules was somehow out of bounds.

"Why don't you wait and see, Peggy?" Jeremy said. He didn't use this name with her often, a university name. A rockabilly pretence she adopted during those days. She wore it the same way he wore his pompadour back then, although she grew out of her pretence more quickly.

"Well, you can't tell me what you really think when she's here," Margaret said, pretending not to have noticed.

Jeremy thought for a minute about the question. Odd how? Well, there's the tongue stud, he thought. Odd because I might have expected to be repulsed by this detail but am not in her case. She's hard and symmetrical and certain. A bit like you, but more compact and more dangerous and, well, just odder.

"She has short white hair and pale blue eyes," he said finally. "She's very smart."

"Jay, look," said Trout, standing next to him now.

Jeremy crouched next to the boy, glad for the distraction. Trout had slipped out of his smock and was wearing his uniform: blues jeans rolled up a turn at the bottom and a white pocket tee. Jeremy wasn't sure he had seen the kid wear anything else in the past three years. Now he took hold of Jeremy's shirt at the shoulder. "It's a dollar," he said.

Margaret came around the Aga to look down on the two of them.

"Very nice, honey," she said to Trout.

An American dollar, painted to fill the middle of an 8 1/2-by-11-inch sheet of paper. Another discernible stab at president Washington. He had the hair right this time, those solid-looking waves of powder white.

"Olli gave him a U.S. dollar after coming back from California about a year ago," she explained to Jeremy. "Trout pinned it to the wall above his bed."

"She made me take it down," Trout said. "Peggy said a dollar would make me greedy if I looked at it all the time."

Jeremy stifled a laugh. Margaret widened her eyes.

"Don't call me that, sweetie."

"Why money, Trout?" Jeremy asked.

Trout didn't offer an answer, and Jeremy didn't know precisely what else to say. He was looking at the painting, feeling the snuffly breathing of Trout next to him. Feeling, as always, the impenetrable nature of what lay behind Trout's fixations.

"I didn't exactly make him take it down," Margaret said when Jeremy stood up. Did she come off hard sometimes? Like a tough mom? She knew she had no perspective on the matter. Self-evaluation in parenting was about the most imprecise science there was, she imagined.

She moved back into the kitchen, leaned and opened the oven door. "Roasted yams," she said. "Stuffed with garlic and ginger. Recommended by Martha."

"Oh, splendid."

"She's wonderful—don't you say a snide word. And quails with grapes. I hope you like quails."

"I love quails. I love to eat little birds. I love ortolans, remember?"

"Oh right, you animal." Margaret said. "Is that what we ate that one time?"

"Sure. Remember putting the napkins over our heads while we ate them?" he asked her, reminded of how they'd gone along with this gourmand convention ostensibly meant to capture the delicate aroma.

"Yes," she said, smiling. It was all coming back. "I think they were pretty good, weren't they?"

"Oh, they're delicious. Silly but good."

"Why silly?"

"Well, to truck in this little bird all the way from France, you know. What's the point?"

"It was fun," she said. Now she was holding a hand gently against her sandy hair as she read from a magazine open on the counter. Silver Palate, he noted and congratulated his nose. "I was going to open a Pinot Gris, Jay. Does that work?"

"It works fine. Was Olli in California again this week?" Jeremy asked.

"Redmond, Washington. The next big thing." She sighed and looked around for a moment, losing her train of thought. She took another sip from her vodka and clumped the tumbler onto the counter.

Jeremy rested the heels of his hands on the edge of the island and watched Margaret corral the quails on the corner of the cutting board and begin to truss them for browning.

"Jay!" Trout yelled from up in the loft.

Jeremy craned his neck back. "What?" he said up into the open air.

"Jay!" Trout yelled again. And Jeremy continued to gaze upwards, waiting for the little face to appear at the railing of the loft. The loft where Margaret and Olli slept in the huge antique sleigh bed. Beyond the bed was a second, smaller staircase that ran up a side wall into the back of the building. Into a small room, separate from the main space, with large rearward-looking windows and a very high ceiling. Here was Trout's spectacular garret. A place where he could contemplate the hive of other lofts rising out of the slopes of Yaletown.

Trout didn't appear, so Jeremy looked back down at Margaret and was startled to find her looking directly at him.

Her hands cupped one of the quails, a bit of string emerging between her fingers, her expression thoughtful.

"Why don't you go up and see him," she said, and she lifted her chin slightly without moving her eyes from his face.

The truth was, all their dates had ended badly. Jeremy drunk and despondent, sucking down a final Pabst in whatever road-house The Decoders had selected to support their rockabilly fantasy that evening. Peggy in her hoop skirt. Bright red lipstick reapplied angrily. They argued endlessly about getting things done, or around this issue. They were both nineteen. She was fantastically impatient and practical, a deep well of potential energy. And taking Jeremy at his word, treated his music seriously too. She could not understand why the Decoder album never got made, and Jeremy played his natural nineteen-year-old nihilism off this pressure. Physically, she had grown into the strength that she now so clearly had. She had been tiny then, and frighteningly soft in his hands. The sex had been erratic. It hurt her sometimes. Other times he couldn't perform, spent from drinking or from some fear she inspired.

From the very beginning they were being torn apart by the strong currents that ran through everything they jointly touched. They made an electric field, certainly, but Jeremy started feeling physically ill. He used to wake in the late morning, missing classes, feeling his heart beat. An unsteady beat he couldn't play along with. It would stop without warning, miss two, three, even four beats. He was reminded of a documentary he'd seen about heart problems in cows raised under power lines, all that electricity running through them day after day.

One doctor's visit convinced him he was at least partly bringing it on himself. The doctor said: "Do you drink a lot?"

Jeremy thought he probably did.

"How much on a weekend night? A six-pack?"

Which meant he was drinking a real lot.

Still, understanding it was self-induced did nothing for the symptoms, which persisted. Walking around campus at one point, ten in the morning, up a little earlier than normal, his heart went into its stuttering, falling two-step. He began to shake minutely and suddenly felt a tremendous certainty that at the end of the two-step his heart would simply stop. He'd never felt as certain about anything in his entire life as he was about the blackness sweeping up underneath his feet to catch him.

He laid down on the grass in the middle of the quad. Simply laid down flat, not caring what anyone might think. He slid an intro art-history text under his head and closed his eyes, whereupon he felt the dying two-step transmute into pulsing shapes. He didn't like that particularly, not wanting to actually *see* the end coming. So he opened his eyes again, looked at the clouds, thought about God and waited for the curtains to fall.

By the end of an hour, flaked out, unmoving, the two-step simply faded away and was imperceptibly replaced by a softer, rounder beat, which Jeremy had to admit felt essentially normal. His heart was beating serenely along, the fibro-palsy having passed on through and disappeared.

But it was a catalyst. They split soon afterwards and adopted what they thought at the time was a very adult post-intimacy friendship, vibrating with aftershock tension. She hung out the available sign and found a boyfriend immediately: Cliff. And Jeremy (disgusted with this choice and possibly acting out a vicarious revenge plot) pushed her together with Olli. The lead singer setting up the girl with the bass player. He drinks even more than I do, enjoy! He knew Olli would go for her.

What he couldn't have known was how Margaret would take to Olli. He made her laugh, she said. And so, assessing her options, Margaret dated Cliff and Olli for a stretch and wouldn't let either touch her. Jeremy watched and shook his head, admiring how cool she was about the balancing act. Two boyfriends: a present perfect and a future conditional.

Present perfect, Cliff: who might be called a solid prospect, handsome, enrolled at medical school, but who by temperament and training was increasingly unsuited to dealing with anything outside the narrowing corridor of his own studies, which were evolving from success to success, from general practice to surgery to neurosurgery, which was simply beyond comprehension.

Future conditional, Oliver: stand-up bass player and computer geek. A clear long-shot. Olli was flying up through very different branches of the Tree of Knowledge than Cliff. He dug machine language, but also networks. This latter part, outside of music, made him interesting and assured his eventual future.

Jeremy found himself jealous of both Cliff and Olli, the two of them being even more jealous of each other. It made for an interesting triangle of male tension at Decoder shows, the serene midpoint of which was the radiant, hoop-skirted, check-shirted, Ked-wearing bopper dancing in front of the stage.

Jeremy would leer at her while singing and smoking and struggling with the huge, semi-functional, hollow body electric he played. Olli was good at ignoring it all; maybe that's what made him irresistible in the end. He slapped the base and grinned at the empty air and let out little snarly rockabilly catcalls.

Cliff stopped coming to gigs eventually; it was just too embarrassing. He didn't even like the music.

So she chose Olli. Not because Cliff gave up, precisely, or because of Olli's interest in machine language but, Jeremy thought with some respect, because it was going to be her choice. It was a binary issue, but on her own binary terms.

Then again, Jeremy sometimes thought, maybe she chose Olli for his athleticism. His clean good looks. There was no accounting for the physical things that drove her taste. She did say once: "He's a perfect mesomorph." Jeremy had to consult the *OED* later. She liked his sandy hair. She liked the way he used to balance on the side of his stand-up bass, standing on it, one foot sticking out behind him, hand slapping away at the neck, cigarette dangling and his fine old butt sticking up in the air. She liked the big leopard-skin clodhoppers. Liked his blond soul patch. Liked that he was more funny than Jeremy. They never fought, she told him.

All these events in the spiralling months before Jeremy's mother died. It had been sudden. Margaret went to his apartment near campus the day she found out. She buzzed three times before he would answer. There was an empty bottle of Jameson whiskey in the kitchen sink. Jeremy was cross-legged on the futon in his underwear. It seemed critical she be there, all of a sudden. She held him, awkwardly at first, but he reached back and clung to her. He cried.

"If you want to talk about her...," Margaret tried. She had no idea if it was what you were supposed to do, only imagined that Jeremy was flooding with memories just then.

At which point he told her a stream of things. Anecdotes tumbling over anecdotes—some she knew, some not—but Margaret had the sense they were the family table of elements. The constituent pieces that had been passed down to Jeremy, that he now construed as making him who he was. Who the family had been. The blank Papier history. Unknowable. Severed. But also how the Professor and Hélène had met in France. How proud she had been to arrive in North America. To have a home and, shortly thereafter, a child.

And more. The stories spilled over one another. How his father's research had continued whenever he was not teaching. In most years he had been gone for months. Her growing resentment. The meals they would cook together during these times—grilled meats, stews with yogurt—food different than their normal fare.

Once, Jeremy told Margaret, when he was just twelve, his mother and he had made a lean-to together from scratch down in the backyard. His mother had gathered fern branches from the forest behind the house. Jeremy had foraged for long, straight poles (he remembered finding a half-rotten oar). And after the lean-to was built, they had waited until dark to build a fire. His mother had defrosted a Safeway chicken, which they ran down a skewer and rotated over the flames. They basted it with oil into which she had crushed garlic and rosemary. He had a glass of wine that night, his first. She told him that before he was born, just weeks before, she had known he was a boy. She had known his name.

They slept out there in the backyard. Her arm protectively around him, old blankets piled over them in a heap. He woke up stiff, he told Margaret. She had been as fresh as the day before. Fresh and dry, somehow.

Margaret hugged Jeremy tighter. She had her own few memories of Hélène, although she didn't speak of them that day. Always, there was Hélène's beauty to consider. Her hair had lightened with the years, her dark skin gently creased. But the mouth was full, her figure still compact and shapely, the hands thin and long. She still walked with a flat-footed nonchalance, her shoulders back, a manner that was at once mischievous and sexual. Jeremy once took Margaret out to the house for dinner on a Sunday. Hélène stewed rabbits, something Margaret had never seen, let alone tasted. They were good and more, they were intriguing. But the Professor had spoken to her almost non-stop, and a real conversation with Hélène did not materialize.

Margaret tried to help clear dishes. She walked into the kitchen behind Hélène. She said: "It was delicious." Not liking herself for sounding shy.

"Your first rabbit?" Hélène had responded.

Margaret remembered liking the Professor. She would see him from time to time on campus, and he would greet her in his not-overbearingly chivalrous manner. He always took great interest in her studies, although engineering was evidently foreign to him. "What kinds of questions would you like to answer?" he used to ask. When her interests had started tending to seismic engineering, he had been fascinated. He told her: "Curiosity about the earth, this crust of dirt and rock beneath our feet, that is one of the most rudimentary curiosities of all. I study how it is that people move across this surface, in groups or singly, or how it is they become stationary. You study how the surface beneath their feet might choose to move first!"

At the time, she thought he was interested in what could only be called a highly theoretical overlap in their disciplines. And, of course, she had been dating Jeremy at the time. But his manner remained on the occasions she'd seen him after they split. "Enchanted," he would say, taking her hand with the tips of his fingers. "Now, you must tell me..."

They went to the funeral, of course, she and Olli. Still outside the chapel, she found herself standing next to a Papier family friend who was a doctor. "Very sudden," the doctor explained to Margaret, tones hushed. "No antecedent symptoms."

He said: *cardiomyopathy*.

And he said: *sudden onset, lethal rhythm abnormalities*.

Jeremy was there, stunned to silence. He smelled like liquor. He accepted their embraces and said nothing. The Professor did not recognize Margaret. He was consumed by the heat of his grief, shrunken in front of her. He extended a small hand.

"Professor Papier, we are so sorry," she had told him.

"Yes," he had said. "Thank you."

"I'm Margaret. This is Olli."

And even as the Professor took Olli's hand, he looked closely at her. Remembering, she liked to think.

The casket was open. Hélène remained tragically beautiful. Margaret stared down and thought only: *lethal rhythm abnormalities.* Her own heart pumping, pumping.

And with that, their lives branched instantly, radically in new directions.

The Decoders never really broke up, they just stopped being. Moss Craven was going to grad school somewhere. Olli's life was raking off in new and exciting directions. He was being scouted by companies in what was then a new place called Silicon Valley, turning them down for all that he felt he could do on his own. Six months after the funeral, he proposed to her. And after she said yes, Olli talked about children immediately, like it was something he needed to get off his chest.

Olli tracked Jeremy down in Dijon, through the culinary institute where he was reinventing himself. "Married. I can't believe it," Jeremy said over the scratchy international connection. But he was happy for both of them.

"She's amazing, you know, Jay-Jay?" Olli said. "She knows what she wants. I am indebted to you for life. You know, man? For life. You my brother, man. You know?" Then he started singing.

*"I gave her a ring…that was wo-oorn by my mother…"*

"What time is it there?" Jeremy asked.

"'Bout ten," Olli slurred. "I'm drunk."

"No kidding."

"But I'm quitting."

The line crackled. The connection to his old band mate was held by a spider-web strand of static. Jeremy looked around himself, at the tiny apartment he was renting with the dark wood floors. Through the small open window he could hear the men and women at the *marché couvert* opening the grates over the stalls. Morning in Dijon.

Olli didn't quit drinking right away. They ended up having the same conversation once again. To Olli's credit, Jeremy supposed, only once more. Jeremy had just returned to Vancouver. An unemployed chef. The Monkey's Paw was still a germinal idea he was going to carry around for a while, thinking of the Relais Saint Seine l'Abbaye, of Patrice, of three paintings in the Rijksmuseum and an epiphany about Blood.

"I gotta quit now," Olli slurred, with a little more conviction than the last time. It was around midnight again. Jeremy was broke and sober.

"What is this?" Jeremy asked. "You've only said this to me once before. Is it a recurring two-year idea?"

Olli told him the reason and Jeremy was truly speechless.

"I went with her to get the ultrasound," Olli spilled into the phone, dropping something in the background. "I could see his little pecker, man. I cried. I wept in the friggin doctor's office."

"Man," Jeremy said. "How's Peggy?"

Olli was breathing heavily into the phone. Restraining maudlin sobs.

"Why is it," he said blearily, "that you call her Peggy and I always call her Maggie?"

They had him over for dinner to celebrate. When Jeremy thought back on this evening, it occurred to him that it was the first time they had him over to their place in Vancouver after his return from France. When Margaret was finally big with Trout, eight and a half months big, she was ready to see him. She had never been scared of him before, quite the contrary, but there had been a distance since his return to the city. He and Olli went out for beers a handful of times. Olli was never allowed to stay out too late.

At that celebratory dinner Olli and Margaret both drank Evian water, constantly topping each other up. Olli eyed the bottle of Concha y Toro but he didn't touch it. Jeremy had to pour for himself, which he did steadily. He was a bit nervous, as if he were applying for a position. The conversation ambled here and there, catching up, covering familiar ground, common friends, the changes in Vancouver.

"So, Jay," Olli said eventually, folding his hands in front of himself and putting his chin on his fists.

Jeremy stopped chewing. The moment had arrived, apparently. Margaret was looking at him too.

"Would you like to be a godfather?" Olli asked. "Maggie's idea. It's a Catholic thing."

The question hung there. He'd been expecting something, but this particular thing surprised him.

"You're the only person we know who even believes in God," Olli said, and Margaret nodded.

The silence grew awkward. "You *do*, don't you?" Olli said finally. "I mean, *I* don't, but I thought you did."

"I do have a sense...," Jeremy began, and then stalled, just like in so many internal dialogues he had had along these lines.

Olli and Margaret waited. Jeremy had a spiralling and sudden vision of the child inside her, as if he could see through her cotton sweater, her skin and the uterus wall. As if he had been selected. Acquired. The thumb came out from between the little translucent lips, the head rolled over to catch his words. He can hear my voice, thought Jeremy stupidly.

"I have a sense...," he tried again, "...about being created. About having a Creator. I don't know, that's it, I guess." And he reddened.

Olli smirked. "That's what I meant."

"So what's the deal? What do I have to do?"

"You have to pray for him," Margaret said. "Technically."

"OK. Pray."

Olli rolled his eyes. "You have to show up for the christening. You have to give expensive, adult-type presents for all of his birthdays. I think cufflinks are nice. You have to sign his passport application without question when he fucks off to Thailand for a year against my wishes. That kind of thing."

Later, when the conversation had moved on, Jeremy asked: "Why Trout?" And Margaret's eyes grew atypically dreamy. "Because he will be the only Trout in any classroom he ever enters. Because he will swim away one day. Because he will be the only Trout he ever meets."

"He'd be the only Skunk too if we named him that," Olli said.

It was their first date that had ended well. He had to date both of them was the trick. Jeremy hugged Margaret firmly at the front door of their apartment. Olli was getting tired and wanted to hit the hay, uncharged by the energy curve of alcohol. His body still adjusting. He seemed happy enough, Jeremy thought. Distracted, maybe.

They kept in steady touch after that. Jeremy attended the baptism in his official godfather capacity. Then, when Trout was three, they had the scare. First came the temperature. Olli and Margaret went through an eighteen-hour cycle of rising panic as children's Aspirin, adult Tylenol, cool water, then ice water, did nothing to stop the escalation. Jeremy got a call from Margaret when they were at hospital already. Trout's body had pumped up the thermostat to 107 by this point, fighting literally to the death with some invisible threat. Margaret wasn't talking too much, just crying into the phone, exhausted with this sudden overwhelming unknown.

Jeremy got there in the afternoon, just as the pediatrician made the call: Kawasaki disease. It was a reasonably rare thing, with no known cause (although according to Dr. Singh, the smart money was on some kind of bacterial toxin). Even so, the source was unknown; it was one of the things medicine blames on "the environment," for lack of any more specific agent.

The symptoms, on the other hand, were well known, and Trout was doing a life-threatening favour for the interns on rounds by offering up a suite of the most typical: fever, lymph-node swelling in the throat, a full body rash and steady, dehydrating diarrhea.

He might have stopped there. Not many parents (or godparents) are prepared to think of a heart attack as being a

risk at this age. But arterial inflammation followed. There was
a coronary aneurysm with blood clotting. His heart stopped at
about 9:30 p.m. while Jeremy and Olli were sitting together
with him. Margaret was in the hospital chapel crying.

Trout disappeared into intensive care in a frenzy of clini-
cians. They formed a valence ring of icy professional intensity
around the stainless steel gurney as it careered down the centre of the hallway. Nurses and patients jumping to clear a path.

Olli ran off to find Margaret, his hair standing straight up
on one side. He'd been napping when the monitor lines went
abruptly flat.

Jeremy went back into the empty hospital room. Stunned.
He remembered sitting back down heavily in his chair. His
face dropping into his hands.

It was a prayer, he supposed in retrospect, though it had
just two words. His face hit the palms of his hand, found that
comfortable personal place that permits pressure on the eye-
balls and the sealing off of all light. And he said aloud, muffled, hot on his hands: "Oh, God…."

"Hello," Jeremy said when he got to the top of the spiral staircase. Trout was sitting cross-legged on the hardwood floor of
the first loft. His newly painted dollar was lying on the floor
next to him, and Jeremy could see past him into Olli and
Margaret's bedroom area. There was the sleigh bed.

"Howdy," said Trout, not looking up. He was pumping the
keys of a Game Boy, using body English to influence the movement of his onscreen character. Jeremy sat down cross-legged
on the floor across from him and put his glass on the hardwood.

"Christ." Trout let the Game Boy flop to his side.

"Hey, language."

"They're all dead," Trout said with a frown, checking the
screen again. "Nowhere near the high score."

"Let me try." Jeremy took the hand-held computer game.

The game consisted of a burning building on the right-hand side of the screen, and two fireman with a catch mat between them, who moved across the remainder of the screen. When the game began, little babies in diapers were thrown from the various windows up the side of the building. You manipulated the firemen to run back and forth across the playing area and catch them. A dropped baby produced a tiny bleat, the same sound you'd get from stepping on a squeeze-toy.

Jeremy looked up at Trout before beginning. "Your dad gave you this?"

Trout nodded.

"OK," he said, launching the game.

It was harder than it looked. While Jeremy scuttled his firemen back and forth across the screen, babies vaulted out the windows of the burning building, falling in their different arcs towards the pavement. He caught one in three at the very most, and within fifteen seconds the screen faded to black to signal his failure. Trout was laughing at his elbow, holding his arm and squealing.

"Is that funny?"

"Yup," Trout answered. And then, no doubt parroting Margaret, he added: "Although macabre."

Jeremy put the game aside. Trout still held his arm, but grew thoughtful. "Peggy says I can't play soccer this year," he said finally, dealing with something that had apparently been on his mind.

"You'd better not call her that," Jeremy said, lowering his voice. Impulsively, he got up and went over to the loft rail. Leaned far over and looked down at her. She was finished trussing the quails.

"How you doing down there?"

She leaned her head back and looked straight up at him. She smiled. "Fine. You?"

He made a face. *Not bad.*

Trout had gathered up the game by the time Jeremy turned around.

"I can't play soccer because I have a damaged heart," Trout said. "When I was little, I got sick with a sickness and part of it made a small damage in my heart. Mom says I can't feel it but I still have it there." He put his index finger in the middle of his chest to show Jeremy where.

"Right," Jeremy said. It made him think of how the imprint of the sick kid made Trout who he was. There was a quiet mystery learned in hospitals, impressed by rough, dry sheets, chrome bars, random pains and intravenous needle bruises. Picked up from the vibration of inarticulate prayer, who could know? Jeremy found himself, on occasions like this one, thinking of Trout as *wise*. Wiser than an adult.

"You're my godfather," Trout announced.

"I am indeed."

"You were there."

Jeremy nodded slowly. "I was there. But you're here now, so we made it." He stuck out a hand, which Trout shook.

"I feel it sometimes," Trout said. "Like a wobble in my heart."

"I think I know what you mean."

"Why, do you have a damage in your heart?"

"Oh, well...." Jeremy stalled on the question. "No, not seriously."

"Does it ever beat funny?"

You had to watch what you said with Trout. It was a bit like being interrogated. He quietly pressed, and before you realized it he was getting somewhere.

"Not any more," Jeremy said. "We should go downstairs."

"I think I remember it. When I was little and I got sick."

"You were very little. People don't remember things from when they're that little."

"I do. I remember things."

Jeremy frowned. Did you encourage this line of fantasy

by asking questions? There were undoubtedly books on the subject, cookbooks for child rearing.

Trout was looking at him evenly, appraisingly. Then, like an adult might if they thought they were boring you or confusing you with a certain conversational angle, he changed the subject. "I'll show you something in my room," he suggested.

He led the way, clutching his game in one hand and his painted dollar in the other. Jeremy followed him up the narrow side-stairs to the second loft at the rear of the building, glass in hand, wondering when Benny would get there.

It was a tall, square room at the top and back of the building, where the huge freight elevator had once been. This structure had been incorporated into the warehouse conversion, with each suite in the building getting a slice of the elevator shaft, the outside wall of which was then replaced with a large, paned window. Since the top of the shaft had housed the elevator winch and motor, the penthouse had a taller, even more dramatic room, below which Vancouver's False Creek stretched out at your feet. The room was dark now. Trout walked to a spot on the wall and pulled a heavy switch that brought on three lamps hanging on cords from the twenty-foot, iron-beamed ceiling.

Jeremy took in the familiar sight from the doorway. The metal walls, planked halfway up. Trout's bunk bed against the left wall. His overflowing toy shelves against the right. Strewn between, across a huge Amish rope rug that covered the polished concrete floor, a drifting chaos of toys and games, childhood equipment across a truly impressive range. Toy cars, a train set, board games, a basketball hoop, an arsenal of Nerf guns, floor-hockey sticks, a soccer ball, monkey bars built into one wall, bubble hockey, foosball, super-destructo dudes of an impossibly wide variety. Plus the tools and the output of Trout's artistic project: watercolours and brushes, an easel, smocks and clean-up clothes, dollar bills strewn through the room randomly. Dropped where they had been finished.

The fourth wall was the window, which started at a low sill and stretched in foot-square panes up to just below the ceiling. Here was Trout's small desk and chair, set up in front of the glass. Empty but for a pad of paper.

Jeremy shook his head. When visiting Trout's domain, he often found himself wondering if the room in total spoke more to the indulgent inclination of parents at this particular point in history, or the scattered, broadband enthusiasms of their children. Both, doubtless. Olli would buy the toys, not Margaret. Trout would play with them in short bursts, curious as to what they had to offer before laying them aside. He would paint when in the mood, and then, for some portion of the day, Jeremy imagined, the boy would drift on his own thoughts in front of the window.

Trout was pulling the soccer ball out of a rubble of Lego. "Jeremy," he called out sharply, snapping Jeremy from his thoughts.

Part of the room against the left wall had been cleared of toys.

"You play goal," Trout instructed, dribbling the ball inexpertly between his feet. Jeremy saw that a goal had been paced off against the wall, with the bed and a stack of books serving as posts.

"Trout," Jeremy said, remembering what he had been told about Margaret's take on soccer. Physical exertion was obviously still a concern.

"Go on," Trout said, waving his hand towards the goal. "Chicken."

"Hey! Me, chicken?"

"I think so."

"Just one shot. Don't run around. Just shoot the ball."

"I don't need to run around."

"And just one shot, right?" Jeremy reminded him.

"I don't need more than one shot either."

Jeremy put his drink down next to the door and moved

across into the goal mouth. When he was standing roughly equidistant from the bed and the stack of books, he turned around to face the boy. Trout was regarding him seriously, motionless, some feet back from the black and white ball.

"All right," Jeremy said.

Trout didn't move, didn't take his eyes from Jeremy's. Like he's trying to hypnotize me, thought Jeremy. Like he's trying to read my mind and guess which way I'm going to move.

"Are you really ready for this?" Trout said.

There were another few seconds of silence during which his godson continued to hold him, locked in a stare. It brought to mind not the psychological battle between goalie and penalty-kicker, but the sense he had known once before of having been selected. Acquired. Trout had turned his head in the womb and regarded him much as he did now, with some kind of steady certainty and knowing.

"Come on, shoot," Jeremy said. "Chicken."

Jeremy didn't play soccer, but he had to guess that the shot Trout then unleashed was somewhere near the top of the power bell-curve for shooters between three and four feet in height. Trout took a two-step run up and fired, his leg making a compact arc. His instep struck the ball squarely. The ball rocketed towards Jeremy. It might have taken half a second in total, but as he raised his arms to catch it (to defend himself, really; it looked like the shot might take his head off) the ball spun sharply to his right, diving down as if guided on wires, and slammed into the plank wall with a dull, resonating boom.

Jeremy hadn't moved. His hands were still up in front of his face. Trout was now circling the room at a sprint, aping the curious vaunting behaviour of soccer players the world over, arms outstretched in front of himself, gesticulating to an invisible crowd, ululating.

"All right, all right," Jeremy said. He was unreasonably winded.

"You have to move one way or the other," Trout said when he stopped running. Not winded. "Right or left. You can't just stand there."

"Oh yeah?" Jeremy said.

"Well, the other guy won't shoot straight at you. That would be dumb."

He had a point. Jeremy retrieved his drink and they went downstairs.

The quails were good, Jeremy thought, although he ate methodically. Not thinking about the food very much at all until he was finished and he remembered to compliment Margaret.

"Excellent," he said, nodding at his plate. She could handle herself fine in the kitchen, although Olli was a little slow to remove the plates after eating. It was something Jeremy drilled into everyone who worked for him: *Remove the remains*. He believed what Claude had once told him: "The finished meal produces a period of natural reflection: Am I full or am I still empty? All this carnage, this evidence that we have tried to fill ourselves, all of it complicates our reflection."

Jeremy was reflecting. Fortunately, Benny and Margaret were hitting it off, and Olli was distracted. By Redmond, Jeremy thought when he caught his friend eyeing the wine bottle.

The conversation swung to Trout in due course, just after he had been sent to bed. About a new school he was attending. About his illness. Margaret explained Kawasaki's to Benny.

"Systemic inflammatory mucocutaneous lymph-node syndrome," she said. "In most cases it passes entirely after a single acute phase. In some it lingers, a persistent chance of recurrence."

"Tell her," Olli said, chiding.

"One and a quarter percent chance of recurrence," Margaret said. "That happens to be the number. After six years, the probability drops slightly."

Across the table from Jeremy, Benny shook her head and made a sympathetic face at Margaret.

"What about a warning if it's about to recur?" Jeremy asked.

"None. If it happens, it happens," Olli said, and he picked a piece of radicchio from his plate. "He turned about this colour the first time—I really don't want to go through that again."

"Does he remember it, do you think?" Benny said.

Jeremy lifted his head from the remains, which continued to complicate his reflection.

"He thinks that he does," he said, looking at Benny, then Margaret. "He told me."

Olli got up to clear plates. "We circumcized him too. I hope he doesn't remember that or things are going to get complicated between him and me."

"Seriously," Jeremy said. "I believe him."

"He's a kid," Olli said, stopping with a plate in each hand.

"He's a strangely wise kid."

Olli frowned at his friend. He got weird on you sometimes without warning.

Benny cut the silence perfectly by getting up to help with the dishes. In the process of scraping quail carcasses into the garbage, she generated an exchange with Olli about which would taste better: seagulls or pigeons. Jeremy stopped listening.

"Why do you believe him?" Margaret said to Jeremy, leaning across the corner of the table and talking under the foghorn of Olli's laughter coming from the kitchen.

Jeremy wasn't sure. But as he considered his answer, he also got a strong, familiar feeling. The slightly cold feeling of Trout bearing down directly on him, and in a rolling instant he was wondering if Trout was at the loft rail directly above his head. Jeremy had to fight the urge to look upwards.

"I guess I don't really know," Jeremy said.

Margaret didn't pursue this; she didn't know either. She wasn't even sure it mattered, although it made her curious.

But now Olli and Benny were back, setting liqueurs on the table: grappa, Drambuie, white port, Essencia, Bushmills for Jeremy. Olli was leading the conversation into work by talking about his trip to Washington State. Benny was handling herself with utter confidence, asking questions about the project that Olli described as "Building Libraries of Everything."

Jeremy had lost the thread. He poured a glass of grappa for Margaret and a Bushmills for himself. He settled back in his chair.

"Massive-scale data architectures," Olli was saying. "We have these tape robots, multi-terabytes each. A little compression software and you can take a snapshot of virtually every page of information the world has ever known. From the Book of Kells to the entire Hooters website. Whatever you can think of."

Jeremy reflected on what seemed like a monomaniacal task. The difference between Jeremy and Olli, it might be said, was scale, that and the fact that Olli had an uncanny sense for making money in the natural orbit he established around such obsessions.

"The thing is the money," Olli continued. "And that's always where partners come in."

"Enter Redmond. Enter Bill," said Jeremy.

"That's right," Olli said, launching himself again through the spectacular constellations of the project. Now he was explaining what it meant to work with this galactic volume of data. Terabyte-sized data clusters. His personal underlying objective: the contents of every library, every museum, every church vault from today back through the mist of recorded history, *disseminated freely*. "Because we can," Olli said.

"Kewl," Benny said, her eyes glistening.

"It gets me hot," Olli said. He poured Benny another Essencia and Jeremy saw it again, a hiccup in the physical releasing of the bottle. There was moment where he poised behind the words, *Just one.*

"Olli wants to know everything," Margaret said. "All knowledge, all places, all the time. Isn't that right, darling?"

Olli defended himself. If it could be done, it should be done, he argued. Feasibility was the imperative. "If it weren't for that drive, we'd be sucking our thumbs in the shade of the Tree of Knowledge, blissed-out in fig leaves."

Margaret rolled her eyes. Benny looked curious.

"It's our project name," Olli explained. "Tree of Knowledge. Remind me later and I'll give you a sweatshirt."

"That's Adam and Eve and the apple, isn't it?" Benny said, wrinkling her forehead.

"A strange myth," Olli said. "The sin should be *not* knowing what is knowable."

Margaret was shaking her head. "The point is, there are some things you can't know. This is part of the architecture of knowledge Olli doesn't like so much." As in seismology, she went on, the use of animal behaviour to predict quakes. It worked on occasion. Haichen, 1975. A 7.3 quake predicted with unprecedented accuracy by watching the sudden migration of monkeys. They evacuated an entire region twenty-four hours before the quake. "A year later in Tanshan," Margaret finished, "no warning of any kind. A 7.6. Two hundred and fifty thousand people dead. No peculiar animal behaviour."

Benny didn't get it.

"It was unknowable," Margaret said. "Even the animals didn't know."

Olli looked across his corner of the table at Benny. "You may not believe it, but we've had this discussion before."

"Trout's Kawasaki episode is an example of the same kind. It is unknowable whether there will be a recurrence. We attach a probability to it, but beyond that we don't know."

"Long live the Human Genome Project," Olli said.

"Which actually scares me more than it encourages me," Margaret said, interrupting Olli. "Something about the Tower of Babel. Sorry. Can't help it."

"My favourite Papist," Olli said, smiling.

"Hey, guilty."

Olli was silent for a couple of seconds. Jeremy took Benny's gaze and smiled at her. She returned the warmth with her eyes, the glass of golden Essencia hovering in the air below her lips. He felt a bootless foot slide across his shoe and settle between his legs, her heel on his chair. Jeremy could see from the corners of his eyes that Margaret was looking at Olli and that Olli was mesmerized briefly—one of those fleeting involuntary meditations—his eyes locked on the glistening heaving liquid in the bottles in front of him.

"I figure that the fear of knowing is like the fear of God," Olli said finally. "And who fears God any more?"

"Godfathers," Jeremy said. "It's our job."

"Besides you." Olli said. "I just think accepting something as unknowable is a cop-out. It was a comforting thought behind which hid the prejudice and intellectual narcissism of a couple thousand years. I can appreciate that there was a certain security to be derived. It provided people with something like roots. But I prefer to celebrate the absence."

"We don't root any longer," Jeremy said. "We hover."

"Not bad. Who needed roots in the first place? Somebody told us we needed them and we believed."

"You root, you lose," Jeremy said.

"It's true," Olli said. "When the future is a promise that we can be anything we want to be, those with roots lose out. The lesson of the Tree of Knowledge is that Adam and Eve should have dug it up, tore it out of the ground and made a raft out of it."

"Blasphemy," Jeremy said. "But then, I'm a bit nostalgic about roots. At The Paw, after all, we're all about reminding people what it was like to be rooted in one place. To eat things from our own soil, know what that soil could produce."

There were times when Olli wanted to tell his friend to just cook and be quiet. That must be the beauty of cooking, he frequently thought: There wasn't much ideology behind it. "How's it going down there, anyway?" he asked.

Jeremy and Benny exchanged another glance. Then a smile. Benny couldn't hold it, and started laughing.

Olli and Margaret smiled politely.

Jeremy straightened his face. "Not altogether smoothly," he said, answering Olli. "Although not without promise."

"Maybe you need new ideas," Olli said, shaking his head a little. But an idea did swim through just as he was speaking. With the restaurant established now, with the money he was making on the Tree of Knowledge. "Like a new look," he finished.

Jeremy was curious; Margaret, dubious.

"I agree," Benny said.

"Money would obviously be an issue," Olli started, and for a moment it crossed his mind to suggest lunch later that week.

Jeremy caught the whiff of something. "Money *is* an issue. And there is a potential investor."

"Oh," Olli said. He should have known. "Do we get to know who?"

"No," Jeremy answered. "But food-wise, he's big. Redmond big."

Margaret wasn't saying anything. The news surprised her, and she couldn't decipher the quality of Jeremy's response to it. The whole idea of a large investor was antithetical. Not to Olli certainly, not in that world. But for Jeremy in the world he was exploring.

"And?" Olli said, exasperated. Even Benny was looking at him curiously, with real focused interest, waiting for this response.

"I'm on the fence, truthfully," Jeremy said at last.

"Take it," Olli said simply. He had a wash of warm feelings for his old friend that he wouldn't want to express in any way other than with these words. Take The Money. Free yourself of the hassles I have watched you deal with, year after year.

"That's it?" Margaret said. "You don't know anything about this guy, and you tell him to take it."

"It sounds really exciting," Benny said.

Olli started to say something to Margaret, who had turned to answer Benny. Jeremy stared around the table at each of them in turn. It had never occurred to him that they would have strong feelings on how he should manage his culinary and financial future. And now everybody was talking at once. Margaret was saying that big is not necessarily beautiful. Talking about personal visions and integrity, and wasn't it important to have independence? Olli chiming in with asides about reality and practicality and economies of scale. He heard Benny say something about the growth of a vision. About how a new look, new people, new money...how these things would facilitate evolution. *At the Inferno Pender, for example....* She continued to surprise him with her sense of the possible, her belief in the future.

The conversation rolled on. He wasn't even included.

Jeremy sipped his Bushmills and leaned back from the table. He let his eyes drift along the length of Margaret and Olli's loft, the sound of their voices discussing the issues surrounding his situation filling his ears. He took in the proud size of the place, the brightly lit cityscape. He let his eyes follow the vestigial crane tracks still hung on the roof. He followed these back to the loft railing. And as he traced his eyes along this structure, his unfocused gaze snagged on a small irregularity at the smooth, stainless steel rail.

It was Trout. He was staring down from above, eyes locked on Jeremy.

It made Jeremy start. It brought him forward in the chair, like he had been pushed from behind. He returned his glass to the table with a cough.

"You OK?" Margaret said, reaching over to pat his back. Benny and Olli stopped talking and were also looking at him.

"Fine," Jeremy said.

They resumed talking. Jeremy cracked another glance upward. Of course, his godson was gone.

When they were ready to leave, Olli made them wait while he ran into the kitchen, opened and shut cabinet doors. He found what he was looking for and returned to the hall.

It was a white mug with green embossing. A silhouette of a tree, with a single pear-shaped fruit and a coiled serpent at the base. Underneath the drawing, the words: *Tree of Knowledge '97. Yum Good.*

"If there's fruit to be eaten...," Olli said to Jeremy, shaking his head.

"Eat it," Jeremy finished.

Olli nodded, wide eyed, as if to say, What else?

Margaret and Benny had a sisterly hug. Then Benny drove him back across town into the West End.

They were parked on Haro Street in front of his building. She'd been up only once, and Jeremy thought it would be an excellent opportunity for a second visit, but she couldn't. Early morning tomorrow at the Inferno Pender.

"You have an early morning too," she reminded him.

"I'm gassing the morning service," he said. "Opening at eleven. Focusing on dinner."

She took this news in. "I'm glad," she said finally.

"You have to move one way or the other," he added, smiling just a little.

She nodded. They looked at each other for a few seconds.

"You think I need a new look," he said, returning to the matter raised at dinner.

"Lose the cowboy boots," she said.

"Hey, these are new."

Benny became serious again. "Sure. There's more you could do with the place. Lots more."

"I feel like something is coming," he said eventually. "Something is about to happen."

"Good or bad?" Benny asked him. She was looking at him calmly, her chin resting on her arms, which were crossed on the steering wheel.

He wanted to tell her about Trout, about the Professor. Trout at the top of the box, at the rail, fixed on him and waiting. The Professor in his tent, in his corner of a strange land. Also waiting. Waiting for his next move, anticipating his next action. About how these thoughts filled him with a sense of the future.

But in the end he only said, "I don't know. Good, I hope, or good ultimately."

She smiled as if she had arrived at this conclusion already and enjoyed him catching up to her.

# THE HELP
# FUNCTION

Wednesday was the turning point. A nadir for Jeremy, even in the most confident frame of mind. As a chef, he was inverted within each working day relative to the norm, starting slow and ending very loud and very late. But his whole week was also upside down. Mondays they were closed; a hungover Jeremy typically slept in. Tuesdays were low-key, foodie nights, when they were lucky enough to get them. By Wednesday the weekend was already looming—walk-in nights, money nights. The future seemed to hinge on Wednesday, and so Jeremy didn't coast down to the weekend from Wednesday like the rest of the world. He struggled up.

The second Wednesday in an otherwise upbeat July was tougher than usual. Despite a fully blooming Vancouver summer—business ticking along in the heat—Jeremy had a message on his home voice-mail from American Express. Somebody named Derek, who didn't state the reason for the call, only said: *We'd like to talk to you at your earliest convenience, Mr. Papier...* He hadn't even received his Amex bill.

Disturbed, but certain he had done nothing wrong, he ignored it.

Dante called the next morning. Just catching up, he said, although Dante was a conversational heat-seeking missile.

Within a few minutes Jeremy realized they had segued from talking about Chicago to talking about The Paw, about business volumes, and then—literally at the moment she walked through the door—they were talking about Jules Capelli.

"You just don't understand," he was saying to Dante as she burst into the kitchen, her expression typically sunny.

Dante laughed and took the cell phone away from his ear. "I don't understand," he said, talking to someone off-line. Then quietly, mouth now very close to the phone, close to Jeremy's ear: "I think I understand that I'm offering you help, yes?"

Jules wasn't waiting for him to get off the phone, exactly; she was beginning the prep routine. But she turned and said hello, and he fussed with things on his desk and pretended to look something up in the phone book, until she finally said, "Who doesn't understand *what?*"

"Oh, you know," Jeremy said, thinking. "Xiang is putting us back on cash again."

"I see," Jules said, wondering why he was lying to her, and about what in that case.

It wasn't a complete lie, in fact. Xiang did put them on cash the previous week. Jeremy had been looking for value, cutting corners, even jeopardizing what they were trying to do with his efficiencies. It hadn't been a great year for wild sockeye, prices were up at the market and farmed Chilean salmon finally made it into the seafood risotto. It didn't taste bad, exactly; it just didn't taste *right*. He was adjusting seasonings when the reason came to him. A fish pen up the coast from Santiago might as well be up the coast from Osaka or Vladivostock or Campbell River. The fish in such a pen lived independent of geography, food chain or ecosystem. These salmon were perfectly commodified as a result, immune to the restrictions of place. There was no *where* that these fish were *from*. And to what end had he made this critical sacrifice, made this culinarily homeless risotto that no amount of saffron butter would resurrect? He had still managed to bounce a cheque. He was paying more in credit card interest than he was in rent to Blaze Properties, and he somehow... well, it happened: A lousy thirty-eight-dollar cheque for potatoes and onions bounced, and Xiang was mad at him. He put them back on cash.

He wondered if Jules was now angry with him too. Or worse, fearful of their future. Her voice had been edged with vulnerability. He knew that he held some key ingredients for their joint future and was himself scared by nothing more than the thought that he could misuse these ingredients and hurt her. She loved this place that they had built together. She had poured her tender intensity into it, and through it into him. There was intimacy in that, intimacy that could be betrayed. They both knew it, although Jules remained outwardly unshakeable. In fact, she chose that moment to suggest that Jeremy cease comping the assiette du fromage to even the *Last Chapter* folks or their most regular foodies, even if they had just polished off the most expensive dinner / wine / dessert combination on the menu.

"It's a bit rookie, isn't it?" Jules said. "A bit eager."

All things considered, he didn't mind the suggestion. And after they were finished a very slow Wednesday evening, with far less kitchen chat than they normally enjoyed, he yielded to temptation and went and drank enough Irish whiskeys at the Marine Club to have a hangover on Thursday. He didn't really remember getting home, but he must have fumbled his keys into the tiny keyhole of his aluminum mailbox because—standing blearily in front of his bathroom mirror holding a mug of coffee the next morning—there was a letter taped to his mirror, unopened.

He looked at it stupidly, letting the coffee do its faithful work and burn a tiny hole down through the middle of his sensory constitution like drain cleaner. It had the return address *Simms, Brine and Lothar* in Toronto, which rang no bells. He pulled it off the mirror and hefted it in his free hand. One sheet, maybe two. He put it down again nervously.

He punched up voice mail instead, stalling.

*You have* [pause] *five messages.* Nellie the computer-gener-
ated voice-mail matron sounded remonstrative about such
a middling number of messages. *One new message* meant:
Someone out there wants to talk to you, be happy! Five were
enough to imply you weren't staying on top of things. He
once heard her say fifteen. Totally different again. She
sounded astonished, impressed. She sounded like she wanted
to meet him.

Margaret. Benny.

Derek.

*Hello, Mr. Papier. Derek at American Express Cardholder Services
calling again. I would really appreciate it if you returned this call
when you got in....*

He had to put the coffee down, but he still found it in
himself to delete the message.

His father had phoned twice.

*Jeremy. It's your father.* There was a long pause, and despite
a screeching bird in the background the Professor's silence
cut the recording off. He phoned back. *Can you spare yourself?
I had hoped...ehem...well... Listen. How about at the lagoon,
Wednesday week? Late is fine. You work until one, two o'clock, I
think. Yes, all right then.... Let's say two.*

Babes in the Wood research, Jeremy thought. Like I have
time.

After he'd showered, his head cleared a bit. He dressed,
pulled on his cowboy boots and went out. He waited at the
elevator and listened as, back down the hall, his phone began
to ring. Perfect. The elevator was coming. It dinged open in
front of him.

They really wanted to talk to him, didn't they? he
thought.

"Hello?" he said, out of breath.

"Mr. Jeremy Papier?" A voice that made it immediately
clear he should not have taken the call. "Doug Acer, calling

from Simms, Brine and Lothar. We're representing Canadian Tire in their claim of...what is it? Well, I guess you owe them three thousand bucks or something. You've received our letter, Mr. Papier?"

Jeremy's eyes fell to the envelope now lying on the coffee table.

"Just a friendly call. I wondered if we could settle this thing up? It's Jeremy, right?" the lawyer said.

Jeremy agreed that it was, sinking down into the couch as he spoke. His face rested on the phone and the open palm of his other hand.

"We can go two different ways on this one, Jeremy," Acer was saying, a discernible edge of meanness in the voice. Acer was bored mean, thought Jeremy. Twenty-five years old, just finished articling. Acer's Wednesday was a zenith, and he was looking down from the peak of his week into the delicious trough of his after-work drinks on Friday and saying, "...so basically, we can pay this thing up right now or go to court, which is kind of a waste of everybody's time, don't you think?"

Jeremy was silent.

"Do you have a lawyer, Jeremy?" Acer asked him. "Should I be talking to your lawyer?"

Now Acer went quiet and waited.

"I'll pay," Jeremy said.

He could hear Acer sit up. "Certified cheque."

"It won't be certified," Jeremy said. "I'll mail you a regular cheque."

"All right, all right," Acer said. "So, we have some interest at 28.8 percent per annum. Let's say four thousand dollars with fees."

Jeremy was awake now, if nothing else. He was thinking through the ways he might swing it. Some combination of advances. He could see fifteen hundred dollars, maybe— two thousand tops—by month end.

"Sooner is good, later is bad," Acer said. "How about today?"

Jeremy wrote the cheque with Acer still on the line. He addressed and sealed shut the envelope after hanging up, and was just about to leave for The Paw, get on with his day (ideas for dinner were already forming) when he grabbed the phone again.

"Mother's maiden name, please," the Amex woman said.

He told her.

"Just a moment, please."

Out towards the park Jeremy could pick up the movement of people down the paths that funnelled into the West End. Slow moving twos and threes and ones, emerging from the forest to enter the daytime and the city. To comb the dumpsters, to hope their hopes, to string together their moments as best they could.

"Yes, Mr. Papier. What kin ah do fer you?" His customer service representative appeared to be stationed in Austin, Texas.

He relayed what he knew: Derek, two calls, his personal spiritual devotion to the card. I am a *member*. A pure, gold card member. I am an original celebrant at the Amex Eucha rist. I carry but do not (normally) use your card. You're not like the others. I carry you inside me, like faith. I am an Amex stoic. Pure and good and Protestant. You could make an advertisement about me. *Chef Jeremy Papier, disciple since 1995*. God may be in his heaven, Jeremy said to the woman, but my comfort shall lie with thee.

Or actually, what he said was: "If there's been any kind of problem or mistake, you know, I would be, of course, keen to immediately clear things up, you know, as soon as possible."

Austin, Texas, went away again for a moment and returned. There was an account manager assigned to the file, she said nervously, who was no longer in the office but would call him in the morning. She was also able to confirm (she sounded pleased, maybe she thought it would please Jeremy too) that the account was frozen and that borrowing privileges had been suspended.

"So it's not *cancelled* exactly, it's jist that you cayn't use the card until this all is sorted out," she said to Jeremy, her drawl like lemon juice in a cat scratch.

"Right," he said to the stinging news, but in the silence that followed, its context, its meaning was weirdly shunted aside by the question that invaded Jeremy's frontal lobes: Why Austin, Texas? Why was he humiliated further by being forced to deal with an American?

"Where are you from?" he asked her. "I mean, on the earth. Where are you located? You're not in Texas, by any chance?"

"No, sir. We're a calling station just outside of Moncton, New Brunswick. That's Canada, sir."

"I know where Moncton is. I'm Canadian."

"Yes, I see, sir."

"And you receive calls from all over?"

"We cover calls from all over North America, yes, sir. Ourselves and several other calling stations. But if I might suggest something, sir, is that you give the American Express public relations department a call. They're open from nine to four and it's a Toronto number...."

"Where are *you* from, though?" Jeremy said. "You're not Canadian, are you?"

"I'm sorry, sir. I cayn't..."

"You're from Texas, aren't you?"

"Sir, I..."

"How did a Texan get up to New Brunswick anyway?"

"Excuse me, sir." A third voice. A different woman. Austin had gone to the help function, although Jeremy could still hear her voice in the background: "I cayn't..."

It all just happened in the ether. These disembodied voices flying over his head. Careering over the world.

"Did he hang up?" said Austin.

"No, I'm here," he said.

"Is there a problem of any kind, sir?" asked the help function.

There was a singing silence filled with the shapes of voices. Like black birds at night. Like bats.

"I just wanted to know . . . ," he started. "I just wanted . . . "

Then he hung up, shaking.

He looked around his strewn bachelor for something to rest his eyes on, but nothing looked good to him. Everything was in disarray. The kitchen was spilling out of itself. Glasses and ashtrays and an overflowing garbage. CDs were out of their boxes. His futon was torn free of sheets, looking like a lumpy beige carcass in the middle of his living room.

He went to the kitchen and looked in the fridge. It was empty except for coffee beans and milk. As he leaned over, his head in the cold yellow-lit interior of the small fridge, he thought about the Great Satan Amex now mobilizing its lesser devils to embark across the face of the world in his pursuit. He hadn't missed a payment—he hadn't used the card in two years before the Fugami purchase—but there they were. They needed no reason. The card wasn't meant to be used. He'd promised himself over the years that it would only be used in an emergency, and even then only when it was clear that he could pay it off immediately. He'd violated his own rules. And by month end, it seemed now quite certain thanks to Doug Acer, he was going to violate the rules of the Great Satan too. And that was worse, because Amex would know. Amex would *know* Jeremy was weak and vulnerable, that he could be taken from the back of the herd.

Just when things were looking up, they tried to beat you down, Jeremy mused. His head was still in the fridge. He thought suddenly: This would be how a chef gives up. Cuts the freon tube and closes the door behind himself. Gas is too pedestrian. A freon cold snap for me.

He called himself a cab instead, now late for work. When he said where he was going, the cab took off without question. Jeremy thought, He knows where it is. He knows my restaurant. At least I have made this small footprint on the landscape.

In front of The Monkey's Paw he reached into his pocket and realized he didn't have any cash. He opened his wallet and looked at the rainbow of cards. He had an almost overwhelming urge to upturn the wallet and shake the cards onto the floor of the car. To see them all (what were there now— eleven, thirteen of them?) strewn in the wet and dirt of the place where countless feet had been. But he resisted.

It took four tries. Diners Club was hopeless. Both Visas were rejected. The cabby was looking a little disgusted (and dubious) by the time he swiped the BMO MasterCard and the authorization number squeaked back through the system, across the telephone lines, through the cell frequencies that crowded the city airwaves, and onto the glowing green screen that sat on the dashboard in front of them like blindfolded Justice herself, beeping irrefutable answers to the questions being posed.

Inside he did some serious prep and set-up. Jules was taking the morning off, and he lost himself in the two soups, carrot-ginger and a curry-leek with yogurt. Today was a one-pasta day, he decided. Rabiata. Hot and decisive, filled with discs of chorizo made by John's Meats and slivers of olives. Zeena arrived in time to help him put together sandwiches on the buns that had arrived from La Baguette. Chevre, chive and onion. Roast beef and horseradish mustard. His own salami. Basic and fast—he didn't think his choices through exactly, but went to the walk-in and reacted to what he saw.

They didn't talk much. Zeena said at one point: "What's up?"

"Nothing is up," he said.

"It's always nothing with guys," Zeena said, musing aloud along a favourite tangent.

He continued with the sandwiches. Zeena started loading them into wicker baskets to put out on the front counter.

"Time?" He asked her.

"Ten-fifty," Zeena answered. "I'll go unlock." And when she was finished with the first load of sandwiches, she carried them out through the portholed swinging doors and into the front. She came back after a few minutes. Jeremy had the second load of sandwiches ready and was over at the range checking his cauldron of rabiata.

"Ready?" he said.

"I'm ready," Zeena answered, but she made no move towards the sandwiches. "I'm always ready."

He looked over at her. She was staring at him.

"What is up with *you*? That's the question," he said.

"Are we OK?"

"OK how?"

"OK here. Us, here. Jules, you, Dominic and me. The Paw. Everything."

"We are fine." He tried to make his voice sound as gentle as it should, although her attention was grating. In the final analysis, he thought, maybe it was best to work with strangers, who would leave what you were thinking alone. People who didn't feel they had personal access to your feelings.

"Well, why do I get the impression that there's, like, this... ," Zeena stalled, and then came up with: "Like the phone's about to ring and it's going to be bad news."

Jeremy said it again. It was nothing.

"Ahh well, there it is," Zeena said, half-turning away. "Nothing. The ultimate out. There's never anything except nothing. I wish I could pull it off myself. Nothing all the time. Never something, just... ," Zeena held a hand up, fingertips together, then spread them sharply open, "poof. Nothing."

"All right, all right. Spare me," he snapped at her finally, not wanting to be mean, in fact forgetting who Zeena was for a second entirely. His friend. *Their* friend. He had showed her the town when she first moved here, given her a job. *That* Zeena.

"Well, sorry," she said, and left the kitchen.

Lunch ended up being slow. Typical, thought Jeremy. Here I am bearing down and where is everyone? They spring out of nowhere when I sleep in or don't show up for some reason.

"How'd we do?" he said to Zeena at about two o'clock, when the trickle had tapered off to almost nothing.

"You did fine," she said, and in her voice he heard something he had never heard before. "You didn't do as well as last Thursday, but you really did OK."

"Hey," he said, and he reached out to put his hand on her thin shoulder. She didn't shake him off precisely, but there was a rigid acceptance of his touch that made him pull back his hand.

"I'm sorry about what I said earlier. I apologize."

"I can't even remember what you said," Zeena answered, just as Jules stormed in surrounded by her high-pressure zone of optimism.

"Hello, my babies," she said, kissing them each in turn. "Look what I have here." And she flourished a copy of *Gud Tayste* and smacked it on the counter.

Jeremy picked it up like it was something he'd never heard of before.

"Page ninety-six," Jules said.

Zeena forgot sufficiently about their tiff to slide in next to Jeremy and lean against him. "What? What? Are we famous?"

"No," Jules said, pinching Jeremy's cheek. "Our baby is."

He couldn't find the page. First he skipped past it, then trying to leaf back, the pages stuck together and he ended up near the beginning of the magazine again.

"Gimme that," Zeena finally said, and took the magazine out of his hands. She turned quickly to a regular front piece called "Hack Your Food."

"New from the Rim," it read. There were entries from Los Angeles and San Francisco.

"'Vancouver!'" Zeena squealed, then read aloud, fending off Jeremy, who was reaching for the magazine. "'And we're not talking Vancouver, Washington. The one north of 49. The Monkey's Paw Bistro. French Chef Jeremy Papier hacks his homeland cuisine with ingredients drawn from the rain forest around him. The scene: groovy, zippie, raver, addict, beemer. Good at: late. Good on: gin.'"

Jeremy finally got the magazine from Zeena. "'French'?" he said. "'Drawn from the rain forest'?"

"That would be the canned peaches they're referring to," Jules smirked.

Jeremy smiled at the ribbing. "So what else do we have here?"

"There's a recipe for soba alfredo at the front," said Zeena.

"Ack," Jeremy said. "Typical."

"Ever tried it?" Zeena said, in a tone that suggested she had just remembered the morning's small abrasion. "They should have said you were the Pacific Northwest's pre-eminent Food Nazi."

Jules laughed loudly, and they walked back into the kitchen together to talk about dinner. She put her arm around his waist as they pushed through the swinging doors into The Zone.

"I've had kind of a shitty day so far," he told her.

"Oh yeah?" she said. They both knew that already. What she thought he didn't know yet was that you needed bad days. You needed bad days to conquer, to make a job into a commitment. "It's going to happen," she continued. "It's mid-week, Thursday. The day we take off again. We always do."

He tried to smile at her, smile into the face he knew so well. That impossibly strong and serene face, the angling confident nose. Jules had pretty ears, he thought. I wonder if I will ever stop noticing these things about her? Will I ever be free of noticing new things about her, recognizing things I've known about her all along?

She smiled back, a smaller smile, and he noticed again:

pale green eyes with an edge of sorrow. The colour of a broken wave. She didn't ask him anything tough at this point. Anything like "What's on your mind?" She didn't ask him anything that would make him lie again.

The weekend was mediocre. On Wednesday of the following week—a cycle of Wednesdays complete—he received the notice in the mail from the Toronto Dominion Bank. They had not honoured the cheque to *Simms, Brine and Lothar*. Custer Quan phoned in the afternoon and gave him a lecture about writing cheques for which he didn't have the funds. Dante's secretary phoned also. Would he phone Mr. Beale that afternoon? She provided a number in Chicago.

When Jules arrived, he explained that he needed to get a little air, and walked over to the Inferno Pender to say hello to Benny.

There was a high sky, clouding over but still bright, and bursts of wind that always made Jeremy think of travelling. It was a get-going wind, a wind full of gusty changes in direction, sudden impulses satisfied. He realized that it felt good just to be walking *away* from the restaurant. Right now he needed to get his head into the breeze and out of the confines of those dark wood walls. The Paw was a place built squarely on his own visions, and he had a breezy feeling of being unloaded, unplugged from the darkness of his own obsessions. Maybe he'd take Benny to lunch. Diva at the Met—one of the cards had to work. He thought he would stare into her eyes over a lunchtime bottle of Merlot and say frank things that would make her young heart beat faster. He thought he might woo her, change things from what they had been into something quite consuming and new.

Benny had seen Jeremy coming from a long way off. From her position on "the bridge" (dubbed thusly by one of the baristas, a *Deep Space Nine* enthusiast), Benny had a clean view: over the espresso stations, over the heads of the customers at the front counter, through the broad sweep of the Inferno Pender's front glass and out into the busy intersection at Granville and Pender streets in downtown Vancouver. Jeremy was walking up Pender. She spied him. She fixed him the second he hove to, hands dug deep in pockets, shoulders folded forward, looking at the ground about twenty yards in front of himself.

My sullen artist, she thought, with an internal smile.

A customer was bantering near her elbow, had been for several minutes and would again tomorrow, the next day. A VSE type: green suit, thin loafers, bad hair.

"Oh, I am sure," she said, in response to whatever had just been suggested, looking down from the bridge and into his watery eyes. But she cracked a glance up again quickly. She kept Jeremy in view. Around her the three baristas in her charge were rapping the orders between them. Latte, frappuccino, Americano. The place was packed. It was always packed.

When Jeremy got to the lights, Benny saw him lift his eyes to the front of the coffee shop. Looking for her. She touched the VSE guy on the shoulder, smiled a brief distracted smile and stepped down from the bridge. She slipped through the crowd, out the front door.

"Hey, barista," he said, slowing his pace as he saw her, smiling now.

She hugged him hard. "Location supervisor," she said into his ear. "I supervise the baristas."

"You run the show," Jeremy said.

"I *am* the show, baby," she said. He didn't quite let go of her but let his hands slip to her waist, his eyes lingering in hers.

So, she thought.

"Let's go," he said.

"Exactly," she said back, which stalled him.

"You...," he started.

"Lunch, my place," she said. Then she kissed him. "I have a craving for Ichi-Ban."

He was smelling her, thinking: CK smelled like citrus, patchouli smelled like loam. It was a promising, protecting and deeply sexy Mother Earth-y combination. Base and acid combined, a total smell.

The wind found them. Down through the towers of the business district, the unpredictable get-going wind was made even more volatile by the deflections and facades, by the downdrafts and the vortexes created in the alley mouths. By the seething traffic. A gust found them standing there, his hands on her hips, just as it had snaked through the trees in a forest somewhere and laid flat a targeted cedar.

They took a cab. She let them in, both of them breathing a little heavily from the jog upstairs. Four flights in a tight, impatient spiral. Up around the glass shaft housing the elevator that took too long to come.

She sat him on the bed, pushed him back. She pulled her own shirt open, button by button, freed her breasts from the white sports bra. She pulled her panties down with a crooked index finger and tossed them into the corner.

With the exception of the round, metallic, blue bauble in her belly button, she was a smooth stretch of golden pink and white.

They rolled over onto the bed, Benny on top of him. She opened her legs around him. No foreplay, no condom. They didn't think of it. There were none. She rode along with the natural arc of the moment, straddling him, holding him tightly with her knees, occasionally leaning back and looking at the ceiling, then back down at him, way down it seemed. She towered, cast a long, curving shadow across his torso.

Jeremy watched her profile as she cleaned herself with tissues that she lobbed into the wastebasket by the door.

Then she rolled back onto the bed next to him, smiled, stretched briefly and fell asleep.

He'd never seen her place before. It was bigger than his, nicer. Immaculate hardwood floors, a separate dining room, and a cute galley kitchen with a gas range and an exposed brick wall. In the living room her stereo was prominent, CDs spread around: P J Harvey, Radiohead, Combustible Edison, Sinatra, *Le Nozze di Figaro,* choral works by Vivaldi. Her books in stacks, used: paperbacks by literary celestials as many light-years apart as Will Self and Flaubert. In the corner of the front hall there was a pile of what must have been dry cleaning: orange sweaters, velvet dresses, trim grey skirts.

The moment had come. He called Dante from the living room. Got him in the car, of course, although the static was particularly bad.

Dante said: "Gotta call you back, Jay. Where are you?"

Jeremy went into Benny's kitchen and boiled water for the Ichi-Ban, a Costco box of which he found under the counter. Three flavours: pork, seafood and miso. It appeared to be the only food Benny had in the cupboards. He picked miso.

Dante phoned back in twenty minutes. Benny was still asleep. The Ichi-Ban water was simmering, and having scoured the fridge and found nothing else, Jeremy was sipping a Coors Light, which tasted metallic and smelled like sulphur.

"What number is this?" Dante's first question, asked sharply. In the background Jeremy could hear heavy traffic, non-stop horns. Dante was lounging in the passenger seat of a rented Jaguar while Philip drove, no doubt.

Jeremy provided an explanation for the strange number. It pleased Dante enormously, disproportionately.

"I was beginning to think you needed a *mujer,* my friend," Dante said, pronouncing the word *moh-hawr* and laughing. "Is she strong? Is she smart?"

"Yeah, well..."

"Yeah, well, I hope so." There was crackling silence for a second or two.

"What's on your mind?" Jeremy asked. The telephony grid rippled with sufficient static to drown out a few words before settling back to the normal sea-state hum.

Dante was mid-sentence, "... Inferno Michigan Avenue. Went to a White Sox game. Then Lowry's, heard of them, Jay?"

"The seasoning salt people. The steak house."

"That's right. I was thinking of ordering tofu, but Philly told me they don't like faggots in the Windy City."

Jeremy laughed dutifully.

"So, instead, I had a little sixteen-ounce steak. USDA prime. A nice light meal. You see, Jay, this is why I mention Chicago, because I'm meeting with bankers down here and moderation is not part of their game. It's a steak or it's your liver they're eating, and either way they use steak knives."

There was another wave of static and talking in the car at Dante's end.

Dante came back on: "Jeremy? I'll call you back." And the line went dead.

Jeremy leaned back in Benny's sofa. Bankers, he thought. Now where might this story be going?

He looked across Benny's living room and through her bedroom door, where he could see the sheeted outline of her shoulder, gently cresting and falling with sleep. There was freedom in that narrow roll, neither dropping nor rising too far. Just the bandwidth of an unconstrained breath. He thought about that breath. He remembered its tiny puffing heat, its very light scent, like a sweet dough, like stollen. He imagined feeling it again. He imagined inhaling enough of it to be partway free himself.

He got up and gently closed the bedroom door, anticipating the phone, which then rang.

"Jeremy," said a voice from the same staticky place. "Philip."

Here's the man." And then there was some hand shuffle and clatter as Philip handed over the cell.

"Had to take another call. Where were we?" Dante was unhurried.

"Steaks," Jeremy tried. "Bankers?"

"Bankers. The reason for my call. Always better partners than bankers. Partners is negotiated co-operation out of mutual interest. Nobody forces you to take a partner, and you can always get divorced, am I right?"

Jeremy didn't even have time to answer.

"Bankers, on the other hand, work with you when times are good and against you otherwise. This is a fundamental principle when it comes to using other people's money: always trade something for the money, always be a partner. Because if you borrow the money, you're renting it. And then you answer for it on bankers' terms."

"Right," said Jeremy. He was now listening carefully.

"All right. I'm going to tell you a short story. Two years ago, a Sunday night, I hear from someone I haven't seen in five or six years... son of Mr. Papier, who has been my neighbour for almost twenty years, my favourite chess companion, loopy but not yet entirely crazy...."

"Dante...," Jeremy started.

"Don't interrupt me. Ten minutes from now I'm at O'Hare, and ten minutes later I'm in the air for New York, and between now and then you and I have to go a much longer distance."

Jeremy had only meant to say: Dante, you don't need to remind me. I remember sitting down with you that day. I remember your generosity. I remember being ashamed that I could not ask my father. I remember. I remember. But he shut up.

"We ate lobster, do you remember that? I had Nova Scotia lobsters flown in that weekend for a party Saturday night. I had two left. We spread newspapers on the picnic table on the deck below the house. It was a beautiful, sunny day looking out over Howe Sound, and we had a proper feed. A big bloody crustacean each and a bucket of Harp on ice. You remember that, Jay?"

"Of course I remember, Dante."

"So the kid has a couple of Mick lagers and starts talking about restaurant ideas, and in an instant, Jay, in an instant I can tell there is a good idea here. I know business ideas—I know when they're too simple and when they're too complicated—and I looked at this kid, back from cooking school in France and working in a hotel kitchen he doesn't like, and I say to myself: He's got skills *and* vision. He's going to take all this classical training he learned from the frogs in the white hats, and he's going to turn the local sow's ear into a culinary silk purse. It's a vision and the kid has got it."

He took a breath and a sip of something. Pellegrino drunk from the neck of the stubby green bottle, thought Jeremy.

"What did the Professor think of you going to France?"

"Ambivalent," Jeremy said, surprised by the question.

"He doubtless thought it a very stupid idea."

Jeremy was left to think about this assessment while Dante took his mouth away from the phone again. When he returned he said: "Philly says I have three minutes or I'll miss my plane. If you charter a plane you might figure the bloody thing could wait for you, but apparently this is not strictly the case. All right, so money. The kid and I discuss money. Eventually everybody talks about money and the kid with the vision doesn't know chalk from cheese when it comes to money but even *he* ends up talking about it. What he says is: Mr. Beale this, and Mr. Beale that...at the end of the day it's something like two hundred grand for a bare bones start-up. I suggest a partnership and the kid says he wants to *borrow* the money. Get me on as a guarantor, but otherwise do it on his own hook."

Jeremy didn't remember it this way exactly, but he did remember that he had welled full of confidence as he spoke and that he had felt possessive about his ideas.

"And I have to tell you, Jay... first off I thought it was going to be more—I'm still amazed what you've done with so little. Second, although I might have liked to be a partner with you, I couldn't help being impressed with what you did there: You said *borrow*. You said *guarantee*. You were talking about *your vision*."

"I don't recall precisely those terms," Jeremy said.

"Well, I bloody well do. You decided you wanted a banker," Dante said, and then he broke off for a moment to take another drink of water. "OK, listen to me. The agreement that we came to over lobsters in the sun in August had the effect of motivating me to do a range of things that my good man Philip thinks were extremely unwise. He might have even used stronger words than *unwise*."

Jeremy thought he heard laughter in the background at this point.

"There was the bank loan. There were the credit cards," Dante rhymed off the obligations. "And when I guarantee somebody else, then I'm *somebody else's* borrower. And if I'm borrowing from somebody, even indirectly, then you're borrowing from me."

Jeremy tried again: "I only wanted to build something for myself."

"Of course you did, and you've succeeded. Only now you've built something with four walls, no door and bars on the windows, and I'm your banker, not your partner, so I guess the question is, How should I respond to a phone call from the Toronto Dominion Bank, a courtesy phone call from a fellow I know, informing me that there are problems with your loan, with your account, and they would like the matter of $230,000 'taken care of'? What do you think, Jeremy? Are they suggesting I might have to pay them? And if I do have to pay them, do you think you could find some way to pay me back at rates of return that satisfy my opportunity cost of capital?"

He was shouting by the end of it.

"So, I suppose I need to know the following at this point," Dante hollered. "Do you need my help or not? Say yes truthfully and I can't be your banker any more, but I will be your partner like I've offered many times before. I'll give you five percent of the place and some freedom. If you say no truthfully, I stay your banker and everyone should be happy. You'll take care of the bank and whatever other difficulties you may have at the moment—and in my experience, these troubles always come in clusters. But if you say no, Jeremy, and you do in fact need help...well, then I'll know very quickly anyway and I'll still be your banker, but I won't be working for you any more. You'll be working for me."

"I understand," Jeremy repeated.

"I remember when your mother died," Dante said, changing tone. And then he let the silence hang as Jeremy did not, could not, answer. "Sudden crisis and everybody ran for cover, didn't they?"

He wasn't wrong, of course.

"I have no family, Jeremy. My family tree is a series of opportunities linked by branches to the main trunk of my life. I see the opportunities, I take them. It's like picking fruit. You might think to do the same. Now, your move."

Jeremy was too tired to think, so he finally said the words: "I need help, Dante. You know it. Just tell me it will be business as usual around here. Free of money problems, we'll go through the roof. Business as usual and you won't be sorry."

Dante sighed. Business as usual, he knew, was code for Capelli. He stalled. "What's with this Derek person at Amex? 'Unusually large purchase.' We sent over a cheque, but why is he calling me?"

"You did what?" Jeremy said.

"It was a sign of good faith," Dante explained. "Now, tell me what I bought you."

"You bought me a knife," Jeremy stammered, and told him about the Fugami. Top end. The very best.

Dante enjoyed the description. "Perfect. Utterly perfect."

"I can return it," Jeremy said.

There was an atypical moment of silence between them. It came to this.

"All right. Business as usual," Dante said.

"You won't be sorry. Jules and I——"

"Don't," Dante interrupted. "I agreed."

"I accept," Jeremy said.

After which the details didn't feel like details. Once the words were released they were simply the operating assumptions, the underlying flavour of a new world into which he had been suddenly born.

It should have been an evening they all enjoyed, he thought, walking across town towards the park. It was 1:45 in the morning now, and he wished he could turn in at any of the bars he passed along the route, Dunsmuir, then Robson, then Denman. The same kind of evening they would have normally kicked through together, riffing at each other, bitching, flirting.

The menu killed. Out front, people were enjoying themselves. Dominic and Zeena carried the comments in from the dining room. Someone liked the wild salmon tartare with grilled oysters on curly endive. Someone liked the black-cod ceviche. (Zeena wrote "Raw Fish Night" on the chalkboard.) They sold out of penne with gorgonzola and only put a few of the rabbit legs in the fridge for Thursday lunch. In all, it was a chemistry Wednesday. A Wednesday to launch them up the rippling back of the wave that would carry them into the weekend.

But Jeremy took little pleasure from it. He struggled to

focus, his mind spinning forward to meeting his father, not looking forward to the very certain reaction his news would provoke.

"Mint leaves, puh-lease." Zeena was back at the pass-through with a trio of sorbets that he had forgotten to garnish. Then, a joke: "Come on, Chef, get with the program."

To which they all heard the Chef respond: "Program?" A kind of dubious snort. It came out involuntarily.

Of course, he gave Zeena (or more precisely the customers) the mint leaves that they were due, and turned irritably to other tasks. But not without catching Jules's eye, catching the look that said...well, he wasn't sure what it said. It was like the single word *no* said slowly, repeated with a changing intonation, from dread, fear, doubt, to more deliberate, emphatic denial, a self-reassuring denial of what had been feared: *No, no, no...NO*.

"Drinks?" she asked afterwards, tentative.

"Believe it or not," Jeremy said, a little angry all of a sudden, "believe it or not, I have to visit with my father this evening."

"What? Where?" Zeena said, sailing into the kitchen. "Weed?"

"Me, please," Jules said. Then: "Nothing, honey. Chef and I are just—"

He had never told Zeena, but why did he even care who knew? "My father," he said, cutting Jules off, "lives in Stanley Park. He lives there at night. He lives there during the day. He eats ducks."

Zeena exhaled a blue cloud of sweet smoke. "Cool."

Bang on two. The Professor was running behind, atypical for him, but the park had become more talkative lately, more distracting. The trees swayed and barked, the residents and new arrivals sought him out. They approached him and held his attention while the hours slipped away.

Notes didn't always do the testimony justice and so the Professor was finding strange diagrams on his yellow legal pads. Circles connected by lines, an evolving complex molecule. The largest circle was in the middle of the page. It was marked "The Woods." There were lines emerging from it running to other circles, one very thick line marked "Caruzo." Another connected to a circle marked "Siwash," a dotted line. Other names, other circles. And then a ring of still smaller circles not connected to the centre at all but clustered at the periphery of the page, as if drawn into orbit by gravity.

Caruzo kept him abreast of new arrivals. "Four," he said, calling from the forest early that week. "Plus dog makes five."

The diagram grew. Earlier that evening he had bumped into Chladek near Prospect Point. Chladek was a displaced Czech journalist-cum-merchant-mariner living under the Lions Gate Bridge. He had already earned his own circle, was approachable, talkative, only rarely incoherent.

Chladek offered a sip of Becherovka, a medicinal Czech liquor in a square green bottle, a shareable portion of which was frequently in his possession. The Professor offered back a package of saltines that Chladek accepted.

"Tell me," the Professor said, after they had sipped from the bottle again. He gestured to take in the entire forest around them. "What is this wilderness to you?"

"Maybe not so much as it is to you," said Chladek, who was capable of being difficult. But he turned the corners of his mouth downwards and nodded slowly, considering the question. "It is Stromovka," he said finally.

The Professor didn't understand.

Chladek smiled. He set the bottle of Becherovka on the pavement with a clink. He spread his arms, palms open as the Professor had just done. "Stromovka," he said again. "The place of the trees."

The Professor pondered this comment at the fire later, time slipping by, sketching lines and erasing them. "Stromovka," he said, looking up into the canopy above, then back down to his diagram. It was no kind of formal science he recognized, but the Professor followed the whisper of an impulse and wrote the word inside the largest circle, the circle at the centre of the page. The Woods. Here he wrote: *Sanctified. Stromovka. The Place of Trees.*

Then he lay back in the ferns to let it all flow over him. Jeremy stood at the centre of his own diagram, the Professor thought. In the thick of his own woods. A joined drama. People turning against the wind, returning to Eden. Those seeking reconciliation with the stable rhythms of the earth, with their own beginnings. Here, in the park, where out of desperation, for lack of options, a living theatre of rootedness had been reborn from distant tragedy. In Jeremy's kitchen, where a sense of lost connection played out in culinary theatrics about the return to a familiar soil.

And just as the thought creased through him—the Professor hoped it might be discussed between them that very evening—he realized it was two o'clock. He jogged to the lagoon, arriving at the cherry trees completely out of breath, his case clutched under his arm. His diagrams folded into a yellow wad and stuffed into his rear pocket.

Jeremy was not at the designated spot, on the city side of the lagoon at the cherry trees. He stood high on the rise above the lagoon, past the tennis courts. The boy had chosen to stand on the lip of grass that was the absolute easternmost edge of the park. The last bit of green before the curb, before pavement and buildings began. The outside. He was looking down.

The Professor climbed up towards his son. The light glanced down from the streetlights across Jeremy's face. It threw shadows under his tired eyes. His downturned mouth. When they were face to face, they stood in silence for a number of seconds. The Professor felt disappointment fill him. "You have not been back to the library," he said.

"Shitty week," Jeremy snapped. But he stopped at that, because in the Professor's eyes, those impervious eyes, there was a colour that he recognized. A shade of bruising. A shade of vulnerability. He lowered his voice. "How is Caruzo?"

"Sends his best."

Jeremy steadied himself.

The Professor spoke first. "There was a woman in the park on the day they died."

Jeremy dropped his head. God.

"She saw something that day... someone..."

Jeremy turned and stepped into the street. The Professor remained on the grass. He held the last inch of his park. "The two are meant to be together," he said, talking to Jeremy's back. "Just as the two were drawn from the same soil, so too must the same soil hold them...."

The strange words.

Jeremy spun, standing in the middle of the empty night-time street. From her expensive apartment window high in the concrete and glass monolith behind them, had the resilient old lady of the West End risen for a nocturnal glass of grapefruit juice just then, she might have looked down and seen a small, charged scene on her quiet street. A rumpled figure, tired, authoritative, holding court on the grass by the curb, his arms crossed, his head back looking at the sky. And opposite him, a leaner, younger frame of a discernibly similar type, angular, also in black, hands in his jacket pockets rigidly, critically, dubiously. Staring at the older cast of himself.

"From the file in the library," Jeremy said.

The Professor pantomimed applause.

"And if you've read it," Jeremy went on, "may I ask why I—"

"Because you are a part of what is going on here."

Jeremy stared. He didn't want to know. He plunged.

"I accepted an offer." Even to his own ear, the words

clanked coldly out into the night air between them, but he couldn't have predicted that the statement would bring the Professor's arms limply to his sides, that it would pull him a step forward. Out of the park. Onto the curb. Into the gutter. The Professor was staring at his son, his blood. Standing in the street, in the city. "Oh, you have made such a mistake."

"It's a good deal. It gives me freedom."

"Freedom. So many things done in this name."

Freedom from debt, Jeremy tried to say, but the Professor was looking past him now. Over his shoulder and up between the buildings. Beyond. He was whispering.

"Too often, I think, the desire for freedom masks the desire for destruction."

The words a thin stream. A last breath.

"You want to destroy everything around you, everything you have created for yourself or been given by others. To be free."

Tapering. Diminishing. Losing angularity, presence, power.

"Natural for you, perfectly natural," the Professor whispered. "Natural to refuse the key that is given. To be blind in the darkness of knowing. To be filled with a dark light that we must shine on the people around us. A light that makes us weep and pull down our own houses."

The wind spoke in the cherry trees, a hissing speech through purple leaves and thin black branches. The city hummed, hypnotic. Winding through the deepest part of a Wednesday night.

"Come stay with me," Jeremy said. He could hardly hear his own words. "Do your research but sleep in a bed. Write your notes at a table. You could shave."

"Stay involved," the Professor said. Back. Alert. "Stay interested."

No second for an answer. He turned. He descended the hill at a determined trot. He threaded through the cherry trees, from the branches of which hung the fruits of their joint linkage to this place.

Around the lagoon went the Professor, dwindling down, then swallowed by the blackness.

# BABES IN THE WOOD

At first, "business as usual" was painfully accurate. A week after coming to his understanding with Inferno International, he was still enjoying a daily flurry of hostile incoming letters and phone calls, complicated by the fact that Dante disappeared to New York City. Meanwhile, there was something like a virus loose among his various credit cards. Business was up enough to permit small payments; he was actually winding the kite in. Still, nobody was happy. Diners Club cancelled the card. *After late payments in seven of the past twelve months . . .* MasterCard sent him a stern reminder about an unpaid delinquency assessment, and it was hand-signed. He'd only ever had correspondence from the computer before.

Then there was the Canadian Tire lawyer. Doug Acer called half a dozen times, each time a little earlier in the morning. He was screening calls by this point, so Jeremy never had to deal with the young lawyer directly, but he was beginning to get the impression it was a sport for Acer. *We should be able to work it out. Let me know a convenient time to reach you. If it's too early, I can try you later in the day.*

Jeremy was forced to track Dante down in New York.

To his credit, Dante provided help quickly. He made one or two power calls of his own on Jeremy's behalf—everybody would be paid out by the end of July—and this precipitation of irritable calls abated immediately. Jules hadn't noticed anything, they were still very much open and business was steady. It was like the sun had come out after a day of rain, which it had, in fact; the weather was brilliant. And then, *Last Chapter* booked a table for twelve for the first Saturday in August. Twelve people, they wanted a prix fixe menu, leaving it to Jeremy to decide. There could have been no better way to start the new "business as usual" era, thought Jeremy. A deliciously good omen.

Here, then, was the happy substance of Plan A as it framed up in Jeremy's mind. By the end of July debtors would be paid out or otherwise mollified. Dante would return from New York and take him for lunch at the Terminal City Club. Maybe Philly would come. In either case, they'd talk pleasantries during the main course, about Chicago and New York. Dante would have stories, and he would tell these without the need for feedback beyond the conversational punctuation of Jeremy saying "sure" or "oh, really?" and thereby demarcating one of Dante's observations from the next. It wouldn't be so terrible. Over dessert, Philly would review the situation. There would be papers to sign. Inferno would buy 95 percent of the business (Paw Incorporated d.b.a. The Monkey's Paw Bistro). The price would be a dollar, and all assets would thereby pass to Dante. In return, Jeremy imagined he would have to sign an agreement relating to his terms of employment, a commitment to work for a couple of years at a modest salary.

The plan offered stability without undue humiliation, but more than that, Plan A, in Jeremy's calculation, meant that Jules, Zeena and Dominic would be kept on. And Jeremy was confident that, by the end of a couple months, anybody exposed to Jules would need no more proof of her abilities. Dante would learn to love her. Jules would eventually tolerate Dante. Everybody would be happy again.

Unfortunately, there was no Plan B, despite the failure of Plan A prerequisites to materialize. First, the end of July came and Dante hadn't played his part. Jeremy tried him at his offices, but no, Mr. Beale was still in New York. He tried the cell number repeatedly, but Dante either had the phone turned off or was deep underground somewhere. Jeremy's signals weren't getting through. He left messages, three in total before he stopped. Was it possible Dante had changed his mind? Jeremy didn't think so. He didn't think Dante changed his mind.

So August arrived without action on anybody's part. Jeremy left his fourth message in a voice mailbox somewhere out there in phone-space; he didn't even know what mailbox he was talking to any more.

*Dante, it's me.* And then he ran out of words, stumbling to a close with: *I'm in Vancouver.*

Brilliant, he thought after hanging up. Of course you're in Vancouver—where else would you be? It's only the Dantes of the world who had unplugged themselves from the planet and were doing their business on a plane that hovered just above the actual surface of the earth.

Living on the plane below that one, where passage over the ground was still measured in some fashion—kilometres, life left in a pair of soles—transactions had a stickier quality. They were tangled more in the social and personal foliage of the place, in the analogue uncertainties of human behaviour. And that might explain why, Dante's lofty assurances not withstanding, on the Friday, the day before the *Last Chapter* party, it seemed that everybody in the Vancouver financial community who had ever had any association with Jeremy or The Paw boiled over at once.

He had just placed the single largest daily order of his life, and paid everyone confidently by cheque: sockeye salmon, Queen Charlotte crab, Saturna Island lamb sides, Fraser Valley ducks and crates of assorted produce from Garrulous Greens. He had walked serenely back through town to The Monkey's Paw. And as he was sipping a coffee and contemplating the uncomfortably large stack of mail, a courier arrived. It was an ominously thin package. Inside, Jeremy read the following on Toronto Dominion Bank letterhead:

Dear Mr. Papier:

Re: Principle and interest due and payable immediately: $233,436.73

It is the duty of this office ...

He didn't finish the first sentence, and his heart was palpitating. A familiar dying two-step with the associated wave of dread—sweeping, systemic dread like only the realization of personal financial ruin can precipitate. And then the eerie prickle as microscopic beads of sweat bristled to the top of every pore, minutely lubricating him for flight in response to the adrenaline coursing through him. He was, he felt emphatically, fucked from a great height.

But he didn't pass out. He hung on. He phoned Dante again, immediately. No answer. And this time, no accessible mailbox either. Instead the robotic femininity of Nellie the mail matron informing him: *This mailbox is full. Please call again.*

Jeremy lost his temper. He made a fist and hit the wall, not hard, just enough to crack the plasterboard and peel a length of skin off his knuckle.

Which only meant that he had a bandage on his right hand as he sat in the downtown Toronto Dominion Commercial Banking Centre opposite a beige individual named Custer Quan. A short man, about forty-five, plumply wedged in his swivel chair, adjusting his round glasses every ten seconds or so with a stubby forefinger and a well-chewed thumb.

Quan was fidgety. There were nine garnishees on the account already that morning. Jeremy's mention of the Inferno payment did not appease. He insisted it would come, and Quan only became embarrassed. His hands, he said, were tied.

Jeremy promised payment Monday. He all but got down on the teal carpet and begged. Monday. End of story. No excuses. Personal commitment. Monday was fall-off-a-cliff day....

Quan agreed eventually, visibly unhappy. But he walked Jeremy out, polite under the circumstances, hedging his bets in case the Inferno assistance really was in the wings.

Jeremy jogged back to The Paw. It was just after lunch. Zeena was bitchy about being left alone over the busy period, even by necessity, with only the sandwiches, salads and onion tarts that Jeremy had managed to prepare.

"Everyone was suitably impressed," Zeena said. "Some people actually look forward to your hot lunch specials."

"I trust you apologized. How'd we do?" Jeremy asked, still trying to re-oxygenate.

"How'd it go with you?" She asked him accusingly.

"How did we do? How much?"

Zeena popped the till open for him and walked slowly into the back carrying the empty wicker basket from the sandwiches.

Jeremy counted out $253 onto the counter. The phone rang.

"Papier," said the familiar voice, tired, amused and mean spirited.

"Acer...," he started, and he thought to himself just then: Here goes, I'm going to let someone have it. Doug Acer from Simms, Brine and Lothar. Couldn't be more perfect.

But Acer beat him to the open air, charging onward, clearly having something to say that he wanted to get out in one chunk. "The cheque you sent me bounced, and I'm sorry to say that the Inferno didn't catch it. I'm in an awkward position here, Papier, a position made more awkward by my discovery that there are twelve other lenders in the picture."

Acer had to stop for a breath, which he did quickly, not knowing that Jeremy was on his heels, also out of breath.

Trying now to slow the heart palpitations, feeling a vertiginous, telescopic expansion of the space between his chin and the floor. He began to stammer a response, but Acer was off again and the words were getting harder. He heard *illegal*. He heard *fraud*. He heard *kite*. He heard *conceivable involvement of law enforcement authorities*. And when Acer was finally finished—and Jeremy had nothing, not a single word to say that might reasonably counter any of what had been alleged—the line ran silent. Acer gave him fifteen seconds of dead phone air to come up with something. Then he hung up.

Jeremy stood quivering, alone in his silent front room. Zeena, he imagined, was hiding in the kitchen.

It was worth one more shot. "Riker." On the first ring.

"Philly!" Jeremy almost shouted.

"Who's calling?"

"Jeremy. Jeremy Papier. What is going on? Nobody has been paid. I have the biggest reservation I've had in my life for tomorrow night. *Last Chapter*. And I'm getting smoked from ten sides here. Quan won't pay the Happy Valley. Says he wants to lock the place up. Acer is threatening fraud charges—"

"Whoa, whoa, whoa," Philly said. "Hang on."

The line crackled as Philly's hand went over the receiver.

"Gimme ten," Philip said.

"Where is he?" He must have sounded pathetic.

"Busy, extremely. All right? Call you back."

He tried to think about dinner during the long minutes that followed. It was one of the strangest undertakings of the week. Everything he had ordered for today and tomorrow had arrived: the gorgeous red salmon, the crabs still squirming in buckets of ice, the beautiful sides of lamb, ready for butchering and portioning, the ducks and all of his greens. And yet he couldn't remember a thing that Jules and he had planned to do with them. He hadn't made any prep lists yet, so he couldn't even use these to jog his memory. He stood in the centre of The Zone, and all he could think of was a roast chicken in the backyard, cooked over a fire just outside their tent. His mother turning it on a stick. And the lamb dish, what was that? She cubed it and left it in a bowl of yogurt and lemon overnight. The next day she skewered it with potatoes and grilled it on the backyard Weber barbecue that was otherwise his father's domain.

"Nomad lamb," he said aloud, just as the phone rang again. It had been more than fifteen minutes.

"Monkey's Paw," he said, trying to sound businesslike.

"You know?" It was Dante. "I never liked that name."

And he didn't sound particularly busy at all.

Plan B was revealed, different in a number of painful ways. The *Last Chapter* dinner, Dante at the very least agreed, would proceed as planned. Jules arrived Saturday morning and they got down to it. She looked tired, wasn't talking much. He asked her if she'd been out the night before, and she nodded but didn't say where. Nor did she look up from banging out small-dice onions for mirepoix. A technique-machine right to the end. Eight vertical cuts, three horizontal cuts, *bam-bam-bam-bam-bam-bam*. Perfect dice.

They had a number of other tables, including Olli and Margaret, which was unexpected. But *Last Chapter* closed the place down. Luke Lucas left a one-thousand-dollar tip. Nobody had ever seen anything like it. Jules just shook her head. Jeremy too. So the servers split it three ways between Dominic, Zeena and the stunned dishwasher. Then they all quietly called it a night.

Plan B formally went into effect the next morning, with Jeremy reporting to Inferno International Coffee corporate offices. They were open seven days a week, it turned out. At the front desk he asked for Dante and got a short, dubious look from the receptionist. Mr. Beale was still in New York. Mr. Riker was back but in a meeting. If Mr. Papier would just wait in the small boardroom off the entrance foyer, someone would be with him straight away.

Jeremy did as he was told, and five minutes later the Inferno delegate arrived. A junior in the legal department he guessed, an articling student. She looked about seventeen, but she had pearl-hard eyes and a brutally direct manner.

"Your signature is required in thirteen places," she said, after shaking his hand and offering the thinnest possible veneer of social preamble. She had fanned out a sheaf of papers on the table, pages marked with purple stick-it notes where he was to endorse the various agreements and terms.

"Can't we...," he stammered, "...walk through it together?"

The young woman thought Mr. Riker might have explained things already. But she took the time, leafing through the pages, explaining how they would file for protection from creditors, push Paw Incorporated d.b.a. The Monkey's Paw Bistro into bankruptcy.

"Bankruptcy?" Jeremy said. Plan B was framing up.

"I understand there were some...," and here the pearl eyes reflected a trace of pity, "...some legal matters. Cheques and so forth."

In any case, *starting fresh* was the term she preferred to bankruptcy. Inferno International Coffee had *started fresh* with a subsidiary corporation to re-establish a restaurant in the same location. Jeremy would be 5 percent owner of this new company, as agreed. 101239 BC Ltd. There was a disclaimer to sign about IIC's involvement in the business before the sale. A certification that all employees of the old company had been properly terminated.

Hello.

Jeremy started to say: *terminated?* But the word didn't make it into his mouth. It lodged in a place between his brain and his throat. Jammed there, half formed. *Term...* And in a swirling, suffocating instant, Jeremy's heart—the physical ticker—was the site of a disturbing convergence of muscle memories. The first, a long ago familiar arrhythmia. A stutter, a partial resumption, a fluttering, failing, vertiginous two-step. The second, the effect of a face, from close. An effervescence behind the breastbone that seemed to lift the heart from its cavity. He was there. He was staring into that perfect face. Her strong green eyes, her magnificent nose and eyebrows and black hair. They were poised above a kiss that was never completed, that might have changed everything but did not. Hovering, Jules and Jeremy, canted an inch towards one another, absolutely ready to do what came next. Kissable over brown-crayon-flavoured coffee at the Save On Meats sandwich counter.

And so, standing in the IIC boardroom, the beats of Jeremy's heart were dissociating and floating from his chest. Perhaps, he thought, reaching out with the fingertips of both hands to steady himself against the boardroom table, this was what it felt like to be *terminated*.

The woman took no notice of Jeremy. She was still talking, meting out words of freezing certainty. A Professional Services Agreement for Chef Jeremy Papier would be signed and would begin immediately. After the restaurant reopened, his remuneration would be augmented by profit sharing. "A share based on profit after interest and tax as outlined in Schedule G," she said. "This is Schedule G. Your initial is required here. And this is the agreement transferring Monkey's Paw assets to IIC. Your signature here."

"Assets," he said, recovering speech and finding only this word.

"Um, yes. Lower-left corner please."

Jeremy nodded numbly and signed in all of the places she indicated. "And the debt is paid off," he said, more to himself than to her, although she primly responded.

"I suppose that could be seen as one of the many bright sides of the arrangement. Once you declare bankruptcy, you don't have to pay anybody."

Jeremy let the words register. "And why would anyone agree?"

She smiled patiently at him, shrugged a millimetre up and down. "Some arrangement?" she said. "The TD Bank is the Inferno International lead lender.... I'm not stating anything directly, of course...."

He left a message for Jules that night, much later. "We're closed tomorrow," he said. "Meet me at two, please. I'll explain. I'm sorry."

He turned off the ringer, feeling empty and foolish. Benny pulled him down onto the couch next to her. "All I wanted...," Jeremy started.

"What?" she whispered, leaning close.

He started to tell her about the *relais*. About the wooden walls and the low light. The regulars and the langue de boeuf à la moutarde. He wanted to tell her everything. About Patrice, resistance fighters, river sources, feelings of Blood. These simple things he had wanted to do with The Monkey's Paw, these things that were put on at every side.

But Benny didn't want stories just then. Benny wanted him to make love to her, and then to sleep next to her between the cool sheets. She said: "Baby." Then again, she repeated: "Baby now, no thinking. Nothing." She took his hand. "Here...."

He was so nervous the next morning that he had to take beta blockers. Just thinking about their meeting made his hands shake. He tried being angry at Dante, bearing down on that feeling. Injustice. Betrayal. Hadn't he been promised Jules would...?

But it only made him feel worse. It was his own fault, not Dante's. It was a cluster of his own failings that had brought them all to this painful morning.

He took sixty milligrams, which was a lot, three pills where one or two would do. Since propranolol lowered your blood pressure, beta blockers had the side effect of producing lightheadedness. It was a complex trade-off between the shakes and passing out, Jeremy realized. In the eye of the observer, he reasoned, the shakes were indicative of moral and emotional weakness, while passing out was a sign of some kind of serious structural flaw. You might go either way depending on who you were facing, and for Jules, right then, moral strength seemed paramount. He sat in the front window and waited for her, and Jeremy did venture to have a coffee, watching himself carefully in the reflection of the glass as he raised the mug steadily to his lips.

"Jules," he said when she came in, smiling weakly. He looked a bit sick, she thought. His eyes were red and bruised from lack of sleep. His hands tremored minutely.

Jules poured coffee and sat. "How bad?" she asked.

Beta blockers also had the effect of slowing his speech, or his perception of its speed in any case. He may have been pumping out the same number of words per minute, but to his ear they emerged methodically, one at a time, and dropped awkwardly into the space between himself and Jules, like blobs of spaetzle dough. "From the top," he said, "understand that none of what has happened is your fault."

Jules established with her eyebrows that the thought had never crossed her mind.

Then he told her the long story. The story in which his kite went aloft and his options grew fewer. His own inability to budget or handle a credit card. The story in which Dante was the only source of assistance on a bleak financial landscape. Dante's promise of "business as usual."

"It wasn't my idea," Jeremy pleaded. "You and I having this conversation."

And then—just as Jules realized fully, unswervingly, that this was the ending she had feared—he did something neither of them had expected. He blamed it on the Professor. The Professor had not been doing so well lately, he said. He described the Professor's living arrangement, his clothes. He described the Professor's smell and his fingernails. Jeremy claimed to have been distracted by this situation. He'd let things get out of control.

Jules listened and did not take her eyes from his face. He was talking about the park now.

"Siwash," Jules said.

He was only trying to illustrate.

"Tell me."

Babes in the Wood. Jeremy gave her the précis.

"Wow."

"Jules. Please."

She let him continue. He described how he thought things had been turning out. How, in a rush, everything had come apart. "The banks came crashing in. Dante thinks we're going to need a transition period."

"Dante," Jules said, testing the word. "Transition to what, do you suppose?"

Of course, he had no answer. He didn't know.

Jules looked out the front window. She didn't see her own reflection; it was unlike Jules to look on herself. Only outward, forward, up the street and beyond. She shook her head a fraction of an inch either way.

"What?" he said. From outside the slender tower of strength that was Jules Capelli, you didn't get a glimpse inside very often.

But she didn't answer, just continued to stare. Up past Victory Square. Past the granite cenotaph with its vaguely accusatory inscription: *Is it anything to you?* Past the sleeping bags that surrounded its base, the kids having a lie-in, enjoying the morning sunshine. Flaked out in an enviable ambition-free drift of what appeared to be more or less satisfied disaffection. Past this scene to the tips of the downtown towers that sprouted along the ridge line, hemming slowly in from the west, appearing to savour the moments before a frontal assault.

It hurt, this news. It surprised her by hurting physically, something like stomach flu. She had seen it coming, although not precisely and not the pain. But what surprised her more was that she was not thinking about Jeremy at all, but about Dante. The coffee baron filled her mental stage. He pushed out all other thoughts. There was only the Emperor of Inferno International and the backhanded compliment he had given her by devouring The Monkey's Paw. The greatest compliment of her career. The greatest affirmation that she had done the right thing to leave The Tea Grill, to come here. To cultivate what they had, give breath to the culinary elements that they both did, fusing ideas that had been theirs alone with ideas they had inherited and protected.

Inferno International Coffee had been drawn to them, despite itself. They had captured the Inferno. Captured Dante. And it didn't matter that the ideas of The Monkey's Paw would not be used, probably not even ruined through improvement but thrown away utterly. She knew they could not be destroyed, and that in the great, culinary meme-pool their ideas were now loose. To some, threatening enough to be feared.

Of course, implied compliment or otherwise, she hated Dante for it.

"They killed a girl who worked in the Money Mart," Jules said, finally.

"I heard about that." He was glad to hear her voice. The worst outcome, he thought, would have been for her to silently leave.

"The guy went running off down Hastings Street with a black plastic bag full of money." She shook her head and looked out the window again. "I heard that there was money coming out of the bag, streaming out onto the pavement behind him. He was carrying so much cash he couldn't even keep in all in the bag."

Jeremy grimaced appreciatively. "Desperate people."

"I hear he courted her. He sent her flowers and other presents for several months just to get to know her. He pretended all that time that he was attracted to her, that he really appreciated who she was."

Jeremy didn't say anything.

"People warned her about this guy," Jules said, shaking her head slowly. "Then he comes to the place at the very end of the night when she's alone. And he shoots her in the head."

"I don't know," Jeremy answered, mistaking this last detail for a question.

Jules turned now and looked directly at him: "No. He did. I'm telling you. He came after hours. She was trying to lock up. He talks sweet to her. She opens the door. Then he *shoots her right in the head.*"

Jeremy swallowed but held her eyes with his own. In the pale green you could also see tiny flecks of brown if you looked closely. He looked for them now but couldn't see them. You had to be closer, he thought. You had to be inside a breath's distance, on the lip of intimacy. They were flecks of something essential and eternally strong. He imagined them distributed throughout her, trace elements of something he connected with this strength, but she looked away firmly.

"Zeena thinks he's the Devil," Jules said.

Jeremy tried to laugh, unclear. "Who are we talking about?"

"Think about it," Jules said. "The way he looks and talks. That whispery mean-streets gangster schmooze. That shark-skinned, cloven-hooved, razor-striped, over-acquisitive,

Thatcher-era, glancey-eyed, price-of-everything, kind of put-the-boots-in bullshit. And he's got pointy ears. Top and bottom, ever notice that? Zeena pointed that out to me once. His ears taper at the top and the bottom. He looks like he should have a tail."

Then she got up and disappeared into the kitchen. Jeremy was left watching the doors swinging and settling. *Thwop thwip thip squeak.* Silence.

He sat in the window for another minute. He wanted to follow her, but the propranolol chose that moment to lick viciously through his bloodstream. He held the table edge, blackness sweeping up under his feet in a cold wave at the same time as the feverish prickling swept over his skin, microscopic, system-wide sweat production moistening the skin along his arms, down the backs of his legs, across his shoulders and over his entire scalp.

He held the table edge long enough to determine that it would sweep on through him and that he could, indeed, stand. And when he had wobbled back into the kitchen, Jules Capelli was gone, leaving the alley door ajar.

Jeremy was afforded the opportunity to discover how an irredeemably guilty conscience expressed itself. After all those years of early mornings and late nights, countless Camel Lights, and maybe more than his share of Irish whiskey, he would have expected a good long swing in the hammock to hit the spot. But not a half-hour went by in those first weeks when he did not think about his betrayal of Jules. The circumstances left him less than drifting—he was becalmed and agitated, a bad combination. And without constructive purpose, the sine wave of his week, of his life, simply switched off. He stopped drinking entirely. The weather turned sour. Clouds lowering the skyline, threatening rain. Not producing until he was well out of the apartment without his umbrella, at which point they would open in short, vindictive bursts. The streets would shine, then dry. The clouds would threaten again. Repeat.

Jeremy tried taking walks but found them dissatisfying. Quite aside from getting regularly doused, there were only two places he ever went. Two places he would end up. One was walking around the lagoon in Stanley Park. He found himself waiting for the Professor to emerge from the woods and was repeatedly disappointed when he didn't. This development was new and depressing. He realized he had no sure way of finding his father, and that without The Monkey's Paw, Caruzo wouldn't know where to find him.

Otherwise he'd launch himself out the front door of the Stanley Park Manor, walk numbly through the streets up through the West End towards downtown. He followed a track like a computer-controlled supertanker on the high seas. Only the end points mattered, the points on the arc were irrelevant. As a result, Jeremy would emerge from the Stanley Park Manor and (having opted not to go to the lagoon) would end up standing at the doors of the locked up Monkey's Paw.

He had keys, naturally, so he would go in and sit in the front room. Or, if it was getting dusty, he would sweep. If there were spiders in the big wash-basin, he would get out the disinfectant and do the entire prep area and the dish pit. He even polished the fish poachers once.

Dante phoned him at home at seven o'clock in the morning. They had spoken only once since Jeremy inked the deal and turned his back on the past. A short conversation, Dante in an airplane somewhere. Jeremy tried to bring up Jules—he found indignation, a small wedge of it—but Dante cut him off with a cold non sequitur before the name was even said.

Dante said: "From where I'm sitting, I can see mountains."

Jeremy said: "Pardon me?"

And Dante went on: "From where I am, I see the mountains. I see all of them. I see the entirety of a single one and the way they join together. I see the way they rise to points and fall away in snow-covered slopes. I see the way people die falling off them."

And then he had to go.

This time—Dante was actually at home, earthbound, porch-bound, in fact—Jeremy was sitting bright-eyed and bored silly staring out across the West End and Stanley Park. Gazing into the grey, sipping Postum. For some ridiculous reason he'd given up coffee too.

"I'm going to have some design people come over this week. What shape is the place in?" Dante asked.

"Clean," Jeremy said. "Real clean."

"All right. I want you to give them their space."

"Can I be there?"

"No. These are the design people. You are the food person."

"I have ideas."

Dante was not soliciting his opinion.

Jeremy forged ahead. "French Bistro."

"Sorry?"

"We make one. It would go down huge and I know the food. We won't need to change the room much."

"Jeremy, please." Dante sighed. "Let the vision emerge. Stay clear for the time being, enjoy your downtime."

He felt isolated by this last statement, but he had to admit he was also impressed. Dante had just opened a reported 25 million dollars' worth of Inferno locations in Chicago (Jeremy had been reading the paper cover to cover lately, even the Business Section) and yet when he gave ten minutes' worth of mental space to this little project of his Dante was able to bring a laser focus to bear. He nailed decisions, flowcharted the future, marshalled resources, delegated and disappeared. He got a lot done.

Authentic French Bistro. Well, he had to suggest something, and hadn't Jeremy been highly vocal over the years about his desire to capture what the Relais St. Seine l'Abbaye had been? What it meant to him to slide up the black iron shutters in the morning, to open up the doors and windows and release the not-unpleasant oaky-winey smell of the previous day? To see the ivy growing up and around the window boxes? To let the golden light flow into the wide, low wooden room? To work devotedly all week and then on Sunday to hear the shuffling rubber boots behind him as the farmers and their families took their places along the tables near the west wall?

"Bonjour," they'd say to Patrice. "Un demi blanc, s'il vous plaît."

And hadn't he regaled Zeena and Jules and Margaret, and anyone else who would listen, with inarticulate accounts of how he wanted to secure the spirit of that thing (the Relais) within the clay vessel of this thing (The Monkey's Paw)? But he never did, did he? Always the foodies and Brollywood types, and never the farmers. Always the polyglot kaleidoscope that was Crosstown and never the quiet, musty uniformity of rural France. The quality of spirit *there*, Jeremy now felt certain, simply couldn't be found *here*. Perhaps it was the right approach to merely capture the physical beauty of the *relais*. To take the clay vessel from somewhere else, as it were, and bring it on over to Crosstown to fill with whatever spirit lived here.

He went out walking after he spoke with Dante. Benny was working longer hours than before, and with The Paw off-limits he didn't feel he had anywhere else to go but the lagoon. Around and around, the water rippling in the breeze, occasionally spackled by raindrops. It took about twenty-five minutes to do a circuit, since Jeremy was walking very slowly and stopping periodically to watch the ducks and the racoons. Or letting himself stand stock-still at the shoreline and gaze out across the papery rushes and the steel-cold water towards the octagonal fountain, a hollowing pull like the force of suction forming within him as he drained empty of every sense but that of being alone.

The Professor was playing God. Silent in his swaying, green heaven, resolved not to reveal himself no matter what the entreaties. The trees stood thickly in their places, leaning and brailing one another with their bushy black-green fingers, forming a wet mass of separateness he could not enter. What would be the point? In the unlikely event he found the Professor's camp without guidance, how would he answer the questions that would then be posed?

"You fired Jules Capelli?" his father would ask, incredulous, his expression the soul of fatherly disbelief. *How could my seed contribute to such stupidity?* Or maybe he would say: "Babes in the Wood?" knowing well that Jeremy knew nothing more.

And so, guilty, irritated and with time on his hands, Jeremy stood in due course in the pizza-fragrant atrium of the library, shaking rain off his umbrella before going inside.

"Back for that Babes in the Wood file," Jeremy said when he saw that Gil was manning the Social Sciences desk.

Gil recognized Jeremy and offered something friendlier than a smirk, although not yet as unguarded as a smile.

"You just can't get enough, can you?" the librarian said.

"I have a problem."

In the carrel he took a deep breath, eyes on the ceiling, before diving in.

He read all the articles, top to bottom. When he finished each one he ticked it off on a separate list he had made and turned the sheets face down on the left side of the file folder. He drew a diagram on another piece of paper, a lopsided Stanley Park. He drew in the Reservoir Trail, where the bodies had been found. He marked the dates of death and discovery: 1947, 1953. He registered the fact that the bodies, thought to be a boy and girl for decades, surrendered the DNA of brothers when examined just a few years ago. He considered Miss Harker's story, plotting her course through the park as he imagined the day. He marked the spots where she had seen the woman with the children, entering the forest here, emerging near the bear cages over here, running through the rose gardens. He sketched the alternate routes she might have taken, looping into the forest and returning.

He turned next to the handwritten notes. They were journal entries, a careful record, although the handwriting was exceedingly scattered. Letters slanted different directions within a single word, words themselves floating free of the lines or sinking into the line below. The pages looked old, although they were not dated with a year. Maybe the writer had been caught up in the precise limits of the moment being lived, and the future (in this case the future reader) had been an impossible abstraction.

Jeremy took a breath, preparing himself, then read.

*Some introductory words:* [the text began]

*It should be understood that my interest in this place is long-standing. I have expected for some time that I should return here once my study achieved a certain focus, and that this return might represent the culmination of all previous work.*

Jeremy leaned back in his chair, rolled his head back and looked at the ceiling.

"God," he said. How had he not seen it coming? These words were, to say the least, somewhat *Professorial*.

Jeremy leaned forward again and considered the page more closely. The only thing wrong was the illegible handwriting, cursive but barely. Each letter, each stroke within each letter, was individual, separate from the word. As if the words might disassociate from one another any minute, the letters within each word disband and fly off the page.

The Professor had only a few pretensions in the material realm, but penmanship and fine writing accoutrements were definitely two. Jeremy recalled him signing field trip approval slips with a LeGrand Montblanc Bordeaux, and for special occasions unsheathing a huge Pelikan fountain pen made of bottle-green glass with inlaid silver birds. His handwriting matched the equipment: elegant, aloof and singular. Broad, flat strokes (only a particular obscure nib would do) leaning distinctly left on the page, despite the Professor being right-handed. It was so dense and consistent from top to bottom that a complete page of his writing had a distinctive uniform brocade. And then there were the touches. The final *r* in Papier, for example. It didn't finish in the little dimpled anthill you were taught in penmanship classes, but formed itself like the printed *r*, a haughtier letter entirely: a short, sharp vertical stroke, with a flaring finish, tapering dramatically up and to the right. The same way, every time.

Someone with bad handwriting and a similar interest? Was there anyone with a similar interest? A colleague?

Jeremy read on.

*What I couldn't have known is that Miss Harker would provide this focus. Witnesses, after all, are not my interest. The murder of the Babes in the Wood, as a murder in itself, was not really my concern. And yet I was interested in this girl, in how she had acted out her heartbreak at leaving Vancouver among these trees on the same day as the murder. And how by doing so she had unwittingly cemented herself into the story, into the landscape from which she had been uprooted, the same landscape of which these children had become a tragic part.*

*I went and interviewed her earlier this year. We had tea, spoke at length. She told me the things I knew already: the woman, the two children. But she told me something else, far more interesting. She told me of a premonition, a vision that unfolded under a cloud of fear. She thought she might have fainted; she found herself on her back, the forest rising above her. The air was suddenly dark and in the darkness the forest was filled with people, with sounds.*

*When she came to, there had been a young man there. Skinny and ragged. He disappeared into the forest, but he had touched her forehead as she lay. She knew so, she said, from a smudge she found there later.*

*Enter Caruzo. I have wondered about his role, and this visit (after many) I am determined to lay this matter finally to rest. I hope he will answer my questions. I hope also that I can last. This work presents a mental and physical test. Tonight, to begin, I will hike across the hillside a safe distance and set up my own camp.*

*August 13*
*Drizzling at seven-thirty in the evening...*

There followed a week of weather reports, while the author waited for Caruzo to reappear. Then, a little further down:

*August 21*
*We aren't talking about much yet, but he has consented to show me around. Caruzo, for the record: tall and heavy, 230 pounds. Age difficult to guess: fifty, sixty even. Large nose. Black and grey, distant eyes; he is caked in evidence of his surroundings. Dirt lines his face and neck and lives under his nails.*

*What I know about his past is limited. He speaks of voices. He was institutionalized at one point. Received electroshock. Schizophrenia, I believe.*

*He carries nothing, has no evident totem. No toby. Talks in riddles, repeating words like incantations. His are mad, angelic ramblings.*

The weather reports and geographic detail resumed as Caruzo slipped out of reach into the forest. Jeremy skimmed down two weeks to find where the story resumed.

*September 9*

*Caruzo has returned. Two excellent days of work. He talks lately of our estrangement: from the earth, from "the garden." He said something very odd: "The two are meant to be together. Just as the two were drawn from the same soil, so too must the same soil hold them, and through it must they be reconciled."*

*He speaks of the children, I'm sure. As if the wrong might be righted by his long presence here. And I sense it is a long time. When asked, he did not appear to know that it is 1987.*

*Will the '90s bring better things for him? I don't think anyone in the city yet understands what he might be saying, what he might represent: the first of a latter-day generation that will live as he does.*

*An aside: Dr. Tully hung up on me this morning. He rejects this data gathering technique. "We do not believe that anecdote is evidence," he said.*

*On other fronts, Hélène grieves. I have broken with my normal practice and begun to call. Each time there are many, many tears.*

Jeremy pulled his head out of the carrel sharply. When it came, he thought, understanding came suddenly.

*1987. Hélène.*

Jeremy hunched back over the yellow pages, reading and rereading the sentences with a new hunger.

*Mid-September*

*I have been granted sick leave.*

*September 24*

*I have begun to feel less like a visitor and more like a resident, an altogether unexpected pleasure. Caruzo has shown me much. He has covered my tent with maple leaves that overlap downwards and spread onto the ground. In the wet they facilitate run-off and minimize flooding.*

*I have lately begun to realize how permanent this arrangement could be. Caruzo has shown me a simple snare for squirrels, a lasso of* copper electrical wire. He has shown me how to catch starlings on a stick with peanut butter and glue. Ducks may be netted, although the technique is fiendishly difficult. I am changed by this selective and respectful harvest. The bounty of the park, given up to those who care to know it, binds us to it.

*Last week of September*

We have had the long-awaited breakthrough. We were eating, talking little. Without prompting, he repeated something he said weeks ago: "The two are meant to be together."

Who? I pressed.

He saw the children. Frankie and Johnny, he calls them. He saw them enter the forest with their mother. He followed at a distance. He saw the girl, Miss Harker, lying in the path. He stopped over her. He touched her face and she woke. Startled him. He ran into the forest. He crashed in circles, became lost. The children were gone.

*October*

He is gone a week and I am afraid for him. For myself. I have pneumonia and cannot sleep for terrible fever dreams.

Last night there were children outside my tent. I cannot describe it any other way except to say that I was awakened by their glow. I was afraid, filled with unknowable fear. Through the nylon walls of my tent I saw the yellow and orange light, and I began to shake uncontrollably. I began to weep.

A boy's voice, a small boy, said: "Come out."

I crawled out into the ferns. He was crouched near the fire pit, with a stick in his hand, poking the coals back to life. The little girl stood next to him, silent. She held a duck, by the neck. It had just been killed.

"Are you hungry?" the boy asked me, looking at me, through me. I didn't answer. I was numb.

He stood away from the fire. He looked like any number of boys I have seen swinging on swings or playing with matches over the years.

The girl held the duck up towards me and smiled.

I woke remembering this scene, disturbed. I climbed from my tent *and down through the forest to the men's room at Second Beach. Caruzo has shown me how a pane of glass can be removed from the rear of the structure, allowing one to use the hot water before the front door is unlocked. I washed at the basin, feeling a strange stillness stretching away all around me.*

*I paused on the trail, walking back, thinking of all that I had learned. I saw myself here for many years, as he has been. As they have been, the two children. And with this thought came another, a sweeping thought of Hélène. In the cool of the morning, in the dew and across cold pavement I made my way to a pay phone. I phoned her, needing to hear her voice. Needing her to understand what must come next. She didn't answer. The phone rang and rang.*

*Part of me wishes to submerge here, to understand perhaps finally the lesson about all places that is buried here. But I will return to my other home instead. Return and repair what damage I may have done.*

*I still don't know if he found the children, but I believe he searched for a very long time. Years even. And at some point, his searching turned to guarding, of a memory, a site of memories that might be made holy through his steadfast watching, through his resolution to remember. Somehow he has remained and become the first, again. Resident zero in the new community that has grown here.*

*I will remember the following strange words: "... meant to be together. Just as the two were drawn from the same soil, so too must the same soil hold them, and through it must they be reconciled."*

*The others are drawn to his vigilance.*

Jeremy was almost entirely numb by the time he had finished reading. Numb and oddly frightened. He walked to the washroom on stiff legs, washed his face at the stainless steel basin. It was as close as he had ever returned to those moments of blinding grief. As he stood at the mirror, water running from his face, he wondered what his father could have felt standing in the men's room at Second Beach that day. He imagined having made the same discovery.

This living theatre of rootedness, born in tragedy and thriving in the person of Caruzo. Ignorant for just those few remaining hours of the strange tragedy that had already fallen in his own life. In their life. He could not know how the two of them were about to diverge. First fleeing one another, and then, brought together again by their twinned obsessions: seeking.

At the Social Sciences desk Gil was atypically gregarious.

"Well . . . ," he asked, "how was that?"

"Fine," Jeremy said. It was necessary to be out of this place.

Gil smiled a narrow smile. "You read the notes. Crazy, hey?"

"No. I don't think so."

"You're a writer," Gil guessed. "A TV writer. You write for *The X-Files* or no, wait, *Last Chapter*."

Jeremy shook his head. "I'm a chef."

Gil was suitably surprised.

"The notes. They appeared in the file one day, unexplained," Jeremy ventured.

Gil nodded. "A few years ago. I assumed they were intended for someone. Maybe you know who wrote them."

"I'm pretty sure I do," Jeremy said.

"Well, take 'em then." He warmed discernibly. He took the file, extracted the notes and handed them to Jeremy. "So, where do you cook?"

"The Monkey's Paw Bistro," Jeremy said, proud to speak of it. "That's my restaurant."

"What kind of food?" Gil asked.

Jeremy was about to explain urban rubber-boot food to Gil. He was about to grow enthusiastic about local bounty, about the soil under their feet, about the richness of knowing what that soil could offer, when it came to him rather starkly that his restaurant was closed.

"That *was* my restaurant," he said. "In fact, it's closed now. It's reopening, eventually. *We're* reopening. I have a partner.

But there will be another restaurant. A new one. New name and everything."

He stopped talking.

"Hey, if you're sure," Gill said, and with that he spun and wheeled away.

He made one last visit to The Paw to remove things from the kitchen that he didn't want touched by the designers, whoever they were going to be. The Fugami blade of course, but also some of his smaller knives and favourite utensils (a green Vaseline glass lemon juicer, by contrapuntal example).

When he was finished he stood for a moment with his loaded box and looked around. The Zone. The blackened range, towering still. The familiar black and white tiles of the floor. The swinging door into the dining room.

"Goodbye," he said aloud, then noticed that Jules had left one of her chef's jackets hanging on the back of a shelving unit. He picked it up and turned it over in his hands. The heavy white cloth was lightly stained at the cuffs and across the front. Stained with some simple dish they had jointly created. He fingered the embroidered *Capelli* on the left breast. He began instinctively folding it, folding in the dirty sleeves onto the breast, doubling down the jacket onto itself.

And then, without warning, he was crying. Bawling, mewling, blubbering. He found himself saying aloud: "What?" As this riptide swept around him, his mouth and nose filling with mucus. "What?" he said, hands to his temples now as Jules's jacket dropped to the floor. His shoulders were shaking with convulsions, eyes seized shut, mouth agape, slick strands of viscous fluid connecting his upper and lower teeth and lips. "What?"

*"You don't like that we might be working on parallel projects,"* the Professor had once said to him. He might have made the

comment years before. They were feasting on a canvasback together. A bird plucked from the lagoon, spit-roasted simply.

His head was spinning. He picked up the jacket and wiped his face with it, paused. He wondered what his father had done, packing away her clothes. He pushed his face back into the safety of that stained cloth. There was a residual smell of her, not perfume of course but sweat. A tired smell, an end-of-the-night smell. The smell of their hugs after things had really worked.

God help me, thought Jeremy, standing with his face still buried.

He lifted his head from the damp jacket, which he stuffed into the cardboard box on top of his knives. Looking up, he saw the lumpy, rain-soaked figure standing there regarding him.

"Jesus!" His whole body jerked back in surprise.

"Hey, hey. Hey."

"Caruzo." He was almost yelling. "Don't do that! You scared me."

"Smoke, Jay?"

So they smoked together, Jeremy's hands shaking. Caruzo was looking around the place, nodding, not understanding why the lights were out. Saying nothing for a long time.

"Hey, Jay. Know something? Wanna know something. I never cry. True. Never cry. Not even once. Not then. Not now."

"Forget it, would you? As a favour, just forget it."

But now Caruzo was staring blankly at him, having moved on from the particulars of the incident. He had something else to say.

"OK, why? Why don't you cry, Caruzo?"

"No ducts," Caruzo said, exhaling smoke. "I got no ducts. No ducts at all. Anywhere in my head. No ducts. My head is defective that way."

"Because you have no ducts," Jeremy said.

"My old man had no ducts neither," Caruzo said.

Jeremy smoked and nodded. "Both my old man *and* I have ducts," he said to Caruzo.

Jeremy might have guessed that was Caruzo's point all along. "You do," Caruzo said to him. "Ducks and ducts. Your old man. You too. Ducts and ducks."

Jeremy began to laugh. It was a satisfactory alternative to crying, although it too required ducts. He laughed until a different kind of tears came down his cheeks. Caruzo laughed along politely with him, a steady dry chuckle.

"You have time," Caruzo said, when they were finished. "You have some time today, tomorrow?"

"I have time," Jeremy said, taking a last draw on his cigarette.

"You coming to the park maybe?" Caruzo said. "Coming on down to the woods?"

I am, Jeremy thought, nodding to Caruzo. I most certainly am.

# STROMOVKA

"Dinner. Yeah?" Caruzo was saying.

The Professor looked at Jeremy.

"Dinner," Jeremy agreed. "I'll cook."

"Hooray," Caruzo said, then crashed off into the bush.

Jeremy glanced after him, then over to his father.

The Professor shrugged. "It's best not to try and understand his comings and goings," he said. "He'll be back."

The Professor had been proudly displaying his new snare. "Observe," he said to Jeremy now. He unfolded a white cane that he had pulled from his knapsack. "The net was a dead giveaway. But it is remarkable, really, how the blind are left alone. Police, especially. It embarrasses them."

"You pretend to be blind?"

"When I walk the park trails near public spaces, I use the cane. It took some trial and error," the Professor said, snapping together the cane into a single 4 1/2-foot length. He paused here for a second. "The original idea was to fasten my Swiss Army knife to the tip like a spear."

Jeremy shook his head.

"Precisely. A violent, uncertain undertaking. I maimed a squirrel, I'm afraid. Never caught him. Caruzo was quite upset with me."

"I read it," Jeremy said, interrupting.

The Professor stopped what he was doing, his hand at the

tip of the white cane. He looked lost for a moment. "You see, the knife was fastened poorly. On impact it did not pierce firmly. It buckled instead—"

"The file, the notes, everything," Jeremy said.

The white cane balanced in his father's hands. "You understand," the Professor said finally.

"I think so. I understand that when she and I came together to Lost Lagoon, when you were away, she came to be near you." He told his father how they had fed eggs to the racoons, about her laughter. "We didn't come the final time in 1987, of course. I was gone myself, too old by then. She was alone."

The Professor nodded slowly.

"Did you come back here afterwards? When I was in France?"

"Oh, no," the Professor said, exhaling a large breath. "I took a long break afterwards."

Jeremy had many other questions he wanted to ask. "Is there any chance Caruzo did it?" he said finally. "Killed the children, the Babes in the Wood?"

"None," the Professor answered.

"But he saw them. He followed them on the day they died, was distracted by the girl, Miss Harker, lying prostrate on the path—"

"Supine, technically," the Professor said.

"—and by the time he remembered the children, they were gone," Jeremy finished. "What do you think?"

"I think this project will be the last major work I do."

Jeremy allowed himself to be deflected from his line of questioning.

"I can't do it forever. It has killed before, and now, appropriately enough, it's killing *me*."

"Don't say that," Jeremy said, exasperated and troubled. He turned away from his father.

"Your work is killing you too. You are younger, granted, so it is killing you at a slower rate. But it is killing you nevertheless."

"Fine," Jeremy said, turning back. "I'm dying at some rate appropriate to my age. I will even accept that I killed something by giving up The Monkey's Paw, my project. What I don't accept is that either of us are dying in any real way, beyond the way that is synonymous with living: day-to-day choices, some bad ones, but continuing. Sure I destroyed something, but I'll create something else far better, far more powerful, just as you have done here."

"I'm a little more tired than before," the Professor said quietly and truthfully.

"Move in with me. I've offered before. Use my apartment as base camp. I want to see this work complete, behind you."

It was always a mixed feeling with those you loved the most, the Professor thought. The boy's words made him proud and worried at the same time. But what different feelings could he possibly inspire in his son?

Jeremy broke the silence with a question. "Had she been sick?"

"In truth, I don't know," the Professor said. "I was told sudden heart failure. *Arrhythmogenic right-ventricular dysplasia.* The heart skips a beat, inserts two where there should be one, syncopates. You die."

He watched Jeremy as these words came out. They were riding back together over the years, full of their joined memories. And observing this reaction in his son, the Professor opened some part of himself that had been closed for a long time.

"She was unique, Jeremy. As a woman, certainly. As a person too. She lived a critical paradox, embodied a complete contradiction. I knew it when I met her—I was drawn to it. I knew it more as the years went by. But I never fully knew it during her life."

The Professor took a breath. Jeremy found he was holding his own.

"In my work, as you know, I have made a lifetime of examining the evidence of the root or its absence. All people, I have observed, will reveal two things in this regard if you look at them from the right angle. The first is an innate polarity, a tendency to either root or move. The second is evidence of the alternative that has been foregone. In my parkade, those years ago, you could say there were only the homeless. Indeed, many people said precisely that, Dr. Tully included. But lived among, talked with, clothed similarly to, *learned from* these homeless were observed to include both the derelict and the celebrant. And each of these, in turn, revealed evidence of the life left behind, tracings of despair and of manic joy, broken and rejuvenated spirits. My job, you might say, has been the mapping of these qualities within the community. For in this topography, I have come to believe, is the seed of how we live. From this relationship people strike with their physical earth, from this intercourse is borne our understanding of many many things: home, culture, language . . . "

The Professor looked at his son for evidence of understanding.

"Food," Jeremy said.

"Crucially, yes," the Professor said, relieved.

"It is trite to observe," he continued, "that in the West we are uprooting ourselves. We know the culprits: information flow, economic globalization. Trite and, for me, not professionally engaging. For me it has always been the individual, the calculated or imposed decision, the personal evidence of allegiance to, or repudiation of, the soil."

The Professor stopped to think. He handled the white cane very gently. Folding it again as he thought.

"She lived in the middle ground somewhere," Jeremy said.

The Professor nodded. "Yes. I think she did."

"She and I built a lean-to once and slept outside," Jeremy said. "I don't think I ever told you this story. In the backyard. 1976 or 1977. We cooked a chicken over the fire. She crushed garlic into olive oil and brushed it on with rosemary branches."

"She was intensely proud of what we had here," the Professor said. "Intensely proud of you, of our house and new citizenship, even of me for a long time. In that sense she was a celebrant of the changes that her family had brought about, happily turned aside from the road life, from itinerant trading, from the *vardo*."

"She missed it more than you realized."

"Not that so much. It was as if she put down roots and they did not take. I understand now that she might have succeeded were it not for me. When it became apparent to her, she fell back into a place of no places. Unrooted but constrained, capable of celebrating neither. And stranded in this way, she became the key to all of what has consumed me, capturing the universe of my studies in the small frame of a single, very beautiful person."

Around them the air stretched cool and still.

"I loved her," the Professor said. "Much more than any of that, I miss her terribly."

They embraced, and they weren't father and son for those moments. Had they been, the embrace would have parted much sooner, each conscious of the many small abrasions that rough the surface of that most complicated of loves. This time they embraced as two people who had set out to travel around the world at the Equator, leaving the same spot on the same day, travelling opposite directions. And who, some time later and quite exhausted, have met again at precisely the opposite side of the world. Face to face again, half the journey complete.

They caught squirrels together and walked down Cathedral Trail towards the sea. The squirrels bounced in a plastic bag against Jeremy's leg. "Returning to the Babes in the Wood," he said.

"A tragedy," the Professor said.

"I'm trying to understand," Jeremy admitted.

"Me too," the Professor said, and some light re-entered his voice. "There are pieces remaining."

They returned to camp by a different route, climbing out along the seawall, then sharply up, climbing cliffs to find an abandoned path. From there, they backtracked into the forest, looping through the falling darkness, finally tumbling between two leaning trees and into the Professor's space.

Caruzo was there. The fire was lit and a grill lay over it, ready for the squirrels. Jeremy guessed the grill had once been the side of a shopping cart.

"You remember the place?" the Professor asked. Gesturing around them.

"Of course, of course," Jeremy said, looking now and enjoying the familiarity of it. "And the tent?"

The Professor gestured silently, and following his finger Jeremy could make out a shape. A leaf-covered shape nestled in at the base of one of the trees. *Facilitating run-off and minimizing flooding*, Jeremy recalled.

"There's been some rain lately," the Professor said, but was interrupted by the sound of leaves crushing. Branches being pushed aside.

Jeremy started, got to his feet, but the Professor motioned him to sit again. "Pieces remaining," he said.

"What about them?" Jeremy asked, as the crashing came nearer.

"I wonder whether you will agree that Chladek is one of them," the Professor said.

And into the orange glimmer, which just managed to push off the darkness of the clearing, stepped the man himself.

Chladek's voice had the clip and precision of an educated Czech, although his face had blunted features, a kinked and flattened nose like a boxer's. He wore a heavy, black woollen overcoat, which he kept wrapped around him. Found footwear.

During dinner there had been only a little conversation. Afterwards, the Professor and Caruzo abandoned them, over Jeremy's objections, crashing off into the bush on some unspoken errand. Jeremy sipped his wine, a sugar-sweet ruby plonk not half-badly suited to the squirrels. He turned to Chladek, determined to draw him out.

Not an unmitigated success. Caruzo was the Patron Saint of Stanley Park, the only statement Chladek was prepared to make on the matter.

"Siwash?" Jeremy tried.

Really, really crazy, Chladek said. He held out his hands about a foot apart to describe the blackened knife that Siwash apparently carried.

Hmmmm. Jeremy thought. What were the chances? His Sabatier now riding around in Siwash's waistband, waiting for the trigger count, the obscure day of reckoning. "And you?" he asked, pressing on. "What brings you here?"

Chladek produced a bottle of Stolichnaya from the folds of his coat. He looked at the bottle, then at Jeremy.

"Let's walk," he said, gesturing with his head into the blackness.

They pushed themselves up out of the cool ferns and off into the darkness, making their way through the brambles and salal bushes, tracing the edge of the cliff. Chladek talked as they picked their way. He was thirty-five. He'd been a journalist at the *Prague Evening* newspaper until the Velvet Revolution in 1989, when he left the country, disillusioned, to ramble the world.

They started up a rock incline that stretched towards the purple night sky.

"I leave Czechoslovakia in 1989," Chladek said over his shoulder. "Sometime after Students' Day. November seventeenth. This is the beginning of our Velvet Revolution. Václav Havel and the students, you know this story maybe?"

Jeremy didn't very well, but Chladek was skipping across the details, homing in on his point. In communist Czechoslovakia, there had been demonstrations and counter-demonstrations on Students' Day for decades. Sometimes violent. But November 17, 1989—with the gale of new ideas blowing through Eastern Europe at that time—was expected to be an especially troubled day.

At the top of the rock face, they climbed over a chainlink fence. "November fifteenth," Chladek was saying, "two days before the official rallies, there is a counter-demonstration in a place called Stromovka."

Chladek looked over at Jeremy, who shook his head.

"Stromovka: the place of trees."

Chladek described a park at the centre of Prague. Very old, very beautiful, loved by many people. And he described how earlier in 1989, the Communists had announced their intention to put a highway through the middle of it.

Jeremy made a sympathetic face.

"Exactly," Chladek said. "But a good excuse for a demonstration."

Things went poorly. The police beat up the demonstrators, along with any journalist impudent enough to cover such an event. Some were jailed, but far more were given the common punishment of being driven five miles out of the city and dropped there. Chladek was swept up among them and found himself on a frozen roadside at midnight, without money and with a very long walk home.

Students' Day, 1989, dawned with portent. The official Communist rally at Vysehard Castle in the middle of Prague drew twelve thousand people, including many of the Stromovka demonstrators and students who had heard about those events. Chladek joined the crowds in his new joint-capacity as victim and journalist. The young people lit candles and sang sad Czech songs. It was beautiful.

"Well," Chladek said, after a fortifying slug of vodka, "you cannot tell twelve thousand Czech people to go home once they have lighted candles and begun to sing sad songs. Everyone now wants to hear Václav Havel speak. 'Havel Havel Havel,' we call out...."

Havel, perhaps wisely, wasn't there. And although a rousing speech from the poet and activist might have satisfied the gathered throng, without him, without his words, the demonstration became restless. It became mobile.

"Now people in the crowd are calling out: 'Václavské námesti! Wenceslas Square!'" Chladek said, pushing the vodka into Jeremy's hands, his eyes glistening with remembrance.

It was forbidden to demonstrate in Wenceslas Square, but even Chladek wanted to see twelve thousand candles lit next to the river. To see the older people leaning out their windows in wonder, up and down the streets connecting to the square.

The crowd entered Národni Avenue, proud but frightened. There were riot police at the top of the avenue, "whiteheads" as they were known for their helmets. They stood in rows, three deep, armed with wooden clubs, blocking the way into the square. Fearing the worst, the students sat in the street, and there followed picturesque moments of uncertainty. Groups of students holding lit candles in their hands. Sitting in front of the ranks of police. Chladek took photos, moving through the crowd.

And then the police fell on them. Through his lens, Chladek saw the clubs rising and falling in the candlelight. He saw students rolled into balls as they were kicked. As they were beaten bloody, as their arms and legs and noses were broken.

"And all the time the students are crying, '*Máme holé ruce!*'" Chladek said, breathing hard. "It means: 'We are bare-handed. We have nothing in our hands.' Do not beat us. *Máme holé ruce.*"

Chladek was pulled from the crowd himself. Pushed against a wall. Three young policemen beat his ribs and his legs, practised and methodical. Broke his nose.

His camera was last. As Chladek described the end of his beating, his hands gripping the railing in front of them, eyes out across the view he was not seeing. His beautiful Leica. The police told him to run and, as he did so, the camera arced over his head and smashed into the street in front of him. It crunched underfoot but he did not stop.

The remembrance of this last detail exhausted Chladek. He took a break during which Jeremy lit them both cigarettes.

"The Velvet Revolution," Jeremy said.

Chladek shook his head. Drank some, smoked some, grimaced. "Very velvet, isn't it?" he said eventually.

They walked up past the flower bed with the marigolds spelling *Prospect Point*. Past the concession, where Chladek stopped at the garbage cans and rifled through the uppermost layer of refuse. They walked in silence down the Park Drive and to the middle of a mossy stone bridge that crossed the causeway, then cut down the embankment and strolled out onto the Lions Gate Bridge itself. The black water of the inlet unfolded beneath them as Chladek picked up the story again.

In the days following the beatings, a rumour swirled through Prague that there had been a martyr. A mathematics student, Martin Smid, beaten to death. Killed for the cause, like students before him. The symmetry of history was tragic and compelling. The country felt changed. Chladek, too, noticed things about himself.

"I felt good," Chladek said, walking slowly towards the crest of the bridge. "I have a big white bandage across my face, and I am limping everywhere, but I feel very, very good. What I think at any time seems right, yes? I understand everything. You know this feeling?"

Jeremy didn't think he did.

Not a bad feeling overall, Chladek said, knowing everything. He woke up that morning, heard about Smid, and half an hour later he understood all that had happened in Czechoslovakia in the past two days, all that had ever happened in Czech history, all that had ever happened, period. World history. The history of humanity.

"So clear to me," Chladek said, remembering.

He wrote an increasing number of articles from this point onward. Three in the single day following the emergence of Smid's story. Seven the following day. Seven again the next day. Ten a day at his manic peak.

"About Smid?" Jeremy asked.

"About the Devil. How he has come again to Czechoslovakia."

He met with his editor on a Monday. The time off that his editor gave him (a reward for excellent work, he was told) allowed him to participate more fully in the events that then followed. Demonstrations daily that grew out of control. Ten days later there were a million people in downtown Prague. The city, the country, stood still.

They had reached the apex of the bridge. Here there was a steel maintenance ladder that lead from the railing down a dozen feet to a catwalk hanging beneath the bridge. Use of the ladder was forbidden in French and English on a small wooden sign affixed to the railing, but also prevented more strenuously with a grating that was secured over the ladder with various locks and shields. Chladek surprised Jeremy by producing a screwdriver from his jacket pocket, and further by how easily he used it to unlock the grate, which swung aside and offered them access to the platform below.

"Chladek. I don't think so."

Chladek disappeared over the railing into the howling blackness.

Jeremy stuck his head over the rail. His stomach dropped even at that, the distance to the water telescoping into countless miles. He'd heard about jumpers. Nobody lived. At this height the Burrard Inlet was like a sheet of concrete. You broke into pieces on impact.

"Come down," Chladek yelled up from the catwalk, his words faint.

"Not a chance in hell," Jeremy yelled back, feeling the vodka swirling in his veins.

Chladek turned and looked out over the water. Then back up at Jeremy. "The park," he said, waving out into the blackness behind him, "as you will never see it."

When he got down, Jeremy's gut was in turmoil, but he turned, hands gripping the railing, and the park did spread out away from him in a way he didn't expect to see soon again. Above them, the underbelly of the Lions Gate Bridge, a sounding board that boomed with traffic. Directly below, the foaming sea, cut just now by a freighter that surged in towards a berth at the terminal. Across the water, the park. The face of the park, Jeremy thought. He had always thought that the park turned away from the city. Presented the tumult of downtown with a turned shoulder. From here, hanging in this sympathetic darkness, displaced entirely from any roadway or city vantage point, transgressing to see this sight. Here the park faced you, its expression one of knowing and familiarity.

Chladek spread his arms in the wind that swept around them, enveloping them in its briny fragrance.

"At one demonstration, Jeremy," he called out, voice raised against the wind, "I remember the people in Václavské náměsti, and a little boy in front of this crowd. He is six, seven, ten, I don't know. A little boy in a white shirt and black hair, and he plays the violin so beautifully that people are crying. A million people weep in Wenceslas Square. And I knew then that an angel has joined the fight. An angel for our Devil, I think. I wrote some more articles."

"And the Communists fell," Jeremy shouted. "Your angel won."

"The Devil won," Chladek shouted back, opening his eyes and grinning. "Smid was a lie."

A real person, just not dead. His death was a rumour spread by the Secret Police, spread to generate dissent and unrest among the students. The rumour was designed to motivate further demonstrations, to provoke riots that would justify martial law.

Chladek pressed the bottle into Jeremy's hands. "We're almost done," he said. "Drink."

Jeremy was now drunk enough that the alcohol was vibrating within him. His eyes felt bright and alert. His thoughts supple, strong, sharp-edged.

And so, Chladek continued, what had begun in Stromovka had now ended like this. He learned the truth about Smid on the seventh day of a week-long period during which he slept not a single hour. He had written over 70,000 words, he guessed, none of them published by the *Prague Evening*. He had phoned every person he had ever known, telling them what he knew.

Then Smid turned out to be a lie.

"Smid the martyr is shit," Chladek said, his eyes filling with dark rage. Then he wound up and threw the bottle out over the blackness. It hung suspended, released a tendril of remaining vodka, then glinted off downward to its faintly audible impact against a bridge stanchion and a glittering distribution of shards over the black water.

"Night cap," Chladek said when they reached his camp—a filthy foam mattress and a tangled pile of clothes spilling out of a yellow plastic milk crate. "You know Becherovka?"

They sat on rocks, opposite one another. Jeremy accepted the heavy green rectangular bottle and took a sip. It smelled of cloves, tasted herbal.

"Why?" Jeremy asked. "Why leave? Why come here?"

After learning of Smid, Chladek went back to his apartment

and slept for fourteen days. By the time he woke up, Havel was the president. The country was already changing, already forgetting.

"Forgetting we win our freedom in a Devil's cheat," Chladek said. He travelled for two years, disgusted. He wrote many more unpublished stories about how it is to be swept up in the winds of history. Chased by the Devil from Stromovka and across the face of the world.

He arrived in Vancouver on a break-bulk carrier riding empty from Hong Kong to fill up with Albertan grain. He befriended a fellow Czech named Kvetomil, who had ingratiated himself with the Filipino captain. Christmas Eve, 1991, they jumped ship at Ballantyne Pier and spent the night at the Balmoral Hotel on Hastings Street. Christmas Day, feeling greatly nostalgic, they splurged for Becherovka and went out looking for a good Christmas meal.

"For a Czech this is a great feast, yes?" Chladek said, sipping from the green bottle. "Goose and ham and many other things."

At the mission on Carrall Street, the two travellers waited patiently in line. They sipped their Becherovka. Kvetomil wiped away tears at the thought of home, and they looked forward to a hot meal. Forty minutes later they were served a bologna sandwich and a box of something called Tropical Splash.

Jeremy laughed loudly.

"Now we are outside and Kvetomil looks like...," Chladek widened his eyes, aping Kvetomil's slow awakening. "'Yes, Kvetomil!' I say to him. 'This is Christmas dinner! Happy Christmas!' I throw my sandwich in the garbage and turn to Kvetomil and I say, 'Fuck!' I scream. I can think of nothing else to say. I say it over and over. 'Fuck, fuck, fuck, fuck, Kvetomil.'"

They finished the Becherovka walking down Alexander Street, heading no particular direction. They spent the last of their money on a six-pack of Molson Canadian that they carried in a paper bag, looking for a suitable place to sit and drink. It was late in the day. A wet darkness was falling. They walked right out of the city and into a dense forest.

"Kvetomil says, 'Look, we are in Alaska.'"

It was raining lightly, but there the water didn't make it to the ground. The forest was an umbrella. It was blue darkness. It was salt, pine, earth. "Look, Kvetomil," Chladek said. "Stromovka. I have returned to the place of trees."

Ducks flew by. There were swans in the water. There were geese just there, sitting up on the lawn, plump on their bellies. Chladek's head was clearing.

"Here is Canada goose for Canadian Christmas."

Chladek stopped talking. He smoked silently for a few seconds.

"Kvetomil says to me, 'We don't need a goose, I have my bologna sandwich still. Now you must thank me for being the smart one.'" Chladek smiled. "So I thank him. I think I even kiss him. And I take his sandwich, and even though the bird will not eat the bologna, he likes the bread very much."

They ate the goose in the forest past Prospect Point, down the embankment near the bridge.

"Not far from here," Chladek said, pointing.

Kvetomil returned to the ship the following day, chastened by a night outdoors.

Jeremy lay back in the leaves and smoked as the story wound to a close. The bridge traffic had slowed to just one car at a time, thumping overhead. In the silent stretches between cars, Chladek's voice grew quieter and quieter. Jeremy finished his smoke and flicked it in the general direction of the sea.

Chladek's speech was now very faint.

"What begins in the place of trees, now ends in the place of trees."

There was silence all around. Filling him and stretching away. Jeremy could feel a distinct rotation, the globe spinning under him, spinning through the blackness, not throwing him off but holding him firmly, as if he were a part of it.

Chladek was snoring.

Jeremy staggered to his feet and off into the blackness. It was not good to be so drunk, he remembered thinking, seconds before sprawling headlong across a root. He scraped his palm but did not bleed. He stood, swaying, and tried to listen to the forest. He imagined that he could navigate through its soundscape, that it would guide him home. And from the trees now drifted the sounds he had heard on nights before, broken up into shards and distributed through the watery air. A piece of a laugh. A fragment of a word. The upper arc of a groan wrung out during sex. Caruzo's foot on dried arbutus leaves, crunching as he ran through the forest. The Professor rolling over inside his nylon sleeping bag. Babies crying under the bruised sky, shifting in this soil.

"Stromovka," he said aloud. "This place of trees."

He fell twice more. The second time he cut open his chin and bled impressively.

He was in a dark place, he was stumbling down a path, then off the path. Through bushes. He was in a clearing ringed with low brush. The moss was deep, his feet sank as if the earth might take him down. Consume him. He slipped again, falling to one knee. He struggled up, now covered in dirt and blood, the ground slick.

There was a person here. A person standing quite close.

"Chladek," he called out. The form was still and glowed light green. It was large.

"Caruzo," he tried.

Silence. It was dark. He was drunk. There was mud in his eyes.

"Say something," he said.

"Something," the form said. And it had a beautiful voice, with deep resonant tones.

Jeremy considered the possibility that he was dreaming.

He sat down on the moss.

"Get up," the voice said, musically, pleasantly. But it was an order.

Jeremy got up. The form regarded him, holding something high in each hand. Something green that glowed, something like blackened chrome that winked at him.

"Do you have any idea where you are?" The figure asked.

"Stromovka," Jeremy tried.

The voice recited numbers. "North forty-nine, eighteen, thirty-two point five," it said.

"What...," Jeremy began, frightened by this flat, impenetrable answer.

"Don't interrupt," the voice answered. "West one hundred and twenty-three, nine, nineteen."

The earth sped up and centrifugal forces overwhelmed those of gravity. Jeremy felt his feet come away from the leaves and the moss as the violence of that spin broke his hold on the earth. His cheek hit the ground before he knew he was falling.

There were a number of voices now. An argument had broken out. Somebody was crashing away into the bush, cursing, hacking at the salal with a stick or a machete.

"Chladek?" he called.

"Jeremy." The word said so quietly. So close.

"Where's Chladek?"

"Get up, come on," said the Professor.

"Where we going?"

"Out. You're going out."

His father had his arm around him now, helping him walk. "Christ, you are pissed as a newt."

"Yes. I am."

"Learn anything?"

"The Devil," Jeremy said, "visits from time to time."

"Ah yes," said the Professor. His voice had been gentle.

"Also: Stromovka."

There was gravel here. Then grass. Then shorter grass. Then pavement, concrete, some more grass. He fell into a hedge at one point.

"Trout?" he called out again.

"It's your father, sorry."

"Professor?"

"The same."

"Promise me something," Jeremy said, looking up into haloed street lights.

"What shall I promise you?" his father said to him.

Jeremy couldn't remember what promise he requested, if he asked for one at all. And now there was afternoon light, and looking around himself, feeling for handholds in the wet earth, he found sweat-soaked futon instead, torn cloth. His head tamped down with the dumb pain of hangover dehydration, the strain of trying to remember how he got there.

Jeremy pulled himself painfully from the futon, made it to his knees and crawled across the carpet to the bathroom. He brushed his teeth, one stroke in, back, repeat.

In the kitchen he drank a glass of water. Then another. Filling the third he noted the cardboard box of items he'd picked up from The Paw still sitting on a chair at the kitchen table. His Fugami lay evilly on top, its black ceramic blade across Jules's white chef's jacket. All of his culinary belongings in a small box. Nothing else remained.

# THREE

# L O C A L
# S P L E N D O U R

It took until the fall for Benny to comment on it, but eventually she did. They'd been closed since the beginning of August, ten full weeks. Mid-October she finally said something along the lines of: "What are you doing with yourself these days?"

Jeremy said: "Reflecting."

Benny pulled the sheet across her chest and sat up. This date was their bi-weekly, aggressive and hungry. Jeremy thought their patterns had normalized in reverse to the convention. With other girlfriends sex had been urgent and obsessive during the early stages, and gradually become more gentle, more relaxed, ending (to date) with the discussion about: What do we really want here? The answer to which had been (to date) enduring friendship.

Benny had inverted this process. The Canadian Tire cash advance scam now struck him as the kind of thing that enduring friends might consummate. Early sex reflected it also; there had been a pervasive gentleness, early trust. He remembered examining her skin as they lay together, running his finger up the almost invisible spider ladder of fur beneath her navel, gently feeling the silver spike through the knot of her umbilical.

By now they were on a Saturday night and Tuesday afternoon routine, a couple of obsessive, sweating hours weekly during which they devoured one another with an intensity suggesting there was a husband on a business trip whose schedule had to be considered.

"I called you late a couple Sunday nights ago. You were out," she said now.

He glanced over at her, trying to get a whiff of her intentions. "Out dancing on a Sunday?"

"Albertini and I are picking out chairs. The Italian rep could only come Sunday."

"Oh yes," he said. Benny's new career. His head rolled back on the pillow. "What have we selected?"

"Golden mohair with high backs from Fiori. What about the other night?"

"Baby," he said, "I am true to you."

Benny answered simply: "I don't doubt it. So?"

So, indeed. They both held something on the other here. She had used the spare key he'd given her and gone to his apartment that Sunday night, and several other nights since. The unmistakable Crosstown blend of patchouli and CK had been hanging in the air on a number of occasions when he got home at two or three o'clock in the morning from evenings in the park. On several of these occasions he had also found a smudge of Benny's scent left on his pillow from the times she laid down to contemplate his whereabouts.

If he needed any other evidence, the tiny slips of paper he had taken to wedging in the door frame had fallen out on these same nights.

He had nothing particular to hide, and he found himself unconcerned by her intrusions. The first time it intrigued him; he hadn't realized she had such an intimate interest in him. The second time he thought about how he held her at arm's length and wondered if maybe the twice-weekly routine had been his passive-aggressive imposition. The third and fourth time she did it (he imagined her sniffing around, like a coyote at the edge of a squirrel path through the forest) he felt strongly drawn to her. This prowling had the effect of making him feel hunted, which made him want to be taken.

"Maybe I was asleep," he said, watching her eyes. Of course she would know that he hadn't been home at all.

"I let it ring and ring," she lied.

"Well," he said, returning a purposefully lame lie, "I was in, I think."

It had been the Professor, Caruzo and himself that particular night, a convivial time. As had become their practice, they snared squirrels for dinner, two reds and a grey, and Jeremy roasted them, spread-eagling the gutted carcasses on Caruzo's grill. He sent Caruzo off to gather huckleberries and dandelion greens and combined these with roasted potatoes (contributed), and they had eaten a robust and flavourful meal: roasted squirrel and potato salad with wild berries and herbs. As they ate, Jeremy found the looks on their faces like a startling memory. Cheeks red and full, smiles easily encouraged.

One comment from Caruzo really pleased him. Caruzo had placed a hand on his stomach and said simply, "I feel good, Jay. You know, feels good."

That stuck with him, although beyond that nobody talked about the food at all. Nobody observed that the squirrels, with their sinewy flesh spread unevenly over bony carcasses, had been perfectly roasted. That the beer marinade he'd applied during cooking had caramelized into a mahogany brown. They were just eating and talking and it was fine. When there had been an extra squirrel or two on these occasions, Jeremy began taking them home to refrigerate. He'd refined his technique in this way, experimenting later. Brown sugar and balsamic vinegar made the marinade both more astringent and yet rounder. A workable gratin Dauphinoise could be fashioned with two potatoes, some garlic and cream, a scavenged hunk of cheese and a square foot of tinfoil.

So ran the course of Jeremy's reflection these days.

Benny was hugging her knees now, thinking. Finally she said: "Dante suggested the three of us go to Seasons of Local Splendour together."

Jeremy didn't bother recounting the ancient Seasons of Local Splendour Snub. He was thinking instead about how fast this happy togetherness had evolved.

The meeting he might have chosen to avoid happened several weeks before. A random Saturday night street encounter downtown. Benny was dragging Jeremy out to meet some of her friends at a dance club. This was her regular weekend scene, but his attendance had been a new idea born of a sud-denly wide-open weekly schedule. He was only glad that Benny's recreational tab of ecstasy had not yet been consumed when she spotted Dante approaching and elbowed him. Slowed her pace.

Jeremy called out a greeting and Dante looked up sharply.

He was wearing a black suit, accompanied by two men in tuxedos whom he did not introduce, but who skated away on patent black loafers to wait under the shelter of an awning in front of a display window full of Fendi bags. They were on the way to the opera, and Dante said only, "Me and my cousins here." Which left it unclear whether they were blood cousins, bodyguards, part of the corporate coffee Cosa Nostra or what exactly.

Jeremy introduced Benny, and they bantered about work-ing for the same outfit. Dante was gracious, even threw out some obligatory polite questions about the Inferno Pender and showed signs of being impressed when Benny said she was location manager.

Jeremy watched the two react to one another. If he were a jealous type, he would have thought Benny were trying for Dante's attention a little more than necessary. On the other hand, Dante wasn't giving Benny very much back, listening but not focusing.

"You must certainly be doing many things well," Dante said at one point. "I hope you'll stay with us for many years to come."

It was Benny who skilfully opened a crack in this smooth conversation.

"I graduated from design school this summer," she said suddenly. "I'm very interested in restaurant design."

Dante had been rocking gently on the toes and heels of his black Crocketts, and Jeremy had just begun thinking about how he could extract Benny and leave Dante to his evening's plans, to his cousins, who were now smoking and looking wordlessly over from the display of expensive handbags.

Now the rocking stopped.

Dante said: "Oh yes?" Voice changing from flat and impenetrable to pliable, enveloping. He canted forward slightly, his hands crossed quietly in front of himself, princely and statuesque in his dark cashmere topcoat and gun-black, double-breasted suit. His eyes were on Benny's face, and they found something of new interest there.

"I actually worked on an Inferno at one point," Benny said. "During a co-op semester with Beekman Schiller. Martin Schiller mostly."

"Marty," Dante said. "We play squash."

"We did the Pender Street Inferno, where I now work," Benny said.

"You've built one of my operations from the ground up," Dante said, shaking his head in frank amazement. "Besides me, I don't know that there's anyone else who can say that, and it's been over fifteen years for me. Too long, in fact, which is why I am so looking forward to starting on our new project."

She handled it well, Jeremy had to acknowledge. It occurred to him, on the other hand, where things might lead. And it occurred to him further that he hadn't uttered a word in this conversation and his impact on where it would end was negligible. His final thought—as the chisel-faced, black-suited coffee magnate took still further minutes out of his evening and swivelled in still more tightly to target Benny—was that Dante already *knew* who Benny was. Knew her human resources record, knew her paycheque deductions. Knew where she lived, her function in future plans, her taste in things from lounge music to piercings to girlish white underwear.

"You know...," Jeremy started, and since he didn't in fact know what he was going to say, it was just as well Dante cut him off anyway.

"Tell me," Dante said to Benny, "what do you think of 'French Bistro' as a leitmotif?"

She had done it and knew it. She answered with confidence. "I think of French bistros as belonging in France," she said.

"You do," Dante said.

"And old. Not the hippest option."

Dante smiled and leaned back, looking straight up into the night sky, then back down to his discovery opposite.

A block later, as they waited for a light, Benny finally asked him: "All right, how did I do?"

"That depends on what you were trying to accomplish."

The light changed and Benny didn't move. "You don't want me involved."

"It isn't that at all, but French Bistro was my suggestion."

Benny was first surprised and then irritated to learn this detail. "Why?" she asked him.

"It just happens to be what I want."

They went out dancing as planned. The following day Benny's area supervisor phoned her and told her to go to Canada Place for a meeting with IIC Human Resources. She called Jeremy in a panic, thinking she'd been fired for making insolent suggestions.

Jeremy said: "I doubt this is how the Inferno fires people."

She phoned him four hours later. "Design assistant...," she said, breathless. "I'll be working with this fabulous New York designer. Albertini Banks."

"Well," Jeremy said. "Nicely done. Where exactly?"

"Surprise!" Benny shrieked. "They're bringing in Banks to do *your restaurant*. Isn't it totally exciting?"

It certainly was. All happily in it together now, they were.

Benny shifted in the sheets opposite, waiting for his response.

"Seasons of Local Splendour," Jeremy said. "Have you been before?"

"No, but it sounds cool. Besides, I think that since you're his partner, you might make an effort to show Dante your commitment to the project."

"Partner is a strong word for it," Jeremy said. "Five percent is more like servitude."

"Make partner the right word. Get in there. Dante is the kind of person who respects assertion."

Jeremy did not doubt that she would know by now, Dante having taken a very personal interest in the project. Back from Chicago and New York, those deals complete, Dante was devoting most of his time to this start-up.

"Power is important to him," Benny said. "Winning."

"Great," Jeremy said. "What does that make me, the person who went bankrupt and whose restaurant Dante was essentially given for free?"

"Dante didn't get your restaurant," Benny said in a kindly voice. "There is no more Monkey's Paw, as good as it was at doing whatever it was you were trying to do. He got a lease, a location. The rest of the future has to be created together."

"A lease?"

"Not even that. He owns the building."

"Dante owns that building?" Jeremy said, sitting up. "I thought Blaze Properties owned it."

"Blaze. Inferno." Benny said. "It's a sister company. Inferno owns them, duh."

"I did not know that," Jeremy said. "He didn't get a lease. He got out of a lease."

"Don't go all paranoid on me," Benny said. "He saved you and is giving you a new place to work. A place that will be simply awesome, the best everything. Do you have any idea what the Inferno budget will be? Try, like, a million."

"Jumpin' Jaysus," Jeremy said.

"He's serious. So realize: Dante will help others win too, as long as he still wins in the process. That's you, get it? The person he's helping."

Jeremy flopped back onto the bed and started at the ceiling. "What about art?" he asked.

Benny made a face like *Whut?*

"Art, as in, for the walls. There were three sculptures in The Paw that I never got back."

Benny sighed and went on, her voice softening: "Can't you also see this opportunity as a way you and I could, you know...build something together?"

He looked across the bed to where she sat on her knees, wrapped in the white sheet. Her perfect small face. The swell of her behind the white cotton.

"So what kind of chairs?" he asked, pulling the sheet away from her breasts.

"Oh, Jeremy," Benny said, rocking forward onto her hands and knees and hovering warmly over him. "They are simply gorgeous."

He agreed they should go together, curious about Dante's interest if nothing else. Dante was a man by whose efforts a uniform commodity was distributed through identical shops to consumers all over North America. There was no difference in process, design or product between any two locations making the Inferno a brutally efficient, market-researched repudiation of the local. Why would this gathering—situated at the intersection of anti-globalization, organic, hemp and all-purpose foodie enthusiasm—interest Dante?

He had a second reason too. In the unlikely event that anyone did remember The Snub, who better to be strutting around with than a new-paradigm heavy such as the founder of Inferno International Coffee?

Dante drove the Jaguar XK8 himself, without confidence. He had learned to need a driver, and Philip was nowhere to be seen. Even at Jeremy's apartment, he was adjusting the electric controls on the tan seats minutely, still figuring them out. An ear-splitting grind of the gears and they were off. It was a forty-five-minute drive, during which Dante drove slowly and held the floor on the topic of "their joint future."

"Now, you don't know it yet," Dante said, addressing Jeremy without taking his eyes off the road, "but we are envisioning something magnificent down there, aren't we Benster?"

"Oh yes," Benny said from the back.

Dante shoulder-checked several times before swerving sharply into an empty lane, then continued: "Our research is just now coming together."

It would be, Jeremy thought and nodded mutely.

"The name," Benny said from the back seat, reminding Dante of something they'd already discussed.

"Right. The name absolutely does not play."

"What name was that?" Jeremy asked.

"Jerry's," said Dante.

Jeremy was blank. "Who's Jerry?" he asked finally.

"You're Jerry," Benny said from behind him.

"Jerry? No one's ever called me Jerry in my life."

"Hardly material," Dante said. "It tubed at survey. Jerry with a J, and people get Seinfeld. Comedy, yada yada yada, aging, single, frustrated, apartment dwellers. Very low food and fashion awareness, which translates as 'bad demos.' Now Gerry with a *G*, on the other hand, is sweet. People get Garcia, who, dead or not, is iconic. Very broad appeal. Garcia is Christ without Revelations. You can really ride a non-brand like Garcia."

"Jerry Garcia spelled his name with a *J*," Jeremy said.

"Crazy, isn't it? People still respond to the *G* and think of him. The customer first, right or wrong. They want a *G*, give them a *G*."

"Fascinating," Jeremy said.

"And I have to tell you," Dante said, "French Bistro also did very poorly. All people think of is French fries, and then they go on to tell you that the best fries they ever had in their life were from McDonald's."

"All right, all right," Jeremy said. Jesus.

But Dante continued. "French simply doesn't cut it any longer as the culinary reference point. Our power-alley demographics, the twenty-five to forty-five-year-old, new economy, urban, food enthusiasts—what we're calling *the fooderati*—they want something wired, post-national, with vibrant flavours. They want unlimited new ingredients, they want grooviness and sophistication, and both purple and gold score very well."

"Fooderati?" Jeremy said. He'd never heard that one before. "The *fooderati* like purple and gold food?"

Dante sighed. "I offer these merely as examples of what we know. Stay with me here. Focus on market-response themes. Think: sophisticated and groovy and new ingredients."

"And purple," Jeremy said.

"And Italy," Benny added.

"Right," Dante said again. "Age clusters right up to sixty-plus take Italy over France every time. Over sixty we're not much worried about—they don't like France or Italy or dishes that are too crunchy."

"Who does like French?" Jeremy asked.

"Put in those terms, nobody really. Anything Italian scores higher. In a nutshell, Jeremy, Bistro is out. Benny was right. We need Ristorante or Cucina or Trattoria or something."

"Trattoria," Jeremy said. "Would someone please remind me again why we are going to Seasons of Local Splendour? These people are fanatically local, more obsessive than I ever was."

"Well," Dante said, smiling to have his point introduced for him, "maybe we can learn something. I personally couldn't tell an organic local carrot from one made by DuPont in a lab orbiting Earth. But I'm under the impression that some people care about what's happening out here today, and that means we should consider it."

Jeremy turned to look at Dante. He had to make sure this wasn't a joke.

"Within reason," Benny said. "I mean, mangoes, right?"

"What about mangoes?" Jeremy said.

"Well, you can't get them here, but we need them."

"Did they score well at survey?" Jeremy said.

"Plus, Dante likes them."

"So," Dante said, trying to return to the matter. "We give these ideas their day in court, as it were."

"I already did," Jeremy said. "Jules and I were highlighting local produce, meats and vineyards for the past couple years. That's what we were all about."

"Yes, of course, you and Capelli," Dante said. Her name jarred him, Jeremy thought. Still. "You guys were great at whatever it was that you did. We're talking about something different here. Something really new."

They were just pulling up to the gates at Garrulous Greens, a pretty farm on a quiet road in Langley with deep frog-filled ditches and high hedges on either side. Once through the farm gate, they were directed up the tree-lined drive by officious volunteers in faux-chef gear, and left into a paddock off the main yard, which had been converted into a parking lot. Dante tentatively manoeuvred the Jaguar in between a Range Rover and a convertible Ford Falcon, which reminded Jeremy of Jules's old car.

They got out and stretched in the cool fall air, then walked through the grass to the main yard, where they exchanged their tickets for a wine glass and a napkin each.

The general idea was to explore at your leisure, from the entrance yard up behind the farmhouse to the working part of the farm. There you found several barns, a greenhouse and a chicken run. The fields stretched away from there to the back of the property, itself lined with the same hedges that lined the road. It was a tidy farm in Jeremy's experience, a bit of a show farm, although Jeremy did not grudge them their mustard greens.

Down the various lanes meanwhile, among the various buildings, visitors would find the food and wine tents. And here, as you wandered slowly and nibbled and sipped, you were encouraged to have your own personal epiphany about the relationship between working farms and the food that you eat. It was contrived, certainly, but Jeremy knew that most people needed the lesson.

There were over thirty tents this year, under the airy covering of which representatives from "the better-known organic restaurants" and most of the local vineyards were busy meeting and greeting and providing samples. Chefs were preparing finger food exemplary of their craft and style, while the vintners were standing at attention with their various Gewürztraminers and Pinot Blancs, Pinot Noirs and the odd Okanagan Cabernet.

Jeremy left Dante and Benny to explore by himself, to chat with the chefs and winery reps he knew. Almost to a person he was greeted with condolences about The Monkey's Paw, and about half of those people tagged on an additional comment along the lines of: "Inferno Coffee, though. Wow." The meaning of the *wow* varied widely depending on the speaker.

He stopped at Valley Vineyards and talked with one of their representatives, who poured him a glass of Gewürztraminer— thirst quenching, with light grapefruit and lychee flavours— before offering his regrets about The Monkey's Paw. After his *Inferno-Coffee-wow* comment, he added: "Very surprised about that, Jeremy. What are you planning together?"

Purple and gold food, Jeremy told him.

"Speaking of Inferno, though," said another wine rep after a parallel conversation ten yards further down the lane, "isn't it something to see them at one of these little events."

Jeremy took a second to process this comment. "Inferno is *here*?" he asked finally.

They were, the rep said. In a kiosk behind the greenhouse, and hadn't times changed vis-à-vis Local Splendour ideological rigour? "Although Inferno apparently waved a lot of money around."

They had also promised to use local dairy products, it seemed.

Jeremy wandered on, sipping a Pinot Blanc, full flavoured and soft in the mouth, perfectly al fresco. He ate a slice of poached sockeye salmon filet, which had been opened and stuffed with a caviar-studded mousse of oyster mushrooms, arugula and cream.

He saw Jules from a few yards off. She was working for the Left Coast Grill. He hesitated, but she spotted him, and instead of turning away she leaned her head forward to emphasize the fact that he had been acquired.

"Don't you go walking by," Jules said to him as he approached the tent. She wiped her hands and came around the table to give him a kiss on the cheek.

"So, you finally made it to Local Splendour," he said. "With a 'better-known restaurant,' no less."

They were busy, so she couldn't take a break. "Word is out, something big and new happening in Crosstown."

Jeremy took the jibe. "I'm getting mixed reactions all around."

He caught her glance for a second, a flash of the titanium-flecked pale green before she pushed her head back with a sturdy swipe of her hand through her hair.

"I saw him," she said.

"Menu espionage."

Jules laughed loudly at that.

"I miss you," Jeremy said, trying to catch her eye again, but she looked away from him, and he hated himself instantly for saying it. It was undeniable, but so was the chasmic weakness in his character it revealed. *I miss you.* What did that mean after you sent someone away?

She didn't answer anyway, but given the growing crowds went back around the table to produce more of the mushroom crostini that the Left Coast Grill was featuring. In front of the work station—a wok on a high gas flame—Jules had arranged her simple ingredients for people to see. Green onions. Chard. Tiny yellow cherry tomatoes. A basket of mushrooms including chanterelle, oyster, shiitake and a magnificent almost-black specimen called blue cluster.

She handed him one of the lightly toasted, ginger-rubbed crostini, piled with its earthy fragrant assortment of mushrooms, the sautéed chard and onions and a single sweet yellow tomato. And then she turned to other people, without saying anything.

He ate the crostini walking through the main farmyard, the familiarity of her flavours making him distinctly lonely. He had red wine after the crostini. A Pinot Noir, the wine glistening ruby in autumn sunlight, smelling clearly of raspberry and strawberry.

He ate a skewer of grilled free-range chicken from Badje's, marinated in yogurt and masala, standing in the middle of the yard.

Badje's owner asked him: "Glad to get some time off?"

It was a nice way to put it. "I am actually."

"You are coming back to all this craziness, of course."

"I will be, yes."

"I'm looking forward to it. I think you will do something interesting."

Jeremy glanced around for Benny and Dante.

They were opposite, at the Chart Room Restaurant tent. They were eating soup out of baked acorn squash bowls, ladling it gingerly into their mouths and comparing notes with a group of seven or eight people who had gathered around them. Dante's face was set to an impassive princely expression as he held very quiet court, the shortest of the men in the group but the core of group attention.

Jeremy noticed something, even at this distance. When others would speak to Dante, or greet him, he would nod hello or exchange brief pleasantries. When Benny pointed her spoon at the squash bowl now—she was guessing at the ingredients of the soup, or commenting on the fact that the tiny squash itself was edible—Dante listened fixedly. Somebody who didn't know Dante, hadn't read first-hand his unearthly post-sexual presence, this might have offered a suggestion of intimacy between them. To Jeremy, it seemed only suddenly clear that Benny had something to fear. That somehow the barista, whose career had blossomed so magnificently, so quickly, would be made to pay.

Dante leaned closer. He was watching Benny's lips as she spoke. She finished. He straightened, took a spoonful of soup and looked around as if nothing had been said.

The Inferno kiosk was opposite. People were standing two-deep in front of the cappuccino maker, waiting for their skinny frappuccinos. And there at the edge of the crowd was Trout, standing quite still and staring up at the Inferno logo on the tent front: the mythic-looking figure and the hair of soft steam, in his outstretched hand a steaming black brew. The coffee deity offering the world a rich cup of Honduran arabica.

He walked up slowly behind the little boy in his rolled-up jeans, white T-shirt, his nylon packsack slung over both shoulders, the buzz-cut head leaned back as he gazed upwards. Trout sensed him coming, turned and held up a hand for a silent high five.

"Who is that?" And here Trout pointed a stubby finger up at the Inferno logo.

"The Devil?" Jeremy suggested.

Trout shook his head. "Nahh," he said. "Too obvious."

Olli appeared just then and Trout scurried off through the barnyard, following the whiff of something. Olli was corporate casual, an expensive merino-wool pullover and khakis. A new Barbour. He was also drinking a glass of wine, Jeremy couldn't help but notice.

"The wise child dispensed wise words, I trust," Olli said.

Jeremy waggled his head. "Not bad, really."

They looked around for a minute at the milling crowds, the foodies eating and comparing notes, the organic-hemp fusion component of the crowd walking slowly and looking up at the sky, communicating wordlessly with the Mother Earth that brought them such bounty.

"I saw Jules," Olli said. If Jeremy took a small measure of judgment from this comment, thought Olli, so be it. The Monkey's Paw closure had disappointed him more than he could tell his friend. He didn't know why it had happened, he only had the sense that Jeremy hadn't tried hard enough in the face of some crisis. How many times in the early years of TroutWorld had he fought bankers? Many. And here Jeremy was supposed to be some kind of culinary artist, according to Margaret, in which case giving up seemed a very bad thing. "I really liked Jules," Olli finished.

They walked over to the fence around one of the fields and leaned on the top rail, looking out over the rows of arugula, mustard, chard, kale, radicchio and other high-end produce.

"Do you still talk?" Olli asked him finally.

"What's that supposed to mean?"

Olli shrugged. "Just wondering."

"I got into some trouble. It was out of my hands. Sure, we talk."

In the middle of the field opposite, there was a woman walking between the rows of arugula and kale. She was wearing black tights and a black sweater, Dayton lumberjack boots.

"Why didn't you come to me?" Olli asked.

"I did once."

"Different," Olli said. "Start-up money. You weren't facing a crisis. You could afford to be turned down."

"I see."

Sometimes he sounded harsher with Jeremy than he wanted to. Olli turned to his friend now and said, a fraction gentler: "I'm assuming it was a crisis this time."

Jeremy nodded. "You ever hear of a kite? I got busted more or less."

Olli raised his eyebrows. "Are you shitting me?"

"No. I had my ass saved."

Olli nodded slowly. "Dante Beale."

"I suppose you can relate to the big partner," Jeremy said.

Olli turned to look back into the field. The woman in Daytons was wandering in a reverie, sipping her Chardonnay. Every five yards or so she leaned dramatically over and plucked arugula direct from the field, elevating a broad ass. When she stood again and ate the arugula, her head was tossed back, blond hair cascading.

"I call it the 'Risk of the Big Heavy,'" Olli said. "Simply put: with heavy partners, the money is good, and that buys some of your freedom. That's the deal, in essence."

Jeremy looked at his friend. These words would be advice, then. "Sure," Jeremy said. "Money for freedom."

"After that, it's ad hoc." Olli was looking around the barnyard now. "The freedom isn't necessarily the whole pay-off. You give up other things. Things you don't negotiate at the outset. Parts of your vision. Parts of yourself. Handle this risk well and the big heavy is your friend. Handle it poorly and they become something else entirely."

Jeremy nodded, chilled by these words. He didn't think his own situation was particularly difficult to evaluate in this regard. The Monkey's Paw had been a spontaneous product of what Jules and he had been together, the sum of their culinary selves. Which part of that vision had he not bartered away?

"What's he like?" Olli asked.

"Dante is a killer," Jeremy said. "He takes care of business."

Olli smiled. He didn't think his friend knew the half of it yet. "And do I get to meet this killer?" he asked.

He did. They all met up in front of the Inferno kiosk. Margaret and Benny found each other at the tent giving out goat's milk gelato and decided to get the group together for drinks. Dante offered his place.

Jeremy was part of the chatty circle that formed but feeling a little zoned out. Olli's observations had put him in a dark enough frame of mind without having to see Jules walk by with a man he'd never seen before, bumping shoulders as they walked, leaning in slightly to hear the words of the other. He raised a hand, started to say hello, but stopped mid-word and brought his hand down. She disappeared around the corner of the greenhouse, the blur of her dwindling down the lane towards the Left Coast Grill tent.

Olli and Dante were appraising each other. Dante's face responded approvingly when he established with whom Olli was now strategically allied.

As they talked, Trout stepped wordlessly between his mother and father, and gazed up fixedly at Dante alone. Dante glanced down, and Jeremy watched as his normally impenetrable facial expression transformed. The hardness went out of it. The blunt came off his eyebrows, the Uzi left the nose, which became merely short and snouted. The bristly dome of his scalp seemed suddenly fragile as a new-born, and he tried for a smile. An unusual, placating smile, as if Trout were an old schoolmate who'd once licked him convincingly.

"Oh, Dante," Benny said, mildly alarmed. She fumbled in her purse and produced a handkerchief. "You're bleeding."

Which he was, a worm of blood having emerged from his left nostril. Dante wadded Benny's handkerchief to his face and tried to laugh through it. "Sorry. Sorry," he said. "Just go ahead to the cars, I'll be along."

Benny hung back. Jeremy noticed the handkerchief reddening as he turned to leave.

On their way to the car, walking between Jeremy and Margaret, Trout said, "Look."

And they noticed the TV crew filming the row of marigolds next to the lane. The heavy-set camera man was holding the camera out, swinging it across the yellow blossoms for a sweeping, dramatic shot that Jeremy imagined opening or closing the segment.

Margaret began to giggle.

"What's funny?" Olli asked.

"They're filming the flowers," Margaret said, laughing louder.

"Maybe they'll ask them questions too," Jeremy said.

They arrived before Olli and Margaret. Dante and Benny went up towards the house, but Jeremy impulsively returned to the street to look back up at the two houses side by side.

The streetscape was familiar. The old house sat next to Dante's, now dark, uninhabited. Both houses were set back off the crescent in a forest of cedars with salal undergrowth. The Professor's house was the more imposing, with a high, shingled roof and dormer windows staring out from between the trees. Dante had the architect's house, an Erikson. His work didn't sit on the ground, it emulated the terrain, in this case forming a low shelf that spread among the trees and traced the lip of an escarpment that plunged to the rear of both properties. Dante's house had a flat tar-and-gravel roof covered with deep green moss.

The Professor's lawn was cut and trimmed.

"I have my landscapers do it," Dante said, who was waiting at the front door when Jeremy returned up the drive.

"Thanks. He's forgetful."

Olli and Margaret pulled up in the Land Rover, waving. Dante looked for a moment like he didn't remember who they were, then turned and went inside with Benny.

"You ever carry a sleeping kid, Chef?" Olli said, from the back door of the Rover.

"Gee. I don't know. Is there a special technique?"

Trout was sitting in place, shoulder belt holding him upright, head lolled to one side. He was snoring.

"Just like carrying a large prosciutto ham I would imagine," his father said.

Margaret smiled, collecting her things from the front passenger's seat.

The house was a sprawling split-level. From the black stone entrance hall, stairs stretched down to the lower level and up to the living room, the upper terraces, the wide-open kitchen and dining areas, and from there to other rooms that spread out to the right and left. In the centre of the house was a fifteen-foot-wide stone chimney with fireplaces in either side, one facing into the living room the other towards the kitchen. The chimney ran through the floor and down to fireplaces on the lower level.

"Come on in," Dante called from the living room as they entered the foyer. He was up in the living room, pulling bottles out of a cabinet and setting them on a folding mahogany table. Scotch, vodka, gin, port. He kept his back to them, calling from the far end of the room: "If Trout wants to play downstairs, there's a box of toys down there some-where."

When he turned, Dante's eyes locked on Jeremy holding Trout.

It hadn't been that difficult after all, Jeremy discovered. Although Trout's head fell heavily across his shoulder and he thought it might have been drool he felt on his neck, at least the kid's legs crimped around his waist in a subconscious grip, sensing true sleep, deep, bed-sleep was near. Jeremy smiled back at Dante. Look what I found.

Trout was still snoring, louder.

"Well, fine then," Dante said, lowering his voice, but his stare did not easily disengage. While Margaret and Olli made their way up into the living room, he continued to stare, processing something. The connection between Jeremy and Margaret? Between Jeremy and Olli? The connection between him and Trout? Was he just remember-ing hearing somewhere, sometime in the past, that Jeremy had a godson?

Dante directed Margaret to an unused bedroom down a hallway behind the kitchen. She motioned Jeremy to follow, which he did. "You'll be talking him back to sleep before this is over," Trout's knowing mother assured. And sure enough, set on the bed, sneakers removed, Trout was awake.

"Hey there, adults," he said, looking from one of them to the other. Margaret got him under the covers and kissed him on the forehead.

"Uncle Jay-Jay's going to say goodnight, then you sleep. Roger?"

"Roger." Thumbs up.

She flicked off the light, leaving only a swirl of orange coming into the room from the hall. Jeremy sat on the bed and looked around. There was a window on the far side of the opening onto a narrow stretch of garden between the house and Dante's greenhouse, where Jeremy knew he kept dozens of orchids.

"So," Trout said.

"So, bedtime," Jeremy said.

"But it's not."

Jeremy pretended to study his watch closely. "But it is. Your. Bed. Time."

"My time, yes. My bed, not."

Clever. "You know who's bed this is?"

Trout said: "The Devil's." His voice rang a bell in the still air.

Jeremy stared down at him.

Trout's mock-serious expression finally broke and he started to laugh. He then produced a credible impersonation of the figurehead in the Inferno Coffee logo. He adopted a stern, regal expression, drew his chin down as if to suggest a lengthy, weighty beard, extended one hand slowly as if it were holding a very deep mug of coffee. When his hand was out as far as Jeremy's chest, Trout's eyebrows glanced up, inviting, beguiling.

"Very funny," Jeremy said.

"Very serious." Trout held the pose.

"Time for Zs."

Trout dropped his arm, settled. He closed his eyes. Sleep was right there.

Jeremy got up gingerly. On his way out he paused at a framed print near the door. A pale sketch on ivory paper, hard to make out at first, but its overall shape drew his eye. A map of an island. A peninsula, with shore lines and topographical marks, trails and road beds. Concessions, beaches all marked. He scanned the image closely now, taking a bird's eye view of the place he was only now getting to know at ground level. Down in the lower-left corner he read the engineers block letters: STANLEY PARK—CITY OF VANCOUVER.

Laughter was coming from the living room when he rounded the corner and rejoined the group. Dante was holding court. Olli was sipping a Scotch. Jeremy looked and looked away, but Olli caught the glance and shrugged very slightly.

Dante was pouring Margaret a glass of red. Firesteed Pinot Noir, no doubt Dante's deliberate choice. Wine from Oregon's self-proclaimed "virtual winery": no vineyards, no winemaking facilities. Firesteed contracted instead with a handful of growers, wineries and winemaking consultants from the Williamette Valley to produce a red of very broad appeal. And Jeremy was rightly confident that Margaret would pick up on it. She accepted the glass, sipped and took immediate note of the label. Undeniably drinkable—well market-researched—with bright fruits, medium body and what wine writers called *approachable tannins*.

Jeremy accepted a Bushmills.

"And such a way with children," Dante said to him, smiling. Trying for warmth, Jeremy thought, and failing. He went and sat at the top of the squared horseshoe that the couches formed around the perimeter of the room. "But seriously and in all modesty," Dante was picking up the thread of a conversation that had been underway before Jeremy entered the room, "it was no surprise that we drew such a crowd. Could our product be more local? We thought it up here."

"And this makes Inferno coffee the product of local vegetables?" Margaret said.

"Droll," Dante said. "Very."

"Kidding. I meant the Local Splendour folks are focused on the local produce angle."

"Certainly," Dante said, turning away from her. Then to Olli. "But conceived here, that's local, don't you think?" Olli protested to be the wrong person to ask, but Dante pressed. "No local on the Net, is that it?" he said.

Olli didn't much like techno-philosophy. It was undisciplined. But he tried for an answer. "The Net still relies on wires and fibres. They need to be strung on poles. The poles need to be stuck in the ground somewhere. Somewhere, that ground is local."

"Then there's wireless," Dante said.

Fine. Olli allowed the point.

"You know…," Dante started, expansive. Host to a large idea. "I think I'm wireless. Culinarily, I mean. Yes."

Jeremy fleshed it out for him: "Where the duck is twice-cooked New England mallard served in a restaurant in Moscow, and the salmon is Chilean-farmed Atlantic planked on Lebanese cedar in a restaurant south of Cork City."

Margaret laughed out loud. Dante glanced at her.

"Precisely," he said. "And so our little Season of Local Splendour, fervency aside, served most in flagging the rules to be broken. Reminding us of where others think we should not go. Maybe I need my young neighbour just as he needs me, to allow us both to take this next step."

Everybody thought it over for a second while Dante refreshed drinks. And then Benny, who had been piecing it together slowly said: "You lived right next door…. Why don't you invite your father over?"

A refreshed drink appeared in Jeremy's hand just as the question aired and he hid a moment's hesitation behind the swirling of his ice, the blunting down of his Irish whiskey, the tentative first sip. Why stall? To protect himself? To protect the Professor? Not quite.

That the Professor might not be disturbed.

"Travelling." Jeremy said. Behind Dante, behind all of them, the plate glass made a perfect mirror. And Jeremy saw there what he knew the rest of them were now appraising, himself by the fire, whiskey in hand, cornered.

"Like, uh, where?" Benny said.

"Stromovka," Jeremy heard himself say. "It's in the Czech Republic."

Everybody said: *Really?* From Margaret to Olli and around

the horn to Benny, four iterations of the word. Amused, impressed, polite and overtly doubtful.

"The Professor is an interesting man." Dante came smoothly to the conversational rescue. "We used to play chess rather often, he and I. He won consistently for several years. After that, he didn't win so much any more. I miss the competition. Joint?"

And here he produced a silver cigarette case from his inside pocket, extracted a very neatly rolled joint and tapped it on the back of the case.

Only Jeremy declined. Margaret said she'd had too much wine, but when the joint got to her she took a toke anyway. Olli was thoroughly loosened up on Scotch. Benny was going to accept whatever Dante offered. Jeremy wondered, in the instant her lips closed on the worm of dope, whether he would ever have sex with her again. Whether he would ever hold her tightly from behind, one hand over each of her breasts. This coming Tuesday would be the next scheduled coupling, a crass thought and he knew it. He wanted her and was also faintly nauseated by the idea.

Dante got up and opened a cabinet next to the TV. "Cooking videos, what do you say?"

Margaret began to giggle.

He popped in a Paul Prudhomme tape, fast-forwarding to the part where the famously fat chef blackens a snapper. The idea was enough, Benny was doubled over on the couch. Olli was guffawing.

The scene cut to a Louisiana back country fair. Prudhomme was in a motorized wheelchair, chatting with a man at one of the kiosks. Behind the man was a rusting forty-gallon barrel of bubbling oil into which descended a sturdy chain, taut with the weight of something hanging below the surface. Turning a winch and hauling in the chain, slowly, minding the splash, the man pulled up a twenty-pound turkey that had been suspended in the boiling fat. The bird glistened brown and hissed audibly as the fat seeped free of the crusted skin.

"I didn't notice Local Splendour had any of that," Dante was saying.

"I think I'm going to throw up," Benny said.

Jeremy only knew he felt the need to leave the room. His face was crimson—he was deprived of oxygen or dehydrated or developing a fever. He slipped out of the room without comment, through the large kitchen and into the hallway that ran past the room where Trout was sleeping. He found the bathroom and closed the door silently behind himself.

His eyes were bloodshot and tired. He ran the cold water and submerged his face in a sinkful, letting the cool seep into his skin and scalp and into his head, chilling and stilling. Prudhomme in the market had been an unsettling sight, in one way. Seemingly overweight to the point of immobility. Talking with the yocals deep-frying their catfish and hush puppies and, yes, turkeys. And for knowing—as Jeremy knew—that this food would be delicious, worth any indigestion, any artery thickening costs that might be imposed, the chef was the clown fool, was he? The room had been shaking with laughter. None of them considered that these backwoods Louisiana locals had something for which they might be profoundly envied. With their bib overalls and greasy ball caps they had a local-ness, ordinary or otherwise, a self that would continue to be the same self long after anyone stopped watching through the lens of a TV camera.

Jeremy pulled his face from the water, hearing it run off him in streams. He took a deep breath and pushed his face back into the sink. He imagined the water was a pool, and that he could dive down into it, swim for a long time submerged, then rise to the surface in a different place entirely. Transformed and clean. He held his breath until it hurt. Holding, holding. And when he finally pulled his face from the water gasping, there was an instant of swimming blackness, flecked with red, and in this blackness there were trees that thrashed in a silent wind. Leaves stripped from the branches swirled towards his eyes. Jeremy thought, Careful now, you're drunk.

Something was missing. Sound. The house had gone silent and black. As if he had slept for a long time, been forgotten, and everybody had left or gone to bed. He stood in the hall, wondering, until he saw the dim glow from the bedroom where Trout was sleeping. The unsteady wink of a flashlight or a candle. Maybe there had been a power outage and Margaret was checking on her boy. A restorative scene of mother and son. He walked numbly across the hall carpet and leaned his head around the door frame.

The black swirled with its flecks of red.

It was Dante. He was standing over Trout, looking down. No flashlight, no candle, but light radiated from the furniture and the walls. From the checkered bedclothes under which the little boy lay. The tall dark posts of the old-fashioned bed frame. The dresser opposite and the far wall where hung the blueprint of Stanley Park with every trail and culvert etched delicately through the forest. Dante was a silhouette in the midst of this scene, the bed shining whitely in front of him and the air incandescent with flying particles of red and now orange.

Trout's eyes opened fully. His bright stare locked upwards on Dante's face.

Jeremy couldn't move his legs properly—he staggered, he stumbled, feet encased in concrete like in a childhood nightmare. And then he was in the bathroom again. He was on one knee on the cold tile. There was water on the floor, water dripped from his face. His hand held the sink edge, knuckles white.

He pulled himself up, plunged his head once more into the basin. Then out, into a towel, which he rubbed briskly over his face and hair.

There were footsteps in the hallway. Voices. Lights came on again under the bathroom door, bright and yellow.

"It's nothing. Terribly sorry." Dante's voice. "I walked into this bloody door frame."

Margaret and Dante were both giggling. "If you woke my child, Mr. Beale, you have to read him stories to put him back to sleep."

"I will I, promise. Ouch."

The voices disappeared into the front of the house again.

Trout's bedroom door was closed when he left the bathroom. When he joined the others, Jeremy found himself carefully taking one of the armchairs furthest from the TV and sitting gingerly, unsure how he would be received.

They were watching a montage of cooking shows now. Dante appeared to have cut together a highlight reel of what he felt were the World's Most Ridiculous Chefs. It was the Italian bread guy with the fake accent at that moment. Something about the way he was kneading a large round of peasant bread was a source of huge amusement. Olli was sniggering. Margaret tittering. Benny hiccuping. Dante sat smiling and pale with a handkerchief pasted to his nose, once again reddening as Jeremy watched.

"Trout fell out of bed," Margaret explained, seeing him come in. "Dante went back to check him and walked into a door. What happened to you?"

Benny cracked only the briefest of glances at Jeremy, openly accusatory.

"I just need a little air," Jeremy said to Margaret, and he went out onto the back porch.

"The Chinese," brayed the Frugal Gourmet after him, "*are the most interesting people in the world.*"

Jeremy sighed. No Emeril, he noted. Dante probably *liked* Emeril.

"Hey."

"Jesus!" Jeremy jumped.

Trout.

"You're up," Trout said.

"Of course I'm up," Jeremy said. "You being up is the issue."

"I got woke up," Trout said. And to divert Jeremy's attention from the fact that he wasn't in bed, he pointed through the trees and went on, "My dad said you used to live there."

The Frugal Gourmet was now squealing from the living room. "Isn't this just *gorgeous...TRIPE!*" (back-dropped by the quartet of dope-assisted hysterics).

"You go back to bed," Jeremy said, looking down at the boy. There were no signs on his face or in his demeanour that anything unusual had happened.

"Over there," Trout said again, pointing to the Professor's house.

"To bed," Jeremy said, more quietly.

And to his surprise, Trout did not object. He recrossed the back of the kitchen, unseen from the living room, and returned to his temporary bed.

Jeremy walked along the west wall, past the brick chimney and circled into the driveway, appraising the empty house. He crossed the gravel to the front walk, to the mailbox the Professor had built a lifetime before. It was a shingle-roofed and cedar-sided miniature of the house itself, with a little door that opened to insert the mail. Reaching in to the very back, he found the bent nail and the key hidden there.

He crossed the darkened main hall, with the stairs winding up to the bedrooms, the hall leading back to the kitchen and family room, and the narrow set of stairs running down to the right to the Professor's study. As a child he had not been allowed to enter this room, so stacked and crammed was it with the fragile bits and pieces of his father's intellectual enterprise.

He descended the stairs and leaned against the study door. It was nearly blocked with something; Jeremy had to apply a shoulder to move the door inward. He slipped through and looked over the sea of yellow foolscap that now confronted him. The ceiling had snowed paper; there were drifts of words. Thousands of handwritten legal-sized sheets. Underfoot where he stood, in the corners, stacked near the wall of bookcases, flowing out of two leather easy chairs and cascading from the desk, from open drawers, thousands more.

He pushed the door shut and walked into the room, shuffling through this drifting chaos. In front of him the desk, covered; behind the desk the book shelves, filled and overfilled with the words of others. He took a sheet from the corner of the desk and examined the familiar handwriting. Not familiar from his early remembrances, not the uniform Pelikan brocade, but the hard scrabble ballpoint and pencil scratch that he had seen at the library. Pages of it, strewn in uneven piles, clipped into indiscriminate clusters.

As he sat on the desk and considered the enormity and confusion of the scene, Jeremy's eyes rose to the far wall. On either side of the door he had just forced open, his father had been pasting pages to the wall. Pages of his own writing, articles from newspapers and magazines, photographs, sticky notes and other bits of paper detritus. A dense, overlapping series of clusters joined by a network of black connecting lines painted directly onto the wall. A flow chart of sorts, branches linked to larger branches carrying larger clusters of pages, which joined to various main stems and then to a single thick squat trunk that ran down the wall and into the baseboard.

He stood and approached this tree-like diorama and began to examine its leaves and branches. There were childhood pictures here. There, a wedding picture he had not seen before. The Pelikan pen itself Scotch-taped to the wall in a cluster that included a letter from the dean of anthropology approving extended sick leave. A page torn from *Will Work for Food*.

No picture of grandfather Felix.

In another place the Anya Dickie review, neatly preserved in laminate. A photograph of The Monkey's Paw, taken on a drizzly day with a shaky hand. A closer photograph of their outside chalkboard: the mains that day were black cod with chive cream and chicken with cognac.

There was a cluster of leaves that centred on a photograph of Caruzo, his grizzled face smiling from the centre of overlapping handwritten pages, candy bar wrappers and a spray of sticky notes, presumably added later as the Professor had other thoughts on the matter. Caruzo with a small skull. Caruzo and a younger Professor. They both looked as dirty as they did now. He pulled this photo down and turned it over. *August 1982. Me and Caruzo.*

Jeremy only nodded numbly and repinned the photo to the wall.

There was a Chladek cluster. *Globe and Mail* articles about the Velvet Revolution. A picture of his camp, the bridge vaulting overhead. A Czech advertisement for Becherovka. Each image grew on the tree in response to the words that had been spoken.

There was more Babes in the Wood material than Jeremy could process standing there. Another photograph of skulls. Newspaper articles. A photograph of a small clearing in the woods. A fragment of what appeared to be bone.

One branch tried to hide itself, bending in an arch away from the main trunk, growing heavier with images towards the tip until it nearly disappeared behind the bookshelves. Jeremy traced it slowly with his finger, memories rising within him. There was the Polaroid snapshot of him lying in the arms of the goddess Sequana at the source de la Seine, the snapshot he had given his father those years before, a present of conciliation the effect of which he had never determined. Next to it, the reciprocal gift. A photograph of a Sabatier taken from an advertisement. A card next to it. An anniversary card from his mother to his father. His mother's squiggly, uncertain script: *We are reminded of our beginnings.*

Jeremy sat cross-legged on the floor and continued to trace the branch. There were more photos of Caruzo and his father at various points in the park. The final photograph of Caruzo alone in front of an anonymous salal bush. It was dated, and this made clear its significance: *October 1987.*

And so, Jeremy thought, here we come to our spiralling conclusion. The beginning of the end. He ran his eyes down to the very tip of the branch. Its last leaf a familiar photograph dangling upside down. His strongest family image, long since burned into his mind's retina: his father beaming, his mother guarded. His own small presence under his father's arm. The three of them staring up through the years, from a fixed site in his memory, and into the shifting uncertainties of their present sorrow.

He collapsed backwards onto the floor and lay staring at the ceiling. He lay on paper, all around him. The Professor's obsessive output of those same years. He grabbed a page at random and pulled it in front of his eyes, threw it aside and grabbed another. Then another and another. He didn't read a word, only scanned the handwriting. All the same. The scribble of grief, of guilt.

He thought of many other things, lying there. Of how, even taken from them, her life had spilled into theirs and theirs into each others. Of what, in total, had been built here in recognition. Their own tree, this Tree of their Life. The core experiences, the clusters and offshoots that were what they had been, what they had done, the offences and betrayals for which they sought redemption. The things they had each become.

But he thought mostly of what must surely lie ahead. Of what must clearly grow from this instant of understanding. This glimpse of life's design. This fragment sense of what was plain.

# THE
# CRITICAL PATH

She finally tracked him down. He wasn't returning her calls, so she had taken to hanging up and phoning again. It finally worked. One afternoon on the third call he picked up.

It had been very rude to wander off from Dante's without explanation, Benny told him. They had all been wondering where he'd gone. They had worried. But when Jeremy offered no excuses for his behaviour she said abruptly: "I hope you're free for half an hour, it's time for you to see something."

In fact, he had plans to go to the park that afternoon. He left an answering-machine message only Caruzo or his father would understand fully. *I can't come to the phone right now. I'm taking a walk around the lagoon, and then I'll be working until after midnight at a private party. Leave a message.*

Benny insisted and offered to pick him up, so they drove together over to the site of the new restaurant, where she parked dramatically across the street, cut the ignition and sat there for a moment. What immediately struck him was that the next building, an almost identical structure one door north of the old Monkey's Paw, had been refitted with the same vaulting front window.

She had keys, of course.

The front room was unrecognizable—three huge, antique chandeliers being only the most obvious reason. The room itself was strangely vast. The old counter against the right wall was gone, the vantage point from which he had watched so many mornings unfold. Instead of one kitchen door there were now two, quilted aluminum with semi-circular tops and port-holes, ten feet apart on the back wall, which itself was wider than possible. And it was only as he approached these doors to look at the kitchen, and stepped up a three-step riser to a new raised section at the back of the room, that it came to him.

He turned to look back at the street, looking at not one vaulted window but two. The north wall had been ripped out cleanly to the roof, twenty feet overhead, blowing the room out to twice its original size. Combining it, he calculated, with what must have been the building next door.

"Same building originally," Benny said, watching his eyes as he took in the changes. She would not remember, he thought, that she was standing roughly on the spot where she had eaten his grenadin de porc au beurre La Fin du Monde. She had sat right there, against the wall that no longer existed, wrapped so beautifully in velvet that he had committed him-self to her, to the shape of her swelling into his Ikea chair.

"He owned the whole thing," Jeremy said, nodding.

"Lucky too. Permits would have been a bitch otherwise. Earthquake upgrades, the whole bit."

Jeremy walked a large circle over the rough planked floors.

"You're covering up these planks?"

"Jeremy," she said, not answering. "Let's look at the kitchen."

It too was double the size, benefiting like the front from a merger with the adjacent room. But it was also gutted. The blackened eight-burner Vulcan-Hart was gone, prep areas and pass-through counters torn out. Stacked against the walls were the workmen's toolboxes and other gear. Sanders and power saws. Electric planers and drills.

"I want you to see it because it's yours," Benny said.

"Albertini and I will listen to you, and give you all the support you need."

Jeremy pivoted in the centre of the room, nodding. Then he walked to the opposite door, went back into the dining room and walked all the way to the south front window. His front window.

Benny followed, and after a short silence said stiffly: "Dare I ask what you think?"

He wasn't sure. Then he decided: "I'm suddenly very tired."

"Well, you can't quit," she yelled at him. This reaction took him by surprise. He turned to respond but she kept going. "You made a deal and you're dropping your end of it. You think I don't notice that you're hovering off somewhere. That you're not around any more. You think I don't notice that your interest in this whole thing started to fizzle as soon as I got involved."

"Benny, no."

"Well, tell me what it is then."

"I have some things going on right now. Unusual things."

"That's what I was afraid of," she said. He raised his eyebrows. She didn't say anything for a while. Then: "I've been in your apartment when you weren't there. At night."

He could pretend to be surprised, offended. But all he said was: "And?"

"I've slept there when you've been out all night."

"Benny," Jeremy said.

"I found a squirrel in your refrigerator."

Jeremy looked sharply to the window. Shit. "It was hit by a car. I took it upstairs."

"To put in the fridge."

"It was alive. . . and I took it upstairs to try and feed it . . . to feed it peanut butter. But it died. I felt terrible. I didn't want to throw it in the garbage. I didn't know what to do with it. I suddenly thought, you know, maybe I should take it to the park and bury it where it came from. I put it in the fridge to keep it until the next day. That's what happened. I buried it in Stanley Park."

She considered this unlikely story for several turgid seconds. Then, slowly, she nodded once. Doubt still read clearly on her features, but also a set of larger concerns that gave her the incentive to let this one go.

"I have a feeling," she said, moving on to these larger issues, "why Dante likes you."

"I'm sort of family."

"It has nothing to do with that. It's because he thinks the two of you will look good working together."

She was right, Jeremy thought. Dante *did* like the idea of them together, the idea of them being seen by the world to be bound in a joint venture. But what grew intense, almost frightening, about this was the follow-up thought that Dante might have liked this idea for *years*. Conceivably, ever since they had that beer and lobster dinner on his deck those years before.

"More to the point, I know my own role is calculated," Benny went on, and sensing his interruption she raised a hand to cut it off. "I know this even if you don't. I was given the job because of what Dante wants from you. To secure your interest. To get your attention."

Again, she was right, and it crossed his mind to warn her about what this might mean for her own future. "The Risk of the Big Heavy." But she plunged on.

"What I'm saying is that I need you to be committed. And you wandering off for three weeks, out of touch . . . you see my problem."

"You don't have a problem. I'm committed."

"I think I know what happens next," she said. Her eyes were wet. "This is the moment we become just friends. Am I right?"

It was the moment. Maybe she was making it happen but that didn't change the fact that his feelings for her were already like memories.

They hugged. "I'm a little worried what Dante will think," Benny said, letting him go.

"I won't tell him. It's none of his business."

She took his house key from her purse and put it on a sawdust-covered windowsill. He took it, pocketed it. Outside she remembered something: "I almost forgot. Philip asked me to give this card to you, for the kitchen. You are to use this for all expenses."

Amex, platinum. *Jeremy Papier,* it read, *member since 1995.* They had apparently forgiven him his previous struggles.

"There will be design team meetings you must attend," Benny was saying, returning to the refuge of business. "I want you there. Show the commitment we talked about."

"I said I would."

"Acceptance," she continued, more sternly. "Joining. That's the only display of commitment that will mean something."

He grew a beard.

"Looks good, Jay," Caruzo said through a mouthful of toasted baguette, stroking his own chin. The fact was, emblems of commitment aside, it was cold out and a bit of face covering helped. His father was shaggy. Caruzo's beard reached his chest (he cut it off blunt with a pair of shears). Even Chladek, who made a dandy pretence of shaving once in a while, for the most part had greater concerns and distractions.

The baguette Caruzo was spraying while he spoke was part of the best meal Jeremy had made for them under the worst conditions. There was a late fall wet over everything, even if it was not raining. Jeremy was wearing three sweaters against the chill, two coats and finger gloves, which made impaling the small birds on the green wood skewers a fumbly challenge.

They had originally set out to catch a swan. "Stinky box does it," Caruzo informed, scratching himself. "Stinky box is all." He shambled around behind the Second Beach concession and returned with a suitably pungent cardboard box, once used to ship hotdog wieners. Jeremy guessed this particular box of wieners had been left overnight behind the concession stand under a dumpster full of broken pickle jars.

"A swan goes for that smell?" Jeremy said, looking around self-consciously. It was just six in the evening, dusky, but the seawall was still full of scuffling sneakers and the sound of nylon track suits, one leg zipping against the other.

"Believe it or not," Caruzo said, delighted to have found something Jeremy didn't know about food, "swans like this smell. Love this smell. OK, so. Here goes."

They walked to the lagoon and stopped near the rushes at the base of an arched stone bridge. The swans were dipping and preening and retrieving bread cubes tossed from the bridge by a scrubbed couple in new Nikes and soccer warm-ups.

"OK. Come on now," Caruzo said, impatiently shifting the box from hand to hand and watching them.

Jeremy looked studiously away, a hand up scratching his temple and hiding his face from view.

"'*And now I singe...*,'" Caruzo said finally, under his breath, and before Jeremy could suggest otherwise he mounted the bridge to ask the young couple for change. Or what he actually did was stalk towards them calling in a loud sing-song voice: "'... *any food, any feeding. Feeding, drink or clothing? Come dame or maid, be not afraid...*'"

They didn't even fumble in their pockets. The young man was already walking, dragging his date behind him. Caruzo was back creek-side, sliding the box across the gravel until it was near the water.

It was an effective technique. The swans redirected as a group and homed in on the unusual smell. One by one they stepped up onto the shore and approached the box, sniffing curiously, until eventually the leader—the largest, fattest male—shooed away the others and climbed into the box himself, flapping his wings proudly. He began rooting, his beak diving into the corners, bobbing in circles.

"I distract him," Caruzo said. "You kill him. Distract. Kill."

"Wait," Jeremy said. But Caruzo was already waving his arms and approaching the boxed swan, which stood higher on his spread black feet. His wings and neck were arching in a ready crouch, beak open and issuing the warning sound that normally preceded a flailing rush, but now, trapped in the box that it had chosen to defend, this hiss only signalled that the swan saw its threat and was committed to its position.

Asselijn's threatened swan stood like this one, with its feet slightly offset. The beak turned to jab. It was a creature of such beauty, then and now. Made more beautiful by the approach of the outsider, made purer. And had Jeremy lived in Asselijn's day, he would have waited until the swan turned to face Caruzo in his confusion, and then he would have killed it without remorse. He would have roasted it in a stone oven and served it in fatty pieces on the porcelain plates of his royal masters, on the pewter of the merchant and the officer, and eaten it himself out of a plain wooden trencher.

Caruzo's arms and hands were outstretched and arched, his neck bent forward, eyes bulging. At the edge of the lagoon the other swans were beginning to bleat and squawk, sensing an impending leadership crisis.

"Caruzo, stop!" Jeremy said, louder.

They walked into the forest silently. After a hundred yards, Caruzo said only: "Little birds?" In the nearby bushes the wrens and robins, the kinglets, sparrows and starlings were flitting and singing in the dusk, preparing for their own tiny morsel of sleep.

He had what they needed back at his camp, and Caruzo led the way along the boardwalk, past the lily-padded Beaver Lake, alive with bird calls in the weak light, and all the way up the hill as far as Reservoir Trail. There had been a salmon hatchery here that had once provided smolt to Beaver Lake, from where they had migrated yearly to the sea.

Caruzo left Jeremy standing in the middle of a maintenance yard and disappeared into a thick cane of salmonberry.
He re-emerged minutes later from a different spot in the
brambles with a Safeway bag swinging from one hand. Back
at the boardwalk, Caruzo brought out a tin of epoxy, a jar of
Squirrel brand peanut butter, a butter knife and a sturdy
length of dowel. The dowel was spread first with the glue
and peanut butter, then planted firmly in the bank and left
extended over the water.

At first they talked only about the hunting, as the birds
began their passes. Black shapes dropped from the dusk and
strafed the area, looking at the stick and the seated figures
with a mixture of bird curiosity and wariness. Jeremy had a
strong sense of the day drawing to a close, of the meal that
would be its final activity. He felt Caruzo sitting next to him,
breathing, at peace.

"Caruzo. The beginning. What's the beginning of it all?"

A starling touched down, planting both feet. The dowel
held, the bird ate, flapping its wings for balance.

"Eden," Caruzo answered.

"Eden."

"A departure. A return."

Clarity or madness. Angelic ramblings. The starling had
eaten its fill and tried to fly again. The wings beat but the
glue held. Other starlings gathered curiously in the night air,
ignoring or unable to interpret the signals, swooping lower
and closer. Gathering.

Caruzo fell silent, watching. Then he began again. "Always
there had been the voices, Jeremy. Questions and demands.
Demands and questions. Mostly demands."

"Demands for what?" Gently.

Caruzo shifted on the bench next to Jeremy. He considered his answer, whether to answer. "Fire," he said finally.
"Mostly fire."

There had been a room. A single room with a bed, a

basin, not much more than that. He did not remember any-thing before this room. Any home, family, place, self. There was a man who operated the door to this room. Who brought food, never books or pencils. He was not allowed to smoke in the room. No matches. A room and voices. And while there were voices, Caruzo said, there had always been this room. The room, in turn, brought the voices very near.

Another starling touched down and began to eat. The first went still. A tiny enactment of starling despair.

He left the room for dinners. Once daily. The last time he left the room had been early autumn.

"Leaves just turning, Jay-Jay," Caruzo said. "Golden. Red."

He remembered it was meatloaf night. Meatloaf and french fries. They were marched across a courtyard to-gether. He and others. He didn't remember how many oth-ers. Perhaps a dozen.

"A hundred maybe," he mused.

The voices grew faint in the courtyard. They always did. It was the best part of going to dinner, the fading away of those internal questions and demands just as the sky bal-looned above him. Forty-five seconds to cross that courtyard. Forty-five seconds of peace and sky.

In the mess hall, the drop tiles clamped down above their heads and the voices returned.

"Fire," Caruzo repeated.

He didn't understand how it started. How it had grown so large. He didn't think the paper napkin thrown onto the stove had been enough. There had been a small flame, a small guttering yellow flame.

"Shouts and voices. Voices and shouts."

Then there had been water, a lot of water.

"From a bucket," Caruzo said.

Jeremy winced.

Something made a very large *woof* sound, and the flames went from a benign yellow flicker to a great angry sheet of orange with billows of white steam and black smoke. Jeremy recognized the result of a bucket of cold water hitting the hot deep-fryer. Fat would have exploded out onto the surrounding griddles, the flaming stove top, seeped into the ovens.

The next sound was more like *boom,* Caruzo thought. Voices turned to screams. Nobody could see anything. He ran in the only direction he knew, back the way he'd come. In the courtyard, again. The sky ballooned, the exultant voices grew an increment quieter.

He remembered pausing, looking back. Black smoke was pouring out the mess hall door. And as he watched, the glass broke outward in one of the kitchen windows. Somebody was crawling free.

He ran for a very long time. There were cars and trucks. Buses. People. Many, many lights. Mountains on his right. Buildings on his left. Running, running. The voices very faint.

When he found the trees there had been no voices at all. He held his hands up now to demonstrate the miraculous silence. "No voices," he said. "Just trees."

It was time to harvest starlings. Jeremy held the dowel while Caruzo plucked them free. The stick twisted in his hands with the force of the many tiny wings. They caught five in the first ten minutes. In the second ten minutes, they caught fifteen. Afterwards they walked. Caruzo held the burlap sack he'd used to drown the birds. They walked slowly.

"And ... ," Jeremy said.

He had been here a week, possibly more. "A month, maybe," Caruzo said.

In the voiceless silence offered by the forest, he had explored, he had learned about the lay of this land. His first shelter was a stone bridge. His second a hollow log. After he recovered from what sounded like a bad case of pneumonia, he had become serious about fires and shelters and eating right.

Caruzo took a deep wheezing breath now.

The children came from time to time, he said. A boy and

girl in matching outfits. They often wore toy helmets with up-turned goggles. Played silently or talked in their own language.

"Brothers?" Jeremy tried.

"Brother and sister," Caruzo said, with unswerving certainty. "Sister. Brother. Playing in the park. Always alone."

Jeremy stopped walking on the path. He put a hand on Caruzo's arm. Through four sweaters, it suddenly struck him that the man was very thin. Caruzo shook slightly. He turned to face Jeremy.

"Frankie," Caruzo said. "Johnny." After a song he remembered. They made fun of him at first. Kids will. They threw stones. "Hit me here," Caruzo said with a smile, pointing at his left temple.

Friendship came, as it will between children left alone a great deal. A sudden, unplanned recognition of common interests. A hard and fervid alliance. They lived with their mother, in a rooming house on Burrard Street. Caruzo thought they were poor and that the rooming house was full of women like their mother. Working women. Poor and desperate women who are very often gone. For a month or more the children came, alone always. They played in the woods, a little wild. Caruzo showed them everything that he had found. Secret trails and trees that had fallen in the middle of the forest where nobody ever walked. An abandoned truck rusting back into the soil far from any road. Birds' nests. Cat bones. Fox dens. Squirrel paths.

They brought him things. Once a cold hotdog. Then a pie, surely stolen. Another time, newspapers. Many other small things to eat or to use. The last item was a quilt with panels of blue like the night sky, a meandering trail of green that repeated itself back and forth across the cloth, and splashes of yellow like constellations and planets. A green land under a night sky.

Then they didn't come for a while. He worried.

Caruzo's voice was constricting as he spoke. His face

wound and unwound on itself. He chewed at his nailless fingers
until Jeremy reached over and put his hand on the old man's
wrist, pulling it down from his mouth.

"They came together again, finally," Caruzo said. "The
three of them."

He followed them that day. Somewhere in his mind had
been the impulse to return to his camp and get the quilt, to
return it to the mother, who he imagined was very angry
with him for having it. But he had been afraid to leave them.
He trailed at a distance instead, an expert by now at walking
silently parallel to the path. Ten yards off in the bush and a
dozen yards behind.

They walked into the forest through the rose gardens,
down Pipeline Road. She pinched a fur coat around herself
tightly, angrily, walking quickly after the children. They entered the bush near Beaver Lake. The children ran ahead,
jabbering in their strange tongue. But then saying something
else. Something he had not heard them say before.

"Caruzo," he said, beginning to visibly shake now. Whispering: "Caruzo. Caruzo. Caruzo."

He encountered a fallen tree, doubled back on his tracks
to find a better route. He got turned around a second time
and then he took the path. Running now.

"Faint voices," he said. "Just now, faint voices."

She was lying in the middle of red path, on her back. "The
mother, I thought. Frankie and Johnny gone. I knelt down.
Just a girl."

He touched her. He thought for a moment she was dead,
and on her forehead he touched her to make a mark with dirt
and bless her passage. But when she opened her eyes and sat
up sharply, Caruzo had been startled. He ran.

"Ran into the bushes, Jay-Jay. Ran for cover." He was a
quarter-mile away before he remembered Frankie and Johnny.

Caruzo seethed with the memory. His face continued to
bunch and relax repeatedly, his shoulders thrusting forwards

and back, his neck twisting and releasing. Jeremy's hand rested on his shoulder while the storm blew through.

He crashed through the bush in no direction, looking for Frankie and Johnny and their mother. "And she did come back. Yeah, she did come back. Here she comes now. She's scared now, Jay-Jay. No kids, no coat. Blood on her leg, Jay-Jay."

And with this detail, Caruzo released a single dry sob.

He looked. Then he gave up. Later he looked again, starting at the spot where the girl had been lying. He followed the points of the compass rose from that spot to the water in all directions. It had been north-west, a little under half a mile as the crow flies. A mossy clearing, strewn with leaves. Low brush all around. The trees leaned in but did not touch that soil. She had covered them with her coat. Buried them under a thick layer of leaves. Her shoe lay nearby. The adze.

"Found them off Reservoir Trail, Jay," Caruzo whispered. "Found them in their spot. The beginning for me, that. Right there. Between those trees. Buried under those leaves."

There was silence for a time.

He didn't touch them further. He left them to lie, to sleep. But he stayed. He set up his hidden camp some short but respectful distance away. For several years he grieved. Then watched. The parks workers came eventually. The man, Albert Tong, had been raking. Something cracked underfoot, not a stick.

Caruzo frowned. "Now the bones are gone. Sure, the bones are gone. But the signs, Jay-Jay. Signs and signals. Signals and signs. Signals to return. Signs to show the way back. I believe in these signs, Jay-Jay. I really believe in these signs."

There were others for dinner. A young man and a woman with a baby. Chladek with another bottle. Others he didn't recognize. They all stood quietly in or just out of the ring of golden firelight. Everybody brought their own plates, produced from backpacks and hidden pockets.

The Professor looked at him curiously when Caruzo and he pulled in with their bag of starlings. He smiled at his father and nodded his head. He felt wonderful.

Dinner came together like on those magical nights when the front is packed and the back is slammed but not a thing you touch will turn out wrong. Everything leaves the frenzy of the kitchen in a warm halo of perfection. The room is stoked; the energy builds and builds.

He plucked and drew the starlings. He ran them down green wood skewers separated by slices of stale baguette brushed with olive oil and rubbed in garlic. Somebody brought potatoes. Another person had foil and onions. There were bottles of wine.

He laid the skewers across the shopping-cart grill and he felt very, very good.

"Hey, Jay," Caruzo said, enthusiastic himself after their cathartic talk, spraying crumbs from a mouthful of toasted baguette. "Beard looks great, Jay."

Jeremy touched it, looked over at his father and smiled again. And then to Caruzo, while still looking at his father, he said: "Give us the poem, Caruzo. The whole thing."

"Oh," Caruzo said. "That. Well . . ." And he rose theatrically to his feet, a piece of bread in one hand, a paper cup of ruby plonk in the other, arms outstretched. He recited the ancient poem he had memorized:

"From the hagge and hungrie goblin
That into ragges would rend ye,
And the spirit that stands by the Naked Man
In the Booke of Moones defend ye.
That of your five sound senses
Ye never be forsaken,
Nor wander from your selves with Tom
Abroad to beg your bacon.

And now I singe, any food, any feeding
Feeding, drink, or clothing
Come dame or maid, be not afraid
Poor Tom will injure nothing."

The Professor came and stood next to him.

"He draws the others," Jeremy said, staring at the ring of faces listening to Caruzo's performance.

"Yes," the Professor said, nodding. "But for me, time here grows short. Having finally read my outline, Sopwith Hill is keen I finish."

"The looming sense of things not done," Jeremy said. "I can relate."

Caruzo was chanting up towards the summit of his performance.

"I know more than Apollo,
For oft, when he lies sleepinge,
I see the stars at bloodie wars
In the wounded welkin weeping...."

When he was finished the group was silent. Caruzo sat, satisfied. He ate a starling with his fingers. And Jeremy thought those seconds before anyone else spoke became part of the poem's passing, an empty space that the words pushed out in front of them.

The design team was working towards its own set of deadlines, meeting weekly. Floor plan, kitchen, menu, linen, flatware, paint schemes, art work—everything had to be discussed and market researched and discussed again. Dante set the third Friday in February for the opening, three months away and they would need every week. They met early, before the trades came in, Dante, Philip, Jeremy, Benny and Albertini Banks, sitting in the torn apart front room of the new restaurant.

This morning was typical. Dante was following a tight agenda, moving through what he called the "Critical Path Issues" as the team woke up over coffee carted in from the new Inferno Hastings. The first Crosstown Inferno location had finally opened around the corner in the space that had been Fabrek's falafel stand.

Albertini Banks was sipping his triple espresso, hungover eyes concealed behind yellow sunglasses with lizard-green frames. (Benny and he had been out clubbing the night before, Jeremy learned. Not their first time.) Banks was, as always, dusted with an urban patina of foundation, mascara and Hard Candy nail polish, corseted with layers of fashion. Today he wore an eight-button, red plaid jacket with a pinched waist and a Nehru collar decorated with silver flashes. A gold neck chain with a Rolex hanging from it. Vintage Gucci loafers with pointy toes beginning to curl upward. Today's hat, a white silk fez with tassel. Karl Lagerfeld does the Turkish Armed Forces.

Benny, too, wore sunglasses, no doubt concealing a hang-over of her own. But she had moulted again, toeing some invisible sartorial line between Dante and her new dance partner. And with only designer New York and Jermyn Street as her points of reference, she'd come up with a black and white nylon tube top under a green blazer with a club crest from the Pall Mall Club. Kinky Knightsbridge. Dante was obviously paying her well.

Philip looked the same as always. Urbanely suited and stubbled. The consummate New Economy Vice-President of Intangibles.

Everybody so far politely ignored that Jeremy was start-ing to look like an Hassidic Deadhead. Overalls, red long johns and a pleasantly thick rabbinical beard that was starting to come down off his chin.

Critical Path Issue #2 had been fabrics, a half-hour discussion that evolved directly into yet another debate about suitable names. This topic had been open for days, but market research had come up with a final proposal.

Dante stood in front of a large swatch of purple velvet that Benny had been showing them. "Gerriamo's," he said grandly.

Everybody loved it. Even Jeremy had to allow it was not too bad an outcome given the short list had included Cucina Gerrissimo, a lemony mouthful of pseudo-Latin pretension if there ever was one.

The only trouble with Gerriamo's was that—as a fabricated word drawn from the consumer intellect revealed through market research—there was wide variance of opinion as to how it should be pronounced. Jeremy took it as *Jerry-AH-mose*. Benny said *SHER-ry-ah-moss*. Dante went with Benny's version or, alternately, something like *CHER-ry-amus*, which sounded simply rude.

"Cherryamus Critical Path Issue #4," Dante said, smoothing his shirt front, straightening French cuffs. "Open kitchens. We should have talked about it earlier. Suddenly I'm getting favourable input on open kitchens."

"I should have thought of that," Benny said, scribbling a note to herself. "I like the idea."

"I find that I can go easy every way," Banks equivocated in his placeless accent. (Jeremy had decided it was the accent you inherited if you were raised speaking Esperanto.) "If we open the kitchen up to the people's eyes from this room, then only I think we use a wide, wooden counter, and over we stack with fresh animals and fishes and vegetables on ice or something, or also have a large flower arrangement to match the one in the centre of the room. This idea could be very opulent. But I see that it will also be very opulent without this open kitchen."

"Jeremy?" Dante asked.

"Closed." He said. "We sweat. We swear. And, I hate to break it to you, but I frequently do not wear the stupid paper hat."

Dante stared at him for a second or two, then said finally: "Closed it is. If we're going to cover up the opening with a flower arrangement, why have the opening in the first place? Second, I want the carpenters out next week not next month. Third, as Jeremy has pointed out, cooks aren't much to look at on the line." Dante reached over and flicked Jeremy's beard with one finger. "Is the chin garnish considered 'grunge'? Grunge is very out, isn't it?"

Jeremy smiled serenely. "Don't you think it makes me look spiritual?"

"Perhaps. But spiritual is hardly one of our market response themes."

"I could die it purple or gold."

"Very droll. You can't cook with that thing, can you? It's not hygienic."

"I'll wear a hairnet."

They turned to other matters. On the opening night guest list, Philip had a confirmation from England. "I am really happy to tell everyone that Kiwi Frederique and *Gud Tayste* confirmed."

"Brilliant," said Dante, turning to Jeremy. "*Quam olim Abrahae promisisti.*"

"I thought you already delivered on that promise," Jeremy said, thinking of the blurb in "Hack Your Food."

"Oh, I have more," Dante said. "How does a feature strike you?"

Jeremy made appropriate noises of enthusiasm and excused himself. He had a meeting with a kitchen designer and equipment supplier. Dante walked him to the front door, where he said: "We should talk menu at some point, yes?"

In this area, as with kitchen staffing, Jeremy had been given some authority. He was obliged only to pay attention to the "market response themes" and table a draft menu at some point well before the opening.

"I don't have anything formal prepared," Jeremy said.

"Just ideas."

"Come on then. Let's have one."

In fact, he didn't have any ideas. But a Monkey's Paw dish came to him then for the simple reason that he'd seen one of its ingredients—which was undeniably groovy at the moment—sold in purple glass decanters. "Prawns sautéed with grappa," he said.

Dante didn't frown or smile. He was merely straining to understand. "Prawns and grappa. That's it?"

Jeremy fleshed it out from memory. "Marinate the prawns in grappa, oil, green onions, salt and pepper. Very lightly sauté. De-glaze with the liqueur and minced shallots. Season. *Monté au beurre*. Serve with watercress and fresh bread."

Dante's lips were slightly pursed. He was nodding his head the way people do when they would really rather shake their head but don't, either out of politeness or because they're fairly sure they can change your mind so why get your defence up prematurely. "I mean, it sounds fine, Jeremy," he said. "But I need you to begin to think in a new way."

Just that.

"I know you can," Dante went on. "But you must. Now: prawns, grappa. These are beginnings. But I do not yet see a completion. I do not yet see an experience about which my fooderati will e-mail their friends in New York City. I do not yet see the vibrancy, the aggressiveness...."

"The purple?"

"Don't be sarcastic with me."

"Shall we add something exotic? Some caramelized, peppered durian?"

"Would that work?"

"No, it would be very unpleasant, I assure you," Jeremy said. "It smells like a sushi fart."

"Then you will, of course, think of something more appropriate. Something that carries with it our messages of newness and sophistication. Grappa, to be clear, I like. But the dish is not hip in total."

It wasn't that terribly difficult to do, to utter a sentence in convincing Crip. How had Jules once said it? "Classic Ingredient A plus Exotic Technique B plus Totally Unexpected Strange Ingredient C." He considered the matter for five seconds and came up with: "Gulf Coast rock shrimp on a spiced ruby yam wafer with vintage grappa and . . . Thai ginger cream."

Dante looked surprised and relieved. "Jeremy, you see that's the idea. Would it taste good, do you think?"

"I'm not going to suggest something that tastes *bad,* not unless *bad* were one of our market response themes."

"All right then, so let's use that one."

"It was just an example. You have to run through these things a few times; there's a natural evolution. The rock shrimp, for example, is not really a sensible choice given our selection of local shellfish combined with what we can get from the Maritimes."

"Now don't regress on me, Jeremy. But fine. That's enough for now. Develop your ideas along those lines."

"I'm on it."

"And bruschetta."

"Sorry?"

"Bruschetta, what about it?"

"Not innovative. Indeed, common."

"As a technique. As a launching point. Put something unusual on it."

"Bruschetta with three strange ingredients," Jeremy said.

"Think about it," Dante said, opening the door for him. "It's a personal favourite."

At the kitchen supply warehouse, he said to the sales rep: "If I had to have a single pot in my hand at the moment of death, what would you suggest? I'm thinking Chaudier."

"Your own death?" the rep said. "Bourgeat copper, I'm sure. The Jacques Pépin Signature Series. Of course, I'm of the view that Pépin *is* God. You might as well be holding his pot when you rise up to meet him in the sky."

"But he's not in the sky yet," Jeremy pointed out.

"Oh, sure he is," the rep answered.

Aluminum-base would cover their needs. Jeremy ran through the Chaudier catalogue and picked out a suitable range of skillets, sauté pans, *saucière*, reducing and roasting pans, stock and sauce pots. But then, acknowledging the point vis-à-vis Jacques Pépin's potentially overlapping relationship with God, he ordered a set of thirty-four Bourgeat pans. These would have to be FedExed in from France, naturally.

They ran through a number of range and grill configurations. In the end, he decided to anchor the kitchen on a twenty-five-foot installation bridge, the main cook top that would centre the room parallel to the front doors. Here Jeremy and his sous chef would work side by side opposite line cooks brought in for the grill, the broiler, hot appetizers and soups. The main work top would have an eight-burner and a grill on either side, a deep fryer, a small secondary prep area and plating counters. Pass-through shelving would run the length of the unit so the team would be able to fire plates back and forth. Behind the unit were some additional work areas and an auxiliary stove top for soups, stocks and sauces. To the far right: cold prep, meat prep and baking stations. Far left, Jeremy was saving square feet for an indulgently large cold room that would sit between the dish pit and the alley doors. Right rear, a small chef's office and dry storage. And just inside the two doors to the dining room would be the hot and cold pick up counters, forming the line across which servers would not pass, where dockets and dishes would be exchanged. The spot from which Jeremy would play point, run the plays, control the action.

"Knives?" the rep said.

Jeremy sighed. No. He had his own.

They worked right through the Christmas holidays. Jeremy was spending nine hours a day in the kitchen, supervising and giving hands-on help installing everything from a Halon fire-extinguishing system (designed for the galley of an American Whittaker-class nuclear submarine), about an acre of Metro shelving, an automated dish pit, the installation bridge and a massive new RapidAir walk-in cold unit.

The walk-in unit inspired unconflicted enthusiasm. No reservation about the menu or the overt artificiality of cooking to market research data could obscure the fact in Jeremy's mind that this was the pinnacle achievement of the global refrigerator-manufacturing community. Never had he seen one as large and perfect. At The Paw, efficiency had been paramount. Leftovers had to be carefully repacked into stacking blue plastic buckets. Storage of anything for more than a day or two was sure to cause log-jams, meaning Jules and Jeremy juggled a very volatile, quick-time inventory. They didn't view the requirement as cramping their style, particularly. They were a fresh-sheet place and couldn't have afforded to carry a large inventory anyway.

But the RapidAir could have been made by NASA, so thoroughly did it provide for all conceivable contingencies. From the outside it looked a module from a space station, all sleek, rounded, white sides with the input console for its Pentium III processor and its flat-screen colour readouts recessed flush into side panels. When you popped the front, using the patented TouchPoint latch-release system, the doors slid aside with a pneumatic sigh. Inside were four distinct compartments, each with separate temperature controls that demarcated the box into distinct climatic zones. The first, a great expanse of crisp, chrome shelving. The second, an open area with hooks for curing ham and sausage. Third, the produce section with clear plastic bins. Last, a wine cellar.

"We call this one the Food Caboose," the RapidAir on-site

installation specialist said. "Only it's closer to the size of a goddamn locomotive."

Indeed, a portion of the alley wall had to be removed to get the Food Caboose into the kitchen. It was the first point in Jeremy's acquisition binge that produced a small frown out of Dante. Even so, he didn't say a word.

Nights, meanwhile, Jeremy was running what amounted to a second kitchen in Stanley Park. Caruzo spread the word, and Chladek found a neutral spot for it, in the forest between their two camps. And people simply began showing up. Most would bring something, and invariably their offerings became a soup or stew, given both the weather and the odd assortment of ingredients. A ring of Polish sausage, a tin of tomatoes, a dozen potatoes or a clutch of starlings or a rabbit. Always a poverty-inspired mixture of items salvaged from dumpsters (from those who had just arrived) or items harvested from the forest around them (from those, like Caruzo and Chladek, whose skills had been honed by need).

In the four hours' sleep he was managing between these two shifts, unexpectedly, there were florid dreams. Just as in France there had come a point when he was swamped with thoughts of the past, thoughts that spurred him on towards the future, so was he now awash in nocturnal recollection. His psyche was taking an inventory of some kind.

"You will be exceptional," Chef Quartey said to him.

"I feel exceptional," Jeremy answered. "The only thing I worry about is if I will forget the things you taught me."

"The things I taught you?" Quartey said, plating a crapaudine.

"Yes, you. Who else taught me?"

"I taught you to cut a chicken like so, to make people comfortable. To pour wine without pretence," Chef Quartey said. "What then can be forgotten? Although it is, I think, very North American to forget like this, no? I forget nothing."

"Where is Patrice?" Jeremy asked Chef Quartey.

Quartey evaporated in steam, shooting skyward with a screech.

"Claude," Jeremy said. They were standing outdoors, on the hillside below the forest. The small sous chef held a Sabatier paring knife in one hand and a leek in the other.

"Ger-ah-mee," Claude said, seeing him for the first time and repeating Quartey's admonition. "Very North American to forget like this, no? Go to her. Go to Patrice, see how she lives."

"I don't know where she is," Jeremy said. And, unexpectedly, he began to weep.

Claude held the knife up now, the blade resting across his Adam's apple. Tears flowed from his eyes too. "Go to her and make up with her," Claude said, the Sabatier beginning to cut his flesh. Jeremy saw the blood bead and spill. "Do you still remember her?"

"I remember," Jeremy said, gasping out the words. "I remember everything. I remember the source de la Seine. We took a picture. I gave it to my father. I remember the source d'Ignon. I haven't forgotten any of it."

Claude stopped cutting his own throat and straightened up. As if he had just caught himself daydreaming when a great many things still needed to be done. "Ah, well then," he said. The leek and the knife were gone and he pulled sharply downward with both hands on the front of his white jacket, as he always did before entering the dining room. "It's not all your fault."

And at his feet the stones bled water. The flow sounded like wind chimes.

Jeremy breathed deeply upon waking, breathed the cold air of his own room. Breathed in Vancouver. Around him the sense of the bed grew firm, the sheets knotted under him.

At Christmas dinner in Stanley Park they had over twenty people in the small clearing. He roasted geese and mashed a cauldron of potatoes, a ring of apples baked in foil around the fire. At first he was self-conscious about the noise they made—no singing and dancing, just the sound that two dozen people will make shuffling and eating in the otherwise quiet forest—but after a few slugs of Chladek's Becherovka he forgot about it entirely. He fed everybody that came, and when he remembered the thought later, he shook his head. It was too wet to be self-conscious. Those who had not returned to their various places to huddle out of the rain were hugging the bases of trees for the little shelter they afforded. Full of geese and potatoes and apples and, for some, a little wine. But cold and still out of doors on Christmas. The rest of the city, the world, was not even looking this direction.

He hugged Chladek before leaving. "Máme holé ruce," Chladek said to him.

He walked with his father through the forest afterwards, the Professor's pace slower than Jeremy remembered. He told his father about a magnificent kitchen coming together.

"Well, this is not so bad then," the Professor said.

No, not entirely. "But come right down to it," Jeremy said, "I'd rather cook here."

He then spoke of his dreams. Chef Quartey with his advice. Claude with his Sabatier. He took a breath and told his father how he had lost his own, lost that special gift.

The Professor looked concerned, but did not reproach.

"And meanwhile I have a Crip menu to write."

To which his father said only: "Something will come up to inspire you."

And he was right. Something did come up to inspire him, namely Jules's three Fenton Sooner sculptures at auction. His guilt at letting Heckle, Jeckle and Hide get out of his hands in the first place was compounded by the fact that he hadn't thought about them in several months. Then, in the mail, he received his auction list from Charmin's Auctioneers (whose speciality was used office and restaurant supplies), and lot number 247 turned out to be *Three Art Sculptures by Fenton*

*Sonar*. He might have missed it entirely had not item 245 caught his eye: *Vulcan-Hart 8-burner, like new.*

"I blew a buffer," Philip said after making some calls of his own to find out. "I just spaced. Had no idea of the value."

"How can you just sell stuff without asking me?" Jeremy said, his voice rising. "I mean, the stove, sure. But art?"

"Jeremy, we bought the hardware," Philip said simply. "You signed a schedule at the time of sale. I'm not saying anything critical here, but you signed."

Jeremy shook his head silently. He considered calling her but, ashamed to see her, he ended up going to the auction alone.

Charmin's Auctioneers was in a warehouse on Terminal Avenue underneath the SkyTrain tracks. The warehouse was stacked with product, an incomprehensible hive of mostly worthless petrified junk, but which was nevertheless auctioned steadily according to the master plan of one Nick Charmin.

Normally, Jeremy knew from experience, it was difficult to get good value at one of Charmin's auctions. Pre-auction viewings were all but useless since Nick only knew for certain where each lot was when it was about to go on the block. The auction list, on the other hand, could only be trusted to give you the most overarching sense of what function an item might once in its history have been able to perform. As a result, you were best advised to wait until a likely sounding item came up for auction, then inspect it hurriedly while making your bids at the same time.

He was glad, in a way. *Three Art Sculptures by Fenton Sonar* was not something anyone would have had the chance to inspect, although collectors would no doubt recognize even the misspelled name.

He scanned down the list of lots, noting that below *Vulcan-Hart 8-burner, like new* came *Prep counters (two metal frame), black aluminum commercial cookware.* A long familiar list. Had he not thought to remove these items himself,

Jeremy was quite sure Charmin would have listed *One black chef's knife* and *One chef's jacket, marked Capelli* as well.

He paid his $1.25 cover charge, which gave him a numbered plastic bidding paddle. He confirmed that they accepted all major credit cards and entered the warehouse. It was more crowded than usual and, scanning the room, his confidence flagging slightly, Jeremy saw Jules. She was wearing a long skirt and boots, a loose sweater that hung over her hips. Her head was bowed in front of a side counter, above which hung a crooked piece of plywood with the word *ART* painted in red letters. With one hand she held her hair back from falling in her eyes. Jeremy could see that the art counter was stacked with dusty oil paintings, costume jewellery in glass-topped boxes, and what appeared to be a series of heads carved out of coconuts. The Sooners were also there, Heckle, Jeckle and Hide, but Jules was studiously not looking at them.

"I'm bidding on the coconut heads, myself," he whispered, standing just behind her.

She spun around, hand on her throat, eyes widened. They stared at each other for a few seconds before she said: "I hope you're not planning to bid against me."

"I was planning to bid for you," he said.

She had recovered by now and turned back to the table. "Not necessary, my dear."

He stood next to her, resisting the urge to put his hand along her waist, as he could have so easily just a few months before. They sifted costume jewellery through their fingers as the first items came up for bid. Finally Jeremy said: "We have an hour."

Over coffee, she made him promise. "I want to buy them myself."

"How much can you spend?" he asked her.

She made a face and looked away. "Fifteen hundred bucks maybe, if I'm nuts."

"They're worth much more," he said gently. "I made some

calls. We're talking about something like three thousand dollars a piece."

"As much as ten thousand for the three of them," Jules said. "Like I didn't check."

"So, basically there are collectors here or not."

"I need a miracle," Jules said.

And she did all right for the first half-dozen bids. Fifty dollars to the man in the black soccer warm-ups. Seventy-five dollars to Jules. Three hundred dollars to the man in the soccer gear. Five hundred dollars to the woman in the long camel coat (bad sign, thought Jeremy). One thousand dollars to Jules. ("Easy now," he whispered.) Fifteen hundred dollars to the woman in the camel coat. Twenty-five hundred dollars to the man in the black cashmere topcoat with the paisley scarf.

It took less than a minute. He thought she might cry for the first time in his memory, and he finally put an arm around her. "Sorry," he said. "I am breaking another promise to you."

The woman in the camel coat dropped when the man with the paisley scarf took her from six thousand to seven thousand dollars.

"You're sure they're not fake," Jeremy whispered to Jules.

"I won't help you do it," she responded.

Sold for eighty-five hundred dollars to Jeremy Papier. The Charmin's crowd, not used to prices rising above two hundred and fifty dollars, applauded wildly. He made Jules take the bow.

Amex came through again. His feelings for the card were beginning to change. Jules asked: "What will you tell them?"

He had no idea.

They looked good in her place, not far from the auction house in east Vancouver. They carried them from the car together and lined them up on the dining-room table.

She thanked him, held each of his hands in hers. She put her next words together carefully before speaking. "You let him take a lot from both of us. Permanently. Not like these."

"I'm trying to make things right."

Her eyes showed a trace of pain. "You'll have to return to your own vision eventually. The one from the very beginning. You all angsty at the Save On Meats, bursting with that one really good idea."

He grew serious remembering their many hours together. Their many cups of drinkable diner coffee. "When we first met in the market," he said, "how did you know that I cooked?"

Jules smiled a half smile. She hadn't thought of their meeting in a long time. "You looked tired," she said.

"Lots of people look tired," Jeremy answered.

"No, no. You looked tired like beat-to-hell tired. Cook-tired. Also, you had a little piece of Elastoplast on your finger right there." She picked up his hand and examined the first knuckle of his left index finger. She remembered exactly where it had been and found the tracing of a tiny scar.

"That's it?" Jeremy asked.

Not quite. "Plus, you were staring at me," Jules said. "I look up and catch this nice-looking young man staring at me. He looks away. Then I realize he was looking at my celery root."

It was nice to hold each other again, even if it was a goodbye hug. And neither of them knew if it was really reassuring, if it really made anything right that Jeremy had made wrong, but they held on to each other for a few extra seconds anyway.

He had the kitchen right by the middle of January. All the hardware had been assembled and installed, the wiring, fibre optics and water lines were in. The RapidAir control system had been tested and retested. The dish pit worked. The prep counters had been levelled and the pass-throughs installed. The eight burners arrived from Germany and were lowered into the bridge. The grill module and the deep fryer came in the following week from Belgium and were slotted into place.

When it was complete and everything had been minutely scoured, the kitchen had a combat-ready gleam. Jeremy was down to a couple hours' sleep a night but still, standing in the middle of it all and listening to the hum of central processors in the dish pit and the RapidAir, he felt pretty much invincible.

He had only a draft menu to worry about, to which Philip had been delegated. They met in the kitchen, sat in Jeremy's office, near the alley doors, and talked about a range of issues: front staff, hosts, servers, bussers.

"And for the back?" Philip asked.

"Six or seven of us for the opening," Jeremy said. "I think we can run thereafter on five."

He didn't have names yet, but he told Philip they would be apprentices. Trained and ready by the day in question. "Be assured."

"Why apprentices?"

"I want kids," Jeremy answered. "Fresh talent, trainable."

"No aging veterans," Philip said with a smirk. "Fine with me."

Jeremy pulled a sheet of paper out of his pocket, unfolded it flat on the desk between them and turned it around to face Philip.

"Kebab of Loch Lommand-farmed salmon on a kimchi bed, with seaweed and smoked oysters." Philip read aloud the first of the appetizers. "Very nice."

Then, the first main. "Beet-marinated, grilled Alaskan goose breast with spiced Turkish couscous." And here he closed his eyes, trying to visualize this plate.

"It's purple and gold, Philly," Jeremy stage-whispered.

"Clever," Philip said, eyes on the menu again. "What's boutifar?"

"A North African boudin. Served split and grilled on a thin crostini with caramelized peppered apple."

"Boudin." Philip thought how to phrase the question. "Is that hip?"

"It's bruschetta. A Dante must-have."

"I see," Philip said, grimacing. "But boudin, that's black pudding, isn't it?"

Jeremy nodded.

"Black pudding as in *blood*?"

"Pigs' blood, normally," Jeremy said, adding in his most reassuring tone: "Blood is perfect for us."

Philip was prepared to be convinced, but dubious.

Jeremy had his speech ready. "Asia, Europe, Africa, the Americas…," he began. There were versions of boudin, literally, around the world. And yet, strangely, pork blood was as close to the pan-cultural forbidden food as you could get, short of cannibalism. Islam, Judaism and Hinduism forbid the use of pork products, of course, but even the Christian Bible outlaws blood.

Philip's expression suggested this was news to him.

"Oh yeah," Jeremy said. "The only food ban in the entire New Testament. And here we show it to reference all of these cultures. Named and seasoned for North Africa, garnished for France, presented for Spain. Our tribute to the polyglot, post-national, transgressive dish."

Philip finally smiled a little, liking the semiotics. "Provocative," he said.

"Millennial," Jeremy answered. "*Teotwawki*."

After Philip left, Jeremy went to wait in the completed front room. Benny and Albertini had managed to create something that inspired in him thoughts of what gazillionaire rock stars might build, people whose long exposure to the very largest amounts of money had made them acutely aware of how quality might be procured.

Gerriamo's wasn't even a room, really; it had moved beyond that to become what designers called a *space*. Golden hardwood floors were covered with thick ivory runners and area carpets. The walls were pale gold, the ceiling the creamy blue of summer sky. The drapes that framed the two vaulting front windows were heavy royal purple velvet, tied back with thick gold rope. The tables were square and blond with thick surfaces and thin, sturdy legs. Heavy white linen covered each. In the raised rear section and against the right wall, the bar glowed with mahogany warmth. Bottles had not yet been put onto the mirrored shelving, but the central decoration had been installed, a deco nude trolling one hand downward as if in the coolness of a stream. Her hair streamed around her breasts. On the lower, round bar tables, there were tiny shaded lamps. Jeremy turned each of them on, then returned to the main dining room and sat in one of the $750 yellow mohair chairs, admiring the effect. Admiring the view of his own kitchen doors, the quilted aluminum and the classic round porthole window.

He felt rich. More than that. He thought he knew, for a moment, what wealth would have felt like in the nineteenth century. Aristocratic wealth. Wealth beyond dreams of wealth. Wealth that liberated you from all human constraints but the final one, and possibly even that if you made the right deal.

Today was Art Day. Spaced evenly around the room were paintings waiting to be hung, face to the wall. And as he sat there, he watched Dante and Benny cross the street together, Inferno Hastings coffees in hand. Dante in crisp black, as he often was these days. Benny in a grey flannel suit, with many small buttons running up to a closed collar, and narrow-legged pants with large cuffs.

"Well, well, well," Dante said after they had entered and seen him sitting still in the middle of the room. "Everybody loves Art Day."

Benny looked apprehensive.

"What's this?" Jeremy asked her, indicating her suit.

"Front staff uniform," she said. "I'm road-testing it. There's a miniskirt version too."

They'd achieved the effect on purpose, he assumed. From the cut of the suit Benny's shape was overtly presented, but the sexiness was balanced by the austerity of the collar. It was the same straight-funky mix that underscored their thinking of the entire space.

"Is there one for me?" Jeremy asked Dante.

"For the kitchen, classic white," Dante said, but then his expression changed as he looked very distinctly at Jeremy's chin. He moved away towards one of the paintings.

"Right then, give us a hand."

They spent a few minutes turning them all face out from the wall. Each painting was framed in heavy gold. There were twelve in total, all still lifes but one, which was a grainy portrait of a naked skinhead.

"Four local artists," Dante said. "Are we not loyal?"

"Well . . . ," Benny said. "Bishop and Nygoyen are actually from Seattle. Kreschkov is Toronto."

"Attila Richard Lukacs is Vancouver, sort of," Jeremy said, motioning to the skinhead. "How much?"

"Jeremy," Dante said, mock disappointed. Then: "Twenty-five thou. I like it at the very back, between the kitchen doors. Thoughts?"

"People will think it's the chef," Jeremy said. "Like a warning."

Dante laughed loudly. "Perfect. The back wall it is."

Jeremy walked around the room slowly, looking carefully at each. Kreschkov's work was beautiful and menacing. The food she depicted was raised on a shining black background, suspended at the top of a void. Much of it was also clearly rotting. The cheese had turned. The shank of meat revealed maggots. The fruit was bruised. But each silky patch of mould, each broken pit, each rejected mouthful was rendered in achingly precise strokes. Jeremy examined the surfaces minutely and imagined that these images of decay had been painted with a brush of a single hair.

Nygoyen worked with multiple panels that assembled to make the whole. One work consisted of four square canvases arranged in a row. Another involved four canvases arranged in a larger square. If the overall image was arbitrarily segmented, Nygoyen at least painted healthy fruit and plump vines that ran from one canvas to another.

The Lukacs was vintage Lukacs, and you either did or did not like phallic National Socialist imagery. Dante had already walked the canvas to the back of the room, where it now leaned in its place between the kitchen doors.

Bishop made no attempt to conceal a debt to the Dutch Masters. The arrangements were familiar: fruit, vegetables, meat and cheese on tables, slaughtered game birds on chopping blocks, even the conical twist of newsprint, out of which spilled a bit of salt and pepper. Still, they all seemed intentionally wrong somehow. The light glanced into the frame from no definite source, throwing shadow in unexpected ways. Perspective was skewed, enlarging a dill pickle until it rivalled a watermelon on the other side of the table. (No amateurish zucchini either—the dill was next to a glass jar full of similar green oblongs, the milky liquid very clearly containing mustard seed and dillweed.)

Benny took charge of the operation and, for half an hour or so, Dante and Jeremy carted canvases up and down the riser, leaning them in various arrangements until they had the configuration just right.

They went into the kitchen afterwards and Jeremy poured iced tea. Dante sat very gingerly on one of the prep counters and waited until he had their attention. "We're almost there," he said, removing an apple from a basket on the counter. He took a bite.

"I'm excited," Benny said.

Dante ignored her, sipped his tea and chewed his apple in silence. He was watching Jeremy, who felt the next part coming with a delicious side-car sense that he doubted he could ever be fired.

"Who is Charmin?" Dante asked, finally.

Benny circled away from them to avoid the conversation. She pretended instead to inspect the kitchen. She ambled behind the pick-up counter and ran a finger nonchalantly along the edge of the front eight-burner.

"Can I help you find something?" Jeremy said to her.

"Benny, up front," Dante said without looking at her. Then to Jeremy: "Oh, fuck it." Uncharacteristic language. He took a last bite from his apple and held it out at arm's length and commenced staring at Jeremy. Benny, returning from behind the range top, encountered Dante's arm with the already browning, half-eaten apple at about eye level. Unsure of its significance for a second, she finally registered the unspoken command when Dante waggled his wrist impatiently up and down.

Benny took the apple between two fingers. She carried it down the room towards the dish pit and dropped it in the garbage can.

"The beard comes off tomorrow," Jeremy said to Dante, whose stare did not waver.

"The eighty-five-hundred-dollar shave," Dante said.

Benny returned from the garbage, expression lost.

Dante shook his head. "Benny, show him."

"Show him what Dante?"

"You like the uniform?" he asked Jeremy.

"I like the uniform fine," Jeremy shrugged.

"Oh don't," Benny said.

"Do it," Dante said. "Show the Chef."

Benny turned to Jeremy, fiddling with her buttons, adjusting the front of the suit. "Albertini's idea. He calls it aesthetic team-building."

"It wasn't Banks's idea," Dante said. "Banks only understood how to implement *my* idea. Now, Chef, I want you to imagine a set of perfect clones. Perfectly beautiful. They are dressed identically. Richly. An almost eerie combination of sex and money. Sensuous and yet efficient."

Jeremy nodded. "Ah yes."

"What did Albertini say?" Dante asked.

"Sexy robotic specimens," Benny answered. Jeremy imagined the quip had been a joke coming from Banks, but nobody was smiling.

Dante finally turned to Benny, expression impatient. She began unbuttoning the front of the suit jacket, her cheeks red. He looked back to Jeremy. "Sexy robotic specimens. I like that. A dozen perfect meat puppets."

Benny's top was now open. She pulled the sides of the jacket away from her chest to reveal the tight top. Black sports underwear, no big deal really beyond the fact that waiters' uniforms did not typically come with standard-issue underwear.

"Cover up," Jeremy said to her. "Sorry."

"Do not cover up," Dante said. He was still sitting on the edge of the prep counter. He had not moved a muscle since this exercise in humiliation and authority had begun.

Benny began unbuttoning the pants.

"The back," Dante said. "It's your ass that interests me."

She turned, dropped the back of her pants. Unisex briefs that came down the leg a few inches. Again tight.

Jeremy was resisting the urge to leave his own kitchen. "What?" he said to Dante.

Dante opened his eyes wider, staring at Jeremy. "The tab, Chef."

He hadn't even noticed. In fact, he had to lean in closer to make out the words embroidered Dolce & Gabbana-style on the waistband of Benny's briefs. She stood, breathing a little raggedly, hand on the prep counter for balance. Dante stared off into the middle distance.

The chef leaned forward across the tiles of his magnificent kitchen.

He read: *Gerriamo's—Welcome to the Inferno.*

# FRANKIE
# AND JOHNNY

He had a sense that it was time to get going. Ideas forming, a swell picking up on his mental seas. He had a sense of the forest around him and everything in it. But he also felt something that he hadn't felt in years, maybe not since those very first days, first months.

Caruzo responded to it. He went to where the Babes in the Wood were. He found the trail. The secret offshoot. The crush of ferns, the leaning trees that did not touch the sacred ground. He went to the edge of the moss. Right there, he put his hands flat on the ground. Both hands, side by side, the thumb and index fingers touching. His heart beat faster, painfully. He sat in the salal. Sat and could not move, his legs sticking out in front of him, temporarily useless. He managed only to pull a hand to his chest. A hand stiffened with weather and age. His hand hurt. His legs hurt.

Everything hurt.

But Caruzo felt a degree of certainty that they were near. First time in a long, long time, this feeling. Them right close.

"Frankie," he said to the fern. "Johnny," to the moss.

They had both been face down. Red plaid jackets. Aviator helmets with toy goggles upturned. Bodies tattered inside their clothes.

It grew dark without Caruzo noticing the day disappear. There was light, then less. Then much less. Deep in the forest he did not see the sunset, did not feel the heat of its orange glow.

He made to move, but couldn't. Or wouldn't.

He pressed his back into bark of the fir tree behind him, pressed his shoulder blades around the trunk, holding it. And finally the smaller lights began to wink out between the trees, pierce the blackness all around. He let the lights penetrate to him, find him.

"Frankie," he said. "Johnny." They were close. They stood in the salal behind him, he thought. Silent as they often were.

Caruzo folded his legs under him, pulling his shins with his hands. It took all his effort and, when he was finished, he clamped his shoulder blades against the tree and did not move again. They were very close now, one on either side. Frankie. Johnny.

There was a way to rise above yourself in this forest, it came to him. There was a way to have your sight carried high above your own head, up and up, through the trees. You closed your eyes and let the tiny hands hold you. Caruzo did this now and he felt them draw near. Still silent. And then the small hands clutched his sleeves and pulled him up, just as he had known they would, through the cedar trunks to the canopy. They held him there, very high.

He could see the Professor from here, curled inside his tent, asleep. He slept on a field of yellow pages, thousands and thousands of tiny words like wild flowers under him. He slept a peaceful sleep tonight. Utterly without dreams.

They carried Caruzo further. They spun him around like a beacon in a lighthouse and broadcast his sight over the entire park. Siwash, always. In the forest outside his bunker. At the edge of the cliff, holding the green glowing box in one hand and his blade in the other. He was weeping in anger. In fear.

Chladek sat in the bridge supports, rocking back and forth. Smoking and thinking, a square green bottle balancing on the I-beam next to him.

Caruzo floated. He turned, smiled to himself. There

were other fires, other people. And to the east there was the city, a blaze of activity, Jeremy in it. He was setting the future just then. Deciding what came next. His face glowed white. Pale and certain.

And for a time these faces and lights and sounds filtered up to Caruzo, and the tiny hands held his arms, and the tiny forms pressed against his sides, holding him high in his impossible perch. He drank in the flow of these sensations like wine. He drank it in until it had been absorbed. He was filled. He was overflowing. He thought to rise again now, up past the trees, out of the forest and into the clear, black sky.

"Frankie," Caruzo whispered. "Johnny."

But their forms had vanished, their light touch fluttered away. Caruzo began to descend towards the earth. The wind picked up on his face; he fell gently. He slid between the highest branches of the trees, through the canopy, skating along the trunks and vines. Bursting through the salal, then the scrub. Plunging faster as the distance to the earth narrowed. Speeding and speeding, the air now pasting his hair to his head, howling in his ears. The ground inches, millimetres, microns away. The red strewn forest floor. The soil with its billion particles.

There were lights all around him. Lights in the forest. Lights in the earth. It all glowed, its shape and every one of its individual grains. A person might slide among these grains. Become a part of the composite. Slide into the leaf, the twig, the earth. Be made one, at last.

Caruzo put his head on the ground. His ear filled with dry leaves that made no sound. A root pressed his cheek without sensation.

The lights and the trees shimmered together. He shimmered himself. He grew warmer for a time. Each of his own grains warm and very, very light.

Jeremy talked to Fabrek for a long time on the phone before convincing him to come downtown. He was trying to sell Fabrek, something he hadn't done before. Sketching plans and envisioning opportunity. "Hey, I'm flattered," Fabrek said. "But I'm busy, there's this new project."

"The Gorilla Grill?" Jeremy said. It didn't sound terribly promising.

"Guerrilla," Fabrek said. "As in: Name a spot, any spot, we'll do the rest. Six people to six hundred. Booze and extras included."

"So, like, totally illegal," Jeremy said.

"So, like, yeah," Fabrek said. But the money was good and they got all kinds of strange gigs. Techno all-nighters. Jungle parties. Yuppie Polynesian lounge nights with whole spit-roasted pigs. The weekend before, Fabrek had been on Gambier Island at a field party for 350 vegan animists.

"How about getting busted?" Jeremy asked.

Fabrek made a dismissive noise into the phone. But he agreed to meet for a coffee.

Now Jeremy was looking out the window of the Rotter-dammer Café, half a block down the street from the papered-over windows of Gerriamo's. Stroking his chin, newly shaven as of that afternoon. It was just nightfall, and the cloud cover had split a seam at the horizon. There was now an orange glow from the west. And this light steadily intensified as darkness descended from the east, blooming upward, refracting, illuminating the clouds from beneath, doming out over the park and the city like the light of a great fire.

Jeremy got to his feet and leaned through the open window of the café. There was a new breeze too. Cold. Salty. It shocked his face and moved his hair.

Fabrek was reclining in the overstuffed couch near the front window. He had a dubious expression as he slowly turned the pages of the menu. A Benny design. Dante loved it. It was a thin cardboard book, the cover divided into four equal blocks of solid colour—olive, black, silver and blood—complementing the room without repeating any tones. It was bound with a white silk rope, tasselled. Inside were four plain, heavy paper pages, the outside edges microscopically gilded. Two pages of food. Two of wine. It was the most elegant menu Jeremy had ever seen.

Fabrek finished and closed the cover with exaggerated care, slid it onto the table in front of him. "I used to make falafels," he announced.

"You had a grill." Jeremy said, sitting opposite his friend. "You made keftes, chicken kebabs, chicken breast sandwiches...."

"Only thing I see on here that's grilled...," Fabrek said, picking up the menu and running a finger down the inside page. "Whazzit: beet-marinated goose breast?"

"So we grill a goose breast. You went to school somewhere."

"No," Fabrek said, mouth bending into a smirk. "I was taught by my baba. She had a Hibachi on the fire escape outside the window of her apartment. She made dinner there every summer night and I don't think she ever put beet juice on a goose."

Jeremy put his palms together, elbows on his knees.

"Where do you buy foie gras anyway?" Fabrek asked.

"This gig is real," Jeremy said. "You could make some money. The opening is going to be special, but if you handle it right it could be a full-time thing. A reputation, a real career. I was thinking of it like a favour."

"Thanks," Fabrek said. "But there's gotta be five dozen apprentices who would jump at this chance."

"I also need special people," Jeremy said. "People I know."

"What's that mean?"

"People I know," Jeremy said. "People who might be prepared to try things a little differently. I don't need fifteen years' experience or anything, just come ready to train."

Fabrek leaned into the window and looked up the street at the front of Gerriamo's. The front awning had been replaced with a longer black one that stretched from the now double doors right out to curbside. On opening night, the tuxedoed valet parkers would stand here on a blood-red runner and make everybody feel like they were attending the Oscars.

Fabrek shook his head. "It's not me," he said. "I'm not *inside* a place like that. I'm cooking on a Hibachi on a fire escape somewhere. You understand?"

Jeremy leaned back in his chair, disappointed.

"But I came down tonight," Fabrek said finally, "because I do know people. Better-suited people. There are these cooking-school kids. They're off until the spring semester, so they'll work."

"What year school?" Jeremy asked.

"You just said they didn't need to be trained."

"How untrained?" Jeremy asked.

"Pretty raw," said Fabrek. "But they roast a decent pig. I know this for a fact."

They walked together around the corner into Hastings Street, Jeremy's turn to be dubious. Half a block away he saw them right where Fabrek said they'd be hanging, at the window tables of Juize 'n' Bluntz. Jeremy had probably walked past them a hundred times. Half a dozen kids in Prada Sport gear and L.A. Eyeworks sunglasses with coloured glass, light blue, khaki, orange, sea-foam green.

Jeremy spotted Henk, whom Fabrek had earlier described. Skinny, with a poofy, natural-red afro. He had a black V-neck shell pulled over an orange T-shirt. He sported a thin gold chain with a tiny eggbeater charm. Timberlands.

"Whassup," Henk said, passing off a joint to a colleague and flopping out a hand to shake, wrist cocked, fingers splayed downward. He spoke very slowly. The leader.

Fabrek shook.

Henk greeted Jeremy the same way, then back to Fabrek: "You workin'?"

"I'm working," Fabrek said.

"You got something for us?" He was still talking to Fabrek, but looking curiously at Jeremy.

Jeremy wondered if Henk had picked him as a roast-pig guy or an all-night vegan jungle party kind of guy.

"It's different," Fabrek said. "This guy here's a chef." Yes, a real executive chef, he explained.

It got their attention. Jeremy was able to observe one of the anomalies of kitchen culture: how working-class kids with born attitude (but who seriously wanted to cook) would sit a bit straighter and even talk nice if they knew they were speaking to an executive chef.

Henk made a very small motion with his hand and his buddy stubbed out the joint. "Are you hiring?" he said. "Chef?"

Fabrek had to go. "Have fun," he said, shaking with Henk and Jeremy again.

"Take care," Jeremy said. "Keep in touch."

"Oh, I'm around," Fabrek answered. "You take care too."

Jeremy had a coffee with the crew, then took them 0around the corner to Gerriamo's. They fell in behind him in a ragged line across the sidewalk and out into the street. They looked like an album cover, all slope-shouldered, sole-scuffing ennui. Henk, Torkil, Angela, Conrad, Rolando and a thick-necked kid with a single black eyebrow visible under the rim of a battered straw hat, who introduced himself by his full name: Joey de Yonker. He was a part-time DJ.

"Joey, OK?" Jeremy said, unlocking the alley door.

The group fell silent behind him. Jeremy turned. "All right," he said. "Joey de Yonker."

They went inside. The kids fanned out around the room, looking, touching, the cool perfection of this kitchen with all its brand new top-end gear slowly sinking in.

"Jayzuz," Rolando said, peering down the gleaming length of the bridge, a long hand to the point of his chin.

Torkil was inspecting the front of the RapidAir, nodding. He looked to be taking mental notes, which Jeremy imagined were instantly memorized.

Angela and Conrad were looking at the Metro shelving full of Bourgeat copper. They were breathing through their mouths, necks craned back. Conrad had to be told to remove his sunglasses indoors. He wore beach slippers and boasted finely chiselled facial architecture. Angela had soft, spoiled but intelligent features framed in blond.

"Whoa," came a voice from the end of the room. Joey de Yonker was grooving on the dish pit.

Jeremy let them poke around for awhile before calling them together again in a way that brought Quartey to mind. A chefly command issued from the middle of a large kitchen. "All right everyone," Jeremy called. "Listen up."

They had fun that first night. They discussed the possibilities. They considered the future.

Jeremy took them up front, and the kids walked gingerly around, looking up at the high walls and the arched ceiling like travellers at the Basilica of St. Peter. Torkil went behind the bar and ran his hands along the wood. Angela, Conrad and Rolando were inspecting a panel of Nygoyen's. Joey, who Jeremy had just decided had to be called something other than Joey de Yonker but hadn't thought of what yet, stood adrift in front of the Lukacs.

Henk stood back by Jeremy, arms crossed, nodding. "Nice space," he said. "Very nice."

Back in the kitchen, Jeremy walked them through stations. They talked about school. They'd done Basic Skills. They knew measurements and knife work. Product ID. Sanitation and Meat Fab. They'd done vegetables, stocks and some sauces. They knew that you didn't sear meat to keep in the juices.

"Whut? Naaah," Angela said when Jeremy suggested it to test them. "It's for colour and for flavour. For caramelization."

The group was nodding, looking at him.

"OK," Jeremy said. "So you knew that."

They talked about the Guerrilla Grill. Mention of it produced sly smiles and sideways glances. Jeremy sensed how delicious the secret was to them.

He learned that Fabrek had alt.celebrity status in the crowd that knew, which at their school was essentially this crowd. Henk had met Fabrek first, at a Dead concert (this event predated the Fabrek's Falafels by a few years). He'd been making portobello mushroom-cap burgers on a Weber kettle set up in the back of his Toyota pickup truck. There was a huge line up, over the heads of which Henk saw this crazed, bald Iranian dancing around in the back of his vehicle, bootleg tapes blaring in the background. And then the burger itself...heaven. The mushroom cap was juicy and hot, rich and complexly flavoured. When the crowd thinned, he went back to the truck and struck up a conversation. Fabrek told him how to make the marinade. (He still remembered: olive oil, balsamic vinegar, minced shallots, parsley, garlic, cumin, mustard powder and cayenne.) The underground economy flourished outside Dead gigs, naturally, but Henk was still impressed.

He told Jeremy how it helped him make up his mind about cooking as a career. "I was going that way," he said. "I just didn't know there could be such individualism involved, such an element of performance. I thought kitchens had to be, you know, straight ahead. Fabrek was a *show*."

The rest of the group agreed. They talked more about performance, saying something individual with your cooking. When the Guerrilla Grill came along they all jumped at the chance. Fabrek had been openly skeptical when Henk showed up with his list of six names. They were kids, Fabrek said. They hadn't graduated Basic Skills I.

"This from a guy who never went to school," Conrad said.

"Anyway," Henk said, looking over at Conrad. "He did start feeding us a little work."

They drove the van. They carried gear into the bush. Eventually Fabrek let them set up the fire pit and tend the pig.

"Showtime," Joey de Yonker said.

They talked about their futures, what they all wanted to do. No surprise to Jeremy by this point that every one of them wanted to start their own place one day. Their own show. In some cases, possibly unrealistic.

Joey de Yonker had a named picked out: The Garage. He thought he wanted to involve a lot of kinetic sculpture. "Metals," he said. "Blow torches."

Torkil was the group baker. He was already selling small-scale to friends and family. He shrugged. Humble. "Chai-thyme rye," Henk said, next to Jeremy. "Stuff rocks."

Angela's idea was Grazer, a high-concept tapas Web bar. Satay, tofu spears, samosas and slivers of super-fusion designer pizza. Caviar and quail's egg was mentioned. The Web part centred on the stand-up tables with shelves for tapas dishes and pop-up, active-matrix, flat screens. Waterproof touch-pad keyboards. The browser favourites file would have links to sites all over the Net, providing background on ingredients. And their own website, naturally.

"Browse the tapas, graze the Web," Angela said. Conrad and Rolando were looking at her very seriously, admiringly.

"Henk?" Jeremy asked.

Henk was thinking about high-end panini street carts. Brie-onion, tomato-chevre. Squashed flat in a two-sided griddle and eaten out of a waxed-paper sleeve while you strolled. A once-humble idea from the Rue Mouftarde, although what Henk was imagining for Canada was more like a panini revolution. Vancouver, Toronto, Montreal, Halifax. Big Time. "Nothing wrong with getting smokin' good food off a street cart," he said, very slowly.

Jeremy told them as much as he could about how the

following weeks would unfold. He could pay them for the three-week training period. He could pay them for opening night, which was going to be a very large, very splashy affair. "We'll be running the kitchen a little hot that night," Jeremy told them. "That's why I'm bringing you all in. But for some of you it could turn into a full-time thing."

They had a glass of Tempranillo to end the evening. They swilled the pleasant wine and talked more freely. Jeremy listened and appraised, already slotting them into stations based on skill and personality.

"We'll bring in a dish pit operator, of course," Jeremy said.

Joey de Yonker looked vaguely disappointed.

At about eleven, when they were gone, he cleaned up and took a last look around. The glasses had run through the dish pit already and were standing in the dryer. The wine bottle was in the recycling rack. The coolers hummed and the floors shone. The knife rack was a phalanx of sharp points, hanging and ready. In the centre, the ageless Fugami. He thought of how he could have used the Sabatier now. The Fugami was here; it *was* this kitchen. The Sabatier might have balanced feelings in him, events he saw upcoming, the same way it would have balanced in his hand.

He pushed his mind to other things. He locked the back door behind him and stepped outside. It was black in the alley, the cloud cover having recapped the sky. It was colder than before. He blew in his hands and turned uptown, ready to walk home and sleep if he could. Pace otherwise. Stare out the window over the blackness of the park and think.

He was almost at the alley mouth when he saw the form against the back wall of the building and stopped. The person pushed off the wall, tiredly. He had been waiting a long time.

"Son?" the Professor said, voice just a little fragile.

He had been sleeping. Not dreaming. Whenever he fell asleep over his work he did not dream, having spent himself. Drained dry.

"It can't have been that late," Jeremy said. They were walking down Haro Street, their pace quick as they passed sleeping walk-up apartment buildings and the oak trees leaned in. They were approaching the park, Jeremy's heart racing, his throat tight.

"I fall asleep early these days," the Professor said.

"Was he sick, did you know he was sick?" Jeremy asked.

The Professor didn't think the question was meant to be accusatory, and so he didn't respond directly and wasn't offended. He returned to telling his story.

Asleep, no dreams. The sunset woke him. Something he had never experienced. There had been a brilliant glow, through his eyelids. It pulled him from sleep.

He crawled from the edge of the tent to look out over the water. The sun had just emerged from under the cap of cloud, making a vein of molten orange at the horizon. Washing over everything around him. It bathed the trees, turned the needles and leaves and fronds of grass into a spectrum of apple green and incandescent violet. An amazing, filtered, vibrant last light.

"I thought of my own endings," the Professor said. "I thought of things being finished."

Jeremy strode along in silence beside him. He burned with a much different intensity now, the Professor noted.

"I went to find him, to talk with him," the Professor went on. "It was suddenly clear to me that the time had come for things to be written, to be finished." He crashed on up through the bush, past Prospect Point, across the causeway to the top of Reservoir Trail. Only by then had the light fallen so low that a uniform blue descended between the trees. The light grew particulate, grainy. You could feel it move across your skin.

In the cane of salmonberry bushes he called Caruzo's name, their comfortable mutual arrangement. He called from the bush a short distance away. No response, do not push on. Go around or come back later.

He waited a long time there. He had never broken the rule before.

"Caruzo," he called again. "Answer me."

Nothing.

His camp was empty, but the Professor felt that he was not far away. He followed the trail he had been shown. Down the hillside to the secret offshoot, the side path. It split out from behind a spray of fern, disappeared into the salal. A short distance along came the mossy clearing. The trees parted, made a place. A place of silence, rest. A place to lay down. Caruzo's holy place.

He was just off the path, short of the clearing itself. His cheek rested on the soil. His eyes closed. He looked asleep, but the Professor felt a weight drop through him. He caught his breath, knelt.

Caruzo was cold.

The Professor grew silent now. They were at the lagoon, still walking very quickly. They were in the forest, climbing Cathedral Trail.

"I always expected a day like this one," the Professor said. He felt very still as they walked. No comparison to the black whirlpool that followed Hélène's death. There was a certain grey tranquility to his emotional seas.

His son vibrated with energy. They were charging up the hill towards the point now, Jeremy maintaining a long, aggressive stride.

"And Siwash was there?" Jeremy asked.

"Later," the Professor answered.

He sat in the salal nearby after finding Caruzo's body. From this spot, the Professor noted, you could not see a single piece of sky. No blue, no stars. The children had been all the light that this place offered. The Professor leaned and touched the moss. He picked up leaves and let them slide through his fingers, brushed the nearby salal. The ancestors of these leaves had covered the bodies in this indentation. Silent and invisible among the trees. To find them you would have had to search very gently, sifting with your hands for a very long time. Searching with tenderness and intent.

He meditated on this quest for a time, as much as half an hour, he thought. It was the green light he noticed first. A small green glow hovering in the trees. It didn't cover any area at all, didn't illuminate. Just made a tiny patch of green where seconds before there had been none.

"Who is it?" The Professor had been startled.

"I," said Siwash from the darkness.

He'd been there a while, the Professor guessed. And in that instant, he wondered if Siwash had played a role in Caruzo's death—the battling evangelists came to mind—although there had been no signs of violence.

Siwash came forward through the leaves. He crouched a few feet away in the salal, regarding the Professor. Then Caruzo's body. He knew, he said, his voice smooth. "I knew the hour and minute," Siwash said. "I knew the second it happened."

He edged a little closer along the path. The leaves rustled under him. He had sheathed his strange green light in a leather holster and withdrawn a knife. Nine, ten inches long. A gleaming blade.

The Professor paid attention to this knife.

"I became unsettled," Siwash said. The knife was extending directly in front of him, silver blade up, black handle buried in his right fist. He was running his thumb along the blade, aggressively. The Professor found himself wincing in anticipation of the cut. The spurt of blood.

"Unsettled how?" the Professor answered.

"I felt that a new wind had risen," Siwash intoned. "And it marked a great disturbance. It marked the great imminence of shaking." And again his deep voice resonated among the trees, shivering the leaves and pine needles. "Of distortion."

The Professor nodded politely, confused. A little frightened. The blade had become uncomfortably active. Twitching in Siwash's hand. Blade up. Blade down. Slashing lightly at the nearby leaves.

"I have not seen it," the Professor said. "This distortion."

"You wouldn't," Siwash said, looking down at Caruzo, cheeks hard. "You need a certain perspective. And you brought it here first. This distortion of views. You brought him in first, and now he comes alone. I see him in the forest with others. I have seen him here, on this spot."

The Professor took a minute to respond. "He's my son."

"The others, the ones on the seawall and in the paths," Siwash said very slowly, rendering judgment. "They come, they go, but they are never truly here. He is not either here . . . or there."

The wind was sighing among the trees. The Professor had the sense that the clouds had thickened. That they were heavy with imminent rain.

"You have reached your number," the Professor said.

Siwash thought the idea over, the knife rotating in his fist, blade turning as if he were twisting it in a wound.

"And did he tell you?" Jeremy asked. They had made their way up into the forest and were now, very quietly, heading towards the spot off Reservoir Trail.

Siwash hadn't said yes or no. The Professor thought he had been taken by surprise that the number was mentioned at all. He turned and disappeared into the dark.

They arrived at Reservoir Trail. Jeremy looked around them both into the same darkness. "He will be back in his place," the Professor reassured. "He doesn't wander as a rule."

Jeremy turned away sharply when he first saw Caruzo's body. He lay with his cheek smeared into the earth. His eyes closed. They both knelt. Jeremy made a move to touch the body, to look at the face and the hands.

"There isn't a mark on him that I can find," the Professor said. "And I had my reasons to look."

"We'll bury him here," Jeremy said.

They found Caruzo's camp a quarter mile away in the salal. They found their way through the maintenance yard first, through his front door. From there the Professor took them through the salmonberry cane, left along a worn but hidden path, between a number of tightly spaced fir trees. It was almost invisible, even standing on top of it. Caruzo had left little physical mark on this place despite his long tenure: a black plastic sheet strung low, a pile of rotting clothes, a faded blanket. A quilt, Jeremy thought, touching it. You could pick out a pattern in the soiled squares, a pattern that was once visible in boldly contrasting colours. There was some peanut butter here. Epoxy. A latrine shovel. No books, no other bags.

They buried Caruzo in the holy clearing. They dug a pit in the moss, sweaty work. They piled earth and leaves over Caruzo and his possessions. A layer of moss was last. He made a green mound in the middle of that place.

They sat on their haunches in the dark afterwards. A few respectful minutes passed. Jeremy was already thinking about what came next.

Siwash Rock wasn't far from the Professor's camp. Jeremy made his way across the park to the familiar cliffside encampment, then another few hundred yards around the hillside overlooking the harbour.

The Professor had strongly objected. What was the point? What could he say? After all that had happened, his father said, their work here was nearly done. Writing could be completed from home, or from Jeremy's apartment, which was closer. So they would leave now, the Professor said, the two of them, finally. They had learned much.

Jeremy looked at his father, impressed by these words. He then impressed his father in return by producing the Fugami from his waistband. He folded back the layers of tea towel he had wrapped around it, and the knife lay darkly across his palms. Even after Jeremy had explained the trade he had in mind, the Professor was unconvinced.

"He is not always stable. Must you have your knife back?"

"Yes," Jeremy said. And more emphatically: "I also don't like the idea of him having it."

After a few minutes of searching the cliff's edge, Jeremy found the path down to the old pillbox. He stood on the sloping grade. Assuming he was already being watched, Jeremy pulled his hands away from his sides, palms out.

He took one slow step at a time, descending the slope halfway without hearing a thing beyond the sigh and scrape of one tree against another in a rising wind. At the bottom of the slope Jeremy could make out the black metal door into the old pillbox. He thought it was ajar.

The sound came from directly behind him. A twig cracked, Jeremy spun around, scattering gravel.

Siwash was immensely strong. Jeremy was on his back, a crushing weight pressed down on his chest. Small rocks ground into his shoulder blades and the towel-wrapped Fugami dug into the small of his back inside his waistband.

"Just be still," Siwash said, persuasive and calm. Deep tones moderated by musical intonation. "Let me have another look at you."

And in this position Jeremy first saw Siwash: bald, serious, skin smooth and seamless as plastic, without wrinkle or pore. Expressionless round grey eyes. Ears impossibly folded, like a boxer's, but cut and ribboned, the earlobe of the left split into two distinct pendants.

The weight on Jeremy's chest shifted painfully. One knee rested squarely on his sternum, the other in his groin. A cold sliver across his Adam's apple remained as well. Jeremy knew the edge.

Jeremy whispered his message. "I brought a gift."

Siwash took several seconds to decide, but when he did, it was final. He pulled Jeremy to his feet, sheathed the knife and commenced vigorously brushing the leaves and bits of gravel off Jeremy's shoulders and his back. Then he led the way towards the pillbox, a rounded rectangle of thick concrete and steel, rusting, moss covered, clinging to a rock outcropping on the cliff. Inside the heavy steel door Jeremy found himself in a tiny, although neatly organized, room. There were stacks of books, a narrow cot, two benches and a stool for sitting. On the walls there were dozens of maps taped up, overlapping, flickering in the light offered by many candles mounted inside soup cans.

They had tea. Jeremy's hands shaking, despite himself. The tea cup rattling. It was China Black, he couldn't help but notice.

Siwash pulled the stool close. He sat and sipped delicately, the Sabatier unsheathed again and balanced across his knees. "You're wondering about the maps, no doubt," he said.

Jeremy hadn't been, but Siwash had decided to talk.

The Mercator projection was familiar to Jeremy. The Miller cylinder might have even come up in highschool geography. The sinusoidal pseudocylindrical projection rang fewer bells, however, and Jeremy admitted defeat with the gnomonic azimuthal. "Not unlike personal perspectives," Siwash said, "we rarely understand map projections that are not our own."

He was on conic projections now: lambert conformal, Albers' equal area. "One of my favourites," Siwash was saying. "Bipolar oblique conic conformal."

Siwash continued to talk while standing and pointing to a map of North America on the far wall. Jeremy could see from where he sat that it was an eccentric projection. If someone had painted a map of the continent on a basketball and (while the paint was still wet) fired this basketball out of a cannon against a canvas, the resultant print might look something like the bipolar oblique conic conformal projection. Compressed and exploded at the same time. It strained to stay on the page.

"The earth usefully rendered in two dimensions," Siwash sighed, sitting. His face clouded. There were projection problems, Jeremy learned. Problems inherent in trying to depict the surface of a three dimensional sphere (or a near-sphere, the world being shaped more like a squashed pear) on the impoverished dimensions of a flat piece of paper. "Distortion," Siwash said, grimacing. "And it gets much worse with scale. You understand?"

Maps of the entire earth were the most distorted, and every projection designed to solve the problem came saddled with its own limitations. Directions weren't true or the proportions got wonky or—as in the case of the globe cut into petals and flattened on the page—it became impossible to get a sense of how anything was connected. "There's no straight line here," Siwash said, stabbing his finger towards a map that illustrated this point. "I know there are straight lines *really*. I can draw one in the soil." He drew one with the toe of his boot in the dust of the pillbox floor. "Proving," he said, eyes wide, "that too much map is *problematic*."

"Smaller maps?" Jeremy tried.

Siwash liked that answer. He leaned back, he smiled. He even drummed his fingers on the blade of the Sabatier lying across his knees.

True. The smaller the map, the less the distortion. "A map of the city is pretty reliable," Siwash said. "But a map of just this room would be better. A map of one square foot of this room better still! How about that? With a map of just one square foot of this room, you'd *really* know where you were."

"As long as you happened to be on that one square foot," Jeremy said.

"Exactly!" Siwash cried, on his feet now, head brushing the ceiling. "Only problem is carrying around all those maps. How many square feet a day do *you* use? I use dozens, and I conserve. But you use more, city people do. Tens of thousands, squander them. Chew them up, spit them out."

Aha, thought Jeremy. Because with his pronouncement, Siwash had flourished the box from his holster, about the size of a TV remote control. He placed it on the stool where Jeremy could see it, turned it on. It had a small green screen that glowed with a string of numbers and letters.

"GPS," Jeremy said, dumbly recognizing the tracking device. Reading the characters that had popped up sharply on the display: N 49.18.32 W 123.09.18.

"Satellites, isn't it?" Jeremy asked finally.

Twenty-four, in fact. In six orbits.

Siwash closed his eyes. "I believe in three segments," he said. "Space, control and user." An incantation. A creed. He took a deep breath, closed his eyes and settled. Jeremy didn't move.

"I believe in a master control facility, in the monitor network and in the signals through which groundtrack is maintained. I believe in earthbound receivers, in the free download of positional data. I believe in the geodetic datum of latitude, longitude, velocity and time. In millimetre accuracy across this ground and in the sanctity of parameters. Forever."

His eyes opened. The air rang.

Between them glowed the GPS verdict on the matter— N 49.18.32 W 123.09.18—and around them stretched the infinite coordinates of a familiar landscape, sweeping away in all directions. Up into the black forest to Caruzo. Along the cliffside to Chladek. Through the trees to all the others. And all these points linked clearly to this one. To Siwash Rock itself, motionless in any breeze, only acknowledging the wind with the slight waving of its single hardy tree.

"You were counting people," Jeremy said, slowly. "And they always said you would reach a number one day."

Siwash raised the knife until it hovered an inch under Jeremy's chin.

"But they were wrong," Jeremy said. "You always had the number. You only counted others to record their passage, to see them move by in thousands. And to see this number glowing, always the same, every day, this has been your reminder that you are not in motion."

Siwash let the knife fall slowly to his side and stood quite still. And with that resignation, Jeremy knew what the Professor had long known: that there were different paths into the same wood. Different views of the same familiar story. Caruzo the first, the guardian, his sense of obligation buried in this place. His quest for redemption and reunion finally complete. Chladek the wanderer, returned at last to his Place of Trees. Siwash the eternal seeker, wanting definition, wanting assurance, certainty on the matter of where he stood. None of them were waiting for anything. They'd found it.

Jeremy pulled the Fugami slowly from his waistband and laid it across his knees. For a moment there were only two things in the room—the Sabatier, the Fugami. The one shone, the other seemed to absorb the light.

"You took something from me," Jeremy said.

Siwash sat heavily opposite.

"Something from the outside," Jeremy went on. "Something that I will need as I return."

It was a friendly exchange, in the end.

Siwash was impressed by the sight of the new blade, its impervious black sheen. But he thrilled at the idea of a blade remaining sharp into the fourth millennium. That kind of permanence—that kind of a clean and undistorted line—could so rarely be assured.

And after Jeremy had his Sabatier comfortably in his hand, he left, feeling the familiar balance of it, the talismanic simplicity of this hand-forged quillioned blade made even before his father was born. He left Siwash to his round room, his ring of flickering candles and his maps providing their various views of what could be known of the world around them.

# GERRIAMO'S

## — DINNER —

KEBAB OF LOCH LOMMAND SALMON ON A KIMCHI BED,
SEAWEED + SMOKED OYSTERS

**SALAD OF PERIWINKLE + TRUFFLE,
ENDIVE WHEATSHEAF, POTATO CREAM**

DANDELION-ROCKET PESTO SOUP WITH CRÈME FRAÎCHE

**ESCABECHE OF SARDINE WITH PRESERVED LEMON OIL**

BRUSCHETTA OF BOUTIFAR WITH CARAMELIZED PEPPERED APPLE

**SAUTÉED FOIE GRAS WITH WHITE-PORT PEAR SAUCE,
GINGER + POTATO CRISP**

TRADITIONAL GAME CONSOMMÉ WITH
GERRIAMO'S SIGNATURE WON TON

**TERRINE WITH PICKLED LENTILS,
BEET CARPACCIO, VARIOUS BREADS**


PRAWNS WITH SPICED YAM WAFERS,
GRAPPA + THAI GINGER CREAM

**FILLET OF TITICACA FLATFISH WITH
WASABI POTATO CRUST + SESAME JUS**

RISOTTO OF WILD MUSHROOMS, SEASONAL LEAVES + HERBS

**ASSIETTE VÉGÉTARIEN**

SQUAB CRAPAUDINE WITH
WILD BERRY CREAM SAUCE + POTATO GRATIN

**DUCK WITH RHUBARB SAUCE, SPAETZLE + LEEKS**

BEET-MARINATED GRILLED GOOSE BREAST
WITH SPICED TURKISH COUSCOUS

**ROAST RACK OF NEW ZEALAND LAMB,
CELERIAC PURÉE, BLACK OLIVE JUS**

PAN-SEARED RABBIT SADDLE WITH SWEET ONION + PANCETTA

**BEEF TENDERLOIN WITH RED-WINE REDUCTION,
LEEK FRITE + CHESTNUTS**

# GERRIAMO'S

## — DESSERT —

A SELECTION OF SORBETS: KIWI, PERSIMMON, LYCHEE

**ASSIETTE DU FROMAGE**

PARFAIT OF WILD BERRY, MINT, CHOCOLATE

**WARM CHOCOLATE CAKE WITH GOAT'S MILK GELATO**

APPLE TART WITH LEMONGRASS +
SMALL-BATCH BOURBON CREAM

# T H E
# G U E R R I L L A
# G R I L L

The days were streaming by. Ideas fully blossomed. And having laid his plans, committed to them, Jeremy wouldn't have minded if time slowed down so he could enjoy himself more. But starting at five o'clock in the morning he was talking with suppliers, time zone by time zone, working his way westward with the sun. Eager suppliers, as it turned out, even some of the international ones having heard about the new ownership and vying to be part of another Inferno success story. He placed his advance orders and took a perverse pleasure in turning inside-out his previous patterns. Dante greased customs. Dante greased everything. All avenues of international supply yawned open and Gerriamo's had credit.

Midday he sometimes took an hour and visited the park. Caruzo's grave first, always. He felt him in the soil. He felt the children too. Part of himself. They were all there and it rooted him. He felt strengthened and pure leaving that place of respectful trees.

Time permitting, he'd pop in on Chladek to see how he was doing. Or Siwash, with whom he might kill a pot of China Black and review projection theory or knife design.

"Have you considered," Siwash said, on one of these occasions, spinning strands of gold with his voice, "living here?"

Jeremy politely declined.

"You *are* a riddle," Siwash said, shaking his head and relighting the candle under his bipolar oblique conic conformal map of North America.

The Professor had returned home to write, and Chladek missed all the action that he and Caruzo used to generate. He told Jeremy: "Without them, the place is less... *glamorous.*"

Afternoons, Jeremy was running the squad through a short but intense training cycle. They came in around two, got dressed in their white jackets and check pants. Then Jeremy took them through drills, stalking up and down the line behind them like a drill sergeant, dressed as they were but for the executive chef colours he'd chosen for a thin band at the neck: blue, red and white. They did a mock dinner, a family meal and a debrief, sometimes over a sip of wine. Although Jeremy didn't want to inflate his head by officially awarding him the title, Henk had become the de facto sous chef. He was blindingly fast, followed instructions and, as it turned out, had a good instinctive feel for Blood cooking.

"This menu is pretty hip, I take it," he said in private to Jeremy after an overarching group discussion about the restaurant's approach. "I mean, we're sorta making a point almost."

"Sorta," Jeremy said. "Like what, do you think?"

Like, Henk tried to articulate, that no pinch of sea salt would do when a combination of spices from eight different countries were available. "It's... ," he summarized, "*copious.*"

"It's copious," Jeremy agreed.

Henk also produced Chico the dishwasher, who for seven bucks an hour was no doubt glad to see the outside of the Juize 'n' Bluntz for a stretch.

Joey would have become their weak link, but Jeremy decided the guy would work out if it killed him trying. He had a serious case of digital spasticity, for one. He was about one in five to drop any given breakable item. Three plates the first day—it was all Jeremy could do not to ask him to leave, right there on the third plate. But Joey grabbed a broom. "Broom," he said, sweeping up. And then he left the broom next to his station.

Presumably to save him time when he breaks the next one, Jeremy thought. *Mise en place.*

There was also the talking-to-himself part. "Onions. Medium dice," he would say, while chopping onions in the way described. "Sauté to golden," he would say five minutes later. "White wine. Reduce."

During which process, invariably, someone would think he was talking to them and answer. Angela would say: "Sorry? White wine?"

And Conrad would say: "What white wine? I thought we did these with port."

And so on, until Jeremy or Henk jumped in and got everyone back inside their own envelope of concentration.

They were working off drill sheets Jeremy had prepared. Detailed instructions for each of the dishes they would prepare. And so the following list of steps hung on the pass-through shelf in front of every station:

### *App. #1—Salmon Kebab*

1) place salmon kebab on the grill
2) warm seaweed
3) warm 3 smoked oysters
4) plate kimchi
5) plate seaweed around the kimchi
6) plate 3 oysters, triangle
7) plate salmon kebab
8) plate chili-oil drops on plate rim
9) plate up (say: "kebab plate up")

Every afternoon Joey de Yonker would come in and look at his lists, squinting, nodding like he thought he might have seen them before.

The rest of the squad was actually better than Jeremy had expected. Speed was going to be a problem when they got well and truly slammed, but Torkil only took a couple of days to get used to the bread ovens and from that point onward was producing very decent bread, loaves, rolls, baguettes, épis. Angela, Conrad and Rolando were figuring out the range tops and the grill. They were burning stuff, certainly. But less stuff the second week than the first.

"Did somebody intend to *watch* these?" Jeremy yelled at one point, looking in on a tray of baguette slices in the oven. They were theoretically becoming crostini; more practically, charcoal briquettes. "You set off the Halon only once in my kitchen, you understand? Once. Now somebody *deal* with it."

There was a trickle of smoke coming out of the oven. Rolando threw his lanky frame into action. He slid his hands into hot gloves, grabbed tongs and a roasting pan, and started scooping the burning bread out of the still-hot oven into the pan.

"The *sink*, please," Jeremy yelled at Conrad, who flashed on the water just in time for Rolando to dump his load of smoking toasts. The water killed the smoke. The Halon did not discharge. Everybody looked sheepish except Henk, who looked angry.

"If you can't remember you got toast in the cooker," Jeremy said, looking at Henk and knowing this message was going to filter down. "You put a goddamn baguette up on the pass-through there. Everybody knows there's bread *in,* so everybody knows it's gotta come *out* sometime."

"Got it Chef." "Right Chef." "Won't happen again Chef."

"OK, let's get back to it. Thanks, Rolando. Fast hands."

So it went. But they were also having fun, and Jeremy knew that with the drills down, the sequence of steps internalized, then the intensity of the opening would melt time. Service would hit and they'd be in the zone. They'd wake up and it would be over, all too soon.

Out front, meanwhile, it was swarming. Servers were being trained. They were stocking the bar and arranging tables and fixing glitches in the cash register and order system. A monitor and printer had to be installed at the pick-up counter in the kitchen, from which Jeremy would announce and distribute the incoming orders. He had intended this counter to be the border between front and back, but Jeremy was fighting a losing battle trying to keep spectators out of his kitchen. As they worked through the menu, the squad was starting to make great smells. Once the menu had been printed and distributed out front, it became impossible to keep out the curious.

They were at day eleven in the countdown, a week and a half to showtime, and Benny came back with Dante and stood watching them run through the mains. The servers were getting menu initiation that day; Jeremy suggested they prepare six goose and six prawn mains for lunch. A chance for a first, live, small-scale test of the squad's grill routine.

"Nice and easy," Jeremy said, leaning on the pick-up counter and looking at each of them. Angela, Conrad and Rolando were on the far side of the main cook top. Henk stood on the near side, shotgun to Jeremy's station. Torkil was at the baking counter, working on pastries. Joey was at the plating station.

"All right, ordering three prawns."

"Ordering three prawns," Henk said and threw on the kebabs, which took two minutes a side. Rolando finished the yam wafers in the deep fryer and Joey fanned these out on the three plates Conrad had prepped with a puddle of warm Thai ginger cream.

"Order three more prawns," Jeremy said.

"Ordering three prawns." Henk flipped the first set of

prawns, plated them in the spiral fashion at the centre of the plate as Jeremy had demonstrated. Chef Papier then walked back to the plating area and finished each dish with diamonds of yellow pepper set carefully at the edge of the cream. Plates to the hot pick-up and they were gone.

The second set of prawns went on, and Jeremy noted that Joey turned smartly to his new plates. Nice mahogany brown wafers. Puddle of cream. Nothing wrong with that.

"Doing good," Jeremy called out. "OK? Order three goose."

"Ordering three goose," Henk repeated.

"Awesome," Benny said to Dante, who watched Jeremy finish the second set of prawns before disappearing into the dining room to eat.

Angela put the pieces of goose breast on the grill to get cross-hatch sear marks on the skin. She grilled them to rare on a medium flame to render the fat and finished them in a skillet in a 450-degree oven. The boys were setting up plates.

"Ordering another three goose," Jeremy said. "OK, pick-up three goose. Doing well everyone."

The pick-up call meant Joey de Yonker had to plate a ramekin of carrot-ginger purée (pre-cooked and waiting in a *bain-marie*), Conrad had to wilt beet greens and lay them out in a bed sprinkled with capers and shredded goat cheese, then back to Joey to plate the Turkish couscous. When the breast was finished, Henk would slice it into seven thin slices per serving, fan these across the beet greens and turn to Angela for a single small ladle full of sauce (made by deglazing the skillet with a combination of white wine, beet reduction and demi-glaze). Last thing on the plate was stuffed Walla Walla sweet onion (which Rolando would have prepared at the order call). Jeremy would artfully garnish with a reef knot of watercress and the entrée was good to go.

So, here Rolando had his onion stuffed with red lentil purée seasoned with roasted cardamom hot from under the broiler, and across the way Joey de Yonker was falling steadily into the shit. Joey grabbed his first ramekin, knocked it out on the cutting surface and replated it at the designated eleven o'clock mark with a metal spatula.

"Plates?" Angela said to Henk, the breasts in their pans now fired and ready for cutting.

The next carrot purée stuck in the ramekin, and Joey tried to dig it out with a paring knife. On the plate it looked like somebody had stepped on it.

"OK, J de Y, let's keep them whole. Take your time and do another one."

Sensing he was falling behind, Joey knocked the next ramekin out directly onto centre of the china plate, which cracked into six pieces. One hit the floor and smashed.

"Hold the breasts on the rack," Jeremy said to Angela, and he jogged around the range to help, but now Joey and Rolando were both trying to clean up and Conrad was starting beet greens (which he'd forgotten at the pick-up). And in this six-armed attempt at catch up, Joey knocked over his container of capers onto the grill, where they bounced and sizzled their way across the hot surface, onto the floor and down into the fire.

"Get more capers," Jeremy said to Joey. Then, when Conrad was back on beet greens where he belonged and Rolando had been redirected to the ramekins of carrot, Jeremy cleaned up the mess himself. Finally: "All right, fire the goose."

They got them out eventually. None with capers, since Joey never returned. Jeremy went looking for him. He went looking out back. Nothing. He poked his head into his office. Not there.

"Chico, you seen Joey de Yonker back here?" Jeremy asked.

"Last I saw...," Chico nodded at the RapidAir.

Joey was still in there looking for the capers.

"Right here," Jeremy said, showing him where they were.

"I screwed up," Joey said.

"In future," Jeremy said, "come back to the kitchen if you can't find something in the cold room. You'll get pneumonia. And if you get in the juice, I want you to take the standing eight count. You know what that is?"

They walked back into the kitchen, Jeremy's arm around Joey's shoulders.

"The standing eight count. You drop a plate, you torch something. I'm yelling at Henk to fire prawns and you realize you are fucked. So. You step back from your station and you tell me what's happening. You breathe deep for eight seconds, no more, no less, wipe down your counter area. Then you get the hell back in there, all right?"

Despite the lack of capers, both dishes went down huge. Dante was effusive; he came back into the kitchen, with some of the servers, saying, "You see? You see? The man is a genius. I loved the purple goose. What was that sauce? Don't tell me. I don't need to know. Sheer *genius*."

Later in the day, they broke down the stations and cleaned. He let the squad go. He went for an early evening walk in Stanley Park. It felt like coming home by now. Jeremy walked the trails with certainty, knowing exactly where he was relative to his destination. For so long his father's camp had been impossible to find, and Jeremy had struggled to understand the topography of the whole. Now, his father at home, writing feverishly, Jeremy found his way in the dark instinctively, feeling between trees whose textures had become individual to him. Western red cedar, western hemlock, Douglas fir, and on the ground too, spiny wood fern and sword fern and foam flower.

Jeremy was home around midnight. He called his father, knowing he would be up.

The Professor gave him the word count for the day. "Two thousand. Not great. Not terrible." He always asked about the restaurant. How was Dante?

"Dante is Dante," Jeremy said. "He pays well."

"No surprise. You made a deal."

"Not forever," Jeremy said. "A year maybe. After that, who knows?"

The Professor was interested. "So that's the plan, is it?"

"That's part of the plan."

"And may I know the rest?'

He told the Professor the rest of the plan. Thinking about it beforehand, he had tried guessing his father's reaction. Now he just spelled it out and waited. And the Professor didn't laugh like it was funny or comic, didn't scold like it were dangerous or wrong. He was only thoughtful.

"Practical matters aside," he said, "it has a certain appeal."

"It's a one-time thing," Jeremy said.

"A Blood overture to Dante's Crip opera," the Professor said.

"Not bad," Jeremy said. "But I was thinking of it more as a tribute."

The Professor was quiet for a few seconds.

"You all right?" Jeremy asked.

"I'm quite all right," his father answered, just a tiny bit choked up was all.

And in this way, the days before the opening flew. The kitchen stocking up steadily, his dry goods, his early orders of dairy started filling the RapidAir. The drills were run and rerun. The squad, improving.

Monday the week of the opening, they had a dry-run dinner for the full staff. It was the full menu for the first time. Out front, the servers would rotate through two simulated sittings, which gave everybody a chance to eat and a turn serving. With significant others invited, it was more than enough people to try all the appetizers and entrées, enough people to slam them thoroughly.

Jeremy went out before service and talked to the group. Aside from the familiar faces of Dante, Benny, Albertini

Banks and Philip, the room was full of identically gorgeous wait staff and their matching J. Crew perfect dates. All the women were blond. All the men black-haired, lantern jawed. It looked like a room full of candidates for the Biosphere, sleek lustworthy specimens in tight grey pinstripes.

"How're the underwear?" he said after Dante asked for quiet, and he got a huge laugh.

"They ride up," someone called from the back. More laughter.

"All right," Jeremy said, motioning for quiet. "I have never said this in front of a group before, but now is the time to thank Dante Beale for what he has done, for making possible what we all have done here, together, in our underwear."

Wild applause. He glanced quickly over at Dante to read whether he was cutting the right line through this material. Dante looked serene and pleased, nodding and applauding with his hands out in front of himself, gesturing towards Jeremy as if to say: *Not me. There's the man deserving applause.*

"I think it's the right time to say this," Jeremy went on, "because I know on Sunday we're all going to be slammed. You always forget to thank people under that kind of pressure. And so: Dante, thanks to you."

Again, enthusiastic hand claps. Dante rose, crossed the room and embraced him. Then, holding Jeremy's face in both his hands, Dante kissed him once on each shaved cheek. When there was silence, he returned a thank you to Jeremy saying: "I have few weaknesses, but this man is one of them. For reasons I have never tried the rationalize, I have known for many years that there are things this chef will do, things this man is called to do, that will be done by no other."

The clapping was tentative at first, but when Dante left it at that and returned to his golden mohair seat, sat, shot cuffs and nodded once, the room erupted.

When things settled down, Jeremy addressed the group with a final encouragement before retreating to the kitchen.

"Please order anything you like off the menu," he said. "Part of the idea is to take the kitchen out for a spin. We're only going to stagger the orders a little bit so we don't get swamped immediately. Complain if you don't like something. Tell us if it's good. That's all I have to say. Enjoy."

In front of the squad, in the tight air of the kitchen, he realized he hadn't given or received a real live pre-service pep talk in a long, long time. Quartey used to do it along the short lines of: "Chicken, fish number one, fish number two, pork roast, everybody? *Bien.*"

"This is just a dry run," Jeremy started, "so nobody panic. The house is full of friendlies. Everyone remember the standing eight count. You're in the shit, you step back for eight, then back in. We'll get through it."

Henk was nodding tightly, poised against the salad prep counter. He looked like a paratrooper getting ready to jump.

"All right: Rolando, Conrad. You guys have two apps: the kebab and the periwinkles. Remember the drill. Order call: Henk starts the fish. Four minutes later he's gotta see those plates. So, Rolando: seaweed in, oysters and toss. Conrad: plate the kimchi, then the seaweed, oysters last. Chili oil and you're good to go. "Periwinkle pick-up" means four-ounce ladle of cream to the plate, wheatsheaf up nice and straight in the middle. Boom."

"Got it Chef." "Right on Chef."

"Henk: escabeche, two minutes a side. Two tablespoons hot marinade a serving. A swirl of preserved lemon oil, spray with chives. Right?"

Henk held up a fist. "Right on Chef!" he said.

"Angela: you and me on bruschetta and foie gras. You've got the toast and the apples. You've got the potato crisps. I need those plates a few minutes after the order."

"You bet Chef."

"J de Y, the terrine you just have to plate. Prepped materials are at your station."

"They sure are Chef."

"I know they are, I checked. And the soups: pesto and consommé. One twelve-ounce ladle, one dollop crème fraîche for the pesto. You have to heat a won ton and add some fresh chive to finish the consommé.

"OK, now the mains. . . ."

And, of course, their timing was terrible. There were something like five standing eight counts. Joey dropped a terrine. Rolando got cocky and dropped three fully prepped periwinkle salads he was trying to hoist onto the pass-through at once.

"Take. Your. Time." Jeremy said to the whole kitchen.

Now there were little black and grey shellfish underfoot. Jeremy stepped on one and it squeaked like a piece of Styrofoam. Joey stopped to clean up. He started picking them up by hand, counting aloud—one, two, three, four—slowing down steadily as it dawned on him that there were probably sixty of them on the tiles and under the range top.

"Chef," Joey called out, holding one arm in the air like a kid in first grade who had to go to the bathroom. "In the shits, Chef. Eight, seven, six, five. . . ."

Mains went well for two tables. Then Torkil, up from the baking station to lend a hand, burned a load of yam wafers that made it onto the plates anyway. Jeremy saw Henk hesitate, looking at them, wondering if they were too dark.

"Those cannot go out," Jeremy said, throwing two more prawn orders on Henk's grill. At which point Joey and Conrad exchanged plates inadvertently and two lambs headed towards the door with spaetzle and leeks, two ducks in black olive jus.

"Come on people," Jeremy yelled, intercepting the plates at the pick-up counter.

"In the shits," Conrad called, holding up his arm. Jeremy made a mental note to talk to them about yelling "in the shits" at the top of their lungs, then sprinted behind the range again to finish plates, still calling out the orders that were coming in to the pass-through. "Order two more lamb. Order one prawn. Order one squab—hey, somebody ordered pigeon! Pick up three ducks."

Henk was firing a lamb, finishing the plate with the celeriac purée. When the lamb was ready Jeremy watched him artfully cut and place the rack, position the zucchini blossom garnish, the drizzle of black olive jus. He was grilling two tenderloins at the same time.

"Order one rabbit, one risotto, one flatfish, another risotto," Jeremy called. Henk shot him a quick look. "Busy, busy, busy," he said, finishing Conrad's goose and prawn plates and jogging back around the range.

There were more meltdowns but, as always, it was over before you thought possible.

"Aaaaah," he said, sighing loudly. "Wine, anyone?" He poured Tempranillo all around. By the time they'd sipped and laughed their way through a glass, there was applause coming from the dining room again. Jeremy straightened his white toque, wiped his hands, pulling sharply downward on his uniform front to straighten himself, took another glug of wine.

"Wash your hands," Jeremy told them. "And get ready for adoration."

The clapping started again as he entered the dining room, but he made them stop with two hands up, palms out. "Now wait," he told the seated group. He went back to the kitchen and pushed open the door.

They paraded in, vamping like runway models, making a point of it. Angela in the lead, the boys following in a line behind her. They stretched their necks upward, pouted, looked hard right or left over one shoulder and then the other. Hands in pockets or arms rigid and held slightly away from the body, hands flared out. They walked out to the top of the riser this way.

Everyone clapped and laughed.

"All right, all right," Jeremy said to the squad. "A little dignity, please."

But he was smiling. Benny could see it. Dante could see it. The Chef was smiling. There was warmth there, pride too.

Dante leaned over to Benny. He whispered in her ear.

"I did not make a mistake, did I Benny?" Dante said to her.

Benny leaned away from Dante so she could see his face. "Of course not, Dante. You thought you might have?"

His eyes were back on Jeremy. "No," he said. "I don't think so."

Back in the kitchen the squad was all grins. They were slapping hands and back to making fun of the standing eight counts.

Henk quieted the group down to ask a question. "How'd we do Chef? Seriously."

Jeremy told them honestly. There was work to be done. Tuesday, Wednesday, Thursday, he was going to continue the drills. Friday and Saturday, if they were ready, they could take off.

"But the kitchen opens 0900 Sunday, the big day," Jeremy went on. "I'll be here earlier. Please, nobody later than 1000. We have mountains of prep. One hundred-plus bodies for an early service about 1900. Dante wants people done and partying by 2100."

"Menu changes, specials?" Henk said.

"I'm coming to that," Jeremy said. "One other thing first."

He pulled out the new jacket that he had made for Henk. He'd picked the throat colours himself, two bands of colour: black and orange. Henk did not want to grin like a kid, but his cheeks were rigid with the effort.

Jeremy helped him on with the jacket. The group gathered around and touched the sous chef colours and smacked him on the arm and teased. It was a group compliment, and Jeremy let them quiet down on their own. He let their comments fly and spark and settle.

"Opening nights are special," Jeremy began when he had their attention again. "After opening night you become a normal restaurant again. You open, you close. You buy, prep and cook. You clean up and restock. Go out and have a drink. Sleep too little. Do it again. But on opening night you put on a play about yourself. Like theatre, like a culinary monologue. You stand out there in front of a new house and you say: This is my kitchen. This is who I am. This is how we have become Who We Are."

And then he gave them every detail on Sunday's performance. A performance about memory, a tribute to the way things once were. He ran down the menu changes, one by one, watching the group expression come to a simmer of new and sharp-edged interest. They did not exchange looks. They were listening only to him.

"It's important to be able to do something like this once in your life," Jeremy said, wrapping up. "Because you're going to learn that in the kitchen, your work is destroyed almost before you know it's finished. It's the nature of cooking, of eating. A six-top, half a loaf of your dill sourdough is gone in minutes."

Torkil nodded. The collective group expression had risen above a simmer now, approaching a gentle boil of Guerrilla Grill enthusiasm.

"This is my work. This is what I do," Jeremy finished. "Maybe it lasts twenty minutes on somebody's plate, but it has to be made. For me. For this house. And the plate is where it belongs."

It was going to be a busy weekend. Chladek and Jeremy met Thursday evening at Lost Lagoon to plan an extensive restocking of the meat, poultry and fish supplies.

"Racoon?" Chladek suggested. "There is certainly no shortage."

Jeremy smoothed the menu on the stump between them.

"What's it like?" Jeremy asked.

Chladek thought for a minute. "It's like dog," he said finally.

"Well, as long as it's not like cat," Jeremy said.

"No, cat is more like chicken."

Jeremy mulled it over.

"Right here," Chladek said, pointing at the last main on the menu. "*Racoon tenderloin with red wine sauce and leek frite.* Sounds pretty good to me."

"You realize, Chladek, we're not actually putting the changes on the printed menu for guests to see."

"How will people... ," Chladek said.

"*Notre gastronomie.* A tribute to Caruzo, to you. To my father. To..." He waited for a memory of his mother to pass on through. "Even as a one-off thing on opening night, I'm guessing people might not partake voluntarily."

When Chladek understood that there was subterfuge involved, his face brightened. "So, here." Chladek pointed again at the menu item. Winking. "*Beef* tenderloin."

Jeremy wasn't sure. "What are our meat options, anyway?"

Chladek rhymed them off. "Cats, dogs, black rats, mice, rabbits, eastern grey squirrel, Douglas red squirrel, skunks. The odd opossum."

"Rabbits?" Jeremy said.

Lots of rabbits, in fact, Stanley Park having been used for many years as a dumping ground for unwanted pets. Whatever their fed-up owners had anticipated, the rabbits thrived. There were probably fifteenth-generation Stanley Park rabbits.

"Are they scrawny?" Jeremy asked.

"No," Chladek said, clenching and pointing at his biceps. "Big and strong. Well fed."

"Fine," Jeremy said. "Rabbit for the rabbit."

Chladek jotted a note in a spiral-bound notebook. "Ducks?"

"Canvasbacks, please," Jeremy said.

"What are you doing for prawns?" Chladek asked. "We could use goldfish."

Jeremy shook his head. "Queen Charlotte prawns is what I'm doing for prawns. They are excellent in the market right now. We need goldfish for the escabeche."

"Right boss," Chladek said. "And lamb?"

"Saltspring Island Lamb," Jeremy said. "They came in this morning."

They went over the rest of the menu, noting the items that needed to be harvested.

"The squab?" Chladek asked.

"How about rock dove?" Jeremy said. "They hang out near the pitch-and-putt. They're a lighter colour."

"Roger."

Jeremy continued itemizing. "Canada geese, OK fine...."

"How about," Chladek said, "for the flatfish we get some of those Beaver Lake carp?"

"I think they're prehistoric," Jeremy said. "Bad karma. Anyway, I thought you said you could buy flounder off those Chinese guys who fish under the Lions Gate Bridge."

Jeremy would take care of all the conventional materials from conventional suppliers.

Chladek looked disappointed. "What about the racoon?"

"All right," Jeremy said. "Three racoons."

"Three only?" Chladek asked.

"Four, if they're small."

And when they had completed these tasks, the kitchen at Gerriamo's had begun to look not unlike how Bueckelaer would have painted it. Friday late afternoon (doors to the dining room now locked) Jeremy surveyed Chladek's first shipment. There was a bucket of dandelion greens and fiddleheads, as well as a garbage bag full of salal, salmon and huckleberries. A dozen plump Canada geese, a dozen grey rock doves, six canvasbacks, four large rabbits, fifteen squirrels (greys, fatter and more plentiful than reds) four huge racoons and a swan.

"Why the swan?" Jeremy said. "I didn't want swan."

"I thought . . . ," Chladek said, "you might . . ."

"Chladek," Jeremy yelled. "I did not want swan! Why did you bring me swan?"

Chladek was confused by the reaction, and clearly hurt, but to Jeremy the swan was ominous. "Take it out of my kitchen," he said. "It's not even indigenous."

Chladek shook his head. "And the grey squirrel? These came from England in a boat."

Jeremy sighed and looked away. Not the point. "I'm sorry, but I cannot have swan."

"Fine," Chladek said. "It'll get eaten, I can tell you. Tonight maybe."

"How's my fish coming?"

"Fish tomorrow," Chladek said. "Goldfish, flatfish, periwinkle . . ."

"Mushrooms?"

"Yes, yes, fungus too," Chladek confirmed. "They're still around but not so many."

Friday night Jeremy worked late butchering, portioning and making stock. The rock doves, geese and ducks all had to be plucked and drawn. The doves he stored for Sunday's crapaudine, the geese livers for the faux foie gras. Duck and geese breasts were set aside for their respective marinades. All the remaining bird carcasses went in to roast.

Squirrels he skinned and boned, then ground the lean meat for the consommé and put it in the walk-in. The rabbit he jointed, removing the two pieces from each saddle and the two rear legs. What was left of these went on for stock, to be combined later with mirepoix.

He turned last to the racoons, opening the first gingerly, peeling away its fur, severing the feet above the claws. Gutted, the carcass was meagre, but Chladek's instinct had been good. There were two tenderloin pieces running parallel to the spine on either side. Jeremy removed one and smelled it. Distinctly gamey, he thought. They'd need pepper to tamp down that flavour. The rest of the meat he divided in two for the terrine. Half went through the grinder and was seasoned with salt, thyme, rosemary, black pepper and Dijon mustard, then moistened with reduced apple cider. The other half he smoked over hickory and ground with diced pork fat. Three large pâté moulds were lined with bacon fat and brandy-simmered prunes. And finally, in alternating layers, Jeremy built his pâté. Seasoned racoon mince, pork fat, minced shallots, parsley and smoked meat. He packed the terrines tightly and put them in the oven to cook in a water bath.

When the duck and geese carcasses were brown and rendered of their fat, Jeremy drained them, added water, caramelized mirepoix, bay, peppercorns and a half-head of garlic, and brought them slowly to a boil. He started a mushroom stock for the risotto with a few pounds of button mushrooms and imported dry porcini. Last, a clear white vegetable stock, which he made with sweated onion, celery and carrots.

It was almost midnight by the time he had the meat stored and the four stocks going at a lazy bubble. It was time for the kimchi, which would need the two intervening days to marinate and develop its piquant flavour. Shredded cabbage, onions, vinegar, sesame oil and chilis. It aged best in clay, he knew, so he rooted for fifteen or twenty minutes after assembling the kimchi, looking to find the urns he'd bought especially for this preparation. They were buried under boxes in the dry storage area, and by the time he found them, filled them, sealed them, put them at the back of the walk-in and turned to his final task of the night, the boutifar, it was one in the morning.

"Damn," he said, noticing the clock and wondering if he should get to bed. But he had the buzz, the zone. He was cooking by feel, instinct. He wasn't tired, so he dug out the two frozen quarts of pigs' blood he'd been sent from the butcher. Just enough to make the sausage he'd need for tomorrow.

He melted the frozen blocks on low heat and steeled the Sabatier to prep the vegetables, swiping the blade down the length of steel. It made a reassuring sound in the silent kitchen: *zing, zing*. He was leaning over the saucepan with the blood, steeling. Not looking. *Zing. Zing.* He didn't even realize he'd cut himself until he moved away from the saucepan to put the steel away. Skimming the Sabatier down the outside of the long, carbon steel rod, he had apparently jumped the guard and cut the first knuckle of his index finger, removing a very neat disk of skin. It was one of those painless, non-life-threatening cuts that bleed a great deal. The ones you do not feel and which require a very sharp blade.

"Damn," he said aloud, startled at the sight of his own blood, now spilling down his hand and covering all his fingers, his thumb. It had dripped down the steel too and onto his pants.

He dropped the knife and the steel onto the cutting board and clamped a hand towel over the cut, applying pressure. He walked the length of the bridge to the first-aid kit and put on a bandage, shaking his head. He went back up the line to clean the cutting board, the steel and the knife. And it was only when he finally turned back to the range that he realized just how much of his blood had been distributed over the stove top. Dime-sized drops, up the front of the unit, across the burners. On the hood.

Splashed all over the side of the saucepan too.

Jeremy groaned. He rolled his head back and looked up at the ceiling. Just what he needed. He should have gone to bed. Any of his own blood in the saucepan and it all had to go into the garbage, of course. He turned off the flame, disgusted with himself, took out a damp cloth and carefully wiped down the stove top. He picked up the saucepan to empty it into the sink, set it down again.

Two precious quarts. There was no more.

He left the pan sitting on the burner and wiped down the sides, using the edge of a paring knife to scrape off the bits that had been cooked hard. He stepped back from the stove, leaned on a prep counter, chin in hand, staring at the pot.

"Jesus," he said aloud. He went out into the back alley and smoked a cigarette, looking up and down the dark shining lane. Black clouds were sifting by overhead.

Boutifar or no boutifar, it was only the thematic core of the whole menu. What were the chances any of his blood got into the pot at all? If so, how much? A single drop? Long since mixed a part per billion with the rest? Boiled?

He flicked his cigarette towards the storm sewer. It made an orange streak through the darkness before hissing out on the wet pavement. He went inside. He set the pot on the side rack to cool. He put a new bandage on his knuckle.

It was a simple sausage, really. Onions and leeks cooked in pork fat, cooled and combined with the blood, some cream, salt, pepper, nutmeg, cinnamon, cayenne and thyme. It took Jeremy about half an hour to fill the casings on the KitchenAid and make a glistening stack of black sausages. Tomorrow he'd poach them. Sunday, on the order call, they would grill and open half a link per serving, sauté sliced onion and apple in butter. At the pick-up they'd broil a slice of baguette, rub some garlic on the crust, brush the sausage with cinnamon-infused olive oil and grill. When it was crisp the sausage would slide onto the baguette slice. Somebody would plate the apple and onion in a ring around it.

Apple blossom garnish and you were good to go.

"This is the speech," Jeremy said, in the kitchen 1030 Sunday morning. "This is the only speech because we're going to be slammed from here down to 2100."

"Go Chef," Joey de Yonker said.

"Thanks for coming on time, everyone," he went on. "Prep lists are at your stations. No surprises.

"Some notes. Henk and Joey, take up the astringency on the rhubarb sauce. Same amount. Try finishing it with a bit of balsamic. The red wine reduction was excellent, same again. Soup same. I'll be making the squirrel consommé and the won tons.

"Conrad, Angela: leeks first, please. Then seaweed, oysters in the smoker, endive wheatsheaves. I'll do the potato cream and give you a hand with anything you need.

"Rolando: you've got yams, potatoes for the flatfish crust, mushrooms to Henk for the risotto. Celeriac dice into a hotel pan of lemon water, please, and then to me. I'll do the purée."

For Jules, he thought.

"New ingredients?" Henk prompted.

"Right," Jeremy said. The Pacific wild periwinkle was more saline than the imported one they had been using, so they needed less salt in the stir fry. The goldfish were larger than the sardine; Henk would need two and half minutes a side. The flatfish were small. Angela's potato crust should be thinner.

"And the racoon...," Jeremy said. "Strong taste. Pepper the tenderloin pieces. I'm not talking about a crust here, but a good grind all over. And remember that these wild birds have been flying distances up until yesterday. They do not have as much fat and don't need to render as long. The goose and duck can grill a little hotter. They'll finish the same as before.

"Questions about any of that?"

There were none.

"Bottom line," Jeremy said, and then lost the words. He felt a flutter of nerves.

"Here's to it," Joey de Yonker offered.

Jeremy pantomimed raising a glass. They all did. "Here's to it," Jeremy said. "Our tribute."

"Our performance," Henk said.

"On which note," Jeremy said. "By 2130 I want to come back here and see this...." Jeremy put a hand above his eyes and looked around the kitchen as if it were empty. Spotless. "I mean clean," he said. "Leftovers go straight into the bins and out to the dumpster. I don't want to find any racoon leftovers in my RapidAir, understand? You can leave at that point or come up front for a drink. Everyone got it?"

They got it, and fell quickly into the routine. For two hours there was little talk in the kitchen of Gerriamo's, just the reassuring sounds of the kitchen humming. Chopping, oven doors thumping shut, Torkil knocking out bread pans, Chico running the dishwasher, the sound of gas flame and scraping pot bottoms. They worked in this familiar cocoon of sounds until mid-afternoon, when Jeremy had everyone take a break together and he made them frittata with pancetta and arugula.

After they'd eaten he walked into the RapidAir and found a bottle of La Fin du Monde. He was at the door, ready to go back into the kitchen, when he thought better of it and grabbed a bottle of Pellegrino instead. He poured off a glass in the kitchen, slugged it down.

"Santé," he said, to nobody in particular.

"A la vôtre." Henk said from nearby.

He went out front later. Staff were jogging everywhere, every movement an urgent errand. Someone was washing the baseboards. Somebody else was brushing the purple drapes at the front of the house. The barman was meticulously redusting each bottle on his massive mirror-backed shelves. Dante and Benny were discussing seating arrangements.

The room looked both opulent and messy—the desired effect, Jeremy was sure. Banks, having seen the zucchini blossom garnish on the lamb he had for lunch on Monday, had strewn the tables with dried ones. To this decorating scheme he'd added open champagne crates set strategically around the room, two dozen of them. Jeremy noticed that the crates contained champagne bottles and, in each, several cabbages: red, white and savoy. Veuve Cliquot and peasant vegetables spilled out of the straw as if the crates had dropped from the back of a very specialized delivery truck.

"You like it?" he asked Jeremy. "We make a joke about rich and poor."

"What's the joke?" Jeremy asked, towering over Banks, his toque adding authoritative feet.

Banks looked confused, and pointed a quivering finger at a Savoy cabbage. "Jeremy, the cabbawge. People laugh at the cabbawge. He is so...green and wrinkled."

Jeremy pretended to be greatly irritated. He said: "Do you mind telling me exactly what you find funny about cabbages?"

Banks squirmed in his cream three-piece suit (under a black cape), his hand fiddling with the huge chrome links of a vestigial watch chain. "Jeremy, is just visual humour. Peoples they look at the cabbawge and the beautiful bottle of the Veuve Cliquot and they will lawf. Is all. Please, Jeremy..."

"Please, *Chef,*" Jeremy said to Banks.

"Please...what?" Banks said.

"Call him Chef," Dante said from a few tables away, without looking up. He was examining a guest list. "It's a courtesy he deserves. Jeremy, you don't like the cabbages?"

"In fact, I love the cabbages," Jeremy said, not lying.

"Good," Banks said, rubbing his hands together with relief. "Good."

Jeremy walked back up the riser towards the kitchen. Just at the kitchen door he was intercepted.

"Chef Jeremy." It was a harsh English accent, chalk to Dante's cheese. Jeremy turned to find a tiny, spiky-haired person standing next to him, looking up. She was wearing a puffy, silver raver's jacket and four-inch orange platforms.

"You must be Kiwi Frederique," he said.

They sat at the bar. Jeremy took another soda. Kiwi took

a Gibson. She slid her Palm PDA onto the mahogany counter, picked up her drink and commenced looking at him intently. Jeremy stared back with a small, expectant smile.

"Who has been your greatest professional influence?" Kiwi asked finally, no preamble.

Over her shoulder, Jeremy was watching the band set up, a large jazz band, octet at least. The stand-up bass player was noodling up and down through scales, and one of three sax players was throwing the riff back and forth with him, bobbing and weaving. It looked like fun. It reminded him of Olli.

"Ray Kroc and Ferdinand Point," he said, returning to the conversation. Chef Quartey would forgive him for lying so egregiously given the circumstances.

Kiwi laughed at what she assumed was an ironic same-breath reference to the founder of McDonald's and that of nouvelle cuisine.

"Seriously," Jeremy said. "In the early part of the century, Ferdinand Point rejected classical French mother sauces. Mid-century, Kroc introduced the first truly global commodity food. Here at Gerriamo's, at the end of the same century, we pay homage to these great revolutionaries."

Kiwi Frederique had decided that he was, in fact, serious and was now making aggressive notes on the Palm. Sometimes when he was throwing things together in the kitchen, not following a recipe, Jeremy felt the same way he felt now. Infallible. Any seasoning he added, any word said . . . any one would work. And punctuating this thought, the piano player kicked in, slapping down magnificently dissonant chords that anchored all the unrelated noodling going on behind him.

"You see, Ferdinand Point was the first wave in a culinary revolution," Jeremy went on. "He broke with French formality; he broke with fat and weighty flavours. He kicked free of the past and floated somewhere new without baggage. Kroc created a second wave with his humble hamburger. He broke the constraints of being *wherever*—McDonald's is the same anywhere in world, right? Who cares where the beef comes from? He created something that lived independent of its ingredients, a huge change."

Frederique continued to scribble ferociously. Slashing down strokes, pounding period marks into the little screen. She was backdropped by eight guys going hard on the band riser. Everybody jamming a different tune, the piano running straight down the core. It was a cacophony of random squawks and squiffs, scales and licks. And yet it swung.

"Which brings us to Gerriamo's," he plunged on, raising his voice above the band. "You have a word for our kind of food."

"International Groove," Kiwi said, looking up.

"We're more than that," Jeremy said. "We claim Point's victory over the past and Kroc's victory over locale. We're beyond international. Beyond globalized. We aren't the restaurant of *all* places—Europe and Africa, Asia and the Americas. This is not *fusion*. We are the restaurant of *no* place. We belong to no soil, to no cuisine, to no people, to no culinary morality. We belong only to those who can reach us and understand us and afford us. Gerriamo's is post-national. . . . Post-National Groove Food."

His grand culinary pronouncement complete, the on-stage jam unravelled to silence and the sound of mikes being adjusted. "Chack . . . ch-ch-ch-ch-chaaack."

Frederique stopped writing, mesmerized. She leaned forward, eyes locked on Jeremy and said breathlessly, "The Third-Wave Culinary Revolution."

Jeremy nodded very slowly. "Complete with the echoes of sorrow for what has been lost in the process, left behind or forgotten. A revolution with memory."

Frederique wrote a word down, then stopped. She picked up her drink. "Like what?" she asked from behind her glass.

He might as well end it there. "It's personal," he said. "The personal part of your involvement with the food. Your memories. Taste and remember for yourself."

Frederique snapped shut the Palm. She smiled broadly. He got her another drink.

"How are we doing, people?" he called out, back in the kitchen. He strolled up and down the lines, checking progress. Conrad and Angela had finished the leeks and were struggling with the endive. Jeremy showed them again how to julienne the heads lengthways, how to make the sheaf of tiny strands tied into a bundle with a blanched chive. You needed to tie the chive with a reef knot, he told them again. A Granny knot would slip. They got back to it.

Rolando was grating potatoes. Henk was roasting pears for the foie gras sauce.

Jeremy felt sudden and profound satisfaction. Kiwi Frederique had heard what she'd come to hear. Now let her eat fully of their efforts. Eat and be unconsciously connected to this place. To himself, to the squad here, working their way through prepping *mise en place* and assembling, straining and reducing sauces.

Jeremy picked up the Sabatier, steeled it, then turned to the celeriac purée.

"Wow," Margaret said, climbing out of the cab and looking up at the front of Gerriamo's.

"Ouch," Olli said. He was still in the cab, sitting forward in the seat to pay the driver, and his tuxedo pants were pinching. He'd complained putting them on earlier.

"Look at this," he'd said, disgusted. "I'm getting a gut."

"You look fabulous," Margaret said. Like all men, he grew a little taller, a little more dignified in the basic black and white cutlines of a dinner jacket. It was true; he was softening. He had pouches above his hips that weren't there when he had time to play squash, when he was just a Vancouver-based entrepreneur-workaholic. Now that he was an internationally commuting entrepreneur-workaholic, he was gaining weight. And sure, he was drinking again. Margaret knew all these things were related, but she was determined not to get squirrelly about it. If she worried, it was only a shadow anxiety about what it meant that Olli had changed his mind on something, so seldom did it happen. The few drinks in themselves...well, he got a little sharper, a little funnier, in fact. And the love handles on the once-lean frame didn't bother her either.

"My God," Margaret was saying outside the cab. She was shielding her eyes and looking up at the two great vaulting windows, the purple curtains just visible from outside, the antiqued wood and slate covering the exterior walls. The hundreds of lights—the entire place was sparkling, flickering. There was a red runner here, a long black awning. There was a man in a uniform and a cap with gold braid, bending over from the waist, talking to her. There were half a dozen valet parkers and a whole lot of photographers standing on a square mat of black carpet set off to the side behind a gold rope. The doorman looked very quickly at the stiff card that was their invitation, returned it, smiling. There was a sudden strobe of camera flashes.

Olli pocketed his change with a little difficulty and pulled himself out of the car using the roof and the door frame as handles. The flashing intensified, bright and hard and white.

"Unbelievable," Margaret said, looking at the cameras. "They obviously don't know who we aren't." But she slipped a hand around Olli's waist and turned him a quarter-turn towards the cameras, squeezed him tight. She was smiling broadly, having fun with it. Olli followed her gaze. The cameras flashed again. Now his eyes were dancing with blue and green dots.

"Jumpin' Jaysus," he said, covering his eyes.

"Don't cover your face," someone said.

Which was all the prompting Olli needed to pull his tuxedo coat halfway over his head. He put his other arm around Margaret's shoulder and, adopting his best wiseguy voice, he hustled up the runner towards the front door yelling: "No pictures, no pictures."

The cameras exploded into action again.

Margaret was still laughing when they got inside, when her sense of being in a movie gave way to the sense that they were actually in an opera. The room was spectacularly packed with tuxedos and gowns. She stared around herself as the maître d'hôtel checked their invitations again and the coat-check girl took her coat. She smoothed her own dark green Donna Karan dress down over her hips. Fitted but simple, it had a square neck and wide shoulder straps. A sexy apron, she thought looking in the mirror earlier. Perfect.

A jazz band was swinging up in the far corner of the restaurant, a metronomic, rolling sound tumbling unstoppably forward. Waiters were trolling through the crowd with trays of champagne and martinis. Cigar girls were popping up at your elbow every ten seconds or so. "Monte Cristo? Romeo y Julietta? Uppman?" They all looked like fitness instructors. Everybody warranted a second look. A man floated by with a magnificent sapphire broach at the throat of his tuxedo. A woman carried a gold lamé riding crop. A tall, black-haired waiter stood nearby in a pinstriped suit designed to fit tight—not so tight that the buttons pulled, but tight enough that he was (Margaret looked away, then back) *visible*. All the light seemed to come from candles, hooded on every table, in aluminum wall sconces between the paintings. And above Margaret the high ceilings vaulted like the night sky, punctuated by three massive chandeliers, constellations of crystal and silver and dozens of beeswax tapers. The light swirled through the room. It glowed and refracted in the yellow linen-painted walls. It danced in darkened air.

"Wow," Margaret said again, this time under her breath.

Olli swept two flutes of champagne off a passing tray and gave her one.

"Is this baroque or decadent?" he asked, from close.

She saw the toque first. One of the quilted-metal kitchen doors had just swung open, far at the back of the room. And above the heads of the guests on the riser, a chef's hat bobbed its way through the crowd. Stopping frequently.

"Chef," people would say, greeting him. A well-educated, fooderati crowd.

"Hello. Hi. Welcome," Jeremy was saying. "Thanks. Thank you for coming. Thanks, really."

Margaret cut through the crowd towards him, pulling Olli in her wake. When she had Jeremy in a hug she said: "So exciting. All this for you."

"Well...," he said, letting her go and taking Olli's out-stretched hand, distracted.

"Well what?" Olli said. "This is the place, isn't it?"

Jeremy nodded and tried to smile. Yes, they were in the right place. Olli tossed down the last swirl of champagne in his glass and swapped for a full glass that appeared on a tray at his elbow.

"You know you shouldn't waste D.P. on me," Olli said.

"They're wasting Veuve Cliquot on you, in fact," Margaret said, pointing out the crates of champagne all around the room.

"Oh," Olli said, sipping, looking around. The band was doing a decent Charles Mingus. "Better Git It in Your Soul." He was beginning to enjoy himself.

"Your father's not here?" Margaret asked, having looked when she came in.

"Oh, he's here," Jeremy said. An answer for which he didn't volunteer an explanation.

"It looks really... dramatic," Margaret said, moving on. But Jeremy just kept stroking his chin and scratching his ear, glancing around the room. He looked pale; had he lost more weight?

"Yeah, it's so dark," he said to her. "Candlelight was Benny's idea—we'll be using electricity after tonight." And then, without warning: "How's Trout?"

"He's fine," Margaret answered, surprised. Pleased. "He was very upset he couldn't come."

"It would've been fine with me." Jeremy smiled and looked into her eyes, finally.

"Is everything fantastic?" she asked him. Ordinarily, he would have told her what to order by now. If not instructed her, at least given her a few ranked options.

"Right...," he said, reminded. He stopped and focused. "Salmon appetizer and pesto soup are great. Prawn main is really good. Olli will love the lamb."

"Baa-aa," Olli said.

She was just going to give Jeremy a good-luck kiss when Dante leaned into the conversation. "Gentlemen, the Chef," he said. Behind him stood two men in black suits with black shirts. Margaret thought they must have called each other earlier to co-ordinate outfits. The short one had sleepy eyes that remained intense, pupils locked on target from under lowered lids. The bulgy, mean-looking one had a taste for silver and turquoise—an earring, a bracelet, a belt buckle. Margaret associated both these qualities with show business.

"Of course," Jeremy was saying. He shook hands with Michael Duke and Luke Lucas. Here they were, *Last Chapter*. He hadn't thought of them since The Monkey's Paw Bistro closing night. "Thank you so very much for coming," he said. He introduced Olli and Margaret.

"Pleasure," Duke said, taking Margaret's hand to kiss it. She gently firmed her arm in resistance, and Duke bobbed slowly back into position for a regular handshake. He turned to Jeremy: "I used to come down to your other place. Loved it."

"The Monkey's Paw Bistro," Margaret said.

"That's the one," Lucas said. "Near here, I think."

Margaret and Olli exchanged the near-invisible glance of people who have been married for a while.

"Very near," Jeremy said.

Dante pulled Jeremy aside. Margaret went off to look at the paintings, leaving Olli to deal with Duke and Lucas. They talked about the show for a few minutes, until a cell phone bleated. Duke did a credible impersonation of a man having an epileptic seizure as he retrieved the tiny phone from an interior pocket and fumbled open the fiddly mouthpiece. Once connected, he signalled *Excuse me* with his free hand and withdrew to the relative quiet at the edge of the room. Lucas turned at the same moment to take a Cohiba off a passing cigar tray, giving Olli three seconds to consider his next move. He slipped into the crowd and over towards the band.

Definitely Mingus. They were doing "Boogie Stop Shuffle" now. An unalterable fact, Olli registered (draining his second flute of dangerously drinkable champagne), despite the fact that the gentleman with the gold cummerbund near the stage was telling his over-perfumed date that it was the theme from *Batman*.

Across the room Dante leaned in close to Jeremy's ear: "What did you say to Kiwi? What is the 'Third-Wave Culinary Revolution'?"

"We are it," Jeremy said, with a smile he hoped was inclusive, soothing. "The restaurant of no place. Post-national."

Dante considered this idea and Jeremy together before deciding his Chef had something. "That is really quite good, you know? Did you talk to Philly about it?"

Jeremy made his way back towards the kitchen. He was just opposite the bar when he saw Benny. She was alone, drinking something clear out of a tumbler, no ice. He judged it wasn't water from the wrinkle that formed across her nose with each sip. The hour was marching down on them—he didn't really have time—but he went over to say hello.

Martini rocks, hold the rocks. Not her first.

"I'm a little high," she said right off, and leaned into him.

"High as in...," Jeremy looked at the drink.

"High as in a tab of E."

What the hell? Was everybody planning to get hammered tonight?

"I was nervous," Benny was saying. "Normally it smoothes me right out. Makes me... *amorous*." She pressed a little harder into him. "Tonight it made me more nervous."

Jeremy put a hand on her shoulder. "Why would you be nervous?" he asked.

"I don't know, Jeremy," she said. "I don't know anything any more."

Now she threatened to go teary on him and there were people around. "Come on, sweetie," Jeremy said, very quietly. "This is the big night."

"For you guys maybe," Benny said, a shade too loud.

"For you too. What is this?" Jeremy asked. "Everybody loves your work."

Everybody loved her work. Sure. Benny sipped. Albertini loved her work, true. Philip loved her work. Dante in his own way seemed happy with what she'd done, and he would probably be happy with her again when next he *needed her*, but in the meantime why didn't she think about a return to the retail side? "The *ree*-tail side?" Benny said. "I knew I was getting used, but I didn't know I was getting thrown out afterwards."

What a time to talk to me about career counselling, Jeremy thought. "You gotta be tough, all right?" he whispered to her. "Dante is playing it close, he always does. Remember: tough."

Benny blew her nose on a bar napkin and looked at him in a way she hadn't in a long time, her breasts still pressing into his arm. "Will you kiss me?" she said. "Please?"

He didn't kiss her. He didn't know why she would have asked, except maybe because the E was kicking in or she wanted to provide him with further evidence that some faintly hysterical energy was sparking through the crowd this evening. His friends were getting loaded, his guests right behind. You simply couldn't calculate these things. But now that the hour was on them, he felt it arrive. He turned away from Benny without saying a word more and began to make his way towards the kitchen doors. He heard her release a muffled sob behind him.

Dante was there again; he was everywhere, apparently. He was teleporting himself around the room, appearing at the elbow of a cabinet minister, a favourite tenor, a clutch of agents, a brace of producers, a murder of Inferno lawyers and I-bankers.

Now, his chef. He appeared and locked his hand on Jeremy's arm. "Everything OK?" he asked.

"Everything is fine," Jeremy said.

"Are you ready?"

Jeremy paused and nodded. "I am ready."

Dante smiled hard, hand still on Jeremy's arm. And when he released, it all began. Dante whispered something to Philip, who had been hovering nearby. Philip turned and whispered to the maître d'hôtel, and the word rippled from there down the chain of command via the telepathic powers people of that important position enjoy. The maître d'hôtel looked briefly around the room—his neck cracked an inch in either direction and he took it all in—and wait staff immediately set down trays, straightened snug jackets and pulled short skirts a fraction of an inch lower over high, round buttocks. They fanned out with that one glance. They appeared at elbows. They murmured, "Dinner is served. Please find a seat." They encouraged. They herded.

Jeremy made his way upstream and burst into his kitchen.

"Time?" he said to Henk, who was standing ready at the stove top. Jeremy strode down the line.

"1903, Chef," Henk said.

They took five, leaned against a prep counter and talked quietly. Exactly seven minutes later, Jeremy heard the printer chatter as his first docket spooled in from the dining room. The narrow paper coiled out of the machine and hung there, quivering in place, waiting for his attention.

Jeremy took a deep breath, as if he were about to dive underwater for a long time. When he exhaled, he leaned over and tore off the docket. Dante's table. They were kicking things off with pesto soup, three salmon kebabs, consommé, a terrine and a boutifar. A tacitly agreed-upon silence hung in the air, enveloping all the kitchen staff. Even Chico stood utterly still in the dish pit without comprehension. A standing eight count of respectful and optimistic silence.

After which Jeremy launched himself off the edge of the prep table, calling the orders as he stalked to his place on the line: "Order three kebab, order pesto, order consommé, order terrine, and order me up some blood sausage."

"Ordering three kebab," Conrad said, nodding down the flat top at Joey de Yonker, whose hands were already in action, one on a plate, one reaching for his kimchi.

"Ordering blood," Henk said, assigning the kitchen name that would stick with the boutifar for the remainder of the evening.

"Order terrine," Rolando said. "Order pesto," said Angela.

"Showtime," said Joey de Yonkers. "Order squirrel soup."

And they were slammed, no surprise. Swamped from the get-go. "Order consommé, order terrine. Order two escabeche."

They had five tables in by 1915. Then seven. Minutes later, twelve.

Jeremy worked with Joey on the consommés. The broth was perfectly clear with a rich golden hue, great flavour. The signature won tons smelled a hint of sesame and ginger. Joey heated them four at a time in a few tablespoons of vermouth and sherry, then floated them into the Chinese bowls Jeremy had filled. The surface of the soup was laced with chives and finished with a single edible Malaysian marigold. It made a pretty dish.

"Order three consommé, order foie gras."

"Squirrel won ton," he heard Joey say, turning to heat the dumplings.

A pretty dish they would run out of quickly. Twenty minutes into the first course Jeremy served the last consommé.

"We're overflowing out there," he said to Henk. "What's the count?"

Henk asked a waiter and reported back: 155 people. Many were sitting at the bar. "We'll be fine. We'll be fine," Jeremy heard himself saying to no one in particular.

Joey dropped a terrine plate that Rolando had very beautifully arranged, the beet carpaccio fanned just so under the two triangles of pâté. He had turned with the plate to give it a spray of minced green onion and ended up distributing the entire dish across the tiles.

"Racoon down," Joey said aloud. But he didn't take the count, just stopped long enough to clean the mess and immediately plate another portion.

"Three bloods, two escabeche and a terrine." The blood sausage was a hit too, as it happened.

"They're in the stretch," Jeremy said when a waiter informed him that the first tables were ready for mains. "Love it, everyone. Good work. Order squab, order duck, order risotto, order lamb."

He got his callbacks. Nothing hit the floor. Conrad flipped his last periwinkle salads on high flame and tonged them out gently in a ring around Angela's endive wheatsheaf. Jeremy gave the plate a once-over and put it up for the server. He noted Angela turn sharply to the duck, searing it off on the grill.

"Order two rabbits, two flatfish and a prawn. Fire the squab and the duck. Fire that lamb, please." Everybody at the range top was making quick, controlled movements between *mise en place* and station. Nothing rushed, just precise. Joey said *bunny* when the rabbit orders came through and *racoon* whenever he had to plate leek frite for the tenderloin, but aside from that they were executing like seasoned pros. In fact, the mains would have gone like the culinary Olympics had it not been for one interruption.

Jeremy was working with Henk on three crapaudine orders. The rock dove had been fired and positioned on the warm plates. Henk had finished the sauce with a tablespoon of cognac and a bit of double cream, boiled it down to consistency and was ladling it over the brown birds. Conrad was cutting thin wedges of gratin Savoyard. And Jeremy had just turned to his *mise en place* for a fresh thyme garnish and found none.

He took a glance around the kitchen. Everybody was bent to a task. Torkil was busy with desserts. Henk had turned to his next orders. And so Jeremy slipped the sauced birds up on the pass-through, called for Conrad to plate the gratin slices and trotted back to get the fresh herbs himself. He did not like leaving the point during service for anything, but here it was, a necessity. He avoided the crowded cook top and took the long way back to the RapidAir. Then, coming out of the cold room—conscious of the cooling squab on their plates, sauced and ready with their gratin—he took the faster route back to the kitchen. He turned left out of the RapidAir, past the alley door, past his office, and right in behind the auxiliary prep tables and the stock stove—a part of the kitchen hidden from his view at the front of the range top.

Which was how he came to find Kiwi Frederique in his kitchen.

They had ended up being included at a sort of head table, emphatically *not* Olli's idea but when Margaret whispered a few words to him after Dante extended the offer, he knew the matter was decided. It was bigger than most of the other tables in the room, and it was set off to one side under a huge bank of still lifes. The captain's table. At least they were near the band.

Benny kissed him on the cheek a little sloppily and sat opposite, between an English woman in a silver down vest, who was writing an article about the opening, and a thin man with a helmet of greased hair, wearing a cream-coloured suit with some kind of superhero cape. "Albertini Banks," the man had said, shaking the very tips of Olli's fingers.

Olli tried politely for the accent: "Swiss?"

"Oh nooo," Banks said, putting a hand over what appeared to be a light-weight anchor chain where his watch chain was supposed to be. His white French cuffs stuck out of his sleeves a good six inches. "Ahm frem New Yowrk."

"Philip Riker," said the other man, who shook everyone's hand before sitting down next to Olli. Dante's secret weapon, his right-hand man. Olli smelled it right away, even before Dante took the head of the table and started calling him Philly, right in front of everyone like he were a pet dachshund. It might have been interesting to talk frankly to Philly about this relationship, Olli thought, but it wasn't going to happen tonight. Olli knew that much about working with heavy-weights. Since you could not convince them of anything directly, you became accustomed to getting your way more subtly. The first casualty of that reality was candour. You simply could not state aloud all that you thought, no matter that the seeds of discontent weeded over your insides after a while.

And here it was. Dante would lob something down Philly's way, and he would answer the same strategic way every time. Not saying all he knew or identifying all that he wanted, just putting the question or the comment back into play.

"This is only the beginning, am I right, Philly?" Dante said. They'd been talking about the time involved preparing the room. The planning, the effort. The future.

"It sure is," Philip said. "And we can go a number of really interesting directions from here."

Olli just smiled widely, laughed or nodded sagely at every-thing anybody said. He had no point to make; it was Jeremy's big night. Margaret only looked at him once or twice, and he knew what that was about. Checking his drink intake, not wanting him to notice. It was Trout who had been on him in his strange way. Just the week before the kid asks him up to look at the dollar bills Olli had been doing his best to ignore.

"There's always more," Trout says.

"That's the thing," Olli told him. "In real life, there isn't always more."

"For me there's always more," Trout insisted. "I just paint more." Then, no warning: "Daddy, you smell different."

What was up with that? He hoped Margaret would lift the embargo on soccer, which Trout so obviously needed to take his mind off how his father smelled.

"I'm fine," he said now, answering Margaret's whispered question. White wine was being poured. The appetizers were arriving.

Dante offered a toast before they began. Around them the food was arriving at tables all over the restaurant, and Olli saw other glasses hoisted. Other toasts being made. Every face ruddy and glowing in the candlelight.

"To the beginning of something," Dante said, and he looked around the table, cycling through each of them in order. "For Kiwi, a discovery, a story. For Monsieur Banks, another notch in the stock of your formidable reputation. To both Benny and Philip, a job so very well done means the beginning of other exciting Inferno projects. And for you, Oliver, Margaret... a striking new adventure for a good friend."

He was back to himself.

"For me, a return to beginnings. The energy of some-thing created anew, something done to the beat of my own heart. Something I have found restorative.

"Ladies and gentlemen, I offer you: Gerriamo's."

"Gerriamo's," they all said. A toast that was picked up

at the tables within earshot and rippled on out from there. In a moment, everybody in the room had a glass raised in the direction of Dante, who toasted the room in return. "Gerriamo's," he said again.

"Gerriamo's," the room answered. Like Mass, thought Olli. He took a sip, set down his glass, then picked it up and took another small sip. Fantastic wine, tasted a bit like grapefruit. Even he could tell.

"Now let's eat," Dante said, sitting. And they did.

Margaret had ordered him green soup, it turned out. It came with a dollop of something white in the middle. "Pesto soup," Margaret explained. "That's crème fraîche." She had a precise shish kebab of salmon cubes herself, which lay balanced just as precisely on what looked like a pyramid of coleslaw guarded by three plump molasses-coloured oysters.

Kimchi. Smoked oysters. Olli was learning something wherever he looked. Each sculpted appetizer defied the next in its oddly original architecture and its mysterious ingredients.

"And what is that?" Olli asked Philip, who was eating silently beside him. He had just forked a tiny triangle of something translucent and purple—a beet?—which lay fanned under a pile of tiny green peas or beans that were providing a fulcrum for a lever of pâté.

It was beet, yes. Pâté, check. The beans were actually le Puy lentils. "The very best," Philip informed, spreading pâté on a tiny wedge of bread. "Expensive as hell."

The soup was good, Olli thought. It tasted like basil. Everybody else at the table was groaning in ecstasy. Benny took one bite of her salmon and forgot about whatever had been so troubling. (Even married to Margaret, who hid her emotions, Olli could tell a woman who'd been crying in the bathroom. Bruised eyes, new makeup.) Now the transformed Benny gushed: "Totally de-*lish*-us." She squirmed on her chair, hugged herself. She took another large sip of martini. Then one of wine.

Banks had taken a microscopic lick of the white salad dressing on his plate and rolled his eyes to heaven. Now he was trying to figure out the impressive sheaf of green in the middle of the plate, knife and fork dancing this way and that, both pinkies quivering erect.

"Are we getting the Philly say-so here?" Dante asked, beaming from the head of the table.

Philip nodded through a mouthful of pâté and bread. When he'd swallowed he said: "Yes, Dante. Definitely. Very, very good."

Dante was eating something black that had been strapped artfully to a piece of toast with a green onion. It was surrounded by a perfect fan of apples. "What did you order, Dante?" Olli asked.

"Blood sausage," came the answer, satisfaction evident.

Margaret looked up. "Blood, you know. . ." She started to say something, changed gears. "Very Jeremy," she said only.

Dante shook his head, crunched up some crostini and swallowed. "My idea actually. I adore bruschetta."

"Well, Jeremy's ideas *are* your ideas," Olli said, hoping to open things up a bit.

Margaret nudged him with her thigh, but Dante took the joke. "Emphatically," he said. "Part of the deal. That was part of the deal, wasn't it, Philly? I got his ideas?"

They riffed along these lines. The ideas of juniors, the credit taken by seniors. Philip thought the strong idea would always win but, at the same time, that there was demonstrably more money and reputation to be made in repackaging the ideas of others.

"I don't disagree," Olli said. "You just gotta get yourself on the right side of that exchange."

Philip returned an almost imperceptible nod of agreement.

Benny thought they were being very crass. Wasn't originality worth anything? Albertini chimed in his support on this matter.

"Well, I guess that's the point," Philip said. "Originality is worth something even if it isn't your own."

The only one not talking at all was Kiwi Frederique, who was sitting on Dante's left, eyes down to her plate, concentrating intently on her food. At the moment her face was about six inches from her oysters. She gently cut one in half, examining the insides. She raised her head an inch further from the plate and put the half-piece gingerly in her mouth, exploring it with her tongue. As she began to chew, her chin rose slowly so that by the time she swallowed, her head was right back, and she was looking at the chandelier overhead. She turned to her second appetizer next, consommé, and did much the same thing. She gently set aside the orange flower, removed the floating dumpling from the middle of the clear soup. She cut it delicately in two, pulled the stuffing out of one half, smelled it gently. She took the other half on her fork and put it in her mouth. She orally massaged this bit before, head back again, her throat waggled in and out and the masticated, well-analyzed dumpling disappeared below.

"Is it good?" Olli finally had to say something.

She looked back down to him as if she'd known he was watching all along. "It was really quite shockingly splendid. Mysterious but yummy." She scribbled something on the screen of her Palm, which was sparked up and running, stylus at the ready, next to her plate. And then, to the rest of the table, she announced: "But I disagree with what one of you was saying before."

Everyone looked in her direction.

"Chef Jeremy's originality cannot be taken by someone else," she said. "What he has created really belongs to him alone."

Margaret was listening. Dante had turned to an inquiring waiter and was ordering more red wine. Benny was finished the small amount of her appetizer that she intended to eat and sat drinking down the white wine that was being continuously poured. Kiwi was now launched through an explanation of something she called the Third-Wave Culinary Revolution. Something Jeremy had apparently invented. Not international, *post*-national. Olli thought he picked up strains of the tune they'd all been playing over at Dante's place those months before. A new place. No geography. Something like that.

"And Jeremy said all that?" Margaret asked Kiwi.

Apparently. "I have a nose for the new idea," she insisted.

The waiter was refilling wine glasses again. A busser was taking away dishes, all but Benny's wiped clean.

Kiwi was back taking notes in her Palm, and Margaret turned to Olli. "Trout won't be in bed yet."

Olli hesitated.

"Go on," she said.

The phone and washrooms were in a plush, blue-carpeted hallway on the north side of the restaurant. There was an attendant in the sparkling white men's room, who passed him a towel after he washed his hands.

Trout answered the phone in his room. Olli asked about the sitter. She was downstairs watching TV. "And you?" Olli asked.

Trout was reading Jacques Pépin's *La Technique*. Olli shook his head.

"You're at Jay's new restaurant," the boy announced. His choice of reading material and his absence at the opening were not unrelated.

"We are indeed."

"Doin' what?"

"Eatin'," Olli said. "Whaddaya think?"

"Eatin' what?" Trout asked.

"Walrus," Olli said. "Elephant."

Trout laughed. "No you're not."

"Oh yeah?" Olli said.

"Tell me," Trout said, threatening to get cranky.

"Green soup," Olli said.

"Green?" But now the boy yawned audibly into the phone and Olli told him to go to bed.

He wasn't tired. What was in that soup?

"I don't know what was in it. I only know it was green and it tasted good."

"Find out," Trout commanded.

"Yes, sir."

"Promise," he said, sleepy. "You really should know."

Olli listened for Trout to hang up before hanging up himself, laughing.

"We really should know," he repeated to Margaret at a whisper as the main courses arrived. She laughed.

The plates slid one by one onto the table. They inhaled as a group, then exhaled their uniform first reaction.

"My God." "Look at this." "Outrageous." "Is so *beyoutifall!*"

The main-course plates were even more fantastically sculpted than the appetizers. Margaret and Olli had lamb racks, the chops carved delicately, mounted in a gravity-defying spiral on top of the puréed celery root. The plate was beaded with drops of black olive jus. Dante and Benny had goose, the colour somewhere between mahogany and purple. It lay thinly sliced around the base of a bright yellow couscous tower studded with clover leaves. Banks had risotto, which spilled out of a hollow acorn squash, the lid set to one side in a field of edible violets and marigolds. Kiwi had duck, the slices propped against a buttery pile of spaetzle, all of it drizzled with a lattice of rhubarb sauce and topped with a julienne of brilliant green leeks.

Philip's dinner won the presentation medal. His tenderloin arrived cut and fanned across a blood red pool of wine reduction, offset by six blueberries at eleven o'clock, a cloud of leek and potato frite at two. It was balanced, minimal. It looked weightless.

"Culinary haiku," said Kiwi, looking intently down the table at Philip's plate. "Although, did you say *beef* tenderloin?

Rather small cow bits, aren't they?"

A waiter appeared like a genie with these words before anyone had time to consider the smallish disks of red meat on Philip's plate. "El Chaco Angus," he explained with an understanding smile. "From the Argentinean highlands. The grown male stands only about so high; he's a miniature. Tastes like a richer, more intense, free-range veal."

Kiwi's eyes bugged out. She almost laughed. But the waiter was nodding deeply, like he'd encountered this reaction before, and she ended up merely shaking her head in amazement. It left them all chuckling over Jeremy's uncanny ability to provision the unexpected.

And with that, they turned to their meals and a short period of table silence descended. Even Dante fell onto his colourful plate of goose with such interest, followed by such enthusiasm, that he overlooked conversation. Olli too, who wasn't sure he'd ever eaten lamb like this lamb before. Roasted to a very precise point, each chop rosy inside, darkened and sweetened outside. Each forkful could be given an unexpected salty kick by trailing it through the olive jus before raising it to your lips.

Half a dozen mouthfuls and a few swallows of wine later, they all became talkative at once.

"Really remarkable." "Delicious, yours?" "Totally." "I'm forever impressed with that young man." "Incredible." "Tarribly, tarribly good," said Albertini Banks.

There were similar comments spilling in from nearby tables as plates were slid soundlessly onto the white tablecloths and the eating began. Indeed, conversation around the room had ebbed and flowed in the same pattern. The volume fell, then rose. The band responded by switching from mellow to mellow swing.

Kiwi was finished first and up with a camera. "May I?" she said. And they all smiled up from the carnage of half-empty plates. Then to Dante: "I was going to try the kitchen next.

What do you think?"

Dante laughed, still eating and growing red-cheeked. "It's fine by me, not by my chef, I'm quite sure. You might try sneaking in the alley door."

They all laughed and returned to their meals. Kiwi sat down and took another few sips of wine, then slipped off her chair and announced the need to powder. Olli was the only one to notice that she didn't go to the washrooms at all, but slipped out the front door of the restaurant and up the street. Off to buy heroin, he thought. Who knew? But he didn't think about it further because he was being offered another glass of wine over one shoulder and, down the end of the table, Dante's conversational radar had swept around to him.

He was asking about the Tree of Knowledge project, predictably. They had earned a blip of press coverage three months before. *Wired* had picked up the story because Redmond was involved. *Newsweek* did a sidebar in a longer article about Internet publishing. Olli accepted the glass of wine and took a stab at a lay person's description. They were archiving Internet development, taking multi-trillion-byte snapshots of the entire thing. The project allowed them to develop tools for the manipulation of huge amounts of data, which in turn... He couldn't think of newer, better words and so out it came, his old vision: "Libraries of everything," he said, and then to emphasize added, "*disseminated freely.*"

It was a point that always got things going, people at the turn of the millennium having developed a fetishistic relationship with data, information. Dante was especially enthusiastic. "Just to bring life to such a tree," he said.

They talked along these lines for some time. The miracle of knowing. But Dante was also drilling relentlessly through the surface to underlying issues. He sensed something and Olli knew he sensed it, because just as his original idealism about collecting and disseminating libraries of everything had now been beaten into to a massive, megalomaniacal archiving project with no express reason whatsoever, so too had the shine come off Olli's pronouncements on the topic.

"And now you archive," Dante said, "but do not disseminate."

True. Things hadn't turned out exactly as he'd wanted on the Tree of Knowledge project. He admitted it when pressed. He let himself be coerced into acknowledging that his ideas had been redirected. And then, recognizing in Dante exactly the kind of force that moulds the idealism of others into service of personal metavision, Olli thought it was a good time to draw another junior into the conversation.

"You know how these things happen, of course," he said to Philip.

Philip smiled without committing. "Not sure I do," he said eventually. "This project turned out more or less as I imagined."

Well, so much for that. Olli hoped the subject would change soon.

"Me too," Benny said. "Despite what Jeremy wanted."

Margaret wrinkled her brow. Olli saw Dante frown a small frown. Benny forged ahead. "He wanted to make us into a French bistro. Not exactly *bleeding edge*."

"Perhaps not thet, 'zactly," Albertini said, looking genuinely confused. "But the bistro is . . . timeless, yes-no?"

"Oh, I don't think so," Benny started up again, and now Dante's frown deepened to frank discouragement, noticeable to all but those whose E was malfunctioning. "He wanted it to be all *French*. French food. French decor. French . . . I don't know. . . bidet."

Philip put up a tent of fingers in front of his face, resting his chin on his thumbs. It covered a small smile.

"Jeremy always talks about that place he worked in France, I know," Olli said to Benny, kindly. He personally did not want to see the girl go up in flames merely because she was loaded.

"But I know he's really pleased with what you've made here."

"As if," Benny snorted. "I almost had to break his arm." She was looking across the table at Philip for support and was getting it with little, barely perceptible, encouraging nods. "You remember, he was talking about beef tongue in mustard sauce."

She said the words just as Kiwi Frederique slid back into her chair. Olli hadn't seen her approach; he was just there all at once. An engaged, conversational aura about her.

"Can you believe that?" Benny was saying, now turned to Kiwi. "Beef tongue. I mean, who eats beef tongue any more?"

And when Kiwi realized the question was aimed at her, she didn't take more than a half-beat to answer. "Oh, I'll bet our chef does," she said brightly.

He had almost stepped on her. He certainly scared her. Kiwi screamed and scrambled to her feet.

"What the...?" Jeremy said.

"Chef——" Kiwi started.

"What the hell are you doing in my kitchen?" He was standing there with his thyme in one fist. There was a tense exchange.

Dante told her it would be OK.

Dante didn't run this kitchen.

She really hadn't been in the way.

He didn't care if she was in the way. And what the hell was she hiding for?

She wasn't hiding. She came in the alley door as Dante had suggested.

"You are not seriously going to tell me that Dante told you to sneak in my alley door," Jeremy shouted. He was going to lose it.

Joey de Yonker poked his head back around the shelving just then. "Everything OK, Chef?"

Jeremy was still glaring at Kiwi. "Give this thyme to Henk and tell him to get those three squab outta here."

"Yes, Chef!" Joey de Yonker said, snatching the herbs from Jeremy's hand and disappearing.

Kiwi stood her ground. "I heard that young cook say *racoon*...," she began.

Part of being on the hot line was being able to respond immediately to the unexpected. Jeremy heard what she said and didn't need a second to compose himself. Kitchen plate code, he snapped. The kid was a jokester, wisecracked all the time. "I do *not* have time for this conversation," he said, turning.

"Later," Kiwi said, following.

By the time Jeremy got back to the point, they were backing up at the pick-up desk. "Order lamb, make that two lamb, order flatfish, order rabbit. Order prawns and another squab. Please." He glared over at Kiwi, who had the nerve to follow him and stand off to the side, out of the way but in clear view. Only now was he beginning to wonder how long she'd been back there and what exactly she had heard.

"How about a picture?" Kiwi called from the sidelines.

"No pictures, no talking," Jeremy barked.

The rest of service was smooth, although one dinner did come back without any accompanying request for it to be heated or replaced. A racoon tenderloin. Jeremy sent a waiter out to talk to the table directly. When he came back he said, "Said it tasted just a bit funny to him. Quite sure it was fine...."

"Not everybody likes El Chaco Angus," Jeremy called out, too loud. "Get him something else. Henk, are we out of anything?"

"Prawns, squab and lamb."

"Rabbit," Jeremy said. "Suggest the rabbit."

"Order bunny," Joey de Yonker said, reaching for his slices of pancetta.

The last orders were being prepared. "Almost there," Henk said without looking up from a last duck breast he was beginning.

"We killed," Jeremy said. "OK, fire everything, you hear me? What do we have here—prawn, squab, duck, and I have the rabbit. These are last orders, last pick-up, people."

Jeremy finished the rabbit order, topped it with the sweet onion ragout and the lightly sautéed pancetta. He sprinkled the plate with a tablespoon of grated Romano, some chives, then slid it onto the pick-up counter.

The waiter was back in what seemed like three minutes with an empty plate and a message from the table that had returned the racoon. "The best rabbit he's ever eaten in his entire life," he said, eyebrows raised.

"Desserts are on the trolleys," Torkil announced from the cold pick-up. "Sauces in serving boats. Gelato is in the reach-in. Servers have been told to wheel them around in fifteen. The bar cappuccino station will be handling coffee orders."

"Henk," Jeremy said, turning to talk privately with his sous chef. They would break everything down, clean it all up. There would be nothing left.

"I understand, Chef," Henk said.

He gave Kiwi about five minutes, standing there against one of the prep counters, the dish pit wailing behind them.

"What was in the won ton?" she tried. She was pretending to be interested in the background of each dish, for the article, of course. He was playing along and giving her bogus answers like: "Marrow." And there was simply no way that was bone marrow in the won ton. Who did he think she was? She told him that he was a terrible liar—very sweetly—that she'd eaten marrow using a spoon made originally for Louis the Sixteenth, and why wouldn't marrow be on the menu in any case?

"Not everything was on the menu tonight *exactly as served,*" he allowed.

"Fascinating," Kiwi said.

The chef sighed. "Listen, off the record?" he said.

"Of course, darling," Kiwi said. He was even cuter when he flushed. The tips of his nice cheekbones went all rosy. She powered down the Palm and put it on the prep counter between them.

"My cooking is always part performance," he told her.

Is that so? How so?

"Well, an actor doesn't give it all to the audience, does he? There are parts you cannot know. Secrets that make the actor who he is. So the audience is ignorant, but the show is better for it."

Kiwi protested. If one agreed to go off the record, she argued, one really expected to learn something. It was only fair.

And my, did she guilt a long speech out of him in response to that. He was all the way back to the Third-Wave Culinary Revolution now, going on about memory. In this brave new world of post-national cuisine, Chef Jeremy left his little reminders about what he thought had been lost. He had a whole list of nostalgic examples: regional tastes, local ingredients, passed-down recipes, family farms.

"Even something of the family itself," the chef said.

And more: Embedded in this cuisine, Kiwi was to believe, were messages about knowing the earth's bounty and your connection to it. Understanding where one stood, understanding loyalty and the sanctity of certain soil.

Kiwi went to the bar before returning to her table. She had a Scotch and talked to a man there about his dinner. El Chaco Angus tenderloin, as it happened. He had never eaten anything quite like it, found it a bit gamey.

"I should think you did," Kiwi said to him. This admission from a man who claimed to have a taste for musk-ox kidneys.

The young girl Benny was on a roll by the time Kiwi sat down. Dante was looking faintly displeased. Banks lost. The nice couple were embarrassed. Only this Riker fellow seemed to be having any fun, and Kiwi had already picked him as a bit dodgy. Unshaven at dinner. How charmingly eighties.

But Benny certainly was on. Kiwi declined a refresh on the white wine and turned to listen to her ranting about the chef's favourite dish, something she evidently found appalling: beef tongue with mustard sauce. She was looking for support on this point, and Kiwi found herself dragged into the discussion.

"I mean, ick," Benny interrupted her. "No offence to anyone French here, but..."

"None taken," Olli said. "Oh wait. I'm not French."

"And he had some other brilliant ideas too," Benny went on, rolling her eyes in Philip's direction again, receiving his subtle encouragement.

"Remember though," Olli tried again, "all his ideas legally belong to Dante."

"No, I mean, like... really off-the-wall stuff," Benny said.

"Like what?" Kiwi said. She turned to look directly at Benny.

Margaret did not like where the conversation was going, quite suddenly. She didn't know why. Call it instinct, but she turned to Dante, actually put a hand on his arm—something Olli did not observe her do often. "Perhaps," she smiled broadly, "you could tell us about your future plans. Other restaurants? Other cities?"

Dante smiled back with some relief and took the offer. He opened his mouth to begin.

"I don't know," Benny blurted. "Like *squirrel*..."

What? Olli thought.

"I'm sorry?" Kiwi said.

"You heard me," Benny said, defiant, although now she also looked like she might start crying again. "Squirrel. I know *for a fact* that Jeremy eats squirrels."

She found one in his refrigerator, that's how. And don't try telling her that it got hit by a car and that he took it upstairs and put it in a *wheelchair* or something, and that it died and he put it in the fridge like his place was a squirrel morgue.

Dante struck Olli as a guy who didn't look really alarmed very often. Like he did now, say.

"Oh, baby," Kiwi said. She didn't reach for the Palm. No need for notes, she'd remember this one. She put a hand on Benny's arm. "Are you for real here? Yeah?"

"Uh, yeah," Benny said. "I saw it. It was grey."

"So brilliant," Kiwi said.

"I am just. . . a bit. . . lost," Olli said.

"Maybe all is not as it seems," Kiwi explained. It wasn't just a meal, it was a performance, she was saying now. A brilliant one too. Jeremy had fed them a range of things, a range of delicious, forbidden things. The chef was challenging the grid. Taste-jacking. He was apparently doing something called *meta-hacking*. For reasons that were not clear to Olli, Kiwi was suddenly using a lot of *Wired* "Jargon Watch" words.

"I ate," Margaret said, tired of it. "I'm full. I'm happy. But the meal was what the sheet said, all right?"

"What did you eat?" Kiwi asked Philip, ignoring her.

Silence.

"El Chaco miniature Angus? Wonderful, but excuse me? I've never heard of it."

"If Jeremy says——" Olli started.

"Then check the kitchen and be done with it," Philip said back to Kiwi. He had been enjoying the fun up to a point, but when she went serious all of a sudden, he pulled right back.

"Go ahead and try," Kiwi answered. "But our performance artist this evening has scoured the place. There isn't a trace of anything. Imagine that. Not a single bit of anything left over."

Everyone took the same nanosecond to consider this detail.

"And it's a tremendous thing, isn't it?" Kiwi drove onward. "In drama, in art. He performed for us. He showed us some things and kept some things secret. Left us to discover the unexpected, strange connections. We should all be *thrilled* to have been part of it."

"What did you eat?" Olli asked her, regretting it instantly as Margaret kicked him sharply under the table.

"That's the whole point," Kiwi said, eyes wide. "I have *no idea*."

Olli was certain she was serious, and that inspired a strange cascade of thoughts. But what was striking him as more unexpected was his sudden impulse to laugh out loud, really loud. What if it were true? On one level—and here Olli cracked a look at Dante, just a half-shade paler than usual, really *thinking*—on one level it would be fucking great. Wouldn't it?

Dante wouldn't have agreed if he'd been asked. Because at that moment, he was rifling through a disorganized stack of thoughts, and he wouldn't have described any of them as "great." He flashed on the Professor, whereabouts again unknown. The mother, glowering at him from the coffin. That woman Jeremy had worked with, the sharp one, overtly hostile. And the young man himself—Dante had tried, Christ had he tried—always faintly resisting. They were like faces staring up at him from the plate, laughing. He had been caught out, fooled, made an example of. He was staring down at his empty plate and he couldn't remember what he'd just eaten. Here these images had skipped across the surface of his consciousness, and all that remained were streaks of purple sauce, a few grains of mocking gold couscous. He felt very full, all at once. Sick full. And braying laughter was coming from a nearby table. The expanse of the room was opening around him, a sense of food in his belly was growing stronger, and everything Benny and this Kiwi person had been saying seemed, just then, very plausible.

Olli watched Dante and only got the sense that if there were a menu handy he would have picked it up and reread what he had ordered. "You were saying...," Olli said, growing serious. Taking a last shot at changing the subject.

But now the room was in motion around them. People were getting up from their tables. Dante was greeted by someone and stood to speak with them, turning his back on

Olli without a further word. Philip disappeared somewhere, to smoke a joint, thought Olli. To get some air. Albertini split to the washroom to regrease his hair, smooth the creases in his cape. Margaret changed seats and sat next to Benny, their exchange having migrated to a sisterly tone. He thought the substance of Margaret's input would obviate anything he could say. *Maybe you should go home, honey....*

He leaned back in his chair. He let his eyes drift around the busy room. Everybody was having a good time. The woman with the gold riding crop was stroking it across some old fart's bald spot. His friends were laughing big, male, locker-room belly laughs. Full and red-cheeked. There was a great quantity of Scotch going down and many, many cigars being waved around.

Olli was offered a Scotch with this very thought, leaning back in his chair thinking about it and watching through the front window as Kiwi hailed a cab and disappeared into the night. Just thinking about that and a voice next to his ear said: "Scotch, sir?"

"What do you have?" he asked by mistake.

"Glenmorangie, Loch Dhu, Balvenie, Dalwhinnie, Glenkinchie, Cragganmore, Oban, Talisker, Lagavulin, Macallan, Laphroaig, Connemara, Glenhaven and Sheep Dip."

They didn't even have Glenfiddich. But he was thinking of Jeremy anyway. Not his taste, Scotch, was it? Ever. Even years ago, years and years. Decoder years when they used to go out together and get right polluted. When life had been a developed, consensual, rockabilly fantasy and that had been just fine.

"You have Irish whiskey?"

Of course they did. Black Bush, Jameson, Paddy's, Power's—

He cut the waiter off. "Bushmills is fine." He pressed a twenty into the man's palm and looked back towards the closed kitchen door. "Bring the bottle," Olli said.

FOUR

# THE  SOURCE

She slipped out of bed in the very early hours.

The Professor knew it. He had been awake himself, thinking. Lying in the heat of mid-summer. Outside the moon was a waning crescent, but still bright, and the thin light of that moon washed the room. She rolled once, awkwardly. Then again, to her other side. Finally she sat up quietly, trying not to wake him. He heard her legs swing out of the bed, find the floor. Heard the springs sigh just a little as she shifted her weight to her feet.

He breathed evenly, didn't say anything. The clock on the bedside table read 2:30.

At 3:15 he went to look for her. He poked his head into the bathroom, the spare bedroom. Downstairs he padded through the living room and into the kitchen. He expected to find her there. She had been eating strange concoctions at even stranger hours lately—pickled cauliflower sandwiches in the wee hours—but there was no one at the counter. No cutlery in the sink. No dirty plate, no left-open jar of mayonnaise. No peanut butter.

He stood in the middle of the moonlit family room for several minutes before walking to the picture window that looked out over the back deck.

Hélène was there, reclined in one of their Adirondack chairs, her dark hair tumbling over the slats, feet propped on a wooden bench. She was looking out over the forested back-yard, down over the expanse of trees to the black and silver water of Howe Sound. Her hands were clasped lightly across her swollen abdomen. Thirty-six weeks swollen, just two weeks more. She had chosen the names. A boy would be Jeremy, the appointed one. They would call a girl Stephanie, after Hélène's mother, who covered up her Romani name with the feminine of St. Stephen, chosen herself on her own tenth birthday. Stephen, who addressed the Sanhedrin council with a history lesson about the homeless, wandering tribes of Israel. *The most-high does not live in houses made by human hands.* Stephen the martyr, dragged out of the city and stoned to death, whose face was transformed before his persecutors into that of an angel.

Most days the Professor was certain Hélène wanted a girl, but not all days.

He slid the glass door open quietly and she rolled her head over an inch, registering his approach. Then she went back to looking over the tree tops, down to the glinting water.

Once, short months after they moved into this house, Hélène had called it *her view.* He liked the sound of that so much that he didn't have words for several minutes. He busied himself with painting the railing or potting seasonals in the planter or whatever they had been doing together at that moment. *Your view*, he said to himself, *please let it be so.* And from that point forward the Professor never referred to it without reinforcing the idea, saying *your view.* Those trees, that slope of green, the sailboats in the water. Even the island in the Sound, Passage Island it was called. All yours.

He took another bench from against the wall of the house and set it near her, off to one side where she could see him, not too close. He smoked a Sportsman plain—he still smoked then, once in a while. Packs went stale but he kept them around for these late nights when everything was silent, inside and out. The cigarette flared peevishly when lit, then settled down to a sullen ember. When it was finished, it surrendered with an angry hiss at the bottom of an empty Coke bottle.

"Hélène," he said. But he knew he could not cross that distance and be with her in front of whatever future she saw lying there. He only knew she saw one, and that it was long, and that it filled her with an irreconcilable mixture of dread and delight.

She didn't answer. She hadn't been answering these past two days. Three, even. At the beginning of the pregnancy they had experienced the joy people typically report. She missed one period, then another. The day that the doctor confirmed she was carrying, she was waiting inside the front door to tell him when he got home from the university. She was shaking with excitement, a measure of fear, nervous energy. They went upstairs. He inspected her minutely for changes. Stroking her still-flat stomach, her breasts. They made love. It was cold outside, just into the new year, and freezing rain was hammering the house in a million tiny strikes. They steamed up the windows.

The middle months were overcast but still. A turgid sky anticipated heat that summer, and May warmed steadily from beginning to end. A shower in the first week. Clouds in the second. Nothing but tight blue from then on. The Professor was away, just briefly, three weeks. When he returned, the summer had begun as spring warned. Grass was watered and did not stay green; the maple out front made shade that was not cool. The Professor wrote up results on his legal notepads, spread out on a card table under a heavy canvas umbrella with a fringe. He drank pitchers of lemonade. Hélène baked on the chaise lounge, eyes closed to her view. He was home from school for the summer, available to watch the day approach, but the closer it came and the larger she grew, the more silent she became.

She shifted in the chair just now, a few feet from him. Not so close that he could reach her with an outstretched hand, but from this short distance he could admire her profile, tired, proud. Her fine nose, the resolution of her set cheeks and her strong chin. Her breasts swollen too, tumescent above the belly where her hands caressed the tight surface of her skin through a thin housecoat. She found her own navel, stayed over it a moment, a finger tracing the circumference of its taut rim. Descended to feel the knot of umbilical chord, to feel the thrumming connection. And with that small motion of her finger complete, she rolled her head over towards him, hands now very still. She told him: "It is a boy. It is Jeremy."

He opened his mouth to say something—to ask how she knew or to say how happy he was—but Hélène was crying. Not sorrow, a different kind of tears. Tears as silver as the moonlight around them and so full, so thick with sudden knowing that they filled his own eyes too. They poured from her and into him. They covered him. He gasped for breath.

He gasped waking, the sheets wet with sweat, not tears.

It was hot. Mid-July. The season for this dream. The room was dark, but there were stars showing. There was a moon not far from the horizon, he guessed. The Professor rolled in bed and confirmed the time: 3:25. Always close. He climbed from bed, went downstairs.

In the kitchen he poured himself a large glass of lemonade over ice. He took the phone from its cradle and slipped it into the pocket of his housecoat. On the back deck he found the now-wobbly Adirondack chair. He lowered himself onto the wooden slats, raised his bare heels onto a rickety bench. The moon above was a waning crescent. In the black night sky, the stars blinked, a little sluggish in the heat.

Her view was unchanged after a decade, although he had to trim the trees back a little each year. No houses had been built below. He folded his hands across his stomach and let his eyes sweep across it. To the southwest, the night was deep over the Gulf Islands and the Strait of Georgia. To the west lay the Sound, Passage Island, the Sunshine Coast beyond. Mountains began to the northwest, snow-covered, silent.

The Professor felt the flat chair-handle next to him. Felt without looking for his lemonade. Felt its heft, the beads of moisture on the outside of the glass, its coldness descend inside him. He set the glass down again and pulled out the phone. He dialed Jeremy's number.

He answered on the first ring. "Nothing is wrong," said the Professor.

He heard his son pull himself up in bed, prop his back against the wall. "As it happens," Jeremy said, yawning, "I wasn't sleeping."

They compared notes on not sleeping. Jeremy sometimes pulled on sweats and a T-shirt, slipped into sneakers and went running down to the seawall and back. The Professor liked the sound of that. The boy flying down through the night air, standing, looking out to sea.

"Although not often, I hope," the Professor said.

"Less, now that I'm in the groove again," Jeremy confirmed. "Tonight, I can't explain."

"Do you remember the story about how your mother knew you were a boy before you were born?" the Professor said. "Just before."

Of course Jeremy remembered.

"Since she died," the Professor said, "I dream that story around this time of year. I dream the part where it actually happened. Once, twice. Then the dream goes away."

He told Jeremy the details. Hélène sitting in the very earliest hours of the day. Looking over her view, her hands on her belly. When the Professor was finished, Jeremy was silent at the other end of the line for several seconds. "Thank you," he said finally.

They talked for a long time after that. They talked about how it is when something is nearly finished. If it has gone well, the moment of understanding about what has been accomplished arrives just before the crest of the hill, just before your objective. Then you reach the summit and for a while there is nothing but the summit. No ascent behind you. No descent ahead. It's all finished and the finishing is everything.

That moment came for Jeremy just as Kiwi left his kitchen. Her last wordless look conveyed incredulity, amazement, curiosity. A dangerous combination in a voracious journalist interested in the avant garde. She kissed him on the cheek. Thanked him. And as the swing door went still behind her, Jeremy imagined her entering the dining room with a brand-new hunger. A hunger for story. An appetite that would not be sated until she knew all the remaining ingredients in the recipe the chef had only partly given her.

She would find out. He didn't care. She had a different role in the scheme of things than did the others—the *celebrants*, he found himself thinking—who had been fed. Fed well. Fed goodness like they had never been fed. And they had eaten it, been delighted, were now satisfied and strengthened and full of unknowable joy. Sanctified by his efforts. It was possible, standing at the top of his evening like that—staring around the empty kitchen, gleaming, ready for the future—to feel briefly messianic. Like he had done a truly great and lasting thing.

Later, Olli was there. He was full of laughter, spilling over with a kind of genuine pleasure Jeremy hadn't seen in him in years, since school. The front room was booming with all the right noises: voices against other voices, bottles on the bar top, the espresso maker howling steam into milk, ice cubes on crystal and jazz thundering over it all. Olli stood inside the quilted aluminum kitchen door, beaming. He had a bottle in his right hand and a long-ago familiar glint in his eye. They drank whiskey out of water glasses and talked and smoked and rambled, sitting on the prep counter. Olli never said a word about dinner.

Two days later, Jeremy was still on the summit, although looking far out, far towards the horizon, there was an undeniable seam of storm clouds ringing, racing in. The restaurant was closed for all of that week and the next, reopening Friday of the following weekend as they had planned. Dante was unexpectedly absent. Philip wasn't answering, and then his voicemail message abruptly changed to a generic Inferno greeting: *The person at this extension is not available.* The receptionist thought they might both have the flu that was going around, which Jeremy had not heard about and found unlikely in any case. He tried Dante at home, tried his cell. Nothing.

He was making phone calls to suppliers. He had just talked to a Hawaiian shark broker about bringing in mako direct. He hung up, leaned back in his chair and heard a knock at the alley door.

Three men. They had municipal paperwork granting them sweeping access to his kitchen, to purchasing records. They wore lab coats, carried clipboards, were monosyllabic and in every way fulfilled Jeremy's fears about the health inspector. One of them appeared to be a stove specialist. He wore a small headlamp on a Velcro headband. The cold-storage man had a down vest. The squad leader did dry goods, work tops, ventilation, fire control and examined the paperwork.

They spent an hour in total. Jeremy sat in his office as instructed. "Well?" he asked when they were finished. "I trust everything...."

Temperatures were good. Storage containers appropriate. Safety measures above standard. No evidence of insect or rodent infestation. Everything was, the man said with marked suspicion, extremely clean. They drove off in a white van without further word. Jeremy got back on the phone. He spoke to his cheese man in Montreal for the next hour, partly business, partly for the pleasurable distraction of it. They talked about an order cycle for a range of unpasteurized Irish cheeses that Jeremy had decided would comprise the next month's cheese plate, and when he hung up he had six voice-mail messages: three oddly enthusiastic well-wishers, two from Kiwi Frederique and one from City Engineering.

He had his first ripple of nerves.

They came around that afternoon and put a lock on the dumpster. Jeremy heard the noise and went outside.

"Can I help … ," Jeremy started.

Don't shoot the messenger. The men loading the locked dumpster onto the back of a flatbed truck had no idea why they had been asked to do what they were doing. They only knew Jeremy had to sign a release before they could remove the dumpster and that the Health Department would apparently be carrying out something called "refuse analysis." Jeremy made some calls and was stonewalled, although a technician at the laboratory to which the dumpster had been directed did confide that Refuse Analysis was a little-known part of the Civic Emergency Plan—a procedure intended for use in instances of viral outbreak. For the first time since the opening, Jeremy had an uneasy night's sleep.

The next morning, the dumpster was back. It still had evidence of yellow biohazard tape on the lid, but the box had apparently passed the screening tests to which it had been submitted. Jeremy took a breath, key in the lock, breathed out and heard the phone ring inside.

Dante had resurfaced. Jeremy went over to the Inferno offices straight away, as it was suggested to him. His first thought on arriving was that Inferno employees were on strike. His second: stark surprise at the idea of Dante allowing them to unionize.

"You going to cross my picket, honey?" said a sharp-faced elderly lady whom Jeremy couldn't imagine working at the Inferno in the first place. She forced a brochure into his hand. The headline read: Vivisection Is Vile.

"I'm sorry?" Jeremy said.

Posters in the hands of the three dozen picketers carried slogans like Embrace the Vegan Village, Living without Cruelty, Choose Soya and, of course, Meat Is Murder. Inferno International Coffee, it seemed, was not vegan-friendly, and worse: the story was circulating that a recent restaurant opening had been a particularly grizzly carnivorous frenzy.

"They flew in exotic and rare animals from around the world," the woman stated, blocking his path. "I have a friend who was there."

"What kind of animals?" Jeremy asked, impossibly curious how this tale had evolved.

Everglade alligators, Kenyan roebuck, platypus, iguana, hyacinth macaw. The list went on. Jeremy's personal favourite was anteater.

"You can't be serious," he said.

"Oh, I am serious, sonny," the woman said angrily, as Jeremy pushed by her. And he heard her voice join in the rising chant at his back: "Chuck out the chicken! Bin the Beef! Trash the Turkey! Shame! Shame! Shame!"

Security guards watched curiously from inside the glass. They frisked Jeremy thoroughly before they let him go upstairs.

"I have one overriding question," Dante said when Jeremy was shown into the boardroom. He was standing with his back to the door, staring out the sweeping windows and down ten stories into the square. Someone was on a bullhorn now, and the words were just filtering through the glass.

"Animal slave traders . . . ." The crowd roared.

Dante listened for many seconds before continuing. "That question being: What have I done to deserve these insults?"

Jeremy opened his mouth to answer and, without turning around, Dante raised his hand sharply, palm open, snuffing out any interruption. "You know what one of them said to me?" he continued. "A young man, as I passed. He said: 'In the beginning, we did not eat meat.'"

Dante finally turned from the glass and looked at Jeremy. All the strength of his face—the fearless lines, the steel-strength suggested by the dome of his crew-cut scalp—all these stood out in disdainful relief against the city that sprawled behind him. The downtown towers stood cap in hand, the West End swarmed nervously behind them, the outer harbour lay in respectful silence beyond. There were ships at anchor there, motionless, meekly waiting for Dante's next words.

"Whatever could have convinced that young man," Dante said finally, "that returning to the beginning had ever been an option?"

They held eye contact.

"Let's keep it simple," Dante finished. "You're fired." There was an envelope at the front desk, and he did not say more. Firm, not angry. Terse, decided. Wanting done with what had to be done.

The settlement was generous. Jeremy held the envelope with his cheque as he passed again through the picket lines. It was only in east Vancouver, visiting Jules the following week, that the full breadth of the rumours began to dawn on him. The Inferno off Commercial Drive had been graffiti-bombed: Do You Smell a Corporate Rat? in very large red letters that began on the side wall and continued around the front, over the windows and the door. The shop was empty.

Jules had saved him an article from the cover of *The Province* the day before. The headline read: "Inferno Victimized by Urban Myth?"

"And then it was over," the Professor said, sipping his lemonade and shifting in the wooden chair. "The ascent, your brief enjoyment of the summit. The descent."

"I suppose," Jeremy agreed. It took a couple of months to depressurize, but he had moved on. Onward towards the next hill. He was cooking again. New kitchen, new neighbourhood, new and improved outlook. "You too," Jeremy said.

The Professor agreed. He was nearly finished the book. Working title: *Stromovka*. "And then, I don't really know. Maybe I'll retire."

Jeremy laughed.

"Or become a restaurant critic."

"That would require actually going to restaurants. You never go out."

"Well, I can't get a table at your place, can I?"

The waiting list was long, Jeremy acknowledged. "But for you, it's a phone call away. Is this the phone call?"

No, no. There was the dream. The Professor had wanted to tell Jeremy about that for a long time. It just happened to be the night. "Sorry about the hour," the Professor said.

"No problem. Dreams will happen when they happen."

The other reason was more mundane. "Happy Birthday," the Professor said.

"You're getting old. My birthday isn't for two weeks."

The Professor waited for him to figure this part out.

Hands on her belly, Hélène had given him life. Three in the morning, the middle of a hot summer. Given life as she touched the chord connecting her to Jeremy and weaving them both into a much longer chord. Two weeks before the umbilical would be severed, that longer chord was as taut as it had ever been, strung tight between heritage and legacy.

They said goodnight and the Professor hung up. He stood and stretched, looked out at her view another time. Swept his eyes from the islands to the Sound to the mountains. All the way from left to right. Further. To his own forest that surrounded his own house. To the forest that formed a thick wall between his house and his neighbour.

His neighbour was up too, it seemed. Just as he looked from the southwest to the north, just as his eyes reached the trees on his own property, an orange light winked on in the Beale household. Four-thirty in the morning, thought the Professor. No rest for the wicked.

But he smiled, thinking that. He smiled thinking of it as something he would have said to Dante at one time. He would have said that, and Dante would have shot back a response. Sharp and mean and funny, laying out a knight fork on the Professor's rook and king. Battling across the chessboard in his explosive fashion, quiet and understated for a long time, with moments of spiking action, throwing long, creative assaults up both flanks at once.

The Professor continued to smile, standing there, his eyes back on Hélène's view. The two of them, neighbours, contemplating this same dark vista.

Maybe thinking about the same kinds of things.

The flight was brutal. The trip had been a terrible idea to begin with but the flight was bloody awful. Arrived at 1350 Vancouver time, fifteen minutes late. Two percent of total flight time from Paris, granted, but without sleep. Not a second's worth of doze. Miserable.

Dante was the first passenger out of First Class. The flight attendant was waiting at the hatch with his black leather Hermès carry-on bag, as instructed. She held it out for him like somebody giving water to a marathon runner. He took the bag and mumbled thanks, then staggered up the ramp and into the terminal. Tired, nothing to show for a week. Furious with himself.

He'd had two hours of sleep in the past forty-eight, and those were in the British Airways First Class Lounge at Heathrow. He couldn't imagine what had gone wrong on that bloody airplane. Crocketts removed, traveller shoe-trees in. Blackout eye patches strapped on, neoprene gel-pack neck brace in place. First Class chair fully reclined, *Tubular Bells* on the Discman, Halcion ingested with glass of warm milk made with a drop of vanilla extract as he had requested.

Not a goddamned wink. Not a minute of undertime. It was all overtime. He hovered above sleep, conscious of sleep. He lay on his seat, conscious of each cushion. He raced above the clouds, and the land below streamed through his mind. Some strange visual fixation he could not expunge. It was like a fever dream. Hedgerows and ditches and roads and little houses flying past inside his eyelids. He was being tortured, strapped to the bottom of a crop duster. Off the continent it switched to water, which was worse. Now the sea went streaming by in one long unbreakable wave. Bits of foam spray flew towards him, fell away.

Somewhere over Kangamiut, bloody Greenland, almost beside himself, he asked for a thermometer.

"Are you sick?" the attendant asked, bringing it back. She leaned over, a little close.

"I rather think I need the temperature to answer that question," Dante snapped. The attendant retreated.

Normal. Completely bloody normal. What now? He hated reading novels on flights; he never finished them and never got around to them later. Hated movies for being stupid.

He had the girl bring over a cup of chamomile tea and every bloody newspaper on the airplane. He read news for an hour. Most of *The New York Times, The Wall Street Journal,* the *International Herald Tribune* and the *European.* And for all that effort, he couldn't have repeated the details on a single top story for a tax tip worth a year's revenue.

He tried sleep again. What else was there to try? There was no part of the holiday he wished to replay in his mind for amusement. And so the waves screamed by in the blackness, so close it seemed the salt was drying his face. He tore off the eye patch. He had to fight the urge to rush the cabin hatch. Dive out the bloody door and into that mocking sea.

"Welcome back, Mr. Beale."

Maurice was waiting outside customs. An ape of a man,

thought Dante. Maurice was apparently some kind of martial arts expert in his spare time; all Dante knew for sure is that he came highly recommended by the same agency that had headhunted Philip out the door to Microsoft and that he was so chiselled, he had definition in his ear muscles. Still, to his credit, his new EA sensed the prevailing mood and did not ask about the holiday. The holiday everybody at the office had undoubtedly been talking about for the past week, getting no work done whatsoever.

"Kind of last minute." "Never known him to take time off." "I heard France." "All *alone?*"

No questions. Maurice proved smart enough to sniff the wind and shut up immediately. He took Dante's bags and they walked quietly out of the airport into a scorcher of a summer day. A limousine was waiting, driver at the open side-door.

"Where's the Jaguar?" Dante asked, trying to keep his voice down. He hated limousines too, just that moment.

The fuel injectors were being replaced, as it happened. Some cretinous vandal squeegee kid had gotten into the tank. The cops called it "yuppie monkey wrenching." They thought the perp probably used Nutella.

"What the ... ," Dante said. He was processing a lot, standing in this beating sunshine on the sidewalk outside the limo. He turned to Maurice. "Terribly sorry," he said. "I'm a bit tired, but what in the name of Christ is Nutella?"

Maurice explained that it tasted like hazelnuts and chocolate and that you normally spread it on toast. It also happened to make just about the best fuel-injection magneto plugging system the mechanic had ever seen.

"Enough!" Dante said. Hand up. Please, no more. His head was throbbing.

In the limo he kept his eyes closed all the way from the airport to as far as the foot of Granville Street. There he tried opening his lids a crack but kept his aching head very, very still.

"All right," he said to Maurice. "Commence talking."

Nothing major to report, and Maurice had thought to leave all of tomorrow and Friday morning clear of appointments. The chiselled one was going up in Dante's books. Friday afternoon, however, was full. "Regular squash game at noon, yes-no?" Maurice said.

Dante said yes. He'd bloody well better be feeling right by then.

Bankers at two. Marketing veeps at three. Regional heads had a conference call on at four, a bad time for the guys down East but the boss didn't take a week off very often. Five was a reception for some mucky-muck or other. Seven dinner with . . .

There was more, but Dante was using efficient listening skills now. The tone of voice revealed the facial expression, and the facial expression revealed whether he needed to know more. In most cases, he judged from Maurice's tone, it was not crucial that he know more. Not now.

The driver took his bags into the bedroom. Maurice gave him his PDA, all his appointments scheduled. "The reminder alarm is set," he warned.

"How do I turn it off?" Dante asked.

"I don't think I will tell you that," Maurice said, testing the waters with a little assertiveness.

Still not a word about the holiday.

"It was fine," Dante said. He had hung up his suit jacket and poured himself a cold glass of water, slugged back three Tylenol. Sleep was suddenly right there. Coming towards him. His mood improved with its advance.

"I'm sorry?"

"My holidays," Dante said, yawning. His headache already diminished. "They were perfectly delightful. I had a very re-laxing time."

"Burgundy, was it?" Maurice asked politely.

"Yes, indeed. Gorgeous country. Really quite exquisite."

Maurice nodded and manufactured a pleased expression. "That's great, Mr. Beale. Really super."

At last, Dante slept. Fifteen pure hours. Deep, deep under, not a fragment of dream. He woke at four in the morning, not fresh exactly, but alive. Functioning. He walked through the darkened house to the kitchen. He poured himself a glass of orange juice and went out onto the deck. The forest swept away black to the water.

He drank down the juice in one pull, went back in and automatically started coffee. It was early, even by Dante's standards, but he was thinking he might as well get back in gear. He walked back onto the porch to look out into the darkness while the coffee brewed.

Dive back in, he thought. That was the ticket. Dante let his thoughts run naturally back to corporate matters. It was a busy time for them, in fact. Next year would be the year of the Eastern Seaboard. They had strat-plans laid out for Boston, New York, Washington, Philadelphia. A grand unfurling of over thirty locations, scheduled over an eighteen-month period. Everybody was going to be busy, no time for distractions.

Maybe he would sell Gerriamo's, Dante thought. Quietly. Sell it with the land. He'd talk to somebody about Asian interest.

Dante went back into the kitchen and considered the pot of coffee, now brewed and ready for pouring. The black liquid heaved in the decanter. It was still very early, wasn't it? Or very, very late depending on how you looked at it. He was considering that he had no meetings today and suddenly felt like having a sip of wine instead. Odd impulse that. Must have something to do with the flight.

He tried to push the thought aside, taking the coffee decanter in his hand. After all, he thought, carrying a full cup back out to the porch, there had eventually been good reviews. Mustn't forget that. And they hadn't begun until after Papier was gone. Dante nodded to himself. *Exactly, I might well have thought of it ten days ago, saved myself the bloody...* Never mind.

The raves started as soon as they brought in... (and then he blanked on the name of the chef they had hired at great expense to replace Papier after the opening).

Reno was it. Renko?

Anyway, he turned out to be worth every dollar it cost to move him in from New York on short notice. Worth every dollar for those reviews alone, impossibly glowing. And the Beale name got mentioned now too. It was like Inferno had invented New Coke then doubled back to Coke Classic and managed to increase market share in the process. He head-faked them. And here he was with—What *was* his name? Some bloody Italian handle. Rezno. Rinko—and the guy was a large degree easier to get along with than that merry, goddamn prankster son of the outdoors enthusiast living next door.

Dante put his coffee down on the porch railing, unsipped. He was all tense again, tired and wide awake.

A glass of wine would go down really well now, in fact. Maybe two. Maybe he'd unofficially extend the holiday another twenty-four hours. Maybe he'd just clean out the system with a bottle of something very, very nice. Go back to bed. Crash another twelve hours. Wake up purified. Start fresh. Newly minted mean on Friday morning.

It was so hot. He let his eyes sweep the horizon, the mountains down across the water, all the way to the southwest and then up through the forest to his left. The forest separating his property from Papier the Elder.

And he was up too. The orange light of his living room winked through the trees. Dante stopped drumming his fingers on the rail and considered this light. He looked at his watch again, knowing well the time by now. He went down to the basement, to the wine cellar. He ran his finger along the bottles. What had they liked to drink together? Dante could hardly remember—had it been that long? A year? More, certainly. Two years even. Claret, wasn't it?

Dante's finger stopped on the bottom of a Latour. A lot of

claret for the old nutcase, he thought. Still, he pulled the bottle down, climbed slowly back up to the kitchen and found two glasses.

It was a firm knock. An aggressive triplet with the knuckles that gave the Professor a start. Not from the front door, but from the steps up to the deck just over to his right. His head snapped around, pulled off the view.

Neither of them said anything right away. Dante was nodding slowly like the scene was exactly as he had anticipated. Both of them sleepless in the middle of a goddamned heat wave. The Professor's expression was bending involuntarily to amusement. Dante had pulled on some kind of Hawaiian shirt and white shorts. He really looked much better in a suit.

Dante climbed the steps very slowly, a wine bottle under one arm, the stems of two wine glasses clenched between his fingers. When he was a few feet away, he stopped. Still nodding.

"Very nice shirt," the Professor said finally. The motif was a pig roast. Here were happy Polynesians on their beach in front of their huts, gathered in an enthusiastic ring around a great pig carcass rotating above the coals.

"A gift," Dante said.

"Oh, thank goodness."

They played chess, naturally. The Professor set up a card table on the deck. Dante set out the pieces, hid two pawns behind his back. The Professor picked white. Once the game was underway there wasn't a lot of talking, just wine sipping and clock punching and the normal brief exchanges of conversational small-arms fire.

It felt to the Professor like the exact same game they had last played, and had many times before that. Dante started classically, taking pawns up the middle, developing his knights and bishops. The Professor built walls. Diagonal defensive ranks of pawns. He castled. He connected rooks. Exchanges began;

they both held back their queens. By the middle of the game the Professor was up on pieces, only to walk blindly into a trap. Dante skewered a knight and rook with his queen.

He sighed audibly. Took a slug of wine. "Not playing much, are we?"

"My opponent lost his appetite for the fight," the Professor answered, moving the knight to protect against what would surely be the follow-up attack on his own queen.

"Ha," Dante answered, taking the rook.

They battled down into the endgame. The Professor extinguishing each assault Dante mounted, each failing at a point closer to the parapet than the last. There was a violent exchange as the perimeter finally fell. Both queens taken. Dante spared a rook. The Professor a knight. One pawn a piece. It was academic.

Dante stood at the rail afterwards and wondered for the first time in the long, episodic chess relationship whether the Professor had thrown the game. He sipped his wine. They talked about work. About being busy, about finishing long projects. The Professor acknowledged that a book was in the works.

Dante turned to lean on the rail, showing interest. "Well, let's have it, then."

Stanley Park. Homeless people. Many more of them than you might think.

"You know, I never really understood what the hell you did for a living," Dante said, giving his head a quick shake.

The Professor laughed. "They say if you can't explain your work to a six-year-old, you need a new line."

Dante didn't think the Professor needed a new line, exactly. He thought the Professor probably lived among the homeless more ably than most people could. Showed more empathy, cared more. "Blessed are the poor and all that, I suppose?" Dante said.

The Professor sighed. When he seemed unwilling to answer,

Dante scratched his chin and looked at him closely. There was another question waiting to be asked. The Professor sensed it.

"Jeremy," Dante said, finally. He had phoned. Out of service. He had written letters. Not at this address. He didn't want to pester the Professor if the boy didn't want to be found. Was that it?

"Not to be petulant," the Professor said, "but you fired him."

"True," Dante said. "But after the opening things were not tranquil."

"So I hear," the Professor said, although Dante now repeated the whole story anyway. The rumours. The Health Department. A phone call from the very nervous executive director of the Canadian SPCA. (That was new, the Professor thought.) Picketers, law suits, graffiti, injunctions, public statements, stories in the local press, accusations, retractions, rephrased accusations, denials. "Inferno Victimized by Urban Myth?"—the question mark in this headline the subject of a heated debate between *The Province* editorial staff and Inferno's lawyers. A debate that Inferno lost, releasing the rumour to public domain.

Jeremy disappeared off the map, Dante said. Yes, it was possible he had been harsh, even unduly harsh. "But if some sort of riddle had been asked in all of it," he said, reasonably, "only Jeremy could have provided the answer."

As it was, nobody could confirm what had happened or had not happened. And meanwhile, carrying on throughout all of it, there was that crazed British journalist running around telling everybody it was performance art.

"Like gasoline on a fire," Dante said, shaking his head. "Not everybody likes performance art. And most people assumed that if it *was* performance art, something disgusting must have happened."

Sure, the *Gud Tayste* article had turned out to be a boon when it finally came out. They got an injunction against the protestors in return for a placating statement about the opening. And in less than a month they were bursting at the seams. Gerriamo's, as it ultimately played, had tremendous crossover appeal. Foodie-scenesters. The monied, urban, young. The hip of every stripe.

So what was the problem in that case? the Professor wondered.

Dante looked out over the water. He gripped the wooden rail. "I just came back from a little vacation," he said.

There had been a restaurant in France of which Jeremy had often spoken. It had been in a small town near Dijon. Dante had gone to Paris for some downtime, on his own, but he took one side trip. He was curious what he'd find. Who he might find. Dante told of the TGV ride out from Paris, flashing through the fields of yellow. He told of how the small town was reached by rented car, driving out a trunk road that wound and dove between the hills. About the town itself. Impossible streets. An abbey. The restaurant was tiny. He wondered how the French made a go of it. Simple food. Good food, but not much to it. He had a piece of duck breast with a sauce made of pears. A salad with chopped up hard-boiled egg and some cheese.

"Good value, I suppose," Dante said.

"You were thinking of buying the place?" the Professor said.

Touché. Before it became clear that Jeremy wasn't hiding out there, hiding in the kitchen behind the protection of his pass-through, Dante was fleetingly inspired to do exactly that. Produce a cheque book, buy the place outright. Offer them so much their provincial French heads would commence spinning. Then take this preciously simple place, this place with nothing to it, and turn it into something that took advantage of the trunk-road traffic flowing through this backwoods on its way from Dijon to Paris.

He'd been stewing over this exact thought, eating cheese, when a huge grey dog wandered out of the kitchen. A male Great Dane, thirty-five to forty inches at the shoulder, massive gear swinging between its hind legs. The dog made its way through the entire restaurant and finally to Dante's table, where it put its chin on the cloth not six inches from his plate. The beast regarded Dante with ageless, yellow eyes.

"And that dissuaded you?" the Professor asked.

Strangely.

The men stared at one another in silence for a moment.

"You can't protect him," Dante said.

"Wouldn't dream of it," the Professor answered. "The Food Caboose."

Dante had to have it repeated a number of times. "What kind of name is that?" he asked finally.

The Professor smiled.

"You're not really going to make me look it up in the phone book, are you?" But apparently that was precisely his intent, and Dante got up and walked into the Professor's house, letting go an involuntary chuckle at the games they inevitably played.

He found a phone book on the kitchen counter. "Food Caboose?" he called back out the patio door, leafing through the pages. And after a whole lot of leafing, he stopped. The Professor was still smiling.

"He's moved out of town," Dante said. He did not even care to conceal his disappointment.

"He hasn't moved out of town," the Professor answered.

Dante looked back down to the book with a frown. "Well he's not bloody here."

Over the top of the house came the first rays of dawn. They lit the Professor's face and all of the vista behind him in brilliant relief, and from the middle of a shining expanse of colour came the Professor's voice. It said: "Oh, he's here all right."

It wasn't inspiring from the outside. A ramshackle, barn-red house at the dead southern edge of Chinatown. The house itself was missing shakes, and some of the thin-slat cedar siding had fallen off.

It had been a grocery store for a while, the owner informed. Back in the early years when a vibrant China-town had sprawled this far south on Abbott Street. In more recent years the colourful community of vegetable stalls and butchers, spice vendors and the sellers of ancient cures had contracted into a few square blocks around Main Street to the northeast. The beachhead of condo development to the southwest had stalled in its advance this direction. Buildings had been torn down and not replaced. The area stopped being part of any neighbourhood at all. A quilt of denuded lots collecting rainwater, a grid of vainly hopeful streets. A place stranded between other places.

The red house was one of the last structures, virtually unrentable. Three months before, the owner had visited the premises and found the front room strewn with hypodermic needles. He broomed them into a pile, pulled on work gloves and counted them. Over 250, a busy shooting gallery. He was out of patience waiting for the redemption of development, out of cash. He was motivated.

Olli hired an engineer. The foundation was hanging in there, the hot and cold water worked and the wiring would not spontaneously combust, at least not in the immediate future. Olli wanted his money out in two years. "Three tops," he said. "Although barring some kind of total economic melt-down I expect to be ahead in one."

"Barring The Big One," Jeremy joked.

"Bring it on. For this price I'm buying land."

Which was not bad considering that the house had the basics. Medium-sized kitchen with a gas range top, the oldest and quirkiest Jeremy had ever seen but functional. There was an open front room with wood planks, a bathroom in the rear. A narrow spiral of stairs corkscrewed up through a hole in the high ceiling and into a sleeping loft at the back of the house. Jeremy's personal quarters.

His for two hundred dollars a month, Olli said. Enough to cover property taxes.

Everything needed work, but Jules helped visualize the finished product, made decorating suggestions. She also produced a drum sander from somewhere and helped him refinish the planks in the front room. He stained the planks mahogany. He finished the front room dark brown to the wainscotting and cream above. He spent almost a week with a box of steel wool and three quarts of Pinesol, cleaning the kitchen, every surface, every corner.

The Professor asked first before contributing anything.

"Pots," Jeremy suggested, and his father came through with Calphalon.

He scraped together everything else on his own. He found a cut-rate set of counters at Charmin's, racks of shelving and an aluminum cold-storage unit, both salvaged off a minesweeper scrapped by the Canadian navy. He tracked down the tables and chairs at flea markets, a case of homemade candles at a craft fair. A box of red-check linen and plain steel cutlery came from Ikea. With half a dozen garage-sale Braque prints—plus Heckle, Jeckle and Hide— Jeremy thought the room had become a pleasantly dark and comfortable place. A place somebody might like to be all alone over the fifteen-dollar prix fixe dinner and a magazine. A place someone else might like to take a special date on a night they wanted to be just a little unpredictable. A place where other people might like to pull two tables together and drink bottles of whichever of the four available wines they liked the most, talk late into the night until the chef had to go to bed.

A place with a Byzantine reservation system, in the end. Jeremy wanted something more straightforward, but Fabrek was the acclaimed expert on all things underground. "No, no," he said over Jeremy's objection. "This is important. I've seen these go down before."

"There are more?" Olli said, looking around the front room. He liked the smallness of it. He liked the idea of coming here regularly and never telling anyone about it. He walked up to the curtained front window and opened it a crack.

Not right here exactly, Fabrek said, but they were around. Alt.repreneurship, the punk economy. No business or liquor licences, no insurance, no regulation, no inspection. Risky but occasionally very good, mostly a lot of fun. Bars, nightclubs, and yes, restaurants.

"Even I've heard about speakeasies," Olli said, in his own defence.

Fabrek told them about two other restaurants, just examples. There was a hip underground tapas bar out in Burnaby somewhere. The best anticucho and live flamenco in the city. There was a Russian place in the basement of an old West End mansion, where you could drink seventeen different kinds of flavoured vodka, quite possibly homemade. Two bucks a shot.

"I was not aware of that," Olli said.

"That's the point," Fabrek explained. "Unless you know somebody who knows somebody, and those two people know each other pretty well, you're never going to get a reference. Forget about the phone number or the address."

"Reference?" Jeremy said.

Sure, that's the glue that held the whole thing together, Fabrek explained. Say a person hears about the Food Caboose and they want to go. Well, in that case they need to find a reference.

Olli looked dubious.

"Like who?" Jeremy asked.

Someone who had reserved before. An insider. A friend of the Food Caboose. That made selecting your first guests all the more important. It was like seeding a stream with salmon fry. Those first guests were going to spawn all the ones that followed.

So (Fabrek went on) a person gets a reference. Now, since

the reference would have actually had a reservation before, they would have the restaurant's unlisted phone number. The reference would phone that number during specified hours and leave contact information in a voice mailbox.

"Like," Fabrek said, demonstrating. "Hey, Jay-Jay. . . yeah, it's Fabrek. There's this guy I know, he heard about the Caboose. Pretty good guy. Give him a call at whatever."

Jeremy thought he understood. "So I call this person with the reservation date."

Fabrek shook his head slowly. "You call him with his waiting list confirmation."

"Waiting list?" Olli said.

Fabrek nodded, eyes closed. "Oh yeah," he said. "Later, when you have room, *then* you call him up and give him a reservation date and a number to call and confirm.

Jeremy nodded. "Got it."

It was a minor inconvenience, but by month six the waiting list was a month long. During the reservation call-back hour, which Jeremy established between 4:30 and 5:30 every night from Tuesday to Saturday, he was typically finishing up sauces at the stock stove he'd bought and set up near the low passageway into the dining room, arm's reach from where the phone also happened to be. And on Sundays, when Jules sometimes came in to cook with Jeremy on her days off, she might answer the phone.

This past Sunday, for example, Jules had come in and brought a stack of new CDs. She was on a Dexter Gordon kick and so they were listening to "The Squirrel," loud, the music hammering, driving away behind them as they prepped. Jeremy answered the phone while he was finishing brown stock. And later—when he was over on the far side of the kitchen reducing this stock to demi-glaze and Jules was roasting walnuts—she answered.

They got their last confirmation at 5:25. Their sixth and last table for their one seating at 7:00 p.m. Another packed house of twenty-four hungry people. Jules hung up and, dipping her head instinctively under a low beam in the passageway, ducked back into the kitchen.

"Booked," she said, taking out the walnuts to cool and turning to the beautiful red sockeye salmon that had arrived that afternoon. Jeremy nodded and continued prepping lamb roasts. Each boned piece of leg was being spread with a mixture of roasted garlic, mustard and ground rosemary before being tied.

When the roasts were in, he checked the bread oven. The baguettes were done. He cracked the oven door and the room filled with that very particular hot and delicious smell. Jules was bent over the food processor. She was seasoning the salmon mousse with salt and pepper. Adding a bit of cream.

Jeremy removed the baguettes to a rack and stood for a moment watching her. There was some kind of cataclysmic drum solo going on in the background, and he found himself smiling uncontrollably.

He went out front later. The little square tables were silent under their checkered cloths. The candles sat unlit in the centre of each. There was a fresh sheet tucked under the corner of each candle holder.

INTRODUCTION: Endive-apple-walnut salad
HOOK: Salmon mousse with arugula pesto + crostini
CLIMAX: Lamb with mint-apricot demi-glaze
DÉNOUEMENT: Sorbet + cheese

The room was warm. There were bottles of red wine on a sideboard. Jeremy lit the candles and glanced at his watch. He turned back to the kitchen just as Jules emerged, wiping her hands on her apron.

"All set?" she said. She came close, slid an arm around his waist, leaned her head over onto his shoulder.

He kissed her hair, breathed in her smell. They stood like that for several seconds.

All set.

## ACKNOWLEDGMENTS

I am grateful to a lot of people who helped and encouraged me as I wrote *Stanley Park.* (None of whom, naturally, should be held personally accountable for what's in the book.)

First and always, thank you Jane.

Thanks to Allen Hepburn, co-editor at *Descant,* for reading an early version of the manuscript and for making persuasive suggestions. Many thanks also to my agent, Dean Cooke, for guidance and for his work in getting the novel published. Thanks Diane Martin and Noelle Zitzer at Knopf Canada for wise editing advice. I would also like to thank Louise Dennys and others at Knopf for believing in this novel.

I would like to acknowledge two chefs who talked cooking with me. Chef Barbara Alexander helped me design the kitchens that appear in the novel. She also made me aware that chefs have many more colourful ways of saying "busy" than merely saying "busy." I am very grateful also to Chef Dennis Blaise, who let me visit his kitchen when they were truly "busy."

Thanks to my brother, Dr. Dylan Taylor, who patiently answered questions on the topic of cardiology and heart disease. Thanks also Ross Crockford for talking with me about Czechoslovakia. Big thanks to the Montana Nelsons: Dr. Kirk Nelson, Helen, Cathy and my buddy Chris Sauvé. The week you put me up in Granny's cabin on Flathead Lake was instrumental. Finally, thanks to the people upon whom I imposed various parts and versions of the manuscript. You were all game: Frances Bergin, Robert Duncan, Chris Elgin, Curtis Gillespie, Zane Harker, David Isenegger, Jill Lambert, John Meier and Kevin Williams.